In the
Australian's Bed

*These sexy men from Down Under
won't be denied!*

*Three sensational, contemporary
romances from three favourite
Mills & Boon® authors!*

In September 2008 Mills & Boon bring back two of their classic collections, each featuring three favourite romances by our bestselling authors…

IN THE AUSTRALIAN'S BED
The Passion Price by Miranda Lee
The Australian's Convenient Bride
by Lindsay Armstrong
The Australian's Marriage Demand
by Melanie Milburne

THE PRINCESS BRIDES
by Jane Porter
The Sultan's Bought Bride
The Greek's Royal Mistress
The Italian's Virgin Princess

In the Australian's Bed

THE PASSION PRICE
by
Miranda Lee

THE AUSTRALIAN'S CONVENIENT BRIDE
by
Lindsay Armstrong

THE AUSTRALIAN'S MARRIAGE DEMAND
by
Melanie Milburne

◎ MILLS & BOON®
Pure reading pleasure™

*Harlequin Mills & Boon Limited,
Eton House, 18-24 Paradise Road, Richmond, Surrey TW9 1SR*

IN THE AUSTRALIAN'S BED
© by Harlequin Enterprises II B.V./S.à.r.l 2008

The Passion Price, The Australian's Convenient Bride and *The
Australian's Marriage Demand* were first published in Great Britain
by Harlequin Mills & Boon Limited in separate, single volumes.

The Passion Price © Miranda Lee 2004
The Australian's Convenient Bride © Lindsay Armstrong 2004
The Australian's Marriage Demand © Melanie Milburne 2004

ISBN: 978 0 263 86133 4

05-0908

*Printed and bound in Spain
by Litografía Rosés S.A., Barcelona*

THE PASSION PRICE

by

Miranda Lee

100 Reasons to Celebrate

We invite you to join us in celebrating Mills & Boon's centenary. Gerald Mills and Charles Boon founded Mills & Boon Limited in 1908 and opened offices in London's Covent Garden. Since then, Mills & Boon has become a hallmark for romantic fiction, recognised around the world.

We're proud of our 100 years of publishing excellence, which wouldn't have been achieved without the loyalty and enthusiasm of our authors and readers.

Thank you!

Each month throughout the year there will be something new and exciting to mark the centenary, so watch for your favourite authors, captivating new stories, special limited edition collections…and more!

Miranda Lee is Australian, living near Sydney. Born and raised in the bush, she was boarding-school educated and briefly pursued a career in classical music, before moving to Sydney and embracing the world of computers. Happily married, with three daughters, she began writing when family commitments kept her at home. She likes to create stories that are believable, modern, fast-paced and sexy. Her interests include meaty sagas, doing word puzzles, gambling and going to the movies.

Don't miss Miranda Lee's exciting new novel, *Bride of Vengeance*, available in January 2009 from Mills & Boon® Modern™.

CHAPTER ONE

'THE ad says the property is open for inspection every Saturday afternoon between two and three,' Dorothy pointed out. 'I'm going to drive up there today and have a look at it. What do you think of that?'

Jake put down the newspaper and looked up at the woman who'd been more of a mother to him than the woman who'd given birth to him thirty-four years before.

As much as he loved Dorothy, Jake wasn't going to indulge her in such a ridiculous idea.

'I think you're stark, raving mad,' he said.

Dorothy laughed, something she hadn't done all that often this past year.

Jake frowned. Maybe it wasn't such a ridiculous idea, if it made her happy.

Hell, no, he immediately reassessed. She was seventy-one years old. Way too old to go buying some run-down boutique winery up in the back blocks of the Hunter Valley.

Still, perhaps it would be wise not to mention Dorothy's age in his arguments. She was sensitive about that, like most women.

Not that she looked her age. Dorothy Landsdale was one of those women who had never been pretty, but had grown more handsome with age. Tall, with broad shoulders and an impressive bosom, she had an intelligent face, with few lines on her perfect skin, a patrician nose and intense, deeply set blue eyes. Her silvery hair, which was dead straight, was always cut very short in a simple yet elegant style.

That was Dorothy's style all round. Simple, yet elegant. Jake had always admired the way she looked and dressed, although he sometimes wondered if she'd had her lips permanently painted red, because he'd never seen her without her favourite lipstick on.

Not that it mattered. Frankly, red lips suited her, especially when she was smiling.

Jake determined not to say anything that would wipe that wonderful smile off her face.

'Look, let's be sensible here,' he began in the same calm, cool, you-and-I-are-reasonable-people voice he reserved for juries during his closing addresses. 'You know nothing about wine-making.'

'Actually, you're wrong there, Jake, dear. You obviously don't know this, but Edward once planned on buying a boutique winery in the Hunter Valley. He fancied going up there on weekends. He collected a whole shelf-full of books on the subject of wine and wine-making at the time. Made me read them so we could talk about the subject together. But then he brought you home to live with us and that idea was abandoned. Though never entirely forgotten. He still dreamt of doing it after he retired.'

Jake experienced a dive in spirits, as he always did when the judge was talked about. He and Dorothy had both been shattered when Dorothy's husband of thirty years had died of a coronary last year, a few short months before his retirement. Jake had taken the news extra hard. If Dorothy was like a mother to him, Edward had been like a father, and more. He'd been Jake's mentor and best friend. His saviour, in fact. A wonderful man. Kind and generous and truly wise.

Jake knew he would never meet his like again.

Edward had left Jake a small fortune in his will, an astonishing document with a written request that within six months of his death Jake was to use some of his cash legacy to buy a luxury harbourside apartment and a yellow Ferrari. Jake had wept when he'd been told this. He'd confided these two fantasy purchases to his friend one night last year over a game of chess, also confessing that he would probably never buy them, even if he could afford to. He already had a perfectly nice apartment, he had explained to Edward. And a reliable car.

But Edward's last wishes were sacrosanct with Jake and he'd taken possession of the new apartment—set on prestigious McMahon's Point—just before Christmas a couple of months back. The Ferrari had come only last week. He'd had to wait ages to have a yellow one imported and delivered.

Both the apartment and the car had already given him great pleasure. But he would give them both back—hell, he'd practically sell his soul to the devil—to have the man himself sitting alive and well at this breakfast table with them.

'So that's what this is all about,' he said with a raw edge in his voice. 'You want to make Edward's dream come true.'

'In a way. But don't get me wrong. This would mostly be for me. I need a new venture, Jake. A new interest in life. Edward would hate for me to be moping around all the time, thinking my life was over because he was no longer here. When I saw that ad in the *Herald* this morning, it jumped right out at me. But it's not just the winery. I simply love the look of the house.'

Jake glanced down at the photograph of the house. 'It just looks old to me.'

'It's beautiful. I love old Australian farmhouses. Look at those gorgeous wraparound verandas. First thing I'd buy would be a swing seat. I'd sit there every afternoon with a gin and tonic and watch the sunsets. I've never had a house, you know. I've always lived in apartments. I've never had a garden, either.'

'They're a lot of work, houses and gardens,' Jake pointed out. 'Wineries, too,' he added, suddenly thinking of another time and another winery.

It, too, had been in the Hunter Valley. But not one of the boutique varieties. A reasonably large winery with acres under vine, producing tons of grapes each season that the anti-machinery Italian owner always had picked by hand.

Which was where he had come in.

Jake hadn't thought about that place, or that time

in his life, for ages. He'd trained himself over the years not to dwell on past miseries, or past mistakes.

But now that he had, the memories came swarming back. The heat that summer. The back-breaking work. And the utter boredom.

No wonder his eyes had kept going to the girl.

She'd been the only child of the Italian owner. Angelina, her name was. Angelina Mastroianni. Lush and lovely, with olive skin, jet-black hair, big brown eyes and a body that had looked fabulous in the short shorts and tight tank tops she lived in.

But it was her come-hither glances which he'd noticed the most.

As a randy and rebellious seventeen-year-old, Jake had been no stranger to sex. No stranger to having girls come on to him, either.

Yet it had taken him all summer to talk Angelina into meeting him alone. He'd thought she was playing hard to get, a conclusion seemingly backed up by the way she'd acted as soon as he'd drawn her into his arms. She hadn't been able to get enough of his kisses, or his hands. He hadn't discovered till after the big event, and her father was beating him to a pulp, that she'd only been fifteen, and a virgin to boot.

Within the hour, he'd been bundled off back to the teenage refuge in Sydney from whence he'd come. The subsequent charge of carnal knowledge had brought him up in front of the very man who'd sent him on the 'character-building' work programme at the winery in the first place.

Judge Edward Landsdale.

Jake had been scared stiff of actually being convicted and sentenced, something he'd miraculously managed to avoid during his rocky young life so far. But he'd felt his luck had run out on this occasion and the prospect of a stint in an adult jail loomed large in his mind, given that he was almost eighteen.

Fear had made him extra-belligerent, and even more loud-mouthed than usual. Judge Landsdale had seen right through him, and also seen something else. God bless him. Somehow, Edward had had the charges dropped, and then he'd done something else, something truly remarkable. He'd brought Jake home to live with him and his wife.

That had been the beginning of Jake's new life, a life where he realised there were some good people in this world, and that you could make something of yourself, if someone had faith in you and gave you very real, hands-on support.

Angelina had lingered in Jake's thoughts for a long time after that fateful night. In the end, however, he'd forced her out of his mind and moved on, filling his life with his studies and, yes, other girls.

Now that he came to think of it, however, none of his girlfriends so far had ever made him feel what Angelina had made him feel that long-ago summer.

Who knew why that was? Up till their rendezvous in the barn, they'd only talked. Perhaps it had been the long, frustrating wait which had made even kissing her seem so fabulous. The sex had hardly been memorable. She'd panicked at the last moment and he'd had to promise to pull out. Then, when she'd been so tight, he hadn't twigged why—young fool that he was. His only excuse was that he'd been totally carried away at the time.

Really, the whole thing had been nothing short of a fiasco, with her father finding them together in the winery only seconds after Jake had done the dastardly deed. He'd barely had time to zip his jeans up before the first blow connected with his nose, breaking it and spurting blood all over one highly hysterical Angelina.

Jake reached up to slowly rub the bridge of his nose.

It wasn't crooked any longer. Neither were his front teeth still broken. He didn't have any tattoos left, either. Dorothy had taken him to the best Macquarie Street cosmetic surgeons and dentists within weeks of his coming to live with her, beginning his transformation from Jake Winters, dead-beat street kid and born loser, to Jake Winters, top litigator and sure winner.

He wondered what had happened to Angelina in the intervening years. No doubt that hotheaded father of hers would have kept a closer eye on his precious daughter after that night. He'd had big dreams for his winery, had Antonio Mastroianni. Big dreams for his lovely Angelina as well.

With the wisdom of hindsight, Jake could now well understand the Italian's reaction to discovering them together. The last male on earth any father would have wanted his daughter to get tangled up with was the likes of himself. He'd been a bad boy back then. A very bad boy.

Not to Judge Edward Landsdale, though. When Edward had first met Jake, he hadn't seen the long hair, the tattoos or the countless body piercings. All he'd seen was a good boy crying to get out, a boy worth helping.

Aah, Edward. You were right, and wrong at the same time. Yes, I *have* made something of myself, thanks to you and Dorothy. But beneath my sophisticated and successful veneer, I'm still that same street kid. Tough and hard and self-centred in the way you had to become on Sydney's meaner streets to survive. Basically, a loner. Such programming is deep-seated, and possibly the reason why my personal life is not as great as my professional life.

A top trial lawyer might benefit from being on the cold-blooded side, from never letting emotion get in the way of his thinking. But how many of my girl-friends have complained of my lack of sensitivity? My selfishness? My inability to truly care about them, let alone commit?

I might be able to argue great cases and win verdicts, along with massive compensation payments for my clients, but I can't keep a woman in my life for longer than a couple of months.

And do I care?

Not enough.

The truth is I like living alone, especially now, in my fantastic harbourside apartment. I like being responsible for no one but myself.

Dorothy, of course, was a responsibility of sorts. But Dorothy was different. He loved Dorothy as much as he had loved Edward. That was why he visited her every Friday night, and why he sometimes stayed the night. To make sure she was all right. Edward would have wanted him to look after Dorothy, and he aimed to do just that.

Not an easy task, Jake reminded himself, if she was living way out in the country.

He really had to talk her out of the ridiculously romantic idea of buying this winery.

But talking Dorothy out of something was not always an easy thing to do...

When Jake's eyes glazed over and he kept idly rubbing his nose, Dorothy wondered what he was thinking about. Edward, probably. Poor Jake. Edward's death had really rocked him. They'd become so close over the years, those two. The crusty old judge with the heart of gold and the cocky street kid with no heart at all.

Till Jake had met Edward, that was.

Impossible to remain completely heartless around Edward. Dorothy knew that for a fact. The day she'd met her future husband, she'd been forty years old. Overweight and on the frumpy side, way past her prime. Edward had been five years younger at thirty-five, tall and handsome and beautifully dressed. He'd come to her aid when she'd been knocked over in Market Place by some lout on a skateboard. He'd taken her for a cup of coffee to settle her nerves and swiftly made her forget that she was a dried-up old spinster with a dreary office job and a bitter cynicism about men, especially the good-looking ones.

She'd fallen in love with Edward that very first day. Why he'd fallen in love with her, she had no idea. He'd claimed it was the heat in her eyes. Whatever, she'd lost those extra pounds she'd been carrying over the next few weeks. In her few spare hours, she'd also smartened herself up. Bought some decent clothes. Had her hair styled by a good hairdresser. And started always wearing the red lipstick Edward had admired.

They'd been married six months later, to predictions of doom from relatives. But their marriage had proved to be a great success, despite their not having any children.

Other men might have resented that. But not Edward. When she'd tearfully questioned him over his feelings about her infertility, he'd hugged her and said he'd married her for better or worse, and that resenting realities was a waste of time. But that was when he'd started working with charities that helped underprivileged boys, and where he'd lavished all his unused fatherly love.

Still, he hadn't become too personally involved with any of the boys till Jake had come along. Jake, of the ice-blue eyes and serious attitude problem.

When Edward had first brought Jake home to live with them, Dorothy couldn't stand the boy's smart mouth and slovenly ways. But gradually, a miracle had happened. Jake had changed and maybe she had changed a bit, too, becoming more tolerant and understanding.

Whatever, they'd both ended up genuinely liking each other. No, *loving* each other. Like mother and son.

Dorothy knew that if she bought this winery Jake would come and visit her up there as much as he did here, in Sydney. The Hunter Valley wasn't all that far away. A two-hour drive. It would do him good, she thought, to get out of the city occasionally. To relax and smell the flowers, so to speak. He worked way too hard. And it wasn't as though there was any special girl to keep him here in Sydney at the weekends. He'd broken up with that last one he'd been dating. A bottle-blonde with a flashy smile and a figure to match.

Why Jake kept choosing girls for their sex appeal alone, Dorothy couldn't fathom. When she'd complained about this side of Jake to Edward a couple of years back, he'd said not to worry. One day, Jake would meet the right girl, fall head over heels, get married and have a family.

Dorothy wasn't so sure about that last part. She didn't think having a family would ever be on Jake's agenda. Damaged children often veered away from having children themselves.

No, she wasn't holding her breath over that ever happening.

'Penny for your thoughts,' she said gently.

Jake snapped back to reality with a dry laugh.

'Not worth even ten cents. So when do you want to leave?'

Dorothy smiled. 'You're going to drive me up there?'

Jake shrugged. 'Can't let my best girl go careering all over the countryside by herself. Besides, I've been dying for an excuse to give my new car a proper spin. Can't do that on city roads.'

'Jake Winters! I have no intention of dying at the hands of some speed-happy fool in a yellow Ferrari.'

Jake laughed. 'And this from the wild woman who's planning to buy some run-down winery in the middle of nowhere! Don't worry, I won't go over the speed limit. And hopefully, once you see this dump for real, you'll be happy to stay right where you are and take up pottery.'

'Pottery! What a good idea! There's sure to be room for a kiln at the winery. The ad says there are ten acres of land, and only five under vine.'

Jake gave up at this point. But he was sure that Dorothy *would* see the folly of her ways and change her mind once she saw the place, and where it was.

'If we leave around ten,' Dorothy said excitedly, 'we'd get up there in time for lunch. Lots of the larger wineries have great restaurants, you know.'

Jake frowned. Mr Mastroianni had been going to build a restaurant at his winery. And guest accommodation. He'd also been going to change the name of the winery from its present unprepossessing name to something more exotic-sounding. Angelina had told him all about her *papa*'s grand plans, but Jake's mind had been on other things at the time and he couldn't remember what the new name was. Or what the old name was, for that matter. Though it hadn't been Italian.

According to Angelina, the winery had belonged to her mother's family. Jake did recall her telling him that her mother had been middle-aged when her father married her. She'd died having Angelina.

'I looked up a few of the restaurants on the internet last night,' Dorothy was rattling on. 'There's this really interesting-looking one on the same road as the place we're going to inspect. It's at a winery called the Ambrosia Estate. Isn't that a wonderful name for a winery? The nectar of the gods.'

Jake's mouth dropped open. That was it! *Ambrosia!*

'What is it?' Dorothy said. 'What did I say?'

'Did Edward ever tell you the story of how I came to be in his court?'

'Yes. Yes, of course. You…' She broke off, her eyes widening. 'Good lord, you don't mean…'

'Yep. The scene of my crime was the Ambrosia Estate.'

'Goodness! What an amazing coincidence!'

'My thoughts exactly.'

Dorothy gave him a sheepish look. 'I—er—I've already made us a booking at the restaurant there for twelve-thirty.'

Jake couldn't help being amused. What a crafty woman she was. 'You were very confident I'd drive you up there myself, weren't you?'

'I think I know you pretty well by now. But honestly, Jake, if you want me to change the booking to somewhere else, it's easily done.'

'No, don't worry. I doubt I'd be recognised. I've changed somewhat since my bad-boy days, don't you think? Though it's just as well *you* made the booking. If old-boy Mastroianni knew Jake Winters was eating lunch in his restaurant, I'd be fed hemlock. Italians have long memories and a penchant for revenge. He might not know my face but I'll bet he'd remember my name.'

Oh, yes. He'd bet the name Jake Winters was burned into Antonio Mastroianni's brain. And whilst Jake really didn't want another confrontation with Angelina's father, the possibility of running into Angelina again sparked an undeniable surge of excitement.

She would be what age now? Thirty-one? Thirty-two? Had to be thirty-two. She'd been two years younger than him and he was thirty-four.

Logic told Jake that a thirty-two-year-old Italian girl would be long married by now, with a brood of *bambinos* around her skirts.

At the same time he reasoned that even if she was married, she'd probably still be living at the winery, with her husband working in the family business. That was the way of Italians. No, she was sure to be there, somewhere.

The desire to see Angelina again increased. Was it

just curiosity, or the need to say he was sorry for what he'd done? She'd been terribly upset at the time.

But what would an apology achieve after all these years? What would be the point?

No point at all, Jake decided with a return to his usual pragmatism. Best he just have his lunch and leave. Maybe he'd catch a glimpse of Angelina. And maybe he wouldn't.

Who knew? He probably wouldn't recognise her. It was sixteen years ago after all.

CHAPTER TWO

'YOU can look for your father when you turn sixteen,' Angelina promised.

'But that's not till November!' her son protested. 'Why do I have to wait that long? It's not as though Grandpa's around any more to get upset. I mean…Oh, gosh, I know that sounded bad. Look, I miss Grandpa as much as you do, Mum. But this is important to me. I want to meet my dad. See what he looks like. *Talk* to him.'

'Has it occurred to you that he might not want to meet you? He doesn't even know you exist!'

'Yeah, I know that, but that's not his fault, is it? No one ever told him. He's got a right to know he has a son.'

Angelina sighed into the phone. She still could not come to terms with Alex's sudden obsession with finding his biological father. Every time she rang her son at school, and vice versa, it was his main topic of conversation.

Of course, when his grandfather had been alive, the subject of Jake Winters had been forbidden. In Antonio Mastroianni's eyes, the tattooed lout who'd seduced and impregnated his daughter was nothing better than a disgusting animal, not worthy of dis-

cussion. Alex's birth certificate said 'father unknown'.

When Alex had been old enough to ask questions,
his grandfather had told him that his father had been
bad, and that he was lucky not to have anything to
do with him. He, Antonio Mastroianni, would be his
father as well as his grandfather. In return, Alex
would carry the Mastroianni name and inherit the
family estate.

To give her father credit, he had heaped a great
deal of love and attention on Alex. The boy had
adored his grandpa in return and, in accordance with
his grandfather's wishes, Alex's father was never
mentioned.

But within weeks of his grandfather's tragic death
late last year, Alex had started asking his mother
questions about his real father, wheedling Jake's
name out of her, then every other detail about him
that she could remember, before finally demanding
that they try to find him.

Just the thought of coming face to face with Jake
again after all these years had put Angelina into a
panic, which was why she'd initially come up with
the 'wait-till-you're-sixteen' idea. But since then,
she'd thought about the situation more calmly and
stuck to her guns.

Because heaven only knew what Jake, the grown
man, would be like. The last she'd heard he'd been
going to be charged with carnal knowledge and
would probably go to jail, something which had

given her nightmares at the time. Till another nightmare had consumed her thoughts, and her life.

At worst, Jake might now be a hardened criminal. At best, Angelina still doubted he'd be the kind of man she'd want her son to spend too much time around. She didn't agree with her father that Jake had been born bad. But maturity—and motherhood—made her see Jake in a different light these days. He *had* been from the wrong side of the tracks, a neglected and antisocial young man, something that time rarely fixed.

'I don't want to discuss this any further, Alex,' she stated unequivocally. 'That's my decision and I think it's a fair and sensible one.'

'No, it's not,' he grumbled.

'Yes, it is. By sixteen, hopefully you'll be old enough to handle whatever you find out about your father. Trust me. I doubt it will be good news. He's probably in jail somewhere.'

Silence from the other end.

Angelina hated having to say anything that might hurt her son, but why pretend? Crazy to let him weave some kind of fantasy about his father, only to one day come face to face with a more than sobering reality.

'You said he was smart,' Alex pointed out.

'He was.' Street-smart.

'And good-looking.'

'Yes. Very.' In that tall, dark and dangerous fashion that silly young girls were invariably attracted to. She'd found everything about Jake wildly exciting back then, especially the symbols of his rebelliousness. He'd had studs in his ears, as well as his nose, a ring through one nipple and a tattoo on each upper arm. Lord knew how many other tattoos he'd have by now.

'In that case, he's not in jail,' Alex pronounced stubbornly. 'No way.'

Angelina rolled her eyes. 'That's to be seen in November, isn't it? But for now I'd like you to settle down and concentrate on your studies. You're doing your school certificate this year.'

'Waste of time,' Alex growled. 'I should be at home there with you, helping with the harvest and making this year's wines. Grandpa always said that it was crazy for people to go to university and do degrees to learn how to make wine. Hands-on experience is the right way. He told me I'd already had the best apprenticeship in the world, and that I was going to be a famous wine-maker one day.'

'I fully agree with him. And I'd never ask you to go to university and get a degree. I'm just asking you to stay at school till you're eighteen. At the very school, might I remind you, that your grandfather picked out for you. He was adamant that you should get a good education.'

'OK,' he replied grudgingly. 'I'll do it for Grandpa. But the moment I finish up here, you're getting rid of that old fool you've hired and I'm going to do the job I was brought up to do.'

'Arnold is not an old fool,' Angelina said. 'Your

grandfather said he was once one of the best wine-makers in the valley.'

'Once, like a hundred years ago?' her son scoffed.

'Arnold is only in his sixties.' Sixty-nine, to be exact.

'Yeah, well, he looks a hundred. I don't like him and I don't like him making our wines,' Alex stated firmly, and Angelina knew her son's mind would never be swayed on that opinion. He'd always been like that, voicing his likes and dislikes in unequivocal terms from the time he could talk. If he didn't like a certain food, he'd simply say, 'Don't like it.' Then close his mouth tightly.

No threat or punishment would make him eat that food.

Stubborn, that was what he was. Her father had used to say he got it from him. But Angelina suspected that trait had come from a different source, as did most of Alex's physical genes as well. His height, for one.

Alex had been taller than his grandfather at thirteen. At fifteen he was going on six feet, and still growing. And then there were his eyes. An icy blue they were, just like Jake's. With long lashes framing them. His Roman nose possibly belonged to the Mastroianni side, as well as his olive skin. But his mouth was pure Jake. Wide, with full lips, the bottom lip extra-full.

He'd probably end up a good kisser, just like his father.

'I have to go, Alex,' she said abruptly. 'I'm needed

up at the restaurant for lunch. It's always extra-busy on a Saturday when the weather's nice.'

'Yeah. OK. I have to go, too. Practise my batting. Kings School are coming over this afternoon to play cricket. We're going to whip their butts this time.'

Angelina smiled. For all her son's saying he wanted to be home at the winery, he really enjoyed life at his city boarding-school. He'd been somewhat lonely as an only child, living on a country property.

Located on Sydney's lower North Side, St Francis's College had come highly recommended, with a sensible balance of good, old-fashioned discipline and new-age thinking. Their curriculum included loads of sports and fun activities to keep their male students' hormones and energy levels under control.

This was Alex's fourth year there and he was doing very well, both in the classroom and on the sports field. He played cricket in summer and soccer in winter, but swimming was his favourite sport. The shelves in his bedroom were chock-full of swimming trophies.

'Good luck, then,' Angelina said. 'I'll give you a ring after you've whipped their butts. Now I really must go, love. *Ciao.*'

She hung up, then frowned. Cricket might distract Alex from his quest to find his father for the moment, but she didn't like her chances of putting her son off till his birthday in November. That was nine long months away.

Nine months…

Angelina's chest contracted at the thought that it was around this time sixteen years ago that she'd conceived. Late February. Alex's birthday was the twenty-fourth of November.

Today was the twenty-fourth, she realised with a jolt. And a Saturday as well. The anniversary of what had been the most earth-shattering day of her life.

Angelina shook her head as she sank down on the side of her bed, her thoughts continuing to churn away. She did not regret having Alex. She loved him more than anything in the world. He'd given her great joy.

But there'd been great misery to begin with. Misery and anguish. No one could understand what it had been like for her. She'd felt so alone, without a mother to comfort her, and with a father who'd condemned her.

Antonio Mastroianni hadn't come round till the day Alex had been born, the day he'd held Angelina's hand through all the pain of childbirth and finally realised she wasn't just a daughter who'd disappointed him, but a living, breathing human being who was going through a hell of her own.

After that, things had been better between them, but nothing would change the fact that she'd become a single mother at the tender age of sixteen. By the time Alex had been born, she'd long left school, plus lost all her school friends. When she'd come home from the hospital, there had just been herself in the house all day with a crying, colicky baby and her father, who tried to help, but was pretty useless.

Some days she'd wanted to scream at the top of her lungs. Instead, often, she'd just sat down and cried along with Alex.

Meeting Jake Winters that summer sixteen years ago had sure changed her life forever. And the thought of meeting him again scared the living daylights out of her.

Not because she felt in danger of falling in love with him again. Such an idea was ludicrous. But because of the danger of Alex falling under his father's possibly bad influence. She hadn't sacrificed her whole life to raise a secure, stable, happy boy, only to surrender him to someone she didn't really know, and possibly couldn't trust. Alex needed good male role models now that his grandfather wasn't around to direct him, not some rebel-without-a-cause type.

Angelina tried to imagine what Jake would be like today. Could he possibly have come good, or had he gone down the road to self-destruction? Was he even alive? Maybe she should start looking for him herself, do a preliminary reconnoitre. She didn't have to hire anybody, not to begin with. She could ring all the J Winters in the Sydney phone book first.

Yes, that was what she would do. She'd get on to that tomorrow. She would try in the evening. Most people were home on a Sunday evening.

Another thought suddenly popped into her mind.

What if he was married, with a wife and a family?

Angelina knew the answer to that as surely and instinctively as Alex had known that his father was not in jail.

No way!

The Jake who'd chatted her up that summer had been a hater of all things traditional and conservative. Marriage would never be for him. Or family life. Or even falling in love. She'd grown up sufficiently now to see that Jake hadn't cared about her one bit back then. All their intimate conversations whilst grape-picking together had been nothing but a way for him to get into her pants.

Which he had. But only the once. And even that must have been an anticlimax, for want of a better word.

Looking back, it was ironic that she hadn't enjoyed the actual event that had ruined her life at the time. She might have borne the memory better if she'd been carried away on the wings of ecstasy to the very end.

Jake's lovemaking had promised well to begin with. He'd been more than a good kisser, actually. He was a *great* kisser. His hands had been just as effective, with a built-in road map to all her pleasure zones. Her breasts. Her nipples. And of course the white-hot area between her legs. Soon she'd been all for him going all the way, despite some last-minute panic over getting pregnant. But the sharp pain she experienced when he penetrated her had swiftly brought her back to earth. All she'd felt during the next ten seconds or so was a crushing wave of disappointment.

Even if her father hadn't watched over her after Jake like a hawk, Angelina had steadfastly refused to become one of those single mums whose son woke up to a different man in his mummy's bed every other week. She'd made her bed, as her father had often told her, and she'd bravely resolved to lie in it. Alone.

To be honest, however, her opportunities for having even a brief fling hadn't exactly been thick on the ground to begin with. As the stay-home mother of a young child, she'd rarely been in the company of eligible men. Her weekly shopping trip to the nearby town of Cessnock had been her only regular outing. In fact, Angelina hadn't been asked out by a single member of the opposite sex till three years ago.

Two things had happened around that time to greatly change her life circumstances. Alex had gone off to boarding school and she'd enrolled in a computer course at the local technical college. She'd known she had to do something to fill the great hole in her life created by her precious son going off to school.

Once she had some computer skills under her belt, Angelina had felt confident enough to try working on the reception desk at the resort. To her surprise, she'd taken to the service industry like a duck to water. Soon, she'd been also escorting groups of guests on tours of the property, serving in the cellar and helping out at the restaurant at lunchtime on the weekends, its busiest time. She just loved talking to people, and they seemed to like talking to her.

Before this, she'd only done behind-the-scenes

jobs around the resort such as cooking and cleaning, hardly esteem-building activities. Not that she'd had much self-esteem by then. Her stay-at-home years when Alex had been a baby and a toddler had gradually eroded her confidence and turned her from an outgoing girl into a reserved, almost shy woman.

Now, suddenly, she had blossomed again, thoroughly enjoying the social interaction and yes, the admiration—however meaningless and fleeting—of the opposite sex.

She'd begun taking care with her appearance again, exercising off some of the extra pounds which had crept on over the years and paying more attention to her hair, her clothes and her make-up.

Of course, her father had noticed her transformation, plus the attention of the male tourists and guests. And yes, of course, he'd commented and criticised. But this time she'd put him firmly in his place, telling him she was a grown woman and he was to keep out of her personal and private life.

Not that there'd been one. Despite her father suspecting otherwise, she *hadn't* taken up any of the none too subtle offers she'd received from the many men who now asked her out. She didn't even want to go out with them, let alone go to bed with them. Maybe it was crazy to use her teenage experience with Jake as a basis for comparison, but none of these men had made her feel even a fraction of what she'd felt when she first met Jake.

Of course, Angelina understood that the intensity of her feelings for Jake had largely been because of her age. He'd represented everything that a young, virginal girl found wildly exciting.

Angelina had no doubt that if Jake himself walked back into her life at this moment, she would not feel anything like she had back then. She no longer found long-haired, tattooed males even remotely attractive, for starters. The sight of him might make her heart race, but only with fear, fear of the bad influence he might have on her highly impressionable and very vulnerable son.

Thinking of this reminded her that, sooner or later, she *would* come face to face with Alex's father again, possibly sooner rather than later, if she started those phone calls tomorrow evening.

The thought bothered her a great deal.

'Damn you, Jake,' she muttered as she stood up and marched across her bedroom towards her *en suite* bathroom. 'Sixteen years, and you're still causing me trouble!'

CHAPTER THREE

THE yellow Ferrari caught Angelina's eye the moment it turned from the main road into the Ambrosia Estate. She stopped what she was doing—opening a bottle of wine at one of the outdoor tables—and watched the brightly coloured sports car crunch to a halt in the nearby car park, her lips pursing into a silent whistle when a dark-haired hunk in designer jeans, pale blue polo shirt and wraparound sunglasses climbed out from behind the wheel.

What a gorgeous-looking guy!

Angelina's gaze shifted over to the passenger side. She could see another person sitting in the car but couldn't make out any details. The sun was shining on the windscreen. But Angelina was willing to bet on it being a pretty blonde. Men like that invariably had pretty blondes on their arms.

The hunk hitched his jeans up onto his hips as hunks often did. Not because his clothes really needed straightening, she'd come to realise during her recent people-watching years. It was a subconscious body-language thing, a ploy to draw female attention to that part of his body.

And it worked. Angelina certainly looked, as did the two middle-aged ladies she was serving. Both widows, their names were Judith and Vivien. They were on holiday together and had been staying at the Ambrosia Estate for a few days.

'Cocky devil,' Judith said with a wry smile in her voice when the hunk started striding round the front of the yellow Ferrari in the direction of the passenger side.

'He has every right to be,' Vivien remarked. 'Just look at that car.'

Judith snorted. 'Don't you mean, just look at that body?'

Angelina had actually stopped looking at the hunk's broad-shouldered, slim-hipped, long-legged body and was frowning over his walk. It was a most distinctive walk, somewhere between a strut and a swagger. He moved as if he was bouncing along on the balls of his feet.

'Jake…'

The word escaped her lips before she could help it, and her two lady customers immediately looked up at her.

'You *know* the guy with the yellow sports car?' Judith asked, grey eyes narrowed. She was the sharper of the two ladies.

'No,' Angelina denied, dismissing the crazy notion that the man could possibly be Jake. 'But his walk reminded me of someone I used to know.'

'A sexy someone, I'll bet.'

Angelina had to smile. 'Very.' She pulled out the cork on the bottle of chilled Verdelho and poured both ladies a full glass. Each one immediately lifted their glass to their lips. They did like their wine, those two.

The emergence of a grey-haired lady from the passenger seat of the Ferrari surprised the three of them.

'Good lord!' Judith exclaimed. 'Not quite what I was expecting. So what do you reckon, girls? His mother? Or do we cast lover boy in the role of gigolo?'

'Oh, surely not,' Vivien said with a delicate little shudder.

'You're right,' Judith went on. 'She's much too old to be bothered with that kind of thing. But she's not his mother, either. Too old for that as well. Possibly a great-aunt. Or a client. He might be her financial adviser. She looks as rich as he does.'

'I'll leave you two ladies to speculate,' Angelina said as she placed the bottle in the portable wine cooler by their table. 'Wilomena will be over shortly to take your orders. Enjoy your meal.' And your gossiping, she added silently.

As she made her way back inside, Angelina threw another glimpse over her shoulder at the man and woman who were now walking together along the path that led over the small footbridge, past the outdoor dining area and along to the main door of the restaurant. The hunk was holding the woman's arm but his head was moving from side to side as though he was looking for something. Or someone.

Angelina found herself hurrying out of his line of sight, tension gripping her insides. Her actions—plus her sudden anxiety—really irritated her. As if it could possibly be Jake! How fanciful could she get?

That's what you get when you start thinking about ghosts from the past, Angelina. You conjure one up!

She resisted the temptation to watch the hunk's approach through the picture-glass windows of the restaurant, though she did go straight to the counter where they kept the reservation book, her eyes dropping to run over the names that had been booked for lunch. There was no Winters amongst them.

Of course not. Why would there be? The hunk just walked like Jake, that was all. OK, so he *was* built a bit like Jake as well. *And* he had similar-coloured hair.

Dark brown hair, however, was hardly unusual. On top of that, this guy's hair was cropped very short, almost in a military style. Jake had been proud of his long hair. He would never have it cut like that. Not that the short-all-over look didn't suit the hunk. It was very...macho.

Jake had been very macho.

It couldn't be him, could it?

Once he came inside and took off those sunglasses, Angelina reassured herself, there would no longer be any doubt in her mind.

And if he *did* have eyes like chips of blue ice? came the gut-tightening question. What then? How did you deal with such an appalling coincidence? What sick fate would send him back to her today, of all days?

The restaurant door opened and Angelina forced

herself to look up from where she was practically hiding behind the front counter.

The hunk propped the door open with one elbow and ushered his elderly companion in ahead of him. The lady was not so fragile-looking up close, her face unlined and her blue eyes bright with good health. But she had to be seventy, if she was a day.

And the hunk? It was impossible to tell his age till he took those darned sunglasses off. He could have been anywhere between twenty-five and forty, although there was an air of self-assurance about him that suggested he'd been around a while.

The grey-haired lady stepped up to the counter first. 'I made a booking for two for twelve-thirty,' she said with a sweet smile. 'The name's Landsdale. Mrs Landsdale.'

Angelina was highly conscious of the hunk standing at the lady's shoulder. Was he staring at her from behind those opaque shades? It felt as if he was.

'Yes, I have your booking here, Mrs Landsdale,' she replied, proud of herself for sounding so polite and professional in the face of the tension that was building inside her. 'Would you like to dine inside, or alfresco? It's really lovely outside today. No wind. Not too hot. And not too many flies.'

The lady's smile widened. 'Alfresco sounds wonderful. What do you think, Jake? Shall we sit outside?'

Angelina froze. Had she heard correctly? Had the woman really said that name?

Angelina stared, open-mouthed, as he finally took

off his sunglasses, her whole world tipping on its axis.

It *was* him. Those eyes could not possibly belong to anyone else.

'Jake,' she blurted out whilst her head whirled with the incredibility of this scenario.

'Hello, Angelina,' he said in the same richly masculine voice he'd already had at seventeen. 'I'm surprised you recognised me after all these years.'

If it hadn't been for the eyes, she might not have. He was *nothing* like the boy she remembered, or the man she'd imagined he might have become. This Jake was smooth and suave and sophisticated. More handsome than ever and obviously no longer underprivileged.

'Goodness, you mean *this* is Angelina,' the greyhaired lady piped up before Angelina could find a suitable reply. 'Jake, you naughty boy. Why didn't you say something earlier?'

He lifted his broad shoulders in an elegant shrug. 'I spotted her through the windows, and decided if she didn't recognise me back I wouldn't embarrass her by saying anything.'

Well, at least that meant he hadn't deliberately come looking for her, Angelina realised with some relief. Still, this was an amazing coincidence, given she'd been thinking about him all morning. She could feel herself trembling inside with shock.

'I—er—didn't recognise you till you took off your sunglasses,' she admitted whilst she struggled to pull herself together. *Think,* girl.

'You do have very distinctive eyes, Jake,' she added, bracing herself to look into them once more. This time she managed without that ridiculous jolt to her heart.

'Do I?' he said with a light laugh. 'They just look blue to me. But now that you *have* recognised me, I must ask. Is your father around?' he whispered. 'Should I put the sunglasses back on, pronto?'

Angelina opened her mouth to tell him that her father was dead. But something stopped her. Some sudden new fear...

This man before her, this grown-up and obviously wealthy Jake might present more of a danger than the loser she'd been picturing barely an hour earlier. This man had the means to take her son away from her, in more ways than one.

She had to be very, very careful.

'You're quite safe in here,' she said, deciding she would tell him absolutely nothing of a personal nature till she'd found out more about him.

But she was extremely curious. What woman—what *mother*—wouldn't be?

The questions tumbling round in her head were almost endless, the main one being how on earth had he come to look as if he'd win the bachelor-of-the-year award in every women's magazine in Australia? And who was this Mrs Landsdale? What did she mean to Jake and how come she knew about *her*?

Despite—or perhaps because of—all these mysteries, Angelina resolved to keep her wits about her. And to act as naturally as possible.

Picking up a couple of menus, she said 'this way' with a bright smile, and showed them to what she'd always thought was the best table outside. It was to the right of the ornamental pond, with a nearby clump of tall gum trees providing natural shade. All the outdoor tables had large umbrellas, where required. But this table never needed one.

'Oh, yes, this is lovely,' Mrs Landsdale said as she sat down and glanced around. 'What a beautiful pond. And a lovely view of the valley beyond too.'

'Papa chose this spot for the restaurant because of the view. And the trees.' Too late, she wished she hadn't brought up her father.

Swiftly she handed them both menus, doing her best not to stare at Jake again. But it was hard not to. Her gaze skimmed over him once more, noting his beautifully tanned skin and the expensive gold watch on his wrist. He had money written all over him. Lots of money.

'The main-meal menu is on the front,' she explained. 'The wine list and desserts are on the back. We don't have a vast selection at any one time, but the chef does change the menu every two weeks. I can recommend the Atlantic salmon, and the rack of lamb. For dessert, the coconut pudding is to die for. I think you—'

'If you're not too busy, Angelina,' Jake interrupted, 'could you find the time to sit down and talk at some stage?'

She wanted to. Quite desperately. But pride—and common sense—refused to let her appear too eager.

'Well, we are pretty busy here on Saturdays.'

'We can't linger too long over lunch either, Jake.' Mrs Landsdale joined in. 'The property is only open for inspection between two and three. Maybe we could come back here afterwards for afternoon tea and you could catch up on old times with Angelina then. Do you serve afternoon tea here, dear?'

Angelina didn't answer straight away, her mind ticking over with what the woman had just said about a property inspection. Was Jake a real-estate agent of some kind? Or an investment adviser? What kind of property was the woman talking about?

There were quite a few wineries for sale in the valley at the moment, from the boutique variety to the very large. Arnold's old place was on the market just up the road. But he was having dreadful trouble selling it. He'd really let the house and garden go since his sister passed away.

There was only one way for Angelina to have all her questions answered. And that was to ask them. Given she'd been going to try to contact Jake anyway in the near future, it seemed silly to pass up this opportunity.

Yet some inner instinct was warning her to do just that, to not let this man back into her life. Not till Alex gave her no choice.

She searched Jake's face for a hint of the man he'd become, then wished she hadn't. The sexual power of his eyes was as strong as ever.

There was no use pretending she could just coldly send him away. She had to at least talk to him.

Fortunately, she wouldn't be alone with him. This Mrs Landsdale would be there as a buffer. And a safeguard.

'We don't actually serve afternoon tea,' she said. 'But the restaurant doesn't close for lunch till four. You are quite welcome to come back after you've inspected this property, if you like. We could have a chat over coffee.'

'I'd like that,' Jake returned. 'Give me an opportunity to find out what you've been up to all these years.'

'Same here,' she replied, pleased that she could sound unconcerned, when inside she was severely agitated. 'Now, since time is of the essence, perhaps you might like to have a quick look at the menu and give me your full order straight away. Either that, or I could take your drinks order now, then send a girl over in a couple of minutes for your meal order.'

'No, no, we'll order everything right now,' the grey-haired lady said and fell to examining the menu. 'Jake, you decide on the drinks whilst I make up my mind on the food. You know my taste in wine.'

'I see you have a suggested glass of a different Ambrosia wine with each course,' Jake said as he examined the menu. 'You know, Angelina…' he rested the menu on the edge of the table and glanced up at her '…I've never seen any Ambrosia wines in bottle shops, or on Sydney restaurant wine lists. Why is that?'

'Oh. We—er—export most of our wine. Here in Australia, we've only been selling bottles at the cellar door. Up till now, that is. Ambrosia Wines does have a booth at next weekend's food and wine expo at Darling Harbour, so hopefully we will be in some Sydney restaurants soon.'

'I see.' Jake dropped his eyes and picked up the menu again. 'These suggested glasses should suit you, Dorothy. You like to try different wines. But I won't indulge myself. Not when I'm driving. So just mineral water for me, thanks, Angelina.'

'Flat or sparkling?' Angelina asked crisply, having extracted her order book and Biro from her skirt pocket.

'Sparkling, I think,' he replied. 'To match my mood.' And he threw her a dazzling smile that sixteen years ago would have rattled her brains and sent her heartbeat into overdrive.

Angelina's heart was still going pretty fast behind her ribs, but her brain hadn't gone to total mush. She flashed him back what she considered was a brilliantly cool smile, the sort of smile she could never have produced at fifteen.

'Sparkling mineral water,' Angelina murmured as she jotted it down. 'Now, what about your meal order?'

When she glanced up from her notebook again, she found Jake staring at her left hand—her *ringless* left hand. Her fingers tightened around the notebook.

'You're not married,' he said, his tone startled.

'No,' she returned in what she hoped was a crisp, it's-really-none-of-your-business tone. 'I'm not.'

'I can't believe it! I thought you'd have half a dozen kids by now.'

'And I thought you'd be in jail,' she countered.

Mrs Landsdale laughed. 'That's telling you, Jake. Now, stop badgering the girl and just tell her what you want to eat for now. Keep the third degree till later. But I must warn you, dear, he's the very devil when he starts questioning people. Not only is he not in jail these days, but he's also a lawyer. And a very good one, too.'

Angelina wished her mouth hadn't dropped open at this news. But Jake Winters...a *lawyer*?

'Yes, I know,' he remarked drily. 'I don't blame you for being surprised. Sometimes I'm a bit surprised myself. But Dorothy's right. We'll keep all this till later.'

Angelina digested this astonishing revelation with mixed emotions. Was this good news or bad news? She supposed it was a lot better than the father of her son being in jail. But a lawyer? She couldn't think. Too many shocks in too short a time. Best she just get on with what she was doing and think about it later.

'Have you made up your mind yet, Mrs Landsdale?' she asked the grey-haired lady.

'Do call me Dorothy,' the woman returned with a warm smile. 'And yes, I'll have the Atlantic salmon. No entrée. I'll save some room for that coconut pudding you mentioned. I'm very partial to coconut.'

'Me, too,' Angelina concurred. 'And you, Jake? Made up your mind yet?'

'The same. I'm easy.'

Angelina wanted to laugh. Easy? If there was one thing Jake Winters would never be, it was easy.

CHAPTER FOUR

SHORTLY after three, Jake jumped into his pride and joy and headed back towards the Ambrosia Estate.

Under normal circumstances, he would never leave Dorothy alone in the clutches of an eager real-estate agent on the verge of making a sale. But he could see within five minutes of Dorothy walking into that darned house that she was determined to have it. On top of that, his objections to her buying a property up here in the Hunter Valley had begun to wane.

The main reason for his change of heart lived less than a mile down this road.

Angelina Mastroianni. Unmarried, and more beautiful than ever.

Like a good wine, Angelina had only improved with age. Hard to believe she was thirty-two. She looked about twenty-five. If that.

Jake smiled when he thought of the way her big brown eyes had widened at the sight of him. Shock had mingled in their velvety depths with something else, that certain something which could not be mistaken.

She was still attracted to him, as he was still attracted to her. The sparks of sexual chemistry had flown between them all during lunch.

Frankly, Jake hadn't wanted to leave. He'd enjoyed just looking at her as she served other people, her lush Italian figure straining seductively against the crisp white blouse and hip-hugging black skirt she was wearing, especially when she bent over a bit, which was often.

As he'd sipped his mineral water, he'd imagined removing that black clip from the back of her head and watching her glossy black waves tumble in glorious disarray around her slender shoulders. Between mouthfuls of Atlantic salmon, he'd thought about slipping open the pearly buttons of her blouse and peeling it back to reveal her full breasts, those breasts which had once filled his hands. More than once he'd stared at her plum-coloured mouth and wondered if she would still be as susceptible to his kisses as she'd once been.

He'd eaten all the food she'd brought him but couldn't remember much of what it tasted like. His mind—and his appetite—had been elsewhere. Dorothy had raved about her meal and the wine afterwards, giving them both five stars. She'd raved about Angelina too, saying what a lovely girl she was and hadn't he let a good one get away all those years ago!

Jake had to agree. Angelina left all the girls he'd dated over the past few years for dead. Where they'd all been entrants in the plastic-beauty parade, Angelina Mastroianni was the real thing. Everything about her was real, from her hair to her breasts to the artless way she'd tried to hide her responses to him.

She'd failed brilliantly, making her even more attractive to him.

He was already planning to ask her out. And he wasn't going to take no for answer.

The only fly in the ointment was her father.

Jake scowled his displeasure at the thought of having to tangle with that old Italian dinosaur once more. But surely, at thirty-two, Angelina could date whomever she pleased.

If she was *free* to date, of course. Just because she wasn't married didn't mean there wasn't some man in her life.

Jake swiftly dismissed the notion of any serious competition. No woman who'd looked at him as Angelina had during lunch was madly in love with another man.

The Ferrari crested a rise and the Ambrosia Estate came into view on its left, stretching across several rolling hills, most of which were covered in vines.

There was no doubt Antonio Mastroianni had made good on his grand plans for the place. The restaurant was fabulous, positioned perfectly on the property's highest point. The guest accommodation, Jake had noted earlier from the vantage point of the restaurant car park, was further back from the main road. A modern-looking, motel-style complex, complete with swimming pool, tennis courts and lush gardens.

Sixteen years ago, that area had been nothing but bare paddocks.

The huge, barn-like structure that housed the winery itself was still on the same spot, not far from where the restaurant stood. But there were several new sheds, Jake noted as he whizzed along the road towards the main entrance. Possibly packaging and storage sheds. There was also a large dam that hadn't been there before, no doubt providing irrigation to stop the vines from becoming too stressed during droughts.

The summer he'd picked grapes here sixteen years ago had been very dry and hot, and old-man Mastroianni had talked endlessly about how stressed the vines were from lack of water. Jake had thought the notion that plants could be stressed was funny at the time. Of course, he'd been a complete idiot back then, in more ways than one.

Hopefully, Angelina would give him the opportunity to show her that he was no longer such an idiot.

His heart quickened as he turned into the restaurant car park for the second time that day. An odd happening for Jake. His heart rarely beat faster, except when he was working out or about to address a difficult jury. It rarely beat this fast over a woman.

Was he worried she might say no to him?

Yeah. He had to confess he was.

Now, that was a first.

Angelina knew the moment Jake arrived back in the car park. She'd been watching out of the corner of her eye, and that bright yellow was hard to miss. This time, thankfully, Vivien and Judith were no longer there in the restaurant to make any comments. They'd not long left after a very leisurely lunch, planning to have naps in their rooms before returning for dinner. Drinking and eating made up the mainstay of their holiday.

There were only two couples left in the restaurant, lingering over coffee. But they were seated inside. Angelina could sit outside with Jake and Dorothy, and be in no danger of being overheard, or interrupted.

She was taking a few steadying breaths and pretending to tidy up behind the counter when Jake walked in, alone. Momentarily rattled, she restrained herself from commenting till they were seated safely outside, having instructed a highly curious Wilomena to bring them both coffee and carrot cake.

'Where's Dorothy?' she asked once they were alone.

Jake took off his sunglasses and relaxed back into his chair with a sigh whilst Angelina fought the temptation to stare at him once more.

'I suspect putting a deposit down on a property up the road,' he replied drily. 'A boutique winery which has certainly seen better days. I would have stayed and tried to talk her out of it if I could. But Dorothy is one stubborn woman once she sets her sights on something. And she's set her sights on this place. The house, anyway. I left her having a second viewing and finding out the ins and outs of everything. The real-estate agent said he'd drop her off here after they were finished. He said he had to pass by on his way back to Cessnock.'

Angelina tried not to panic at this unexpected development. 'Is this house…um…white, with wide verandas?'

'That's the one.'

'Good lord, that's Arnold's place!' If Dorothy bought Arnold's place there was no hope of keeping Alex's existence a secret. The vineyard community up here was like a small town. Everyone knew everything about everyone.

Her exclamation sent Jake's dark brows arching. 'You know the owner?'

'He…um…he works for me. He's my new wine-maker.'

'I thought your father was the wine-maker here,' Jake said with a puzzled frown.

Oh, dear. Impossible now to keep secret that her father was dead. Still, everything was going to come out, sooner or later. She might as well start with the lesser revelation.

'Papa died last year,' Angelina said, and tensed in anticipation of Jake's reaction.

He said nothing for several seconds. Perhaps he was mulling over why she hadn't told him about this earlier when she had the chance.

'I'm sorry to hear that,' he said at last. 'Truly. I know how hard it is to lose someone you care about. A very good friend of mine died last year. Dorothy's husband. You don't realise how much you miss someone till they're not there for you any longer.'

Angelina was touched—and somewhat surprised—by Jake's sentiments. But at least she'd had one of her questions answered. In part. She now knew who Dorothy was. The wife of an old friend.

'How did your father die?' Jake asked. 'Had he been ill?'

'No. He was as healthy as a horse. It was quite tragic, really. He was bitten by a snake. A King Brown.'

'Good lord. That is tragic. But isn't it also unusual these days? To die of snake-bite? Don't they have antidotes?'

She nodded whilst she struggled to get a grip on herself. She hated talking about that awful day. After all, it wasn't all that long ago. Three months and a bit.

'He might have lived if he'd been bitten on the hand,' she explained. 'Or a foot. But he must have been bending over and was bitten on the chest, not far from the heart. He…he stopped breathing before the ambulance arrived. They tried to revive him but it was too late.'

Tears flooded her eyes as all the turmoil and torment of that day rushed back. Jake's reaching over the table to cover her hand with his catapulted her back to the present, and made her hotly aware that she'd been wrong this morning. Jake, the man, still had the same effect on her as Jake, the boy. When his long fingers started moving seductively against hers, a charge of electric sensations shot up her arm.

'Don't,' she snapped, and snatched her hand away from under his, clutching it firmly in her lap with her other hand.

He searched her face with thoughtful eyes. 'What's wrong, Angelina? Are you still angry with me for what happened sixteen years ago? I wouldn't blame you if you were. I was thinking earlier today how much I wanted to say sorry to you for how things turned out that night, so if it's not too late, I'm truly sorry.'

'No need for an apology,' she bit out. 'I was as much to blame as you were.'

'Then what's the problem? Why snatch your hand away like that?'

Angelina could hardly tell him the truth. That just the touch of his hand fired up her hormones as no man had in the past sixteen years. Not even close. Even now, she was looking at his mouth and wondering what it would feel like on hers again; wondering what making love would be like with him, now that he was older and so much more experienced.

Jake would be only too happy to accommodate her, she knew. Angelina had seen the way he'd looked at her during lunch today. She'd been on the end of such looks from men a lot lately. Invariably, they were followed up by some kind of pass.

She wouldn't mind betting Jake had organised leaving Dorothy behind for a while so that he could be alone with her. The realisation that he thought he could just take up with her where he'd left off all those years ago infuriated Angelina.

'You look as if you've changed, Jake,' she said sharply. 'But you haven't changed at all. You still think you can have any female you fancy.'

He smiled the most heart-stopping smile. 'It would be hard not to fancy you, Angelina. You were a gorgeous-looking girl, but you're one stunning-looking woman.'

Angelina gritted her teeth to stop herself from smiling back at him. Damn the man, he was incorrigible. And almost irresistible.

Wilomena arriving with the coffee and cake was a godsend. But she was gone all too soon.

'This is great cake,' Jake praised after his first mouthful.

'Glad you like it,' she remarked snippily.

He took another mouthful, followed up by some coffee. She watched him, her own appetite nil, her frustration growing. Who did he think he was? It would serve him right if she upped and told him right now the result of his last encounter with her. Finding out he had a fifteen-year-old son was sure to wipe that satisfied look off his far too handsome face.

But she didn't tell him. She couldn't be sure of his reaction, and there was no way she was going to upset Alex this year. Angelina aimed to delay Jake finding out about his son as long as possible.

'So!' Jake exclaimed, dabbing at his mouth with a serviette after polishing off his slice of cake and most of his coffee. 'Is there a current man in your life, Angelina? Or are you footloose and fancy-free?'

Here comes the pass, she thought irritably. Well, he was in for a surprise because she intended to head him off at the pass. As much as Jake still had the power to turn her head—and turn her on—Angelina wasn't about to fall for his smooth but empty line of patter twice in one lifetime.

'Yes, of course there's a man in my life,' came her blithe reply. Alex was almost a man after all.

Jake muttered something under his breath before searching her face again with those hard, sexy blue eyes of his. 'So what's the score? Is it serious? Are you living with him?'

'Sometimes.'

'Sometimes.' Jake looked puzzled. 'What does that mean?'

'He lives in Sydney most of the time. Comes up here for holidays and the occasional weekend. And I go down there to see him every once in a while.'

'What about next weekend? Will you be seeing him next weekend?'

'Nope. I'll be attending the food and wine expo at Darling Harbour.'

'You mean you'll be in Sydney and you're not going to see each other, not even at *night*?'

Angelina couldn't decide if she found Jake's shock amusing or annoying. Clearly, his priority in a relationship was still sex.

'Alex will be away next weekend,' she said coolly. Actually, Alex was going to a special swimming training camp in preparation for the big interschool swimming carnival the following weekend. He was the captain of the team. 'I'll be seeing him the following weekend.' At the swimming carnival.

'Where are you staying this weekend in Sydney?'

Angelina almost laughed. Obviously, Jake didn't aim to go quietly off into the sunset. She should have known.

'I've booked a room at the Star City Casino for Saturday night,' came her composed reply. 'It's the closest hotel to the expo.' In truth, she wasn't strictly needed at the expo. The marketing agency who now handled the Ambrosia Estate account had hired professional sales people for the weekend. But she thought it wise to check personally on how her money was being spent. This venture hadn't been cheap.

But Angelina knew you had to invest money to make money these days. It had been her idea for the winery to get a web site two years ago. Her father had argued against the idea, but she'd had her way and it had brought them in a lot of business.

'Are you planning to marry this Alex one day?' Jake asked abruptly.

'No.'

Jake shook his head, his expression bewildered. 'That's what I don't get with you, Angelina. Why *haven't* you got married? I thought marriage and children were a must with Italian girls.'

'Not with me. I have other priorities.' *Like our son.* 'Now that Papa's gone, I'm solely responsible for the running of this place. That's a lot of work. But enough about me. What about you, Jake?' she asked, swiftly deflecting the conversation away from her own personal life and on to his. 'Are you married?'

The corner of his mouth tipped up in a wry smile. 'Come, now, Angelina. I told you way back when I was seventeen that I would never get married. I've had no reason to change my mind on that score.'

Her heart sinking at this news annoyed her. What had she subconsciously been hoping could happen here? That he would fall madly in love with her this time, marry her and they would live happily ever after, the three of them?

Dream on, Angelina.

'What about children?' she couldn't resist asking. 'Haven't you ever wanted a son? Or a daughter?' she added quickly.

'God, no. I'd be a simply dreadful father. Just the thought of being responsible for a child's upbringing gives me nightmares.'

Oh, great, she thought. He's going to be thrilled when he finds out about Alex. It was as well Alex was almost grown up, if that was Jake's attitude.

'Why do you say you'd be a dreadful father?' she asked, though she suspected it had something to do with his childhood. He'd never told her specifics all those years ago, but she'd been left with the impression of serious neglect.

Angelina's father had always been a right pain in

the neck, but he'd never left her in any doubt that he loved her.

'I'm way too selfish for starters,' he confessed. 'And damaged, Dorothy would say. You know the theory. An abused child often becomes an abusive parent. But let's not talk about life's little nasties,' he swept on, brushing aside any further explanation. 'Let's talk about you instead. OK, so you don't want the traditional role of wife and mother. I can accept that. I guess you have got your hands pretty full running this place. A lot of women these days are into the business scene. And careers. Don't go imagining I'd ever judge you harshly for that.'

'How generous of you,' came her caustic retort.

He just smiled at her again, as though amused by her impertinence.

'So when are you going to dump that loser you've been seeing and go out with me?'

Now Angelina did laugh. The man had the hide of an elephant. Exasperated, she decided to prick his ego some more. 'Alex is no loser. He's just as good-looking as you are. And just as successful, I might add. In fact, he's the only son and heir to a veritable fortune.' Besides being worth millions—property-wise—the Ambrosia Estate ran at a tidy profit each year, with their resort and restaurant very popular, and their wines in high demand over in America and Europe. If Angelina's plans for expansion into more markets bore fruit, profits could be even higher in future.

'Not impressed,' Jake countered confidently. 'Money

is nothing. Attitude is everything. He's a loser. Because if you were my woman,' Jake said, and leant closer to her across the table, 'I'd make damned sure I wasn't away if you were going to be in Sydney next weekend. You wouldn't be staying at some hotel on Saturday night, either. You'd be staying at my place.'

His eyes locked on to hers and for the life of her, she could not look away. In the end, she laughed again. It was the only way she could safely draw air into her suddenly starving lungs.

'But I'm not your woman, am I?'

He leant back in his seat again, still holding her eyes firmly captive with his. 'What if I said I wanted you to be, more than anything I've wanted in a long time? What if I told you to tell this Alex he's history? What if I asked you to stay at my place next weekend instead of the Casino?'

She should have protested at that point. But she was too enthralled with thinking about what it would be like to spend next weekend with him, staying at his place.

'I have this wonderful harbourside apartment with all the mod cons and only a short ferry ride to Darling Harbour,' he went on when she foolishly stayed silent. 'We could paint the town red on Saturday night, or stay in, if you prefer. Then on Sunday we could have lunch down on the waterfront somewhere. You must surely get a lunch break. Unfortunately, I have to be in court first thing

Monday morning, or we could have made it a long weekend.'

Angelina finally found her voice. 'What is it you expect me to say to these extraordinarily presumptuous suggestions?'

'Right now? Nothing. I wouldn't like to be accused of rushing you into anything, like last time. I'll call you later this week. Or you can call me earlier than that, if you'd like. Here...' He whipped out his wallet from his jeans and extracted two business cards. 'You got a pen on you?'

She did, in fact. She kept one in her skirt pocket. She fished it out and gave it to him. He flashed her a quick smile before bending to the task of adding some numbers to the first card before handing it over. 'That first number is my private and unlisted number at home. The second is my cellphone. Now, write yours down for me on this...' And he handed her a second card, along with the Biro.

She stared down at the white card which said simply 'Jake Winters, Lawyer' in bold black letters, along with an office address and phone number in smaller lettering underneath.

She turned it over and jotted down both her numbers, all the while thinking to herself, what *was* she doing?

She wasn't going to say yes to his invitation. How could she? OK, so she was tempted. She was only human. What woman wouldn't respond to what Jake was making her feel at this moment? As if she was the most beautiful, most desirable girl he'd ever met.

What had he said? That he wanted her to be his woman more than anything he'd wanted in a long time.

The devil would be proud of him!

Sixteen years ago, she'd fallen for such a line, hook, line and sinker. Well, she *had*, hadn't she? But sixteen years had taught Angelina to recognise the signs of a dedicated womaniser. You didn't have to have jumped into bed with that type to recognise their trappings. Jake had them all. The car. The clothes. And the charm.

Angelina knew beyond a doubt that being Jake's woman was only a temporary position, whereas her being Alex's mother was forever. Allowing herself to be seduced a second time by Alex's father was just not on.

At the same time, she *was* curious to learn a little more about him, and his life. This was the man she was going to have to entrust her son to, possibly sooner than she'd anticipated. After all, once Dorothy moved up here and found out dear Angelina at the Ambrosia Estate was a single mum with a fifteen-year-old son who just happened to be the dead spit of Jake, the cat would be out of the bag. And as much as Jake might try to abdicate his responsibilities where Alex was concerned, Angelina knew that her stubborn son would not let him get away with that. No, Alex would force himself into Jake's life whether Jake wanted it or not.

'I'm not promising anything,' she remarked coolly as she handed back the card. 'But you're welcome to ring me. I might agree to have lunch with you. Alex wouldn't mind my having lunch with an old friend.'

'I'm sure he won't,' Jake said as he tucked the card back into his wallet. 'It's hardly a grand passion between you two, is it?'

'You know nothing about my relationship with Alex.'

'I know enough,' he stated with an arrogance which was as unsettling as it was wickedly attractive. Why, oh, why did she have to find him so exciting?

Maybe she shouldn't agree to lunch with him. Even lunch might be a worry, especially down at Darling Harbour, with its air of away-from-home glamour and glitz. Sydney could be a very seductive city. Angelina often found herself losing her head a bit when she was there and spending more money than she should. Especially on clothes. She had a wardrobe full of lovely things she rarely wore.

She would have to weigh up the pros and cons of lunching with Jake before his call. If she thought there was any danger of making a fool of herself, she would not go.

'I'll look forward to ringing you,' Jake said, and slipped his wallet into the back pocket of his jeans. 'Meanwhile, surely you have some questions for yours truly? Don't you want to know how come I'm a lawyer and not in jail?'

Angelina shook her head at him in frustration. He was like a rolling bulldozer, difficult to stop.

'I'm sure you're going to tell me, whether I want to hear or not.'

'You *want* to hear,' he said cheekily. 'You know you do.'

So Angelina listened—yes, in rapt silence—whilst he told her everything that had happened to him since that fateful night. She marvelled at his good fortune, and couldn't help feeling a bit proud of him. Both Dorothy and her husband had clearly been wonderful, but Jake must have worked very hard to accomplish what he had.

Not that she intended telling him that. He was smug enough as it was.

'And to think I worried myself sick that I'd been responsible for your going to jail,' she said when he finished his tale of miracles.

'Did you really? Oh, that's sweet. But you were sweet back then. Very sweet.'

'Don't count on my being so sweet now, lover-boy. I've grown up. I might not live in the big bad city but a number of Sydney's more successful swinging singles have stayed at the Ambrosia Estate over the years. I know all about men like you.'

He laughed. 'Tell me about men like me.'

'You work hard and you play hard.'

'True.' He picked up his coffee-cup again.

'You like your own way and you don't always stick to the rules.'

'Mmm. True, I guess.' And smiled at her over the rim of the cup.

'You're all commitment-phobic sex addicts who change girlfriends as often as you do your cars.'

Jake almost choked on the last of his coffee. 'Now, wait here,' he spluttered. 'That's not quite true.'

'Which part is not quite true?' she asked tartly.

'I've only had two cars in the last few years. A navy Mazda and the yellow Ferrari I'm driving to-day.'

'Surprising. OK, so what's the girlfriend count during that time?'

He looked a bit sheepish. 'I don't have that many fingers and toes. But what about you, Miss Tough Cookie? Or shouldn't I ask?'

No way could she let him find out there hadn't been anyone since him. His ego would probably ex-plode. And his predatory nature would go into full pursuit mode.

'You can ask, but I'm not into the kiss-and-tell scene,' she tossed off. 'Let's just say I'm a big girl now and I run my own race.'

'Even when your father was alive?'

'After my not-so-successful rendezvous with you, I learned to be more sneaky.'

'You'd have to be with a father like yours around,' came his rueful remark. 'So! Did your dad *like* this Alex of yours? Or didn't he know about him?'

'He adored Alex.' Too late, Angelina wished she hadn't started that silly subterfuge.

'An Italian, is he?' Jake said drily.

'Half. Now, no more questions about Alex, please. Aah, Dorothy's back,' she said, spying the lady herself walking along the path towards them, accompanied by a portly, grey-haired man in his fifties. 'She seems to have brought the real-estate agent with her.' Fortunately, not one Angelina knew personally.

But when Dorothy swept in with the news she had secured the property and that she was here to get the owner's signature on some papers, a panic-stricken Angelina jumped to her feet and offered to find Arnold for them.

'But why don't you want them to know about Alex?' Arnold said when she cornered him in the barrel room of the winery five minutes later.

'The man with the woman who's buying your place is Alex's father,' Angelina explained reluctantly. 'All right?'

Arnold's eyes rounded. 'Heaven be praised! Just as well Antonio isn't here, or there'd be hell to pay. But he's not here, Angelina, so why keep the boy a secret?'

'Only for a little while, Arnold. I will tell Jake. But in my own good time. OK?'

'Has this Jake turned into a decent kind of chap?'

Decent. Now, decent was a subjective word.

'He's a lawyer,' she said.

'Nothing wrong with lawyers. At least he's got a job. Things could be worse.'

Angelina nodded. 'You're so right. Things *could* be worse.'

But not much.

CHAPTER FIVE

'YOU don't look too pleased,' Dorothy said within seconds of leaving the Ambrosia Estate. 'Did the lovely Angelina surprise you this time by saying no?'

Jake's hands tightened on the steering wheel. 'Things didn't go exactly according to plan. But I haven't given up yet.'

'Good.'

Jake's eyes slanted over towards Dorothy. 'You mean my old flame has your tick of approval?'

'She's a big improvement on your last few girl-friends,' Dorothy said in her usual droll fashion. 'And she'd be very convenient, considering where I'll be living soon. I'll have no worries about seeing you regularly if you start going out with a local girl.'

'I have to get her to drop some guy named Alex first.'

'You've never had any trouble getting your girl-friends to drop their old boyfriends before.'

'This one sounds formidable. A poor little rich boy. Very good-looking. Lives in Sydney. Too bad I didn't find out his last name. I could have had him investigated. From the sound of things, they don't get together all that often. He's probably two-timing her with some city chick. Guys like that are never faithful.'

'You'd know.'

'Dorothy Landsdale, I'll have you know I've always been faithful to my girlfriends!'

'Oh, I don't doubt it. They don't last long enough for you to do the dirty on them. Every few weeks it's out with the old and in with the new.'

Jake didn't like the flavour of this conversation. Dorothy was making him sound as if he was some kind of serial sleazebag where women were concerned. Angelina had inferred the same thing.

'I can well understand Angelina not jumping at the chance of being next in line,' Dorothy went on before Jake could defend himself. 'She might like a bit more security in her relationships. And a possible future.'

'I'll have you know she's no more interested in marriage and having a family than I am. She told me so. She's a career girl.'

'What? Oh, I find that hard to believe. That girl has marriage and motherhood written all over her.'

'You're just saying that because she's Italian.'

'Not at all. I've known enough career women in my life to recognise one when I meet her. If Angelina Mastroianni is a career woman, then I'm…I'm Marilyn Monroe!'

Jake laughed. 'In that case, perhaps I should be relieved that she said no to me.'

'Perhaps you should.'

But he wasn't relieved. He was annoyed. And frustrated. And jealous as hell of this Alex bloke.

Angelina belonged to *him*. She'd always belonged to him.

The sudden primitiveness—and *possessiveness*—of his thoughts stunned Jake. This wasn't him. This was some other man, some caveman who believed that his taking a female's virginity gave him the rights to her body forever.

Logic told Jake this was crazy thinking. But logic wasn't worth a damn beside the passion and determination that was firing Jake's belly at this moment. She was going to be his again. That Alex guy was going to be history, no matter what it took!

Angelina watched the yellow car till it disappeared from view, then she turned and walked with slow steps back down the path to the restaurant.

Wilomena—who had no doubt been waiting with bated breath to collar her alone—pounced immediately. A tall, rake-thin brunette, the restaurant's head waitress had sharp eyes to go with her sharp features.

'All right, fess up, Angelina? Who was that gorgeous hunk in the yellow Ferrari?'

'Just a guy I used to know. No one special.'

'Just a guy you used to know,' Wilomena repeated with rolling eyes. 'Did you hear that, Kevin?' she called out to the chef, who was the only other staff member left in the restaurant at this hour. The rest of the evening's waitresses wouldn't arrive till five-thirty, which was almost an hour away. 'He was just a guy she used to know. No one special.'

Kevin popped his bald head round the doorway that connected the body of the restaurant with the kitchen. In his late thirties, Kevin was English and single and a simply brilliant chef. He'd been on a working holiday around Australia a few years ago, filled in for their chef, who'd been taken ill, and never left. Since his arrival the restaurant's reputation had gone from good to great.

'Amazing how much he looked like Alex, isn't it?' Kevin said with a straight face. 'If I didn't know better, I would have said he was Alex's father.'

Angelina groaned. It was no use. She had no hope of keeping Jake's identity a secret, not even for a minute.

'It's all right,' Wilomena said gently when she saw the distress on her boss's face. 'We won't say anything. Not if you don't want us to.'

'I don't want you to,' Angelina returned pleadingly. 'Not yet, anyway. The other girls didn't notice, did they?'

'No. They're too new. And too silly. All they can think about on a Saturday is where they're going tonight, and with whom. So! Does he know about Alex? Is that why he was here?'

'No. He has no idea. He just dropped in for lunch by sheer accident and he…he…. Oh, Wilomena, it's terribly complicated.'

'Why don't you sit down and tell me all about it?'

Angelina looked at Wilomena, who at thirty-eight had a few years on her. Divorced, with two teenage girls, she lived in Cessnock and worked long hours at the restaurant six days a week to support herself and her kids. Angelina realised she could do worse than confide in Wilomena, who was both pragmatic and practical. And she needed someone to confide in. The only friends she had now were the people she worked with. Her father had been her best friend. Still, this little problem wasn't something she'd have been able to talk to him about. He'd been totally blind when it came to the subject of Jake Winters.

'OK,' she said with a sigh. 'Let's have a glass of wine and I'll tell you all.'

Wilomena smiled. She was really quite attractive when she smiled. 'Fantastic. Let's go into the kitchen so Kevin can hear. Otherwise, I'll just have to repeat everything after you've gone.'

Angelina laughed. 'You two are getting as thick as thieves, aren't you?'

'Yeah,' Wilomena said with a twinkle in her quick blue eyes. 'We are.'

Half an hour later, Angelina made her way slowly along the path that ran from the restaurant and past the cellar door before branching into two paths. One led to the winery, the other followed the driveway that led to the resort proper, a distance of about a hundred metres. She headed for the resort, her shoes crunching on the gravel, her head down in thought as she walked down the gentle incline.

Kevin had advised her to tell Jake the truth as soon as possible, especially since Alex himself wanted to meet his father. He'd said he would want to know if he had a son and would be seriously annoyed if such news was held back from him.

'And that's bulldust about this Jake saying he'd be

a rotten father,' Kevin had pronounced. 'Lots of men talk like that. You wait till he finds out he has a son for real, especially a great kid like Alex. He'll be falling over himself to be the best father he possibly can.'

Wilomena hadn't shared Kevin's optimism. There again, she had more jaundiced views about the opposite sex and their ability to be good fathers.

'What fantasyland do you live in, Kevin?' she'd countered tartly. 'Obviously, you've never been a father. From my experience, lots of men these days soon get very bored with the day-to-day responsibilities of fatherhood. Guys like Jake, especially. He admitted to Angelina he was selfish. And damaged, whatever that means. I think Angelina's right to be careful. I don't think she should tell him anything for a while. If nothing else, it gives Alex time to grow up some more. It'll be weeks before this Dorothy lady moves up here. Meanwhile, Arnold's not going to say anything.'

They'd argued back and forth, with Angelina a bemused onlooker. In the end, Kevin had thrown up his hands and told Wilomena it was no wonder she was still single, if she was so distrusting and contemptuous of men.

Angelina had done her best to smooth things over between them but by the time she'd left, there'd been a chilling silence in the kitchen. She was relieved she wasn't working there tonight. Or on the reception desk. She'd already planned to take the evening off, to do some female things, like have a long bath, shave her legs, put a treatment in her hair and do her nails. It would be good to be alone, to think.

'Angelina, Angelina!'

Angelina turned to find Wilomena running after her.

'Sorry about the ruckus in there,' Wilomena said on reaching her. 'Don't worry about it. Kevin will be fine later tonight. And yes, before you ask, we are sleeping together.'

'I...I wasn't going to ask.'

Wilomena frowned. 'No, you wouldn't, would you? You're not like other girls. It almost killed you to tell us what you told us in there, didn't it? I mean, you're not one to gossip, or to confide.'

'No, I...I guess not.' When you spent the amount of time *she* had spent alone, you lost the knack of confiding in other people. You tried to solve your problems yourself.

'Look, I just wanted to say that I think you should go out with Jake, but without telling him about Alex. Aside from having a bit of long-overdue fun, you can go see where Jake lives, and how he lives. See what kind of man he is.'

'But how did you...?'

'Yeah, I know, you didn't tell us he'd asked you out. But I didn't come down in the last shower, honey, and I watched you two today. Both times. He asked you out all right and you said no, didn't you?'

'I haven't actually given him an answer yet.'

'What does he want you to do?'

'Stay at his place when I go to Sydney for the expo next weekend.'

'Wow. He's a fast mover all right. It took Kevin two years to ask me out, then two months to get me in the sack.'

'It took Jake about two minutes the first time,' Angelina said drily.

'Ooooh. That good, eh?'

'His kisses were. The sex itself was not great. I froze, and he just went ahead.'

'But you wouldn't freeze this time,' Wilomena said intuitively.

Angelina stiffened. 'I have no intention of finding out if I would or I wouldn't. And I have no intention of staying at his place next weekend.'

'But why not? I wouldn't be able to resist, if it were me. The guy's a hunk of the first order.'

Angelina didn't need to be told that. Jake, the man, had even more sex appeal than Jake, the bad boy. And *he'd* had oodles.

'If it was anyone other than Alex's father, I would.'

'If it was anyone other than Alex's father, you wouldn't want to,' Wilomena said. 'I've known girls like you before, Angelina. You're a one-man woman. And he's the man.'

'That's romantic nonsense!'

'Is it?' Wilomena probed softly.

'Yes,' Angelina said stubbornly whilst secretly thinking that Wilomena could be right. Why else hadn't she accepted dates with other men? It wasn't as though she hadn't been asked. She couldn't even claim to be protecting Alex any more, now that he was at boarding school most of the time.

Wilomena shrugged. 'Have it your way. So, you're really not going to see Jake next weekend? Not at all?'

'I...I might go to lunch with him.'

The look on Wilomena's face was telling.

'Just lunch!' Angelina insisted. 'As you yourself said, I need to find out some more about him.'

'Sounds like an excuse to gaze at him some more.'

'I didn't gaze at him today. I was just shocked at how much he looks like Alex.'

'Who do you think you're kidding?'

Angelina groaned. 'I did stare, didn't I?'

'Don't beat yourself up over it. The man was worth a stare. I ogled myself. So did every other woman in the place.'

'Which is why I can't risk being alone with him again. The man's a right devil where women are concerned. He always was.'

'Mmm. But aren't you curious over what it would be like with him now? I mean, he's sure to be very good in the sack. If what you say about him is true, he's had plenty of practice.'

'Too much practice. No, I'm not curious about his lovemaking abilities,' she lied. 'Only about his character and whether he's going to be good for Alex.'

'You know, Angelina, you're a woman as well as a mother. Do you ever think of your own needs?'

'Yes, of course I do.'

'But I've never known you to go out on a date. Not during the time I've worked here, anyway.'

'Dating is seriously overrated. And so is sex.'

'Don't knock it till you try it.'

Angelina flushed. 'Who says I haven't?'

'I have eyes, honey. And ears. If you'd slept with someone around here, I'd know about it. Look, your father's gone now and Alex is almost grown up. Time for you to live a little.'

'Maybe. But not with Jake.' *I'd probably fall in love with him again and then where would I be?*

'Yeah, perhaps you're right. If you slept with him, it could be awkward once he finds out about Alex. He might think you were trying to trap him into marriage.'

'I'd be more concerned over what Alex thought.'

'I dare say you would. You're a very good mother, Angelina. You put me to shame sometimes.'

'Nonsense. You're a great mother.'

'I try to be. Talking of kids, I have to go and ring mine. See what the little devils are up to.'

'And I have to ring Alex and see how he did at cricket today.'

'Being a mother just never stops, does it?' And with a parting grin, Wilomena hurried off.

Angelina sighed and made her way down the rest of the path and through the covered archway that provided protection for arriving guests. A green Jaguar was parked there, with a middle-aged couple inside booking in. Angelina slipped through a side-gate just past Reception that led into a private courtyard attached to the manager's quarters, a spacious two-bedroomed unit with an *en suite* to the main.

She and Alex had moved in there two years ago after Angelina had started doing night shifts at the reception desk. The excuse she'd used for the move was that the old farmhouse where they'd been living, and where she'd been born and brought up, was a couple of hundred metres away, far too long a walk for her at night. Or so she had told her father. Papa had not been happy with their move at first, but he'd got used to it. Besides, when Alex came home on holiday, he'd often stayed with his grandfather in his old room.

Angelina rarely ventured back there, the house not having all that many good memories for her. She'd been a lonely child living there, and an even lonelier single mother. She much preferred her memoryless apartment with its fresh cream walls, cream floor coverings and all mod cons. She liked the modern furniture too, having never been fond of the heavy and ornate furniture her father had preferred. Now that her father was gone, Arnold was living in the old farmhouse, free accommodation being part of his contract as Ambrosia's wine-maker.

Of course, Alex hadn't liked that at all, having someone else living in his grandfather's house. But that was just too bad.

Another sigh escaped Angelina's lips as she let herself in the front door. What a day it had been so far. And it wasn't over yet.

She moved straight across the cream carpet to the

side-table where she kept the phone, sitting down on the green and cream checked sofa and calling Alex on his cellphone. He should have finished playing cricket by now.

'Yes, Mum,' he answered after the second ring.

'You lost,' she said, knowing that tone of voice.

'I don't want to talk about it,' he grumped.

'Never mind. You'll wallop them at the swimming carnival.'

'We'd better. They'll be insufferable if they win that, too.'

Alex had a killer competitive instinct. He was the one who would be insufferable.

'So how's things up there?' he asked.

'Everything's fine. Arnold sold his place today.' *And your father showed up out of the blue.*

Alex groaned. 'Does that mean we're stuck with him forever?'

'Alex, I'm not sure what your problem is with Arnold. He's a really nice man. You could learn a lot from him. Your grandfather said he was brilliant with whites. You know Papa was not at his best with whites. He was more of a red man. But no, we're not stuck with him forever. He said he's going to buy a little place over in Port Stephens with what he gets for his place, with enough left over for his retirement. He's well aware how keen you are to take over and is more than willing to stand aside when you feel ready to take on the job of wine-maker.'

'Good. Because I intend to do just that as soon as I finish my higher-school certificate.'

A prickle ran down Angelina's spine. He sounded like Jake had today. So strong and so determined.

'I won't stand in your way, Alex,' she said. 'This place is your inheritance, and the job of wine-maker is your right.'

'And I'm going to find my father, too. Not in November. I can't wait that long. I'm going to start next holidays. At Easter.'

Angelina grimaced. Easter! That was only a few weeks away. Still, maybe it was for the best. She couldn't stand the tension of such a long wait herself.

'All right, Alex. You'll get no further argument from me on that score. Come Easter, we'll go find your father.'

'Honest?' Alex sounded amazed. 'You're not going to make a fuss?'

'No.'

'Cool. You're the best, Mum.'

'Mmm.'

'Got to go. The dinner bell's gone. Love ya.'

'Love you, too,' she replied, but he'd already hung up.

Tears filled her eyes as she hung up too.

'Lord knows what you're crying over, Angelina,' she muttered. 'Things could be worse, as Arnold said.'

But she wasn't entirely convinced.

CHAPTER SIX

JAKE paced back and forth across his living room, unable to eat, unable to sit and watch television or work or do any of the other activities that usually filled his alone-time.

The sleek, round, silver-framed clock on the wall pronounced that it was getting on for half-past eight. He'd dropped Dorothy off at her place in Rose Bay at seven-thirty, an hour earlier. The drive back from the Hunter Valley had taken a lot longer than the drive up. They'd been caught up in the Saturday-night traffic coming into the city, slowing to a crawl near the Harbour Bridge.

'I won't miss this when I move to the country,' Dorothy had declared impatiently, which had rather amused Jake at the time. She should see how bad the traffic was in peak hours on a weekday. If there was an accident on the bridge, or in the tunnel, the lines of traffic didn't crawl. They just stopped.

But that was city living for you.

Jake had declined Dorothy's invitation to come in for a bite to eat, and now here he was, unfed and unable to relax, becoming increasingly agitated and angry. With himself.

He'd handled Angelina all wrong today. He'd come on to her way too strong, and way too fast.

That might work with city babes in wine bars on a Friday night, but not girls like Angelina. Even when she was fifteen, she hadn't been easy. She'd made him wait, forcing him to make endless small talk that summer before finally agreeing to meet him alone.

He could see now that her still being attracted to him in a physical sense wasn't enough for her to drop her current boyfriend and go out with him. She claimed she was a modern woman who'd been around, but he suspected—like Dorothy—that Angelina was not as sophisticated as she thought she was. She had an old-fashioned core.

She was going to say no when he finally rang her. Nothing was surer in his mind. And the prospect was killing him.

He had to change his tactics. Hell, he was a smart guy, wasn't he? A lawyer. Changing tactics midstream came naturally to him.

Go back to square one, Jake. Chat her up some more. Show her your warm and sensitive side. You have to have one. Edward said you did. Then you might stand a chance of winning, if not her heart, then her body.

And don't wait till tomorrow night to call. Do it now. Right now, buddy, whilst she can still remember how it felt today when you touched her hand, and looked deep into her eyes and talked about spending a whole weekend together.

If it was even remotely what you felt—what you are *still* feeling—then she has to be tempted.

Jake's hand was unsteady as he took out his wallet

and extracted the card where she'd written down her telephone numbers. He had it bad all right. It had been a long time since he'd felt this desperate over a woman. Damn it all, he'd *never* felt this desperate before!

Except perhaps that summer sixteen years ago. He'd been desperate for Angelina back then too. No wonder he'd been hopeless by the time he'd actually done it with her.

Jake craved the opportunity to show her he wasn't a hopeless lover now.

But first, he had to get her to say yes to seeing him again. Even lunch would do. She'd said she might go to lunch with him. It wasn't quite what he had in mind but it was a start.

He dragged in several deep breaths as he walked over to sweep up the receiver of his phone. His hand was only marginally steadier as he punched in her number but he consoled himself with the fact she could not see it shake.

As long as he sounded calm. And sincere. That was all that mattered.

Angelina was sitting on the sofa and painting her toenails, her right foot propped up on the glass coffee-table, when the phone rang. The brush immediately zigzagged across her second toe onto her big toe, leaving a long streak of plum nail-polish on her skin.

The swear-word she uttered was not one she would

have used if Alex had been home. Or if her father had been alive.

By the time she replaced the brush in the bottle, poured some remover on a cotton-wool ball and wiped off the wayward polish, then leant over to snatch up the phone from the nearby side-table, it had been ringing for quite a while.

'Yes?' she answered sharply. She hoped it wasn't Wilomena with more advice. She was all adviced out. Besides, she'd already made up her mind what she was going to say to Jake when he finally rang.

'Angelina? It's Jake. Have I rung at an awkward moment?'

Jake. It was Jake!

'You weren't supposed to ring till later in the week,' she snapped, hating it that just the sound of his voice could make her stomach go all squishy.

'I couldn't wait till then to apologise,' he said. 'I wouldn't have been able to sleep tonight.'

'Apologise for what?' Her voice was still sharp.

His, however, was soft and seductive.

'I was out of line today.'

'Were you really?' Now her tone was dry, and sarcastic.

No way was she going to be all sweetness and light. She was still seriously annoyed with him for turning up in her life at this particular point in time and making her make difficult decisions.

'I was pushy and presumptuous, as you said. My only excuse is that I didn't want to let you get away from me a second time. I really liked you sixteen years ago, Angelina, but I like the woman you've become even better.'

She laughed. 'Wow, you've really become the master of the polished line, haven't you? But you can save the flattery for another occasion, Jake. I've already decided to have lunch with you on Saturday.'

The dead silence on the other end of the line gave Angelina some satisfaction that she'd been able to knock him speechless. Unfortunately, now that she'd voiced her decision out loud to him, the reality of it shook her right down to her half-painted toes.

But the die had been rolled. No going back.

'Great!' he said, sounding much too happy for her liking. 'I'm already looking forward to it. But does— er—Alex know?'

'I spoke to him earlier this evening. We talked about you.'

'What did you say? I'll bet you didn't tell him how we first met.'

'Alex already knows all about you, Jake. There are no secrets between us.'

'And he *agreed* to your going to lunch with me?'

'Why should he object to a platonic lunch between old friends?'

'Old *flames*, Angelina. Not old friends.'

'Whatever. A lot of water has gone under the bridge since then, Jake.'

'I'll bet you didn't tell him everything I said to you today.'

What could she say to that?

'You didn't, did you?' Jake continued when she

remained silent. 'No man—not even your pathetic Alex—would willingly let his girlfriend go to lunch with another man who'd declared his wish to make her *his* woman.'

Angelina could not believe the passion in Jake's words. And the power. How easy it would be to forget all common sense and tell him that she had changed her mind, that she would not only go to lunch with him on Saturday, but she would also stay at his place on the Saturday night.

Dear heaven, she *was* going to make a fool of herself with him again. Or she might, if she went to lunch with him on Saturday as things stood. If he could do this to her over the phone, what could he do to her when she was alone with him in the big bad city?

She had to tell him about Alex. Right here and now. It was the only way she could protect herself against her susceptibility to this man.

'Jake, there's something I have to tell you,' she began, then stopped as she struggled for the right words. He was going to be shocked out of his mind. And furious with her for playing word games with him. How she could possibly explain why she'd done such a thing? She was going to look a fool, no matter what she said, or did.

'Alex doesn't know you're going to lunch with me at all, does he?' Jake jumped in.

'Er—no. He doesn't.'

'You realise what that means, Angelina. You're

finished with him, whether you admit it or not. You're not the sort of girl to two-time a guy.'

'I don't consider lunch a two-timing act,' she argued, panicking at the way this conversation was now going. Instead of finding sanctuary in the truth, she was getting in deeper. And deeper.

'It is when you know that the guy you're having lunch with wants more than to share a meal with you,' Jake pointed out ruefully.

'But what *you* want is not necessarily what *I* want,' she countered, stung by his presumption.

'That's not the impression you gave me today. We shared something special once, Angelina. It's still there. The sparks. The chemistry.'

'Men like you share a chemistry with lots of women, Jake. It's nothing special. Which reminds me, is there some current girlfriend who should know that you've asked another woman out to lunch?'

'No.'

'Why not?'

'I'm between girlfriends at the moment.'

She laughed. 'Am I supposed to believe that?'

'You sure are. I'm a lot of things but I'm no liar.'

'Such as what? What are you, Jake Winters, that I should worry about before daring to go to lunch with you?'

'You don't honestly expect me to put myself down, do you? I'm no saint but I'm not one of the bad guys, either. I don't lie and I don't cheat. There is no other woman in my life. But I *am* a confirmed bachelor. And I aim to stay that way. Which should

please you, since you're not into wedding bells and
baby bootees. Or did I get that wrong?'

'No. No, you didn't get that wrong.'

*If I can't marry you, then I don't want to marry
anyone.*

The thought burst into her mind. Shocking her.
Shattering her. This couldn't be. This wasn't fair.
Not only that, but it was also crazy. He'd only been
in her life a few short hours this time.

She couldn't be in love with him again. Not really.
She was being confused and corrupted by the ro-
mance of the situation. And by desire. His, as well
as her own. She wasn't sure which was the more
powerful. Being wanted the way Jake said he wanted
her. Or her wanting him.

Angelina still could not believe the feelings which
had rampaged through her when he'd simply touched
her hand.

Wilomena was probably right. She was a one-man
woman.

And Jake was the man. Impossible to resist him.
She could go to lunch with him next Saturday, pretending that it was a reconnaissance mission to find
out what kind of man he was. But that was all it
would be. A pretence.

'Tell me about your job,' she said, valiantly re-
solving to put their conversation back on to a more
platonic, getting-to-know-you basis. 'What kind of
lawyer are you?'

'A darned good one.'

'No, I mean what kind of people do you represent?'

'People who need a good lawyer to go in to bat for them. People who've been put down and put upon, usually in the corporate world. Employees who've been unfairly dismissed, or sexually harassed, or made to endure untenable work conditions. I have this woman client at the moment who's in the process of suing her boss. She worked as his assistant in an un-air-conditioned office with him for years whilst he chain-smoked. She repeatedly asked him to put her in a separate office but he wouldn't. Yet he was filthy rich. She now has terminal lung cancer and she's only forty-two. We're suing for millions. And we'll win, too.'

'But she won't,' Angelina said. 'She'll die.'

'Yes, she'll die. But her teenage children won't. She told me she'd die happier if she gets enough money to provide for them till they can provide for themselves. Her husband's an invalid as well. That's why she had to work and why she stayed working for that bastard under such rotten conditions. Because the job was within walking distance of her house, and she didn't have a car. She couldn't afford one.'

'That's so sad. I hate hearing stories like that. Don't tell me any more, Jake.'

'All right,' he said gently. 'You always did have a soft heart, Angelina. I remember the day we found that bird with the broken wing caught in the vines. You cried till your dad promised to take it to a vet.'

He was getting to her again. 'I only have a soft

heart for poor birds with broken wings,' she countered crisply. 'And poor people dying through no fault of their own. Not smooth-talking lawyers who go round trying to seduce old flames just for the heck of it.'

'Is that what you think I'm doing?'

'Come, now, Jake, you ran into me today by sheer accident. You haven't given me a second thought all these years.' Unlike herself. Even if she'd wanted to forget Jake, how could she when his eyes had been staring back at her on a daily basis for years? 'Your dear old friend Dorothy is buying a place up here,' she swept on. 'You spotted me again today, liked what you saw, and thought I'd be a convenient lay during your weekends up here.'

'That's a pretty harsh judgement.'

'I think it's a pretty honest one. Please don't try to con me, Jake. I won't like that. Be straight with me.'

'OK, you're right and you're wrong. I admit I haven't actively thought about you for years. But that doesn't mean I'd forgotten you. When I realised where I was going for lunch today, everything came flooding back. The way you made me feel that summer. The things that happened. I really wanted to see you again. I told myself it was just curiosity, or the wish to say sorry for being just a chump back then. But when I actually saw you, Angelina...when I saw you I—'

'Please don't say the world stopped,' she cut in drily.

He laughed. 'I won't. It actually sped up. At least, my pulse-rate did. Do you know how beautiful you are?' he said, his voice dropping low again. 'How sexy?'

Don't fall for all that bulldust. Keep your head, honey.

Angelina could almost hear those very words coming from Wilomena's mouth.

'You're not the first man to tell me that, Jake,' she said in a rather hard voice.

'I don't doubt it.'

'City men are amazingly inventive, especially when they're away from home. The Ambrosia Estate has become a popular venue for conferences,' she elaborated. 'Lots of them pass through all the time.'

'You sound as if you've been burnt a few times.'

'Who hasn't in this day and age?' came her off-hand reply. If he thought she'd jumped into bed with her fair share of such men, then all well and good. No way did she want him thinking he was the only man she'd ever known.

'I'm sorry but I really must go, Jake. I was in the middle of something important when you called. I'll see you on Saturday at the expo. I'm sure you can manage to find the right booth. Shall we say twelve-thirty?'

'Noon would be better.'

'Noon it is, then. Bye for now.' And she hung up.

Jake was grinning as he replaced his receiver.

Alex, old man, he thought elatedly, come next weekend, you're going to be history!

CHAPTER SEVEN

ANGELINA couldn't stop titivating herself. If she'd checked her make-up and hair once, she'd checked it a hundred times.

Not for the first time this morning, she hurried into the hotel bathroom so that she could stand in front of the cheval mirror that hung on the back of the door.

The dress she was wearing was not casual. But she knew she looked good in it, which was the most important thing to her right at that moment.

Light and silky, the sleeveless sheath skimmed her curvy figure, making her look slim yet shapely at the same time. Its scooped neckline stopped just short of showing any cleavage, the wide, softly frilled collar very feminine. The hem finished well above her knee on one side and dipped down almost to mid-calf on the other, as was the fashion this year. The print on the pale cream material was floral, the flowers small and well-spaced, their colours ranging from the palest pink to a deep plum, her favourite colour. She'd matched the dress with open-toed cream high heels and a plum handbag. Her lipstick and nail-polish were plum as well. Strong colours suited her, with her olive skin and dark hair and eyes.

Her hair—which had been up and down several

times so far this morning—was finally down, its natural wave and curl having been tamed somewhat with a ruthless blowdrying, but it still kicked up on the ends. Shoulder-blade-length, it was parted on one side and looped behind her ears to show her gold and pearl drops. A gold chain with a single gold and pearl pendant adorned her neck. The floral scents of her perfume, an extravagant one she'd bought during her last shopping trip to Sydney, was only just detectable on her skin. Angelina didn't like it when a woman's perfume preceded her into a room like a tidal wave.

She stroked the figure-hugging dress down over her hips before turning round and looking over her shoulder at her back view. Her scowl soon became a shrug. Nothing she could do about her Italian lower half. She had wide hips and a big bottom, and that was all there was to it.

Angelina turned back and looked with more approval at her front view. At least she had the breasts to go with the backside. They were a definite plus. Just as well, however, that her nipples were hidden by the wideness of the collar, because she could feel them now, pressing against the satiny confines of her underwired bra, making her hotly aware of how excited she was. How incredibly, appallingly excited.

A small moan escaped her lips, Angelina stuffing a closed fist into her mouth and biting on her knuckles in an effort to get some control over her silly self. But she was fighting a losing battle. The truth was she was dying to see Jake again. She wanted to see that look in his eyes once more, the one which made her feel like the most beautiful girl in the world.

Oh, she knew that he'd probably looked at a hundred different girls that way over the years. There were no end of lovely-looking girls here in Sydney, model-slim girls with more sophistication and style than she had. But no matter. She could pretend she was the only one, just for one miserable lunch.

Surely there was no harm in that. Lunch was safe. They wouldn't really be alone. Impossible for him to get to her sexually during lunch, no matter what his secret agenda might be. Sharing a meal was also a good opportunity to find out more about him.

Her eyes went to her wrist-watch. It was ten-past ten, still almost two hours to go before noon. The minutes were dragging, but then, she'd been up since dawn.

She hadn't slept well, and she couldn't even blame the hotel bed. She hadn't slept well all week, her mind never giving her any peace. She'd been tormented by regrets and recriminations.

Of course, in hindsight, she *should* have told Jake about Alex straight away last Saturday when he'd come back to the restaurant. And she shouldn't have begun that silly charade, letting Jake think Alex was her boyfriend. No, not boyfriend. Lover. It had only made Jake even more determined, it seemed, to win her. She'd become a challenge.

By Friday her nerves had been so bad that she hadn't felt capable of driving down to Sydney, let alone coping with the inner-city traffic. Whenever she came down to visit Alex at weekends, she always stayed at the Rydges Hotel in North Sydney, which was near his school. There was never any need for her to drive over the Harbour Bridge. If she wanted to go shopping in the city during her weekend trips down, she caught the train over the bridge. She never attempted to drive. For a country-raised girl, driving in that congestion would be a nightmare.

But getting to the expo, and the Star City hotel, would require her to go over the bridge and negotiate all those confusing lanes that went off in myriad different directions. Her father had brought her down to a show at the Star City theatre last year, and even he'd taken a wrong turn. Much easier to catch the train down and get a cab from Central. Much easier to come down on the Friday, too, rather than wait till the Saturday morning.

Arnold had kindly driven her into the station yesterday morning and she'd arrived in Sydney just after two, giving her enough time after booking in at the hotel to go for a walk and locate where the weekend expo was being held. It was down on a nearby wharf, in a building that had once housed the old casino.

The finishing touches on the Ambrosia Estate booth were being made when she arrived and she'd been very impressed. It looked like a little piece of Italy, with vines climbing over a mock-pergola, from which hung big bunches of grapes—not real but very lifelike. The right side of the booth was dedicated to white wines, with the red wines on the left. Each side would have its own team of pretty female demonstrators for wine-tasting, she'd been informed by the man running the show. Cheese would be offered with the reds, slices of fruit with the drier whites, and exotic sweets with the dessert wines.

The only negative during her inspection tour was this man himself. He was a typical salesman. Thirtyish and suavely handsome with a moustache and goatee beard, he just couldn't help flirting with her. Not too strong for a first meeting. But Angelina had had plenty to do with salesmen at the resort, and she knew as sure as the sun was already up and shining that morning that today would be a different story. Today, he was going to come on much stronger. Today, he was going to be hands-on.

Which created a dilemma for Angelina. She didn't want to encourage the guy by turning up again today. At the same time, she didn't want Jake to think her presence wasn't required at the expo. She needed to actually be there at the booth, doing something constructive, when Jake showed up. Which meant she'd have to leave the sanctuary of her hotel room soon and make an appearance.

Angelina sighed. She hoped that Wayne—he must have told her his name ten times—didn't think she'd dolled herself up for him. Yesterday she'd only been wearing jeans and a simple white shirt, and he hadn't been able to stop eyeing her up and down.

The telephone suddenly ringing startled Angelina. As she hurried from the bathroom, she wondered who it would be. Unlikely to be Alex. The team wasn't allowed any outside calls during their weekend camp. The focus was to be all on swimming. Angelina had called him last night from the hotel and they'd talked for simply ages. Mostly about the expo. Alex was all for advertising their wines, unlike his grandfather, who'd been old-fashioned in his ways.

No, it couldn't be Alex, she thought as she crossed the hotel room and scooped up the receiver. Hopefully not the dreaded Wayne, wanting to know where she was.

'Yes?'

'Do you always answer the phone as if it's bad news?'

Jake. It was Jake. Angelina's stomach started to swirl.

'How did you know to ring me here?' she said.

'I was just talking to the chap running your booth at the expo and he mentioned you'd arrived yesterday. You yourself told me where you were staying, Angelina.'

'But what are you doing at the expo this early? You said noon. It's only just after ten.'

'I didn't want to risk not being able to find you later, so I thought I'd do a preliminary sortie. I'm glad I did. This place is a madhouse. You should see it. Which reminds me. Why aren't you down here, selling your wares? It wouldn't be because you don't really need to be here, would it? You couldn't possibly have lied to me about that too, the way you lied to me about when you would be arriving in Sydney?'

Angelina didn't know whether to be annoyed with

him, or charmed. 'I didn't want you pestering me any more than necessary.'

'Pestering! Wow, you really know how to take the wind out of a guy's sails, don't you?'

'Sorry. That was a bit harsh. But you know what I mean. Is there a purpose to this call, Jake, or is it just a softening-up trick?'

He laughed. 'I can see I'm going to have to be very careful with you.'

'Yes, you are. I'm fragile.'

He laughed again. 'You're about as fragile as Dorothy. OK, so I won't confess I just wanted to hear the sound of your voice. That would probably go down like a lead balloon. The second reason for this call is to check that you don't get seasick.'

'Seasick,' she repeated blankly. She was still thinking of his wanting to hear the sound of her voice.

'Yep, I'm planning on booking us a luncheon cruise on the harbour. That's another reason for my early arrival over here. I wanted to find out what was available.'

'Oh. Oh, how…lovely,' she finished, having almost said how romantic.

'I thought you might never have done that, living where you do.'

'No. No, I haven't. That's very thoughtful of you, Jake.'

'I cannot tell a lie. It wasn't thoughtful. It was my next best softening-up trick. After this phone call.'

Angelina smiled. 'You really are shameless.'

'And you really are beautiful. Yes, I know, I shouldn't have said that, either. I can't seem to help myself with you. My mouth has a mind of its own. Have you told Alex about us yet?'

'There is no *us*, Jake.'

'About lunch with me, then?'

'No.'

'You're only delaying the inevitable.'

'Yes. I know that.'

She heard his sharp intake of breath. 'Does that mean what I hope it means?'

'Let's just take one day at a time, Jake,' she said.

'Fair enough.'

'See you at the booth at noon,' she said, and hung up before she could say another single silly word.

CHAPTER EIGHT

JAKE watched her from a safe distance, Angelina totally unaware of his presence. He was a good thirty metres away from the Ambrosia Estate booth, with the milling crowds providing the perfect cover for his observation post.

She looked even more beautiful today than she had last Saturday. That dress was a stunner. But then, Angelina would look stunning in anything.

Woman was the right word to describe Angelina. So many girls these days were like stick insects. But not her. She was all soft curves and lush femininity. The two skinny blonde demonstrators working next to her in the booth looked positively anorexic by comparison.

Jake had been thinking about Angelina all week. She'd constantly distracted him at work and disturbed his sleep with dreams of the most erotic kind.

Last night had been especially erotic. He'd woken and reached for her in the bed—so real was the dream. But where he'd anticipated finding her warm and naked next to him, there'd only been a cold emptiness.

And to think she'd actually been *here*, in Sydney, last night, staying at the Star City hotel! This revelation had frustrated the hell out of him. If he'd known, he could have persuaded her to at least have dinner with him.

And she would have come. She'd virtually admitted to him over the phone this morning that she'd decided to give Alex the brush-off in favour of him.

Unfortunately, she'd also made it clear that he was still on probation. One day at a time, she'd said. He could not afford to rest on his laurels just yet. Or presume that she would say yes to more than a meal or two today.

Never in the last ten years had Jake had to be this patient with a woman. And never had he felt *less* patient.

His body was on fire, aching to be with her in the most basic way.

As his eyes roved over the silky dress she was wearing, his loins stirred alarmingly. He shifted away from the wall he was leaning against, taking several deep breaths and willing his flesh back to a semblance of control, and decency.

Suddenly, Angelina's eyes started to search the crowd as though she was looking for someone. Despite it only being ten to twelve, Jake instinctively knew she was looking for him. With rather anxious eyes, he thought. Perhaps because that Wayne fellow was being a pest. Ever since Jake had taken up his vantage point five minutes earlier, the sales rep had been chatting away to Angelina, his slimy dark eyes all over her.

When the sleazebag actually had the temerity to reach out and lay a hand on Angelina's bare arm,

Jake decided that waiting till noon was not on. He forged forward, amazed at the wave of fierce emotion which had consumed him.

Not jealousy. He didn't think for a moment Angelina fancied the guy. Jake had read her body language. He just couldn't bear for any man to touch her like that. Or to undress her with his eyes the way that guy had been doing.

The thought that *he'd* been doing some undressing with his own eyes was a sobering one. Though Jake quickly dismissed any guilt with the added thought that it was different with him. He *cared* about Angelina. It wasn't just a question of lust.

Her eyes lit up at the sight of him, making him feel almost ten feet tall.

'Ready to go, darling?' he said, firmly staking his claim.

Fortunately, Angelina didn't give him one of those don't-go-getting-carried-away-with-yourself looks she'd bestowed upon him last Saturday.

'I just have to get my handbag,' she replied eagerly.

Within thirty seconds, he was shepherding her away through the crowd, his hand resting possessively in the small of her back. Once they were out of sight of the booth, he rather expected her to tell him to keep his hands to himself.

But she didn't.

Angelina knew she was being foolish. But ooh…the touch of Jake's hand on her body was electric. His palm was like a hot iron, burning its way through her dress to her skin beneath. Heat radiated through her, making her feel as if she was glowing all over.

'Thank you for rescuing me from that creep,' she said as he steered her through the throng towards the exit.

'My pleasure.'

'I can't stand touchy-feely men.'

'Oops!' His hand promptly lifted away.

'Not you,' she hastily assured him with an upwards glance. 'I didn't mean you.'

Their eyes met and Angelina knew she'd just crossed a line, that line which she had taken such pains to draw earlier, but which was now in danger of disintegrating entirely.

Her eyes ran over him, and she thought how utterly gorgeous he was looking in his trendy city clothes. No jeans for him this time. But not a suit, either. His trousers were a bone colour, not dissimilar to the cream in her dress. Very expensive by the look of their cut, and the lack of creases. His shirt was made in black silk, worn open-necked, with its long sleeves rolled up to his elbows. Casual, yet sophisticated and suave, the epitome of the man about town, such a far cry from the Jake whom she'd ogled just as shamelessly sixteen years ago.

Only his eyes were the same. Still that same hard, icy blue, and still with the same intent. To get her into bed.

'That's a relief,' he said, and his hand settled right back where it had been.

A shiver ran down Angelina's spine. How would it feel if she had no clothes on at all? If she was lying with him, naked, in a bed, and he was sliding his hand down her back whilst the other was…?

She gulped the great lump which had formed in her throat and tried to find reasons for why his making love to her should never be allowed to happen. But none came to mind at that moment.

'Did that guy say or do anything really offensive?' Jake asked as he guided her out onto the wharf and into the sunshine. 'Do you want to me go back and sort him out?'

Angelina drew in some blessedly fresh air and tried to get herself back on to an even keel. 'Lord, no. No, that's not necessary. Wayne's harmless, really. Just too full of himself. And it's not as though I have to see him again.' Too late, she realised she'd made another blunder.

Jake pounced on it immediately. 'You don't have to go back to the booth today?'

'Not if I don't want to.'

'And do you want to?'

'Hardly.' Silly to say that she did. 'I thought I might do some shopping after our lunch,' she added, hoping to retrieve lost ground.

'Shopping for what?'

'Clothes.'

His gaze travelled slowly up and down her body. 'More clothes to drive men wild with lust?'

She flushed. 'That's not my intent when I buy a dress.'

'It might not be your intent,' he said drily. 'But the result's the same. I have to confess I do understand where poor Wayne was coming from. You'd tempt a saint, looking as you do today. And not many men are saints. But I doubt you'll have much time for shopping after our luncheon cruise. The one I've booked takes three hours. Most shops close at four on a Saturday. Besides, I was hoping you'd agree to come back to my place for a while. I live over in that direction there on MacMahon's Point,' he said, pointing straight across the expanse of sparkling blue water at the distant skyline of high-rise, harbour-hugging apartment blocks. 'I've already organised for the boat's captain to put in at the wharf there and let us off afterwards.'

'That was presumptuous of you, Jake,' came her surprisingly cool-sounding remark. Inside, she felt far from cool.

He shrugged. 'I didn't think you'd mind. I thought you might like to see where I live. I'm happy to drive you back to the hotel later in the afternoon. If you want to change for dinner, that is. But you look perfectly fine to go out with me exactly as you are.'

She laughed. 'You have today all planned out, don't you?'

'Being a lawyer has taught me that it's always wise to have a plan.'

'And do things always go according to your plans?'

'On the whole. But there are exceptions, of which

I suspect you might be one,' he finished with a rueful sigh.

She smiled, gratified that he thought she had more will-power and character than she actually possessed at that moment.

'You said one day at a time,' he reminded her. 'This is just one day, Angelina.'

He was right. It was. But she knew how Jake aimed for this day to end. All she could hope was that, when the time came, she had the courage to say no to him.

CHAPTER NINE

'YOU hear people saying how spectacular Sydney Harbour is,' Angelina said as they leant against the deck railing of the cruiser. 'I've admired it from afar many times. In movies and on television and from hotel-room windows. But it's not till you're on the water itself that you appreciate its beauty, and its size. Thank you so much for this experience, Jake.'

'I thought you might enjoy it.'

She truly had. Every bit of it. The views. The food. But especially the company.

Jake had to be one of the most intelligent and interesting men she'd ever talked to. Even if he wasn't drop-dead gorgeous and she hadn't been madly attracted to him, she'd have enjoyed his company these past three hours. They'd chatted about so many different topics, getting to know each other as the adults they'd become, not the teenagers they'd once been. She'd discovered they had similar tastes in books and movies, thrillers being their entertainment of choice. After agreeing to disagree on what kind of music was best, they'd argued happily about politics, discussed the world's leaders failing with peace and the environment, and in general had a great time, solving everything themselves with sweeping words of wisdom.

None of this would have been possible, Angelina realised, but for the other people on the cruise. Mostly tourists, with cameras which were whipped up at every opportunity to snap pictures of the bridge, the opera house and the shoreline. Their constant presence had allowed her to drop her defences and be more relaxed with Jake than she had been since he'd walked back into her life. It had been good to forget the threat of being seduced for a while and just enjoy Jake, the person, and not Jake, the sexual predator.

She was even beginning to reassess that judgement of him. Maybe she'd been harsh in thinking he was that shallow when it came to relationships. Just because he didn't want marriage and children didn't mean he wasn't capable of caring, in a fashion. Of course, his track record with women wasn't great. Even he'd admitted to that. But even men like Jake could change, couldn't they? Maybe he was getting to that age when he was ready for commitment.

But was he ready for a ready-made son, complete with mother attached?

Angelina felt that was too large a leap of faith.

No. Jake, the man, would still not be pleased when she finally told him the truth. Which was perhaps why she couldn't tell him yet. For one thing, she didn't want to spoil today. Surely she deserved one day of being totally selfish, of just being Angelina, the woman, not Angelina, the mother? It was so nice to be squired around by Jake, to have him lavish attention on her, to feel desired and wanted.

Of course, it was risky. But it was worth the risk to feel what she was feeling at the moment. Not in sixteen years had she experienced anything like it. This fizz of excitement dancing along her veins and through her head. Her very *light* head, she suddenly realised.

Her laugh sounded rather girlish, even to her own ears. 'I think I've had too much to drink.' The white wines served up with the buffet lunch had been excellent, and so easy to swallow.

'I'll make you some coffee when we get up to my place,' Jake offered. 'It's just a short walk from the wharf. Come on, this is where we get off.'

He hadn't lied about the shortness of the walk. But it was still far too long with her hand warmly encased within Jake's. By the time they'd strolled up the hill to his apartment block, and ridden up in the lift— alone together—to the fifteenth floor, Angelina was desperate to put some physical distance between them. She was glad when he dropped her hand to unlock and open his front door. But that was only a short respite. She needed longer.

'I—er—have to use your bathroom,' she said as soon as Jake shut the door behind them.

He gave her a sharp look, as though he knew exactly what she was doing. And why.

'This way,' he said crisply.

Her five-minute stay in the bathroom helped, although not the sight of the bathroom. How many people had bathrooms which had black marble right to the ceiling, not to mention real gold taps and corner spa baths big enough for two?

Angelina recalled that the living room—which she'd followed Jake across on her way to the bathroom—also had black marble tiles on the floor, not to mention thick white rugs, red leather furniture, sexy steel lamps and a television as big as a movie screen. Then there was the far wall, which was all glass, beyond which was a wide terrace and a view to die for.

The place had 'seduction palace' written all over it!

'This is a very expensive apartment, Jake,' she said when she finally joined him in the kitchen. It, too, had the same black marble on the bench-tops, and the latest in stainless-steel appliances. Above the double sinks was a wide window that overlooked the terrace and caught some more of the brilliant view of the harbour, and the bridge.

'It was all Edward's doing,' he said as he spooned the coffee into attractive stoneware mugs. 'He insisted I buy a flashy harbourside apartment with some of my inheritance.'

'Well…this is flashy all right.'

He looked up from his coffee-making, his expression disappointed. 'You don't like it.'

'No, no, I do. What's not to like? It's just… well…it does have "bachelor pad" written all over it.'

'True. But then that's what I am, Angelina. A

bachelor. I thought that was one of the things you liked about me. I fitted in with your priorities in life.'

She looked away before he glimpsed the truth on her face, walking over to slide open one of the glass doors that led out onto the balcony. 'Could we have our coffee outside?' she threw back at him, deliberately directing the conversation away from her priorities in life.

Jake shrugged. 'Whatever you fancy.'

Leading words, and one which Angelina struggled to ignore. If only he realised how much she fancied *him*. So far, she'd done a good job of keeping her desires hidden, but the fact she was even here, with him, alone, had to be telling.

She was standing against the glass security panels that bounded the terrace, her hands curled tightly over the top railing, when he joined her with the two steaming mugs.

'I remembered how you liked your coffee from last Saturday,' he said. 'I hope I got it right. Black, with one sugar?'

'Perfect,' she said, and went to take it from him. Stupidly, not with the handle. On contact with the red-hot stoneware, her hand automatically jerked back. At the same moment, Jake let the mug go and it crashed to the terrace, splintering apart on the terracotta tiles, some of the near-boiling black coffee splashing onto her stockinged legs.

Her cry of pain was real, Jake's reactions swift. Shoving his own mug onto a nearby table, he scooped Angelina up in his arms, and carried her with long strides back inside and over to the kitchen. There, he sat her on the marble counter, stripped off her shoes and swivelled her round to put her stock-inged feet into the larger of the two sinks. Turning on the tap, he directed the cold water over her scalded legs.

'That water's freezing!' she cried out, and stamped her feet up and down in the sink.

'That's the idea,' he replied. 'It'll take the heat out of your skin and stop it from burning. Now, stop being such a baby.' And he kept swivelling the tap back and forth across her lower legs.

'You're getting my dress all wet,' she complained.

'I have a drier. Besides, there's coffee on that very pretty skirt, anyway. You'll have to take the dress off and soak it, if you don't want the whole thing to be ruined.'

Take her dress off! If she did that, then she'd be a goner for sure.

'Was this part of your plan for today? Spill hot coffee all over me so you could play knight the res-cue and get my dress off at the same time?'

His blue eyes glittered with amusement. 'I'd love to say that I thought of it. In fact, I might put it away in my mental cupboard of plans for seducing difficult old flames. But given you dropped the mug, Angelina, might I ask you the same thing? Was this *your plan*,' he countered, his voice dropping to a low, sexy timbre, 'to spill coffee all over yourself so you could take off your dress in order to seduce *me*?'

If only he hadn't been so close, or his hands hadn't

been on her legs as well, or his eyes hadn't been searching hers.

'Could be,' she heard herself say in a faraway voice, her head whirling. But not with the wine this time. With desire. For him. 'Has it worked?' she murmured, her eyes drowning in his.

His hands stilled on her legs. Then slowly but surely, he turned off the tap and scooped her back up into his arms.

'Absolutely,' he said.

Jake's heart pounded as he carried her down the hallway towards the master bedroom.

This was the moment he'd been waiting and hoping for. There was no stopping him now.

Yet her eyes slightly bothered him. They seemed kind of dazed. Was she still tipsy from the wine she'd drunk over lunch? Surely not. She'd hadn't consumed that much.

He angled her through the bedroom door and carried her across the expanse of white shag carpet towards the king-sized bed with its gold satin quilt and matching pillows. Her calling the apartment flashy popped back into his mind. If she'd thought the rest of his place flashy, he wondered what she'd make of this room.

But she wasn't looking at the room. She was just looking at him. With those huge, liquid brown eyes of hers. Still dazed, they were. But also adoring.

Had there ever been a woman look at him quite like the way she was looking at him?

Only her, all those years ago, when she'd been just a girl. His heart flipped over at this realisation. Dear God, let him do this right this time, he thought, and laid her gently down across the bed.

She sucked in sharply when his hands slid up under the damp hem of her dress.

'Just taking your wet stockings off,' he explained softly, and made no attempt to do anything else as he peeled them off her and draped them over a nearby chair. Despite his own intense need, Jake knew instinctively not to go too fast. Or to do anything even remotely crude. Or aggressive.

Angelina was not like any other woman he'd known. She was different. Special. Fragile, she'd called herself this morning. He'd laughed at the time but he could see that she was right. She *was* fragile.

'Do you want me to take your dress off?' he asked. 'Or do you want to do that yourself?'

She just stared up at him for a few moments before rolling over and presenting her back to him.

The naivete behind this trusting gesture touched him, and reaffirmed his new assessment of her. His very first instinct about Angelina had been right after all. She might talk tough, but she wasn't tough. Or all that experienced, either. He suspected she hadn't had as many lovers as she'd implied. How could she have, with that eagle-eyed father of hers?

The thought made him even more determined to do this right.

The zipper on her dress was long, opening up the back right down to the swell of her buttocks. The sight of nothing but a thin white satin bra strap and the beginning of what looked like a matching thong did little for his resolve to take this as slowly as possible.

'Roll over,' he ordered a bit abruptly.

She did so, and those eyes were on him again. Wide now, and dilated. Her lips fell apart as her breathing quickened appreciably.

He tore his eyes away from hers and bent to ease the dress off her shoulders and draw it down her arms and over her hips, down her legs and off her feet. He tried to remain cool and in command, but the sight of her soft, curvy body—encased in sexy satin underwear—was unbearably exciting.

Hell, how *was* he going to control himself in the face of such temptation?

His hands were unsteady as he reached to unhook the front bra clip, hesitating for a moment before exposing her breasts to his increasingly lustful gaze.

They were as perfect as he'd known they'd be. Full and lush, with dusky-tipped aureoles and large, hard nipples seemingly begging to be sucked.

But he knew that would have to wait. If he started sucking her nipples now, he would become hopelessly lost in his own desires. Hers were the ones he wanted to satisfy this first time. His male ego demanded it. And something else, some part of him which he couldn't quite grasp yet.

'I have to sit you up for a sec,' he said, and did so with a gentle tug of her hands. The action had her breasts falling deliciously forward, twin orbs of erotic promise that he steadfastly ignored as he eased the bra off her body.

'You can lie back down,' he suggested as he moved over to put the bra on the chair with the dress and stockings.

She did, her face now flushed, her eyes still wide.

The decision to leave her with her G-string on was more for his composure than her comfort.

Her eyelashes flickered wildly when his hands went to the buttons of his shirt. Her lips fell further apart.

He undressed slowly, seemingly casual and confident in his actions, but inside he was going through hell. Never had a woman watched him so intently as he removed his clothes. There again, never had he done such a deliberate strip for a woman.

Jake knew he had a good body. Mostly God-given, but also because he looked after himself, having always worked out regularly. There was a gym and a swimming pool in the apartment complex which allowed him to keep fit nowadays with the minimum of effort. So he had no reason to be embarrassed once he was in the buff.

He had to confess that he could not recall being this turned on before. Yet he hadn't even kissed her.

Drawing on protection at that point was premature on Jake's usual standards, but it seemed a good idea to be prepared. Jake had an awful feeling that once he started any form of foreplay with Angelina, he would enter the danger zone. It proved strangely awkward, with her watching him with those almost awestruck eyes of hers.

He was relieved to join her on the bed, stretching out beside her and propping himself on one elbow so that he had one hand free. His right hand.

'Wait,' she whispered, and before he could stop her she wriggled out of her panties and tossed them away, her face flushed by the time she glanced back up at him.

He didn't dare look down there. Or to think about how much he wanted to slide over between her legs and just do it. Now. *Without* preliminaries. He ached to be inside her, to feel her hot wet flesh tight around him.

At least he could touch her there. And his free hand stroked down the centre of her body and slid between her legs.

Her moan echoed his own feelings. Already she was panting, her legs growing restless, her hips writhing as a woman's did when release was near. The selfish part of Jake wanted to stop so that he could be inside her. But experience warned him that things didn't always work out that way for a woman. Better he give her a climax this way first.

'Jake,' she cried out, her eyes dilated and desperate.

His mouth crashed down onto hers, smothering her cries as she came apart under his hand. He kissed her with a desperation of his own, his tongue echoing what he would rather be doing to her with his body. Its job done, his hand moved to play with her breasts, his still wet fingertips encircling her taut nipples. Jake kept kissing her, and playing with her nipples, elated when in no time her back began to arch away from the bed in that tell-tale way. Moaning, she clung to him, her left leg lifting up onto his hip, inviting him in.

Jake needed no further invitation, groaning as his flesh slid home to the hilt. The sensations as he pumped into her were a mixture of agony and ecstasy, for he could not possibly last very long. Yet he wanted to, wanted to feel her come again with him inside her.

Her muffled moans were encouraging, as were the movements of her body. She followed his rhythm, her hips rising with his forward surge and sinking back when he withdrew. He stopping kissing her and cupped her face instead, looking deep into her glazed eyes.

He didn't say a word, just concentrated on her, slowing his rhythm appreciably but going deeper with each stroke.

She gasped, then groaned.

'Good?' he asked.

She nodded, then grimaced.

He was in his stride now, no longer balancing on that dangerous edge, determined to make her come again. She drew in more sharply with each successive stroke, her mouth falling even wider apart. Her hands tightened around his back, her nails digging into his flesh.

He felt no pain, only pleasure. The pleasure of pleasing her.

Her climax was imminent. He could feel it, deep inside. The tightening. The quivering. The rush of heat that always preceded the first spasm.

'Jake. Oh, Jake,' she cried out, and then she was there. But so, astonishingly, was he. Instantly. Brilliantly.

Poets often spoke of stars exploding when two people in love made love. Jake always thought that was just so much crap.

But this time, it *was* not unlike stars exploding. His body trembled and his head did cartwheels. His mouth found hers again and he knew that this was where he wanted to be for the rest of his life. With her. No one else. Just Angelina. And he didn't mean living together, either. He wanted her as his life partner. His wife.

Angelina Winters. Till death them did part.

It didn't occur to Jake till much later, when he was lying quietly with her sleeping form in his arms, that Angelina might not be altogether cooperative in his achieving that goal.

'I might not want what you want, Jake,' she'd said to him earlier that day.

Jake thought about all she'd told him about herself so far. Her insistence that she was independent-minded career woman. Her claim to not want marriage and children.

And then he thought of her eyes today as he'd carried her into this bedroom.

Bulldust, he decided. All of that other stuff. Dorothy was right. Angelina had marriage and motherhood written all over her. She'd been burnt, that was all, by the wrong kind of man. Some sleazebag, probably. All it needed was the right kind of guy to come along, someone who really loved her.

'*Me!*' he pronounced out loud.

Jake still wasn't sure about becoming a father, but heck, he hadn't thought till now that he'd ever fall in love, or want to get married himself. But he did. And when Jake wanted something, he made it happen.

Angelina Mastroianni was going to be his wife, no matter what she thought she wanted. Because Jake knew what she really wanted. He'd seen it just now. And felt it. What he needed to do was make her feel it again. And again. And again. He had one weekend to cement his position in her life, and in her heart. Given that was a pretty short time span, Jake decided that the best way he could achieve that was through her body; her warm, luscious, possibly neglected body.

That pathetic boyfriend of hers hadn't been doing the right thing by Angelina. Jake was sure of it. Which was fine by him. It gave him an advantage.

Just thinking about making love to her again turned him on. Retrieving a condom from where he'd shoved a few under the pillows, he slipped it on, amazed but pleased to see that he was as hard as he'd been earlier, confirming his belief that this was a once-in-a-lifetime relationship.

Scooping her naked body back against him in the spoon position, he gently stroked her breasts till she stirred in his arms, then his hand slid slowly further down her body.

'Oh,' she gasped when his fingers started softly teasing the centre of her pleasure.

But there was nothing soft, or gentle, in Jake's mind. It was full of hard resolve, as hard as his desire-filled flesh.

As soon as she moaned, and began wriggling her bottom against him, he eased himself inside her from behind.

Angelina stiffened for a second, only to melt as soon as he started rocking back and forth inside her. She would never have conceived of making love like this, on their sides, with him pressed up against her back and his hands on her front, playing with her.

It was nothing like last time; that tender and romantic position where Jake had kissed her all the while and held her like a true lover. This was entirely different. This felt...decadent. Yet oh, so exciting.

Her head whirled as a wanton wildness overtook her.

'Harder, Jake,' she bit out in a voice she didn't recognise. 'Harder.'

He groaned, then increased his tempo.

'Yes,' she groaned, her body immediately rushing towards the abyss. 'Oh, yes. Yeesss!'

CHAPTER TEN

ANGELINA knew she was in trouble the next morning. Deep, deep trouble.

It was not long after sunrise, Jake was still fast asleep in the bedroom and she was curled up on the red leather sofa, her naked body wrapped in Jake's bathrobe, her hands cradling a not-too-hot mug of coffee, her eyes taking in the sun-drenched terrace, and the bridge beyond. The traffic on it was only light at this early hour, she noted.

But not for long. The day promised to be as bright and warm as yesterday.

Yesterday...

She took the mug away from her lips and sighed. Dear heaven, what had she done?

A small, dry laugh escaped her lips. What *hadn't* she done? more like it. Her behaviour in bed was bad enough, but it hadn't been confined to Jake's bed, had it? She'd been bad in the spa bath as well, and in the kitchen whilst he'd been microwaving them a meal. And here in this very room, on the rug, in front of the television.

It was as though Jake's making love to her that second time had released something in her, and suddenly she was hungry for it all. Every experience possible with Jake.

He hadn't minded, of course. Though she'd had the impression he was a bit surprised at one stage. Not with what she did. Perhaps he was just surprised that *she* would what she did, and with such avidness.

But as much as Angelina was worried sick by where this would all end, she could find no real regrets in her heart for the actual events of last night. How could you regret something that made you feel the way she felt this morning? Like a real woman for a change. A desired and desirable woman who had been made love to very, very well.

At least now she knew what Wilomena meant by having fun. It *had* been fun. At least, it had been with Jake. The man was the very devil with women all right. If she'd shocked him once, he'd shocked her a dozen times. Thrillingly, though.

The memories made her quiver with remembered pleasure.

'What are you doing up this early?'

Angelina almost spilt her coffee again, her whole body jumping at Jake's sudden appearance behind her.

As she glanced up over the back of the sofa at him, he bent to kiss her, one of his hands sliding down the front opening of the robe at the same time.

Angelina didn't know how she *didn't* spill the coffee this time.

'Mmm,' he murmured by the time he'd straightened. 'I know what I'm going to have for breakfast. Fancy a shower together?'

'Not till I've finished my coffee,' she replied with

creditable control, considering. Angelina had already decided that, whilst yesterday had been marvellous, today was another day entirely. Today, she had to start getting some control back over herself.

Watching Jake walk over to the nearby open-plan kitchen didn't exactly help that resolve, given that he was stark naked. She told herself not to look, but look she did. By the time he'd made his coffee and returned to sprawl in an adjacent chair, sipping his coffee with apparent nonchalance, her control was definitely at risk.

Gulping down the rest of her coffee, she uncurled her legs and made some excuse about seeing to her clothes, which Jake had actually popped into the washer and dryer at some stage last night. She was just hanging her fortunately crush-free dress on a coat hanger in the beautifully appointed laundry when Jake's arms went round her waist from behind.

'Methinks the lady is suffering morning-after syndrome,' he whispered as he started unsashing her robe.

'Not at all,' she lied coolly. 'I'm just a bit concerned about today, that's all. I really need to go over to the hotel this morning, change into some casual clothes and check out. Then I have to drop in at the expo and see how we're doing.' She really couldn't go home without knowing if this venture had been a success. Arnold would ask, and so would Alex.

'When's check-out time?' Jake asked, those busy hands of his not missing a beat as they drew erotic circles around her stiffening nipples.

Angelina swallowed. She really couldn't allow him to seduce her again so easily. But of course that was his talent, wasn't it? Seduction. And sex. Tender sex. Rough sex. Imaginative sex. Whatever was required. But still just sex. She had to remember she wasn't anything so special. Just more of a challenge than his usual chicky babe.

Or she *had* been.

'Ten-thirty,' she told him, swallowing again. Why didn't he stop that? On the other hand, why didn't *she* stop him? She was just so weak where he was concerned.

Was it love making her weak? Or could she take some comfort in hoping this was just sex for her as well? In a way, this made some sense. She'd lived a celibate life for so long that surely it was only natural that she'd go mad for sex, now that she'd discovered it. Maybe she wasn't madly in love with *him*, after all.

'We have plenty of time yet,' Jake said throatily, cupping her breasts and pulling her back hard against him.

She could feel his hardness through his bathrobe.

'I'll drive you over to the hotel around ten,' he murmured as he pulled the robe further open and nuzzled at her neck. 'And take you personally to the expo. Then we can go have lunch and do some shopping.'

'Shopping?' she echoed somewhat blankly, having reached that point when intelligent thought was nigh-on impossible.

'Didn't you say you wanted to go shopping?'

'Did I?' The robe slipped off one shoulder, then the other, before dropping to the floor. Suddenly, she felt more naked than she ever had been with him. And more vulnerable.

He was smiling when he turned her round in his arms.

'I dare say you've changed your mind, like a typical woman. But I have a fancy to buy you something really sexy to wear. Something…naughty.''

She stared up into his eyes, which were gleaming hotly down at her.

'You're still a very bad boy, aren't you, Jake?' she choked out.

'I haven't noticed you objecting,' he replied with a devilishly charming grin. 'Now, come have that shower with me, gorgeous.'

She went.

'Sydney really is a beautiful city,' Angelina said as they walked, hand in hand, through Hyde Park.

Jake glanced across at her, thinking how beautiful *she* looked today. Beautiful *and* sexy. Those jeans hugged her curvy body like a second skin. Too bad about that loose white shirt she was wearing over them. Though perhaps it was as well she wasn't wearing anything too revealing on top. Jake's possessiveness of her had increased overnight, along with his desire. He only had to touch her and he wanted to make love to her again.

Jake thought of what was in the plastic shopping

bag he was holding. The sexiest black corset he'd ever seen. Angelina had refused to try it on in the shop, but he knew there would be no such objections once he got her home.

'Sydney always looks great in the summer,' he agreed, very pleased with the way things were going.

'I guess the good weather is one of the reasons the expo has gone so well,' she remarked.

'Perhaps. But it always pays to have a good product. Your wines are going to be a big hit down here in Sydney, by the sound of things. Wayne was over the moon with the orders they'd already taken and the interest shown.'

'Men like Wayne are exaggerators,' Angelina said drily. 'But it does look promising.'

Jake had to admire the way Angelina's feet were firmly on the ground when it came to her business. She was no pushover, in lots of ways.

Sexually, however, she was putty in his hands. Jake couldn't wait to get her alone again.

'I work not far from here,' he pointed out. 'My office is in that tall bluish building over there. If the sun's out, I come over to the park and eat my lunch here. Right here, in fact.' And he pulled her down onto a seat under a huge tree that provided almost an acre of shade.

His arm wound round her shoulders and his lips pressed into her hair. 'Want to make out?' he whispered.

'Jake Winters, behave yourself. I don't think we

need to make out in public, do you? We've been at it like rabbits. A breather is definitely called for.'

'Not rabbits,' he said. '*Lovers*. Once is never enough for lovers.'

'Once! How about one times twenty? I didn't know it was possible to have so much sex in one weekend.'

'Amazing, isn't it?'

Angelina glanced up into Jake's grinning face and took a mental photo of it for her memory bank. He looked so handsome today. And so happy.

She doubted he'd look quite so happy once he found out about Alex.

'What?' he said, his grin fading.

It constantly surprised Angelina, the way he seemed to pick up on her inner feelings, without her having to say a word. It was almost as though he could read her mind sometimes. He certainly knew whenever she wanted him again.

Unfortunately, this was almost continuously. She simply could not get enough of him. Even now, she wanted him to take her home. She wanted him to strip her off and lace her into that decadent-looking corset and do whatever it was he had in mind to do to her whilst she was wearing it.

Hopefully, he couldn't read her thoughts. She seriously needed this breather so she could think.

'What is it?' he repeated. 'Tell me true.'

'Nothing much. I was thinking how handsome you were. And how much I like you with short hair.'

'And I like you with long.'

She flushed as she thought of what he had done with her hair on one occasion last night. He really was a wicked man.

No, not truly wicked, Angelina conceded. But seriously naughty. A very good lover, though. Very knowledgeable about women's bodies, and totally uninhibited when it came to using that knowledge. How on earth was she going to find the strength to tell Jake about Alex, when it meant she would have to give up his lovemaking?

Because it was all going to end once the truth came out. If there was one thing the last twenty-four hours had proved to Angelina, it was that Jake only had one need for a woman, and that was as his sexual partner. His plaything. Even his calling her his lover just now was telling. Why not girlfriend? Lover had that for-sex-only connotation about it.

No, Jake hadn't changed in that regard. His aim had been to sleep with her. And now that he had, any complications would have him running a mile.

And Alex, let's face it, she thought, was one big complication.

'What a shame today has to end,' she said with a sigh.

'Does it have to?'

'Time marches on. Nothing can change that.'

'You could always stay the night with me, go home tomorrow.'

She was seriously tempted. If she'd been in bed

with him at this moment, with his hands on her naked body, she probably would have said yes.

'Sorry,' she said crisply. 'No can do. I have to get back home tonight. Work tomorrow.'

'Yeah. Same here. I'm due in court first thing in the morning.'

'On that case you told me about?' Angelina asked, grateful for the opportunity to get her mind off sex. 'The lady who's dying of lung cancer?'

'That's the one. I have to deliver my closing address.'

'Are you ready?'

'I should hope so. I've been living and breathing that case for months.'

'Do you memorise your speeches?'

'Not really. I do write my ideas down. But I never try to remember them word for word. That's the sure way to go blank and stuff it up. No, I prepare well and then I talk from the heart. You do make the occasional stumble over words that way, but the jury never minds that, if they know you're being sincere.'

'I hope you win,' she said with feeling.

'Don't worry,' Jake returned with a little squeeze of her shoulders. 'We will.'

Angelina abruptly jumped to her feet. 'Come on, let's walk some more. I want to go see St Mary's Cathedral.' And she yanked a groaning Jake to his feet.

'More walking? Can't we just sit here and cuddle?'

'You've had more than enough cuddling for one weekend. *Up!*'

'Wow. I like it when you're bossy. Would you like to be on top when we get back to my place?'

'Get that bag and come on!' She was already off, walking in the direction of the cathedral, not giving him the opportunity to take her hand again.

'Oh, look!' she exclaimed when they emerged from the park directly across from the main cathedral steps. 'There's a wedding car just arriving. Let's go over and watch, Jake. I love watching weddings.' Anything but going back to his place yet.

'Why?'

'Because!'

'That's no reason from a girl who says she doesn't want to get married.'

'I don't want to be an astronaut, either,' she argued, 'but I like watching their exploits.'

'I suppose you could compare marriage to flying into space.'

'It's certainly a risky venture.'

'But risk can be exciting.'

Angelina arched her eyebrows. 'This, from a man who said *he* never wanted to get married?'

'Maybe I've changed my mind.'

Jake saw the shock reverberate in her eyes. 'You... you don't mean that,' she said stiffly.

Jake immediately regretted his possibly ill-judged words. If he rushed her, he might lose what he

wanted most. After all, this was just their first weekend together. Best stick to sex for now.

'Never say never about anything,' he remarked
nonchalantly. 'That's my motto.'

'For the record, I never actually said I would *never*
get married. I just said it wasn't a priority of mine.'

Jake felt heartened by the carefulness in her word-
ing.

'That's good,' he said with a smile. 'I like a girl
who keeps her options open.''

Her hitting him playfully on the arm broke the
tension he'd foolishly created.

'I'm just a sex object to you, aren't I?' she accused.

'Absolutely. So, do you want to go look at this
wedding, or do you want to go home? Don't forget,
we've only got four hours before I drive you home.
We'll have to set off by eight if I want to be back
in Sydney by midnight. I'm a Cinderella kind of guy
when I have to be in court in the morning.'

'Decisions. Decisions.'

'Yeah, life's a bitch, isn't it? So what do you
reckon? Which is it to be?'

Angelina knew he thought she'd opt to go home.
And she wanted to. She wanted to so much it was
criminal.

All the more reason not to.

'I think it would do you good to see that there is
more to a relationship than just sex. That couple in
there are about to promise to love and cherish each
other till death them do part.'

'Until divorce them do part, don't you mean?'

'You're a cynic, do you know that?'

'Takes one to know one.'

'Point taken. But I still want to see the wedding,' she said firmly, and walked over to press the button that would change the traffic lights. 'Despite the fact that the bride has already gone inside.'

'Fine by me. I not only like to watch sometimes, but also to wait. Waiting whets the appetite further.'

'You have a one-track mind.'

'Where you're concerned, I have.'

'You'd better behave yourself in this church.'

'I'll be an angel.'

'Don't be facetious.'

The lights changed and Angelina launched herself across the road, Jake hot on her heels. She could hear the organ blaring out the *Wedding March* even from that distance.

'No wandering hands during the ceremony,' she warned him as they skipped up the steps.

'Definitely not. I know you. You won't be able to control yourself.''

'I will!' she countered, but blushingly.

'No? Pity. Well, let's hope this isn't one of those long ceremonies. I'm not sure I'll be able to sit on a hard pew for more than twenty minutes, max.''

She laughed, not a good idea since they'd just entered the vaulted interior of the cathedral, right at the moment when the organ stopped. Her laughter echoed up into the cavernous and unfortunately silent ceiling. Several heads whipped round to glare.

'Sorry,' Jake apologised to them. 'I can't take her anywhere.'

'Stop it,' Angelina hissed. 'Just shut up and watch.'

He shut up. But not for long.

'Hard to see much from this far back. Want to get closer?'

'No! I can't trust you to behave.'

'True. I've always been a bad boy in churches. Can't stand all the hush-hush nonsense. Makes me want to break out.'

'If you embarrass me,' she whispered, 'I won't go to your place with you afterwards at all. I'll make you drive me straight home to the Hunter Valley.'

'Don't think so,' he returned just as softly. 'You left that pretty handbag behind, remember? We'll have to go collect it. Although, perhaps not. You could always collect it next weekend.'

Angelique frowned. She'd been trying not to think about tomorrow, let alone next weekend. 'I...I have to have lunch with Alex next weekend.'

'You don't *have* to do anything of the kind. Call him. Tell him it's over by phone.'

'No.'

'I knew you'd say that,' he muttered. 'OK, go to lunch with him if you have to. But that's just on the Saturday during the day. As soon as you're finished with him...*permanently* this time...I will expect you at my place. Shall we say four? Five?'

'Make it six.' The swimming carnival wouldn't finish till five.

'That's one hell of a long lunch. I sure hope it's

going to be somewhere public. All right, all right, so I'm acting like a jealous fool. Six, it is. I'll book us a table for dinner at eight. You can stay over till Sunday night, can't you?'

Angelina swallowed. She really shouldn't let this fiasco continue. It wasn't right. She should tell him the truth.

But she just couldn't.

'All right,' she said with a sigh. 'Now hush up.'

He hushed up, but a small boy several rows up from them didn't. He started whinging and whining about wanting to go outside. Several warnings from both his parents to be quiet and to sit still had no effect. Finally, the father lost his patience, swooped the child up in his arms and headed with swift strides back down the aisle, past Angelina and Jake.

Angelina smiled a wry smile. She remembered full well the trials and tribulations of taking a small boy to church.

Jake's suddenly leaping to his feet startled her. 'Be back in a minute,' he said. 'Got to check on something.' And he was off, bolting down the aisle after the man and child.

Angelina jumped up as well, and hurried after the three of them, catching up with Jake on the cathedral steps. He was standing there, staring, an odd confusion in his eyes.

Her hand on his tensely held arm was gentle. 'You see?' she said quietly as her gaze followed Jake's to where the father was happily lighting up a cigarette whilst he watched his son enjoying himself im-

mensely jumping up and down the steps. 'No need
to worry.'

'I thought…'

'Yes, I know what you thought,' she said softly.

She actually felt the shudder run all through Jake.

'Can we get away from here?' he said, glancing
around at all the onlookers who were gathering to
see the bride emerge.

'All right.' She tucked her arm through his and
they just walked in silence for a while, finding their
way across the road and back into the park at the
next intersection.

'Is that what your father did to you, Jake?' she
asked gently at last. 'Hit you?'

'No, not my father. I never knew my father. He
did a flit before I was born. It was my mother who
did the honours. Man, she had a punch on her, that
woman. Not a day went by that she didn't lay into
me for some reason. Just about anything would set
her off, especially when she'd been drinking.
Sometimes it was just the way I looked at her. I can
still remember how scared I was to go home after
school, right from the time I was in kindergarten.
Although weekends were the worst. No school to escape to those days.'

Angelina was both horrified and saddened by his
story. What kind of a mother would do that to her
son? 'But didn't the teachers notice?' she asked. 'I
mean…there must have been bruises.'

He shrugged. 'I'm a boy. Boys get bruises all the
time. If they did notice, they just looked the other

way. Teachers weren't always as conscientious in reporting such matters back then as they are now.'

'But what about you grandparents? Your aunts and uncles? Neighbours? Wasn't there anyone who cared?'

'Not that I knew of. Mum was estranged from her family. And the neighbours we had were just as bad. It was not a salubrious street.'

'So what happened in the end? Did you run away?'

'I put up with it as long as I could. By the time I was in high school, I didn't go home much so I didn't get hit as often. I spent more and more time on the streets after school. Got into a gang. God knows how I didn't get arrested for shoplifting. I thought I was smart but I was just lucky. Anyway, one day when I was around fifteen, I came home late and Mum started swinging at me with this frying pan. Great heavy thing it was. Collected me a beauty. I'm not sure what happened next but it was Mum who ended up on the floor. Made me feel sick afterwards, I can tell you. But then…aggression breeds aggression. That was when I walked out and never went back.'

'But where did you live?'

'On the streets, of course.'

'But…'

'Look, I survived, OK, thanks to Edward and Dorothy. Let's not get into this. It's all dead and gone, even the lady herself. I looked her up last year when Edward died and found out she'd passed away years ago. Hepatitis. I didn't grieve, but I needed to know what had happened to her. Closure, I guess.'

Closure? The man who'd started shaking at the sight of a father showing even a small amount of impatience with his son was a long way from closure. Angelina was so glad that she had never used corporal punishment on her son. She'd never allowed her father to hit Alex either, no matter what.

Poor Jake. All of a sudden, she wanted to hold him and love him, to make up to him for everything he'd suffered as a child.

'Let's go home, Jake,' she suggested softly.

He stopped walking to throw her a speculative glance. 'Home, as in your home or my home?'

'Your home.'

'Now you're talking.'

But she didn't do much talking on the way home. She kept thinking of everything Jake had suffered as a child.

It explained why he didn't want to have children himself. Clearly, he was afraid he'd be a bad father, that the cycle of physical abuse would continue. Angelina didn't believe that it would for a moment. Not with Jake.

Still, it was what Jake thought that counted.

It was going to come as a terrible shock when she told him about Alex. Perhaps it was as well, Angelina realised, that their son was a teenager and not a baby.

'You've gone rather quiet,' Jake said as he unlocked his front door and ushered her inside. 'Is something wrong?'

'Wrong? No, no, nothing wrong.'

'It's Alex, isn't it? You're worried about him.'

'Alex will be fine,' she said. And he would be, too. He was going to be thrilled to have a father like Jake. It was Jake's reaction that worried her.

'So what is it?'

'I'm worried that I might be getting addicted to this.'

'To what?'

'To being with you.'

He dropped the shopping bag, kicked the door shut behind them and drew her into his arms once more. 'There are worse addictions, you know,' he murmured as he bent his mouth to hers.

Angelina wasn't so sure. Already it was responsible for her changing her mind about telling Jake the truth. And possibly for longer than a couple of weekends.

'This is one addiction which I would happily subscribe to,' Jake muttered against her lips. 'Come on, gorgeous,' he said, taking her hand and scooping up the shopping bag at the same time. 'Your breather is up.'

CHAPTER ELEVEN

'THURSDAY,' Angelina muttered to herself as she set about making her bed.

Four days since she'd seen Jake. Four long, boring, lonely days. And two more till she saw him again.

Coming round to the other side of her double bed, she picked up the pillow on that side and held it against her cheek. This was where Jake had laid his head the other night.

Could she still smell the scent of him on it?

Angelina imagined she could.

It had been quite late by the time Jake had driven her home last Sunday. She hadn't thought he would want to come in with her; hadn't anticipated it. But he'd insisted on walking her to the door, then claimed he needed to come inside to use the bathroom before driving back.

Her panic had been instant, and intense. For how could she let him come in? The place was full of Alex memorabilia. Photos everywhere. Trophies in his bedroom. Stuff on the fridge.

She'd finally managed to stall Jake at the door, saying that the place was a mess and she'd die of embarrassment if he saw it like that.

'Just give me one minute,' she'd begged. 'Please, Jake.'

He'd seemed amused. 'Don't tell me you're not perfect,' he'd said.

'Hardly,' she'd replied. 'Who is?'

Her dash around the rooms had been like something out of a farce. She'd scooped all the photos on top of the sideboard into the top drawer. The same with the ones on her bedside chests. She almost missed the reminder for Alex's swimming carnival on the fridge door, shoving it on top, along with the magnet photo of him as a baby. Alex's bedroom was a lost cause so she just closed that door, then flung open the bathroom door so that Jake wouldn't walk into his son's room by mistake.

He hadn't. But neither had he left after his trip to the bathroom, as she'd expected him to. He'd kissed her again, and soon she was ripping at his shirt and pulling him into her bedroom—the two-hour drive enclosed in that sexy car with Jake had done dreadful things to her resolve to be good—and the last thing Angelina remembered was falling asleep in his arms.

When she'd woken in the morning he was gone.

Mid-morning that Monday, a huge arrangement of red roses had arrived, with a card attached saying, 'Next weekend can't come quickly enough. Jake.'

The flowers were still alive and utterly gorgeous, sitting on the sideboard in place of the still absent photos. She didn't dare put any of them back up yet. In fact, since last Sunday, she'd locked Alex's bedroom door, and hidden anything else that might give the game away if Jake ever showed up here again. After his phone call last night, Angelina wouldn't be at all surprised at his driving up tonight. He'd been so excited after winning that case.

And missing her terribly, he'd said.

Angelina sighed. He wasn't the only one.

Jake sat down on his favourite seat in Hyde Park, placed the banana smoothie on the grass at his feet, then proceeded to unwrap his king-sized roll. This was the first time he'd had the opportunity to eat lunch in the park this week. Not because of the weather. Sydney had continued to be dry and warm. Circumstance had been the guilty party.

Monday, he'd been too wrecked to eat lunch. He'd had to call on every reserve of strength he had to deliver his closing address in court that morning, the weekend finally catching up with him. After the jury had retired to consider their verdict, he'd gone home and just collapsed into bed. Tuesday, he'd been far too agitated to eat. The jury had still been out. Wednesday, he'd been much too elated. At eleven that morning, the jury had found for the plaintiff to the tune of fourteen million dollars.

Now it was Thursday and the bedlam of the last couple of days was hopefully behind him. If another television station showed at his office, wanting another damned interview, he was going to go bush, preferably to the Hunter Valley.

Jake loved being a litigator. Loved having victories over the bad guys. Attention from the media, however, was not one of his loves. He hated having cameras and microphones shoved in his face. Of course, the law firm he worked for didn't mind one bit. But that kind of publicity was not Jake's bag, even if it did result in his being offered a partnership.

Strangely, Jake wasn't sure if he wanted to become a partner in Keats, Marsden and Johnson. Neither did he fancy being pushed into taking on the inevitable rush of perhaps not-so-worthy clients who thought they could make a mint out of suing their bosses over supposedly adverse working conditions. He'd only won this case because his client had a genuine complaint. Copycat cases rarely had the same integrity, or sympathy.

Jake munched into his salmon and salad roll—man, it tasted good—and wondered if now was the right time for him to make a move, start up a practice of his own. He'd be free then to take on only the clients he really wanted to represent. He wouldn't be influenced by money, which a big law firm invariably was. Of course, this would mean forgoing his six-figure salary plus bonuses, not to mention his generous expense account. It would also mean a lot of work. Starting up your own business involved a lot of red tape.

On the plus side, he would be his own boss. And the temporary loss of salary wouldn't be any great hardship. He still had a small fortune in cash left over from Edward's legacy.

Maybe he'd run the idea by Angelina tonight. She

was a businesswoman. She would know what was involved. See what she thought.

Aah, Angelina…

Already, he was looking forward to talking to her tonight. Their nightly chat was the highlight of his day, something to look forward to after work. He would ring her a lot more than that, but Angelina had forbidden him to call during the day, claiming she'd never get anything done if he did that.

Possibly true. Once they were on the phone together, they sometimes talked for hours.

Of course, he *had* broken the rules and called her as soon as the verdict came in on the Wednesday. But that was a special occasion and he hadn't kept her on the line for long.

The salad and salmon roll duly disposed of, Jake picked up his banana smoothie and started to sip.

How soon, he wondered, could he tell her he loved her and wanted to marry her?

Not too soon, Jake suspected.

A couple of times last weekend, she'd fallen silent on him. Suspiciously silent. You could almost hear the wheels turning away in her brain. Yet she'd been unforthcoming when he'd asked her what was wrong.

In a way, she was secretive. She rarely opened up to him about herself in any depth. And she never talked about her feelings for him.

In the past, he hadn't been able to stop women telling him their feelings, especially how much they loved him. Angelina never went near the subject of love. She said flattering things about his lovemaking but that wasn't the same.

Already addicted to having sex with him, she'd said last Sunday.

Jake frowned. He didn't like the idea that she might be only coming back to see him this weekend for more of the same. There was no doubting she liked sex. After his initially thinking she was pretty inexperienced in bed, she'd turned into a veritable tiger.

Once his mind took that tack, the worry started up that she hadn't been totally truthful over what she was up to this coming Saturday. To put aside a whole day to tell any man she was breaking up with him seemed excessively kind.

Maybe she's not going to break up with him at all, a dark voice whispered in his head. Maybe she's going to spend the whole day at Alex's place, in Alex's bed. And then come on to *his* bed for the rest of the weekend.

The idea revolted him. But it was possible, wasn't it? She had a very high sex drive. But was she capable of that level of deception?

He wouldn't have thought so. Still, his buying that huge diamond engagement ring yesterday afternoon now struck him as being ridiculously premature. Amazing the things a man in love would do! Fools did rush in, as the saying went.

The buzzing on Jake's cellphone had him sitting up abruptly, his banana smoothie slurping back and forth in its cardboard carton. Setting the drink down, he fished his phone out of his trouser pocket, clicked it on and swept it up to his ear.

'Yes?'

'Sally here, Jake. Sorry to bother you, but if you've finished your lunch perhaps you should get back here. You have a visitor.'

'A visitor. What kind of visitor?'

'A young man. Name of Alex.'

Alex! Jake didn't have any colleagues or acquaintances named Alex, so presumably this had to be *the* Alex.

Jake frowned over Sally calling him young. Of course, Sally thought anyone under forty was young, but it sounded as though Angelina's Alex was what was commonly called a 'younger' man.

Jake tried to ignore the instant stab of jealousy and focus on what the fool was doing, showing up at *his* office.

All he could think of was that Angelina had changed her mind and broken up with Alex over the phone, plus told him the identity of the guy she'd thrown him over for.

Jake groaned. As much as he was happy to find that his paranoid thoughts about Angelina two-timing him were just that...paranoid, the last thing he wanted was a confrontation with a furious ex boy-friend.

'I gather you know who I'm talking about,' Sally said.

'Possibly. Does my visitor have a second name?'

'Mastroianni,' Sally supplied.

'Mastroianni!' he repeated, totally taken aback.

And then the penny dropped. Alex was some kind of relative. Angelina had said he was half-Italian. Maybe that was what she'd meant about her relationship with him being complicated. If he was a cousin or something, she would have to explain things more fully. She couldn't just dump the guy without giving him a reason.

'I think you should get back here, Jake. This is something you have to attend to personally, by the look of things.'

'OK,' Jake said with a sigh. 'Tell him I'll be there shortly.'

The offices of Keats, Marsden and Johnson were spacious and classy, occupying half of the tenth floor of the building Jake had pointed out to Angelina the previous Sunday. Their main reception area was set directly opposite the lift well, behind a solid glass wall and two equally solid glass doors. Sally reigned over the reception desk and the waiting room, and had done so for many years. Although not unattractive for her age—she had turned fifty last month—Sally was the exception to the rule that highly visible Sydney receptionists should be curvy blondes with seductive smiles.

Jake, for one, enjoyed the wonderfully pragmatic and no-nonsense atmosphere Sally brought to the firm. Actually, Sally was one of the reasons he just might stay. He'd miss her if he left.

'Well?' he said as he strode in. 'Where is he and what am I in for?'

Sally glanced up, her no-nonsense grey eyes sweeping over him from top to toe in a critical survey, as though she were meeting him for the first time. Jake found himself automatically straightening his tie and wondering if his fly was undone.

'A shock, I would think,' she said drily. 'I put him in your office to wait for you.'

Jake ground to a halt beside her desk. 'What did you do that for? And what kind of a shock? Don't tell me he's a big bruiser.'

'He's not small,' she said, her grey eyes now gleaming rather mischievously. 'But then, neither are you.'

Jake wasn't sure if he was getting the subtle meaning behind this interchange.

'Looking for a fight, is he?'

'I wouldn't think so. More likely some answers to some questions.'

'Do you know something here that I don't know?'

Her finely plucked eyebrows lifted in feigned innocence. 'Know? No, I don't *know* anything. But I am a highly observant person, and a darned good guesser.'

'Sally, remind me to have you fired when I get to be partner.'

'Aah, so you've changed your mind about going out on your own, have you?'

He just stared at her. The woman had to be a witch in disguise. He had never discussed that idea with anyone in this firm.

'How did…? No, no, I am not going to ask.'

'Like I said,' she threw after him as he strode off down the corridor towards his office, 'I'm a darned good guesser.'

Jake hesitated at his door, irritating himself when he started checking his clothes again, as if he was going in for a bloody interview. Comforted that he looked his best in one of his newest business suits— the charcoal-grey mohair-blend—Jake still slicked his unslickably short hair back from his face before reaching for the knob.

'Sorry to keep you waiting,' he ground out as he opened the door and walked in.

The only other occupant of Jake's office immediately spun round from where he'd been standing at the corner window.

He was tall, though not as tall as Jake, or as solidly built. He was very good-looking, with strong facial features and an elegantly athletic frame. His long-lashed blue eyes reminded Jake of someone, but Jake couldn't remember who. His hair, which was dark and thick, was cut very short. Short was the fashion at the moment.

The only thing wrong with Jake's visitor was that he was dressed in a school uniform.

A shock, Sally had said.

She'd been right there.

This *couldn't* be the Alex Angelina had talked about. As sexy as Angelina was, he couldn't see her in the role of conscienceless cradle-snatcher. This boy could not be a day over seventeen. Eighteen, at a pinch.

Then who was he? Her ex-lover's younger brother? His son, maybe? Alex Mastroianni junior? If so, what was he doing here? And why was he staring at *him* as if he'd seen a bloody ghost or something?

Certainly, he wasn't in the mood for this!

'You wanted to see me?' he said abruptly, and continued round behind his desk, which sat adjacent to the window. 'Sit down,' he said with a gesture towards the two upright chairs that faced his desk. Then sat down himself.

The boy just stood there, staring.

Jake sighed.

'I gather your name is Alex Mastroianni,' he said. 'I'm Jake Winters.'

'Yes, I know,' the boy said, finding his voice at last. 'I saw you on the news last night. Twice. First on Channel Nine. Then later on Channel Two.'

'Aah yes, the news. We haven't met before, have we?' he asked, his mind teasing him again with that vague sense of recognition.

'No. Never,' the boy said.

'So what can I do for you, Mr Mastroianni?'

Jake decided to play this straight, as though the teenager before him was a potential client, and his name just a weird coincidence, which it very well might be. Life was sometimes stranger than fiction.

'Are you in need of a lawyer?'

The boy smiled. And again, reminded him of someone.

'Please call me Alex,' he said with a cool assurance that surprised Jake. Having found his tongue, he seemed to have found a degree of confidence as well.

'Very well. Alex. Please, do sit down. You're making me nervous, standing over there.'

The boy laughed. 'Not as nervous as I am.'

But he did sit down.

'You don't look nervous,' Jake said.

'Yeah, well, trust me, I am.'

'You don't have to be nervous with me. You can tell me anything. There is such a thing as client-lawyer privilege. I can't divulge anything you tell me. Like a priest.'

The boy just sat there a while longer, looking at him a bit like Sally had looked at him earlier, as though he was trying to see something in his face, or perhaps in his eyes. Was he wondering if he could be trusted?

Jake decided not to press. He didn't have any appointments for a while. He had the time to be patient, and, quite frankly, he was curious. Very curious.

'Do you remember a girl named Angelina Mastroianni?' the boy asked after a minute or two of tension-making silence. 'In case you've forgotten, you picked grapes at her father's vineyard in the Hunter Valley sixteen years ago.'

Jake snapped forward in his chair, his hands reaching for the nearest object. A Biro. He gripped it tightly and prayed this kid wasn't going to say something he didn't want to hear.

'I remember,' he returned tautly as his fingers

tightened. 'So what is Angelina to you? A cousin? An aunt?'

Stupid question, that last one, Jake. Angelina doesn't have any brothers or sisters so how could she be an aunt?

'No,' the boy denied. 'Nothing like that.'

Nothing like that. Then what?

'She's my mother.'

The Biro snapped. Clean in two.

'Your mother,' Jake repeated in a numb voice.

'Yes.'

'That's impossible! Angelina isn't old enough to be your mother!' He knew for a fact that sixteen years ago, she'd been a virgin. One and one did not make two here.

'I look old for my age. I'm only fifteen. I don't turn sixteen till the twenty-fourth of November this year.'

Jake's mind reeled. Only fifteen. And his birthday was in late November. He quickly counted backwards and landed on late February as the date of his conception. If Jake had been reeling before, he now went into serious shock.

It wasn't possible. He'd pulled out that night. Sort of. Well, maybe not in time. OK, so it *was* possible. But just as possible that Angelina had gone from him to some other guy. These things did happen once a girl had lost her virginity.

His gaze raked over the handsome boy sitting before him as he tried to work out all that Angelina had told him since they'd met up again. The lies.

No, not lies. But definitely verbal sleight of hand.

She'd deliberately kept Alex's true identity secret from him, and the question was why? It wasn't as though single mothers were uncommon these days. Even Italian ones.

'And your father?'

Even as he croaked out the question, Jake saw the truth staring back at him. Those eyes. They were *his*. So was the chin. And the hairline. Even the ears.

'Why, it's you, of course, Mr Winters,' the boy said with some bemusement in his voice, as though he was surprised Jake hadn't realised already. '*You're* my father.'

CHAPTER TWELVE

ANGELINA was behind the reception desk, booking in the Williams family, when Jake's yellow Ferrari shot down the driveway and braked to an abrupt halt under the covered archway on the other side of Mr Williams's sedate navy sedan.

Her heart began to thud.

So Jake had decided he couldn't wait till the week-end, either!

'Wow!' Mr Williams exclaimed. 'I've always wanted to cruise around Australia in a car like that.'

'In your dreams, darling,' his wife said. 'Where would we put the kids for starters?'

'With your mother, preferably,' he quipped back.

Jake, Angelina noted, did not get out of the car and come inside. Instead, after glancing over his shoulder at the reception area—which was clearly visible through the mainly glass front wall—he just sat, drumming his fingers on the steering wheel. Waiting, obviously, till she was alone.

A swirling sensation began to eddy in Angelina's stomach. But she didn't let her excitement show.

'Here are the keys to your suite,' she said with a smile as she handed them over. 'If you follow the driveway round the back, you can park right outside your main door. The pool is heated and open till ten.

The tennis court is available till the same time. Dinner starts at six in the restaurant. Did you see the restaurant as you drove in?'

'Sure did. Looks fabulous,' the wife gushed.

'Breakfast is in the same place from six-thirty till nine-thirty,' Angelina went on briskly. 'We don't cater for meals in the rooms here, I'm afraid. I've booked your free tour for tomorrow, starting at nine. Best to do it early in the summer before it gets too hot. Your guide will be waiting for you at five to nine at the cellar door, which is not far from the restaurant. Just follow the signs. I think that's all I have to tell you but please, feel free to ring and ask if you have any problems at all.'

'Oh, I'm sure we won't,' the wife beamed. 'This is all just so lovely.'

'Come on, kids,' the father said to his son and daughter, who looked about eight and ten respectively. 'Let's go and find our cossies. That pool sure looks good after our long drive. Thanks, miss.'

'Angelina,' she told him, pointing to her name tag.

'Angelina. Pretty name.'

'Pretty girl,' the wife said, but without a trace of spite, or jealousy. Angelina decided she liked her very much.

'OK, kids. Back into the car.'

Angelina had tried to keep her cool during the five minutes it had taken to go through her resort spiel. But all the time, she'd been watching Jake out of the corner of her eye.

No sooner had the navy sedan moved off than he

was out of the car and striding towards the reception room.

Angelina's gaze raked over him admiringly as he approached. It was the first time she had seen him in a suit, and my, he did look well in one. He looked well in any clothes, she conceded. And even better in nothing.

Angelina groaned and dropped her own eyes to the desk. She'd accused Jake of having a one-track mind last Sunday, but she was no better where he was concerned. One glimpse, and she was aching to rip his clothes off.

The small bell on the door tinkled as he pushed it open, Angelina pretending not to have noticed his arrival till that moment.

'Jake!' she said on looking up. 'Goodness, what are you doing here?'

He eyed her quite coldly.

'Cut the crap, Angelina. You saw me drive up. I know you did. I suggest you get someone else to take over here,' he commanded in a peremptory fashion. 'We need to talk.'

Angelina felt as if he'd punched her in the stomach. What was going on here? And who did he think he was, talking to her like that?

'I...I can't,' she replied, flustered by his rudeness. There *is* no one else. Not till five.' Barbara would take over at five for the night shift.

They both glanced at their watches. Five o'clock was fourteen minutes away.

'Is your place open?' he asked abruptly. 'I'll wait for you in there.'

Angelina hesitated to let him go into her home by himself. He might start looking around.

Though why would he...unless he'd found out something...?

The arrival of another car outside Reception forced her to make up her mind.

'Yes, it's open. Go on round and I'll be with you shortly. But what is this all about, Jake? You seem upset.'

'Upset,' he repeated, as though considering the word. 'No, I'm not upset. I'm bloody furious!' With that, he marched out, leaving Angelina to stare after him.

Has he found out about Alex? came the immediate question. But if so, how so? Had Arnold let something slip in his negotiations with Dorothy?

Angelina knew that the sale of Arnold's property was going ahead at a great rate. Money had been no object and Dorothy had had her lawyers rush through the searches. Contracts were being exchanged next week and she was going to move in a fortnight later.

Fortunately, Barbara arrived ten minutes early for work, Angelina relieved to let her take over so that she could bolt round and see what Jake wanted. Unfortunately, even in that short space of time, her nervous tension had reached dangerous proportions.

She hurried in to find Jake in her kitchen, making himself some coffee and looking as if he'd lost his case this week, instead of winning it.

'I'm here,' she said, unnecessarily, since she was standing in the same room, not ten feet from him.

His head turned and those icy blue eyes of his cut through her like knives.

'How long,' he ground out, 'did you intend to keep our son a secret from me?'

Angelina sagged against the kitchen sink. He knew.

'How…how did you find out?' she choked out, then slowly shook her head. 'Arnold, I suppose. He must have let it slip to Dorothy.' Alex was right. Arnold could be a bit of an old fool.

'Alex told me himself, in my office, just over four hours ago.'

Angelina gaped at him. This she had *not* expected. Oh, Alex…

'Naturally, when I was first told I had a visitor named Alex,' Jake ground out, 'I assumed he was your ex-lover. Imagine my surprise when I encountered a schoolboy. But I won't go into that, or even try to understand your sick reasons for letting me think such a thing. I am here because of the real person, the real Alex. Our son. Seems he saw me on TV last night and realised that I was the Jake Winters his mother had said was his father. No doubt because we look exactly like each other!'

Angelina groaned. So that was what had precipitated their son's actions. If only she'd thought of something like this happening. She herself had seen Jake on the news. What an idiot she was! But, of course, her mind had been on other things since last weekend. Her son had ceased to be her top priority for once.

Her remorse was acute.

But once she saw Jake's body language, the mother tiger in her came back with a vengeance. 'If you acted like this with him, Jake,' she bit out, her eyes narrowing, 'I won't ever forgive you.'

Jake's nostrils flared. 'Do you honestly think, after what *I* went through as a child, that I would do anything remotely hurtful to *my* son?'

Angelina was taken aback by the possessiveness in his voice. And the sheer emotional power.

This was not a man who was repulsed by the discovery that he was a father. Sure, he was shocked. And yes, he was angry. But only with her.

She smiled. She couldn't help it. 'He's wonderful, isn't he?'

'Bloody hell, Angelina, how can you smile at me after what you've done? Look, I understand why you didn't tell me about Alex when he was born, and during the years since. Aside from your father's natural hostility towards me, why would you? If I'd been in your boots I wouldn't have told me, either. But after we ran into each other again the way we did and you saw that I wasn't some kind of deadbeat, you should have told me then. Why, in God's name, didn't you? Especially when Alex was already pestering you to find me. Oh, yes, he told me all about that. Not one to hold back, is Alex. Unlike his mother,' Jake bit out.

Angelina remained guiltily silent.

'I asked you a question, Angelina. I expect an answer. Why didn't you tell me on that first Saturday? You had every opportunity, especially when I came back a second time.'

'I guess I was afraid to.'

'Afraid! Afraid of what?'

'Of your not wanting Alex!' she burst forth. 'You said you didn't ever want children.'

'Alex is a *fait accompli*,' he muttered. 'That's a different matter entirely.'

Angelina winced. He was right. She should have told him. 'You…you didn't tell him about us, did you?' she asked plaintively.

'What do you take me for, a complete fool? No, of course I didn't tell him about us. You have nothing to worry about. I made all the right noises. Did a better imitation of a father thrilled to discover he had a fifteen-year-old son than you'd see in a Hollywood movie. I also told him that I would come up and see you personally and smooth things over. He was worried sick how you would react when you found out he'd looked me up, since you had a deal to wait till Easter. Though might I add he seemed chuffed to find out I wasn't the jailbird you'd told him I was sure to be. He said he told you I wouldn't be, but you didn't seem to have the same blind faith in my character.'

She flushed, but lifted her chin defiantly. 'You have to appreciate it was a one-in-a-million chance that you'd turn out to be any good.'

'I'm not blaming you for that judgement call. You

did exactly what I would have done in your position. I suppose I could even forgive you for not telling me about Alex straight away. What I find *un*forgivable is that you didn't tell me the truth by the end of last weekend. What could you possibly have been afraid of by then?'

'Well, I…I…' How could she tell him that she was afraid he'd stop wanting to make love to her? It sounded so…selfish.

His sudden paling had her panicking.

He's guessed the truth. And he's totally appalled.

'It was that incident with the kid, wasn't it?' he said, startling her. 'And my telling you about my childhood. That's why you went all quiet on me. You were worried I might hit Alex like my mother hit me.'

'No! No, nothing like that at all! I'm sure you wouldn't do any such thing!'

'What, then?'

There was nothing for it now but to tell him the truth. In a fashion. 'I…I wanted to tell you. Really, I did. But I was afraid that it would change things between us. I thought…' She bit her lip and tried to find the right words.

'What did you think?'

'All kinds of things. At first, when I agreed to have lunch with you, I just wanted to find out what you were like, what kind of man you were, *before* I told you about Alex. You have to appreciate it was a terrible shock to me, Jake, when you turned up in my life, *and* when I found myself as attracted to you as

I was when I was just a girl. I thought I could control how I felt about you. But of course, I couldn't. Then, when the sex was so fabulous between us, I didn't want it to end. I wanted you to keep looking at me the same way. And making love to me. It was selfish of me, I know, but I…I've never felt anything like I do when I'm with you.' Tears pricked at her eyes. 'I'm sorry, Jake. Truly. I didn't mean to hurt you.'

'Well, I am hurt, Angelina. Do you have any idea what it was like, finding out we had a fifteen-year-old son like that?'

'I'm sure it was a shock.'

'That's an understatement.'

'I…I don't know what to say.'

'There's nothing you can say. The damage has been done.'

Angelina's heart sank. But then defiance kicked in. And resentment. Had what she'd done been that wicked, or seriously unforgivable?

Hardly.

'Well, I happen to think there is a lot I can say,' she threw at him. 'I've stood here, like a typically pathetic female, humbly listening to your poor-little-me tale. I've even been feeling sorry for you. But you know what? I think I'm all sorried out. Where is your sympathy for me? Do you have any idea what *my* life has been like? How hard it's been for *me*?'

'I have some idea. Alex told me. In fact, he told me more about you in the two hours I spent with him today than you have in two weeks. I know the sacrifices you've made for him. I know you've been a good mother. I know you never laid a hand on him, no matter how naughty he was. I know he thinks the world of you. I also know you don't date. *Ever.*' He glowered at her. 'It seems you've become a master at deception in a lot of things.'

'What do you mean?'

'You keep secrets from *everyone*, not just me. *I* know you've had lovers. You told me so. Yet your teenage son says there's never been another man in your life after me. He thinks you're a cross between the Virgin Mary and Mother Teresa. He even has this romantic idea that when you and I meet up again this time, we'll fall in love once more and get married.'

'Oh…' It wasn't so far removed from the romantic notions she'd been stupidly harbouring this last week.

'Yes, *oh*,' Jake said drily. 'Our son has to receive a reward for optimism, doesn't he?'

'He certainly does, considering who his father is. But for your information, Mr Smarty Pants, I have not had lovers. And I never said I had. You just jumped to that conclusion, probably because you couldn't conceive of anyone choosing to lead a celibate lifestyle. Which I did. For our son's sake. Don't think I didn't have offers. I've had plenty. So Alex was right. There's only been the one man in my life. *You!*'

Now that she'd blurted out the whole truth, Angelina rather enjoyed the shocked look on Jake's face.

'You can't seriously expect me to believe you haven't had sex in sixteen years?'

'No, I wouldn't expect you to believe that. Not *you*, a man who has a different girlfriend every other month and who can't even roll over in bed without reaching for another condom. But perhaps if you think about it a little more, you'll see I'm telling the truth. Why do you think I couldn't get enough last weekend? Because I was so frustrated, that's why.'

Jake stared at her. 'Frustrated.'

'Yes. Frustrated!' Her hands found her hips. 'I deserved a break after being such a goody-two-shoes for so long, don't you think? I could do with a few more, too. But I guess that's out of the question now. I always knew that as soon as you found out about Alex, everything would change between us. I'm no longer lover material, I'm the mother of your child. The *single* mother of your child. And, as such, to be treated with suspicion. It wouldn't take a genius to know that the invitation to come to your place this weekend is off.'

He looked stunned. 'Well, I…I need some time to think.'

Her smile was laced with bitterness. 'How come I'm not surprised? You can run but you can't hide, Jake. Alex has found you now, and if I know my son he won't let go. You're his father. Get used to it.'

'It's only been half a day, Angelina. Give *me* a break, will you?'

She laughed. 'You were right. You are going to be a pretty rotten father. Oh, I don't doubt you'll give lip-service to the role, but you just don't have what it takes in here…' She patted her hand over her heart, that heart which was breaking inside.

But be damned if she was going to show it.

'Alex's inter-school swimming carnival is on this Saturday,' she announced. 'It starts at one. Can I tell him you'll be there when I call him tonight? Or do you want time to think about that too?'

'I've already told him I'll be there.'

'No kidding. You've surprised me.'

'I surprised myself,' he muttered. 'Look, I'm doing my best, all right? I don't really know the boy. And I see now that I don't really know you.'

'Men like you never know anyone, except themselves.'

'That's a bit harsh.'

'Is it? I suggest you go home and have a good look in the mirror, Jake. If you can see past the shiny, successful, sexy surface, you just might not like what you find.'

'Angelina, I—'

'Oh, just go,' she snapped, and, wrapping her arms around herself, she whirled away from him to stare steadfastly out of the kitchen window.

She felt him staring at her. Felt his hesitation. But then he started walking. 'See you on Saturday,' he muttered, leaving his coffee untouched behind him on the counter.

By the time Angelina heard the Ferrari growl into life, she was crying her eyes out.

CHAPTER THIRTEEN

'I STILL find it hard to believe,' Dorothy said during dessert.

Jake, who always lost his appetite when he was stressed, or distressed, put down his dessert fork, his slice of lemon meringue pie still intact. 'You and me both,' he said with a weary sigh. 'I didn't sleep much last night. I kept seeing Alex's face when he called me Dad. He made me feel like such a fraud. I'm no hero, Dorothy. I'm just a man.'

'You're not *just* a man, Jake. You're an exceptional man. And you'll make an exceptional father.'

'How can you say that, knowing where I came from?'

'Because I know you. There's not a violent or a mean bone in your body. Angelina more or less said the same thing.'

'Angelina! Don't talk to me about Angelina!'

'Why? Because you're in love with her?'

Jake stiffened in his chair. 'I am not in love with her. I don't fall in love with liars.'

'She explained why she lied. And I, for one, understand her reasoning perfectly. So would you, if your male ego wasn't involved. She's a mother first and foremost. She was protecting her child.'

'She deceived me.'

'For the best of reasons. She wanted to get to know you first.'

'Yeah. In the biblical sense.'

'Oh, for pity's sake, will you get off your high horse? The girl obviously fancies you like crazy. She always did. You pack a powerful physical punch, Jake. She's a healthy young woman whose hormones have never had a chance. I don't blame her one bit if she wanted you.'

'Dorothy!'

'Goodness me, who do you think you're talking to here? A nun? I'll have you know I know exactly how Angelina must have felt last weekend. I was forty years old when I met Edward. OK, so I wasn't a virgin but as good as. I went to bed with Edward the very first night and we didn't sleep a wink. *All* night. Damn, but it was good.'

Jake just stared. He would never understand women. They could look so soft and malleable on the surface, when all the while, inside, they were tough as teak. And so damned surprising.

He hadn't expected Angelina to stand up to him the way she had yesterday. He'd expected her to wilt under his anger and beg his forgiveness. Instead, she'd read him the Riot Act and given him his walking papers.

She obviously didn't fancy him that much. *And* she sure as hell hadn't fallen in love with him last weekend as he'd foolishly hoped she had.

His goal to marry her now seemed even further away than ever. Perverse, considering they shared a child. Which brought him to the problem of Alex. Not that Alex was a problem child. He wasn't. He was a credit to Angelina. *He* was the problem. The father. The pathetic and panic-stricken parent.

He didn't know what to do or what to feel.

'Just go to the swimming carnival, Jake,' Dorothy advised, 'and let nature take its course.'

Jake shook his head. That was another thing about women. They were mind-readers. And weirdly perceptive. Look at how Sally had known Alex was his son at a glance. And then there was her knowing he was thinking of starting up his own business. How had she guessed that? Maybe the whole sex was in league with the devil.

'Stop thinking about yourself and *your* feelings,' Dorothy said sternly. 'Think about Angelina for a change. And what *she's* been through. Much more of a challenge than anything you've ever faced. Being solely responsible for looking after and bringing up a child is a massive job. She might have had her father for support but I doubt he was such a great help with the day-to-day problems of child-rearing. She did it all by herself, Jake. And she did a wonderful job by the sounds of things. The reason you've fallen in love with her is not just because she's physically beautiful. You've had oodles of good-looking girls before. It's because she's a beautiful person, with character and spirit. And you know what? I think she loves you for the same reasons.'

'Yeah, right,' he said drily.

Jake winced when Dorothy gave him one of the

savage looks she used to give him when he'd first come to live with her. 'I never took you for a coward, Jake Winters, but you're beginning to sound and act like one. You *do* love Angelina. And you love your son, even if you don't know him yet. Because he's your flesh and blood. And he loves you for the same reason. The three of you should be together, as a family. The reason Angelina got so stroppy with you yesterday is because that's what she wants too and she's afraid it's not going to happen. She's afraid her son is going to be hurt. She's afraid *she's* going to be hurt.'

'Have you finished?' Jake said ruefully.

'For tonight,' Dorothy returned as she stabbed her piece of pie with her dessert fork. 'There might be another instalment at some time in the future.'

'God forbid. Did Edward know you were like this?'

'Of course. Admittedly, he hated it when I was always right.'

Jake laughed. '*I* hate it too.'

Dorothy's breath caught. And then she let it out very slowly. He did love Angelina. Thank goodness.

'So what are you going to do about it?' she asked, feigning a composure she was far from feeling.

'Back off, Dorothy. This coward is still a male animal and likes to do things his way.'

'I don't really think you're a coward.'

'I know,' Jake said more softly.

'Er—do you think I could come to the swimming

carnival with you tomorrow?' Dorothy asked. 'I would dearly love to see the boy.'

'Only if you promise not to interfere.'

'Would I do that?'

'Yes. Now promise.'

Dorothy sighed. 'I promise.'

'OK,' he agreed, and Dorothy beamed.

She rose and scooped up Jake's untouched dessert. 'Coffee?'

'Mmm. Yes, please,' he said, watching blankly as Dorothy left the room. He was wondering what Angelina was doing and if she really might love him, as Dorothy said.

'I hate him,' Angelina muttered as she slammed the plates into the dishwasher.

'Hey, watch it with the crockery there, boss!'

'Let her break a plate or two, Kevin,' Wilomena advised from where she was scraping the remains of tonight's meals into the bin. 'Better than her breaking them over a certain person's head. Besides, they're her plates. She can do with them whatever she damned well pleases.'

'True,' Angelina growled, and slammed a few more in.

None of them broke. But then, they weren't as easily broken as other things. Like her heart.

'The bastard,' she grumped. 'How dare he say he had to *pretend* to be nice to Alex? As if anyone ever has to pretend to be nice to Alex.'

'Geez, Angelina!' Kevin exclaimed. 'Give the man a break.'

'That's exactly what she'd like to do,' Wilomena said drily. 'Across that stupid skull of his.'

'You women expect too much of a guy.'

'No kidding!' both women chorused.

'He'll come round. Just give him time.'

'Like, how long? A lifetime?' Wilomena said waspishly. 'That's how long it takes for some men to come to the party. If ever.'

'I think he sounds like an OK guy. He's going to Alex's swimming carnival tomorrow, isn't he?'

'Big deal,' Angelina muttered.

'Yeah, big deal,' Wilomena echoed.

'Women!' Kevin huffed. 'Impossible to please.'

'He could please her all right,' Wilomena said after Angelina had gone home and she and Kevin were stacking away the last of the things. 'He could tell her he loves her for starters, then ask her to marry him.'

Kevin laughed. 'You think that would please her? You know what she'd do? She'd throw back at him that he didn't really love her and he was only marrying her for the kid's sake. And then she'd say no, like a typical female.'

'Rubbish! She would not! Not if she loved him. And she does. Trust me on that. Women who love guys don't say no to a proposal of marriage.'

'You know, I'm glad to hear you say that,' Kevin said, and, drawing a small velvet box out of his white coat's pocket, he dropped to one knee then flipped it open. The cluster of diamonds in the ring glittered like his eyes.

'Wilomena Jenkins,' he said, 'I love you and I want you to be my wife. Will you marry me?'

Wilomena didn't say no. She didn't say a single word. She was too busy crying.

CHAPTER FOURTEEN

ALEX stood behind the starting blocks with the rest of his relay team, nerves making him shift from foot to foot. He swung his arms in circles to keep his muscles warm, and tried to focus on the race ahead, deliberately keeping his eyes away from the stand where he knew his parents were sitting together watching him, along with the old duck they'd brought with them.

'Dorothy's an old friend of mine,' his dad had introduced her before the meet began.

Old was right. And brother, had she stared at him.

Of course, that was because he looked so much like his dad.

His dad.

Alex scooped in a deep breath and let it out very slowly. It was still almost too good to be true, finding his father like that. He'd been confident that his dad would not be in jail. But he'd never dreamt he'd be a top lawyer. How cool was that? And what about that simply awesome car he drove? The guys at school had been green with envy when he'd rocked up on Thursday in a yellow Ferrari.

He'd felt so proud, introducing his dad around to his friends and teachers. He must have gone to sleep that night with a permanent smile on his face.

Now today was his chance to make his dad proud of him. Alex knew he wasn't good enough at his school work to line up for too many academic prizes. But he was his school's best swimmer. He'd already won the hundred-metre sprint. And the two hundred. Now he was lining up for the four-by-one relay, the last race of this meet, and he was swimming the anchor leg.

Kings were in front on the scoreboard. But only by a couple of points. If St Francis's could win this relay, the cup would be theirs. The trouble was, their second-best hundred-metre swimmer had come down with a virus that morning and they'd had to bring in the first reserve, who was three seconds slower. On paper, they couldn't possibly win, not unless they all swam above themselves.

Alex wanted to win. He wanted to win so badly.

They were being called up for the start. Alex felt sick. As team captain, he'd made the decision to put their slowest swimmer first, employing the tactic that sometimes a swimmer could swim a personal best if they were chasing. Of course, sometimes the chase theory didn't work. The behind swimmer tried too hard on the first lap and went lactic in the second.

The gun went off and their first and slowest swimmer was in the water, doing his best but possibly trying *too* hard. After he'd come in to the changeover several lengths behind, Alex wished he'd made the decision to go first himself. But he soothed his panic with the knowledge that Kings had sent their second-best swimmer off first.

By the second changeover, they'd caught up a couple of lengths. But then disaster happened. Their third swimmer's foot slipped on the starting block at the changeover, losing them another precious length. By the time he turned to come down for the second lap, he was trailing the Kings boy by a good five lengths. He dug deep, however, and came towards the wall only three lengths behind.

But even as Alex readied himself for the changeover, logic told him that three lengths were still too much. Sure, he'd won the hundred-metre race earlier in the afternoon. But only by a length. How could he possibly find another two lengths?

And then the voice came to him, across the pool, loud and clear.

'Go for it, son!'

He went, with wings on his feet, making up half a length in the changeover dive alone, coming up with the Kings swimmer's feet in his sights. There was no holding back. He wasn't close enough for fancy tactics, like riding in the other boy's wash. He put his foot down, his big arms slicing through the water, his even bigger feet churning with a six-beat kick right from the start.

You have to nail the turn, he lectured himself as the wall loomed into view. His lungs were bursting. He'd forgotten to breathe. No time now. He would breathe later, after he'd turned. He tumbled. His feet hit the wall and he was surging forward under the water. Up he eventually came, gasping for air but still swimming like a madman. He had no idea where the Kings boy was now. His head was turned the other way. All he could do was go like the hammers of hell.

His arms were burning. So were his legs. He'd never known such pain. Or such determination. He was going to win, not just for his dad, but also for his mum. He wanted to make her proud as well. Alex knew she'd given up a lot for him, and he wanted her to see that it had been worth it.

Not far now. He could hear the screaming. It had to be close. Just a bit more, Alex. You can do it. Stroke harder. Kick faster. The wall was coming up. Time it right. Dip down, stretch those fingers. You've got your dad's big hands. They have to be good for something.

He touched then exploded upwards, out of the water. He looked up, towards his mother. She had her hands over her face and she looked as if she was crying. His heart sank. He'd lost. He'd given it his all and he'd lost. But then the boy in the next lane was tapping him on the shoulder and congratulating him.

He looked up again. His mum was now wrapped in his dad's arms and the old duck next to them was grinning like a Cheshire cat, with her hand held up towards Alex in a victory sign.

Alex grinned back at her, his own hand punching up high into the air as he yelled, 'Go for it, Dad!'

CHAPTER FIFTEEN

'Is it always like that?'

Angelina lifted her head at Jake's question. They were back at his apartment, Angelina having driven there at Jake's request after the swimming carnival was over. She was sitting on the sleek red leather sofa once more, with a Malibu and Coke cradled in her hands, wondering when she could possibly get up and leave. Just being in this place with Jake, alone, was killing her. She'd thought she hated him this past week but of course she didn't. She loved him.

'Always like what?' she asked, her voice sounding as dead and drained as she was feeling.

'When your kid does something great. Does it always feel like that?'

'Like what, exactly?'

'Like your heart is going to burst out of your chest. Like you're on top of the world, a world bathed in everlasting sunshine.'

Angelina's own heart squeezed tight as all the fears which had been gathering that afternoon suddenly crystallised into one big fear.

'Yes,' she said flatly. 'Yes, it always feels like that.'

Jake sat down on an adjacent armchair with his

own drink in his hands. Scotch on ice, by the look of it.

'We have to talk,' he said, his tone serious.

'About what?' Angelina took a sip of her drink.

'You. Me. Alex.'

'Let's just stick to Alex.'

'I think we should start with you and me. After all, that's where Alex started, sixteen years ago.'

'A lot of water has gone under the bridge since then, Jake.'

'Yes. It certainly has. We're different people now, you and me.'

'One of us is, anyway,' she bit out, then took another sip.

Jake gritted his teeth. She wasn't making things easy for him. When she'd cried back at the swimming carnival and he'd taken her into his arms, he'd thought that everything was going to be all right. Alex had clearly thought so, too. *And* Dorothy. But the moment they were alone together again, she'd withdrawn inside a cold, hard little shell that he just couldn't penetrate.

Jake decided that a change of tactics was called for.

'So you're going to do it again, are you?' he said sharply.

That got her attention. 'Do what?'

'Lie to me.'

'I never lied to you,' she said defensively.

'Yes, you did. By omission. And by implication. Now you're doing it again.'

'I don't know what you mean.'

'You're pretending you don't care about me. That you don't love me.'

He watched her mouth drop open; watched the truth flash into her eyes.

'You *do* love me,' he ground out, his voice thick with emotion.

'I...I...' She shook her head from side to side, clearly unable to speak the words.

'You love me and you're going to marry me.'

'*Marry* you!' She jumped to her feet, her drink sloshing all over the rug. 'I am not going to marry you. When and if I marry, it will be to a man who loves me as much as I love him. And *not* because he covets my son. Oh, yes, I saw the way you looked at Alex today, Jake Winters, and I knew. I knew in my heart that you wanted my boy, not just for a weekend here and there but all the time. That was why I was crying so much.'

Jake snatched the glass out of her shaking hands and rammed it down on a nearby table along with his own drink before glowering at her with fury in his eyes and frustration in his heart.

'I've heard enough of this rubbish!' he roared. 'I *do* love you, woman. I probably love you even more than you love me! If you don't believe me, then come here...' Grabbing her hand, he dragged her with him into the bedroom, where he yanked open the top drawer of his bedside chest.

'I don't think that showing me how many condoms you've bought is proof of love,' she said scathingly as she tried to tug her hand out of his. But he refused to let it go.

His producing a ring box and flipping it open to show a spectacular diamond engagement ring shut her up. But not for long.

'Good try, Jake. Good move, too. I've got to hand it to you. You're clever.'

Jake dropped the ring box on the bed, grabbed a piece of paper from the drawer and shoved it into her hands. 'That's the sales receipt. Care to check the date?'

Angelina's eyes dropped to the date. Wednesday. He'd bought the ring on Wednesday.

She looked up, tears in her eyes. 'You bought this *before* Alex went to see you?'

Jake had to steel himself against his own rush of emotion. 'I wanted to tell you I loved you and wanted to marry you last weekend. But I was afraid of rushing you. I thought you needed time. I was prepared to give you all the time in the world. But then I walked past this jewellery-shop window and saw this ring and I just had to buy it for you. When I put it in this drawer, I told myself I didn't care how long I had to wait till you wore it, as long as you eventually did.'

'Oh…' More tears rushed in, spilling over.

He wiped them away with his fingers, then curved his hands over her shoulders. 'I love you, Angelina Mastroianni. And you love me. So I'm not going to give you any more time. We've already wasted sixteen years.' He reached to extract the diamond ring from the box and slipped it on her left hand. It fitted perfectly. 'We're going to be married. Not hurriedly. Magnificently. Next spring. In St Mary's Cathedral. But that's just a ceremony. From this moment on, you are my woman, and I am your man, exclusively, till death do us part.'

'Till death us do part,' she repeated dazedly.

'Now tell me you love me.'

'I love you.'

He sighed and drew her into his arms, his lips burrowing into her hair. 'I think you should show me how much.'

CHAPTER SIXTEEN

SEPTEMBER—the first month of spring down under—
was an iffy month for weather in Sydney. Often cold.
Often rainy. But occasionally brilliant.

St Mary's Cathedral had never looked better than
it did that September afternoon, bathed in sunshine,
the nearby gardens just beginning to blossom. But
nothing could match the splendour of the bride as
she carefully mounted the cathedral steps.

Her dress was white chiffon, with a draped bodice
and a long, flowing skirt that fell from straight under
her impressive bustline. Her dark hair was sleekly
up, with a diamanté tiara as decoration. Her veil was
very long and sheer. Her neck was bare, but delicate
diamond and pearl drops fell from her lobes.

She looked exquisite. She also looked nervous,
which enhanced that glorious air of innocence that
often clung to brides, even those who were secretly
five months pregnant.

'I never appreciated till now,' she said to
Wilomena, 'just how nerve-racking weddings are. If
I hadn't had your help today, I'd never have been
ready in time.'

'That's what bridesmaids are for,' Wilomena returned, busily fluffing out the bridal veil. 'I'll be re-

lying on you for the same help when Kevin and I tie the knot later in the year.'

Angelina smiled at the girl who had fast gone from employee to confidante to best friend. 'My pleasure. And might I say that burgundy colour really suits you, despite your doubts? The style, too.'

Wilomena's dress was chiffon as well, calf-length, with a low neckline, spaghetti straps and a long, flowing scarf that draped softly around her throat and hung down to the hem at the back

'Mmm. Yes. I'm forced to agree. Kevin said he can't wait to get it off me later tonight,' she whispered.

'Come on, Mum,' Alex said, and took his mother's arm. 'Stop the girlie chit-chat. We don't want to keep Dad waiting too long. He was champing at the bit this morning.'

Angelina looked up at her son. So handsome he was in his tuxedo. And so grown up. He'd matured considerably since Jake had come into his life. The two of them spent as much time together as they possibly could, obviously trying to make up for lost time.

Angelina might have been jealous if both the men in her life hadn't been so happy. Besides, Jake still found plenty of time for her. Quality time. In bed and out.

The *Wedding March* started up, snapping Angelina out of her thoughts. Wilomena took her place in front of the bride and began the slow walk up the aisle, just as they had rehearsed. Angelina's arms tightened around her son's when her bouquet started to shake.

'Relax, Mum,' her son advised.

'How can you be so calm?' she cried.

'Well, there's nothing to be nervous about, is there? I mean...we all love each other here. Not only that, if I'm going to do Grandpa's job, I want to do it with dignity and panache, like he would have.'

Angelina's stomach tightened at the mention of her father. 'Do you think he'd mind my marrying Jake, Alex?'

'Grandpa? Nah. He'd be happy, I reckon. Especially now.'

'You mean because Jake's turned out to be such a good man?'

Alex stifled a laugh. 'Come on, Mum. This is me you're talking to. Because of the *baby*, of course! Dad told me all about it.'

'He *told* you!'

'Yeah, there are no secrets between Dad and me. He said it was all his fault, as usual.'

'Oh...'

'He also said if I ever get a girl pregnant this side of twenty-five, he's going to skin me alive,' Alex added with a grin. 'Hey, we'd better start walking. Wil's halfway up the aisle.'

They started walking, Angelina's head whirling. Jake had told Alex about the baby. And there she'd been, trying to hide her pregnancy, worried sick about what her son would think when he found out.

'You don't mind?' she whispered out of the corner of her mouth.

'Why should I mind? I always wanted a little sister.'

'You know it's a girl as well?'

'Yep. Dad's tickled pink.'

Which was true. Not that Jake had really cared if it was a boy or a girl. He just wanted them to have a baby together. He'd told her he wanted to experience fatherhood right from the start.

'Smile, Mum,' Alex ordered.

She smiled. And then she smiled some more. Alex was right. They all loved each other here. There was nothing to worry about.

Jake's heart lurched when she smiled. Then lurched some more when her smile broadened. God, how he loved that woman!

'What a babe,' Kevin muttered beside him.

'You can say that again,' Jake returned before he realised Kevin's eyes were on his fiancée across the way.

Those two only had eyes for each other. Jake knew that for a fact. Since quitting his job, he'd been spending a lot of time up at the winery, helping out there till he worked out what he was going to do, career-wise. Probably start up his own law practice. Sally had already indicated that she was for hire, at the right price.

He and Kevin had hit it off right from the start and when Angelina said she'd asked Wilomena to be her one and only bridesmaid, Jake had no hesitation in asking Kevin to be his best man.

'Angelina looks pretty good too,' Kevin added, and Jake laughed.

He caught Sally's eye in the third pew and gave her a wink. She winked back.

Then he smiled at Dorothy, who was looking just a little tense.

Dear Dorothy. *Smart* Dorothy as well. He would be forever grateful for the solution she'd come up with for a problem he had about names. The names of his children. He wanted both of them to have the same surname. *His*. But Alex was adamant about keeping Mastroianni as his surname and Jake could appreciate that. Still, with Dorothy's help, he'd sorted that all out. He hoped Angelina would be pleased, he thought as his gaze returned to his lovely bride.

Dorothy was determined not to cry during the ceremony, but she clutched a white lace-edged handkerchief in her hands, just in case. What a beautiful bride Angelina made. But what a handsome groom Jake was. Most touching of all was the way he was looking at the woman he loved as she came down the aisle. With so much tenderness. So much love.

Oh, Edward. You would have been so proud of him today.

But no prouder than she was. Maybe she wasn't his mother by blood, but she was in her heart. And now there was a baby coming as well. A dear little baby girl for her to help mind. And to love.

Oh, dear. She dabbed at her eyes.

Jake tensed when the priest got to the part which he knew would come as a bit of a surprise to his bride.

'And do you, Jake Mastroianni, take…?'

Angelina reached out to touch the priest's arm. 'No, no,' she murmured. 'You've got it wrong. It's Jake *Winters*.'

'Not any more,' Jake whispered to her. 'I had my surname changed by deed poll. With Alex's approval, of course. I'm a Mastroianni now.' And he glanced over his shoulder at his son, who nodded to his mother with a wide smile.

'You've taken *my* name?' Angelina asked, looking pleased, but stunned.

Jake sighed with relief. He'd done the right thing. After all, he had no real attachment to his own name. His poor mother had died some years back and he'd never known any of his other relatives. But it was rather ironic that he was to be called Mr Mastroianni from now on.

I'll try not to discredit your name in any way, came his silent promise to the proud Italian man who had once broken his nose.

'Please go on,' Jake directed the priest.

The ceremony was a bit of a fog after that, Angelina not surfacing till Jake lifted the veil from her face and kissed her.

His lips on hers felt slightly different this time. Softer. More tender. More loving.

She looked up into her husband's eyes, those beautiful blue eyes that could look so hard at times. But not today. And certainly not at this moment. They were soft and wet with tears.

'Mrs Mastroianni,' he choked out, and she realised, perhaps for the first time, just how much he *did* love her.

'Mr Mastroianni,' she returned softly, and touched his cheek. 'My sweet darling. My only love.'

THE AUSTRALIAN'S
CONVENIENT BRIDE

by

Lindsay Armstrong

Lindsay Armstrong was born in South Africa but now lives in Australia with her New Zealand-born husband and their five children. They have lived in nearly every state of Australia and have tried their hand at some unusual – for them – occupations, such as farming and horse-training – all grist to the mill for a writer! Lindsay started writing romances when their youngest child began school and she was left feeling at a loose end. She is still doing it and loving it.

Don't miss Lindsay Armstrong's exciting new novel, *The Billionaire Boss's Innocent Bride,* available in January 2009 from Mills & Boon® Modern™.

CHAPTER ONE

STEVE KINANE turned off the highway, swore beneath his breath and pulled his Range Rover off the dirt road towards the girl thumbing a lift on this isolated outback road.

Country ethics dictated that you didn't ignore any travellers in distress but it had been a long day and he got the feeling he was about to be taken out of his way. Then he noticed—and this slightly qualified his 'damsel in distress' reading of the situation—that she had an efficient and fit-looking bodyguard: a blue heeler with black points on a lead. While only medium-sized dogs, their devotion to duty was legendary.

He opened his door cautiously and the dog barked but, at one word from its mistress, sank silently to its haunches, Steve firmly in its sights.

'Hello,' he said, approaching the girl. 'Where are you headed?'

She was a cool, young blonde—in her early twenties, he guessed. Her hair was long, fair, curly, and tied back under a blue linen sunhat. Her eyes were grey and direct and her figure in jeans and a T-shirt—his eyes widened—was slim and curvy.

'Afternoon,' she replied. 'Thanks for stopping. I'm headed for Mount Helena station. I think it's about ten miles down the road.'

He frowned. 'Are they expecting you?'

'Does that mean you know it?' she countered politely, taking in his stained, frayed jeans, his bush shirt, battered boots and dirty hands.

He looked down at himself and said, not entirely truthfully, 'I—work there.' Then immediately wondered why he was being selective with the truth—obviously some instinct he couldn't pinpoint was directing him.

But the girl seemed to relax. 'I'd really appreciate a lift, then. This isn't the busiest of roads, is it?' She looked nervously at the empty landscape before turning to look straight back at him. 'I'm Charlotte Winslow, by the way,' she said without dropping her gaze and while confidently putting out her hand.

He took it, noticing that her arm was lightly tanned with skin as smooth as silk. The dog growled warningly.

'It's OK, Rich,' she murmured, but instantly withdrew her hand.

'I'm sorry, but Charlotte Winslow doesn't ring a bell,' he said.

'Please call me Chattie, everyone does,' she invited. 'Uh—they may not have had time to discuss me with—uh—you.'

'They may not have,' he replied sardonically and allowed his cool, dark gaze to drift down her figure again.

She took a sharp breath as she suffered the paralysing experience of being mentally undressed before his eyes narrowed and focused on hers again. 'Are you after Mark Kinane, by any chance?'

She hesitated. 'What makes you think that?'

'It's been known,' he replied. 'Are you?'

Chattie debated for a moment, and decided the simplest way to go would be to admit to it and let this man make whatever he liked of it. 'Yes.'

'How come?'

She chewed her lip. 'We, that is, Mark, talked a bit about the place and he issued an open invitation, so here I am!' Surely he can tell I'm lying, she thought.

'How the hell did you get this far?' Steve Kinane asked incredulously.

'I got a lift from Brisbane with a friend who was going through to Augathella. He would have brought me the whole way but it wasn't a four-wheel-drive and he didn't want to risk his suspension off the highway on this kind of road.'

She looked expressively westward along the dusty red road with its potholes, gutters and ridges.

'What would you have done if no one had come along?'

She shrugged, hopefully disguising her own surprise that her friend had just abandoned her here. 'I was going to give it another hour, then walk back to the highway. I'd have had no trouble getting a lift to the nearest town and—tomorrow is another day.'

'OK,' he said at last. 'The dog can go in the back with your bag.' He heaved up her holdall.

Five minutes later they were all aboard and under way with the dog planted alertly in the back seat. To his irritation, Steve could feel it breathing down the back of his neck.

Chattie, on the other hand, couldn't help but be impressed by his expert handling of the vehicle on such a difficult road and it came to her unwittingly that this employee of Mount Helena station, with his strong hands and long lines, was rather a fine figure of a man. She even felt herself blush as these thoughts brought back the memory of his visual exploration of her body earlier.

Stunned by the direction of her thoughts, she immediately and sternly told herself she must be out of her mind, this was not the time or place for anything of that nature, and she concentrated fiercely on the countryside instead. Still vast, it wasn't quite so empty now, she noticed, with some interesting rocky outcrops and more trees.

Then her lift said, 'How long have you known Mark, Chattie Winslow?'

She thought back carefully. 'A few months, I guess.'

He flicked her a glance. She'd taken off her hat and her profile was delicious. A short, straight little nose, lovely curving mouth, delicately sculptured jaw and a smooth, slender throat. Even her ear, and it occurred to him he'd never really considered ears before, was pretty with that riotous fair hair tucked behind it.

I have to hand it to you, Mark, he thought, you sure can pick 'em, although why do I get the feeling you may have bitten off more than you can chew here?

'How did you meet Mark?' he asked.

'At a party,' Chattie answered honestly but conscious at the same time that, in her quest to keep things simple, she was presenting herself in the light of Mark Kinane's girlfriend, which could complicate things for her. She added, with a smile curving her lips to take the sting out of it, 'Why do I get the feeling you're interrogating me?'

A corner of his mouth twitched; it had been an enchanting smile. 'Just interested. I guess you're a bit of a diversion from damn cows.' He waved a hand at a mob of cattle gathered around a small dam. 'Sometimes they're enough to send you stir-crazy.'

Chattie looked ahead and laughed, an attractive musical sound. 'I guess I can understand that. I believe Mark felt the same.' She stopped and bit her lip. Until she found Mark Kinane, she didn't want to discuss him with anyone, let alone an employee, so why did she keep bringing up his name?

'I could tell you something about me,' she offered. 'I'm a teacher.'

The Range Rover veered off course briefly until he corrected it.

'What's so surprising about that?' she asked, amused at his reaction.

'You don't look like a teacher.' He flicked her another glance, but this time she met it and their gazes caught and held for a brief, but telling, moment.

Trying not to sound as shaken as she felt, she said, 'Thanks, but your ideas about teachers could be a bit outdated.'

'Perhaps.' He shrugged. 'What do you teach?'

'Domestic Science—as in cooking and sewing, which is rather lucky because I love to do both.'

Curiouser and curiouser, Steve Kinane reflected. His brother Mark's taste in women didn't run along domestic lines, or hadn't to date. Models and starlets had featured prominently in his love life: beautiful, flighty creatures with few practical talents that he'd been able to detect, at least.

Yet, although this girl had the looks, she not only taught down-to-earth, practical subjects, but, if the way she'd got herself this far into the outback and the way she'd trained her dog was anything to go by, she was both practical and down-to-earth herself.

'Is there anything wrong with that?' Chattie enquired as the silence stretched.

'Not at all,' he denied, but added the silent rider to himself—Just doesn't make sense.

'I also paint and play the piano,' she offered gravely, but now he got the distinct impression she was laughing at him.

'What do you know about Mount Helena?' he asked abruptly.

Chattie searched through her knowledge of the place and found it to be minimal. 'Er—not a lot.'

He glanced at her suspiciously. 'Mark must have told you something!'

Chattie detected both the suspicion and the fact that he was less than amused. On the heels of this discovery came the realization that he might only be an employee but he was also tall and tough and quite capable of questioning her right to be ferried to Mount Helena. And equally capable of turning back and dumping her on the highway if he decided she was less than legitimate.

'Uh—I gather that Mark hasn't decided whether he wants to be a cattleman yet but he did say it was quite a place. I've never seen a cattle station.'

'Go on.'

It was definitely an order and Chattie bristled. 'What more do you want to know? He has an older brother who runs the place and goes around like a dictator, but if you work there you probably know that as well as anyone.'

Whether prompted by her tone or his, Rich growled softly as if to back her up.

Steve Kinane looked irritated beyond words but the glint of suspicion died out of his eyes, although he did say, 'You obviously have no qualms about foisting your dog on unsuspecting hosts?'

'He's trained to sleep outside, if necessary, and I'd be more than happy to introduce him to anyone he needs to know so they needn't be scared of him. He's actually a very friendly dog,' she said evenly.

'So long as no one raises a hand or their voice to you.'

Their gazes clashed briefly.

'When I found Rich he'd been abandoned as a puppy in a box in a building rubble dumpster,' she said coolly. 'How he wasn't crushed I'll never know. I had to climb into the bin and literally dig him out. He's been my constant companion ever since.'

'As well as suitably grateful and devoted,' Steve commented, but as her eyes flashed added, 'Don't get your hackles up, I would have done the same.'

He turned the wheel and drove through a set of wire gates and they trundled over a cattle-grid. The legend on the gates—MOUNT HELENA—was not flashy but the road improved immediately.

'Nearly there, I gather?' Chattie hazarded.

'Yep, about a mile to go.'

They drove the last mile in silence until Steve pulled up outside a garden fence.

Chattie looked through the windscreen at the sprawling white-painted house with a red tin roof beyond the fence. It was surrounded by lawn and shrubbery and neatly fenced off, everything was neat and trim for that matter and although the house was old, it gleamed with new paint. Behind it were several water tanks smothered with bougainvillea and allamanda, and the land rose from there to a series of low hills cloaked in gold grass studded with blackboys.

Marvellous colours, she thought, taking in the red-gold soil, the sky, the grass and the house again, and she heaved a sudden sigh of relief.

Steve Kinane glinted a question at her.

She smiled with a touch of embarrassment. 'It looks quite civilized.'

'You expected to have to rough it?'

'I wasn't quite sure, to be honest. Mark, well, most men,' she amended hastily, 'aren't very good at describing houses, are they?'

Steve didn't reply but had she thought to check his expression, Chattie would have discovered it to be rather grimly thoughtful.

Then he shrugged and opened his door. 'I'll drop you off here. The—uh—housekeeper should be around somewhere—oh, there he is. I'll just have a word with him.'

Chattie blinked. The 'housekeeper' was a tough, leathery-looking man in his forties with a bald pate and grey pony-tail. Steve met him at the garden gate but their conversation was inaudible, although Chattie did observe that there seemed to be an aura of incredulity about it. There was certainly a bit of head-shaking on the part of the housekeeper.

Then her lift—it was at this point that Chattie realized she didn't know his name—brought the other man over to introduce him.

'Chattie, this is Slim,' he said through the window.

'He's in charge of the house and he'll look after you until…things get sorted out.'

'How do you do, Slim?' She stuck her hand out of the window to have it taken in a strong grip. Rich barked.

'Howdy,' Slim said in a deep, gravelly voice as he ducked his head to look in at her. 'Well, I'll be…' He didn't finish as his gaze ran over Chattie and the dog. 'That is to say, welcome to Helena, miss.'

'Thank you,' Chattie replied. 'Is Mark around?'

'Not at present,' Slim replied.

'Oh.' She looked uncertain.

'Doesn't mean to say we can't make you comfortable,' Slim offered. 'Let's get your gear out. Is the dog house-trained?'

Chattie explained that it certainly was and received the information that the house was between dogs at the moment but there would be no objection to a suitably trained one taking up temporary residence.

She couldn't help herself from raising her eyebrows at the man who had driven her here, only to be ignored, and not much later she was installed in a guest suite beneath the red roof of the Mount Helena homestead.

Slim had provided her with afternoon tea on a tray. He'd also advised her that dinner was scheduled for seven o'clock and recommended that she not bother about unpacking but have a rest instead.

Her lift had disappeared before she could thank him or discover his name.

Her question to Slim about when she could expect to see Mark Kinane had been answered with a shrug and a negligent wave of his hand—as if to say she shouldn't bother her head about it. Then she'd been left alone.

She sat down on the vast bed and Rich sat at her feet with his head on her knee. 'Why—' she stroked his nose and spoke with a frown '—am I getting strange vibes? Don't tell me I've come on a wild-goose chase and Mark isn't here?'

She looked around. Although rather old-fashioned, it was a large, comfortable room with a covered, screened veranda and its own bathroom.

In fact, everything in the bedroom was on a grand scale. Big bed, large mahogany wardrobe with an oval mirror in the central panel, divine chest of drawers starting small at the top, the drawers, and graduating to full width towards the floor. Pretty curtains in an old-fashioned floral cretonne with twisted cord tie-backs and a rose-red sumptuous silk-covered eider-down on the bed.

The bathroom appeared to have been modernized recently, the veranda had two comfortable cane chairs and a table on it and the whole was spotlessly clean and polished.

But as she poured then sipped her tea gratefully her thoughts turned to the predicament, or one of them anyway, she appeared to have got herself into—suspected of being Mark Kinane's girlfriend, in other words. Of course, she acknowledged, the whole reason for her being at Mount Helena had all the hallmarks of a tragic predicament, but for her sister Bridget.

Mind you, she sighed, since she and her younger sister had been orphaned and placed in the care of an aunt who had found them burdensome, Bridget had been a predicament in her own right. Even now, at nineteen, absolutely lovely and training to be a model, she was as vulnerable and defenceless as she had been from the time of the loss of their parents.

Or, Chattie suddenly wondered, was she always destined to be the same? Warm, loving, generous, scatty and staggeringly unwise at times without me to lend a guiding hand?

And was I always destined to feel responsible for her, to sometimes feel a hundred years older than her although I'm only twenty-two?

She sighed again and put her cup back on the tray. Whatever, when Mark Kinane had entered their lives at a party and completely bewitched Bridget with his good looks and fun ways, she had done her level best to keep Bridget's feet on the ground. Her utmost to prevent her sister from being swept *off* her feet and then her warmest and wisest when Mark and Bridget had broken up and she'd been left to pick up the pieces.

The only time she'd lost her cool had been when Bridget had shown her a positive home-pregnancy-test kit and announced that it was Mark's baby and she would never love anyone else.

'*Does he know?*' she'd cried with utter frustration. And—'How did it happen?'

He didn't know because Bridget had not known herself at the time. How it had happened had been typical Bridget, a tale of mixed-up dates and forgotten pills, or perhaps the one night they'd both got so carried away it hadn't entered their minds?

For the first time in her life, Chattie had been really stern with her sister and she'd dragged the whole story of the breakup out of her rather than the edited version she'd suspected she'd been favoured with to date.

Mark Kinane, who was the same age as Chattie, was a mixed-up young man, it emerged. He'd already suffered a broken engagement, he wasn't sure what course his life should take and he'd been ordered home to an outback cattle station by his disapproving older brother.

As it transpired, Bridget laid a lot of the blame for Mark's difficulties and insecurities at the dictatorial older brother's feet—he'd been their father's favourite, according to Bridget.

He was forcing Mark to be something he didn't want to be, he was perpetually undermining his confidence, but with she, Bridget, at his side, her sister had declared passionately, along with the responsibility of a family, things would be very different.

Chattie had reviewed Mark Kinane in her mind's eye and not been so sure at all. Charming he'd been, yes. Hard to resist, yes, but how much substance there was to him and whether this news would be welcome were another matter. One thing she couldn't dispute, however, was that he had a right to know and Bridget's baby had a right to some kind of support.

It had been when Bridget had decided categorically that she could only deliver this news to Mark in person that Chattie had decided otherwise. Bridget was looking fragile, haunted and starting to suffer from morning sickness—there was no way she could go chasing what might turn out to be moonbeams beyond the black stump. Chattie would go herself.

The outpouring of love and gratitude from Bridget had been moving but Chattie had taken two precautions. She'd rung the station and asked for Mark Kinane only to be told he was out on a muster and would she like to leave a message? She'd declined, saying she would call back, which she'd had no intention of doing but at least she'd established where he was—she guessed now it was Slim she'd spoken to. And she'd installed a good friend in their rented cottage to keep an eye on Bridget while she was away, just in case things took time...

'Perhaps I had a premonition? Or, perhaps I'm imagining things. If he was here two days ago, surely he's still here?' she said to Rich, now curled up at her feet.

He opened an eye and thumped his tail.

She smiled. 'None of the aforementioned answers the question of what to do about being mistaken for Mark's girlfriend, though.'

This time the dog scratched his ear and she laughed softly. 'I know, it's a right old conundrum! Oh, well, maybe I'll just play it by ear. If the guy who picked us up is anything to go by, they're a pretty cagey lot.'

This conjured up a mental vision of their 'lift' and she frowned. Was it her imagination or had there been something...she couldn't find the right words...but something more to him than a worker on a cattle station not precisely beyond the black stump but certainly in remote western Queensland?

She pictured him again in her mind's eye, searching for that elusive quality, but could only come up with: dusty and dirty he might have been, but rather dishy with thick dark hair, dark eyes and a fine physique.

'Probably got from throwing a lot of calves,' she told herself dismissively, only to find that he wasn't so easy to dismiss from her thoughts. In fact it was difficult to think of him at all without thinking of his hands, his tall strength and the curious fact that being undressed mentally by him had annoyed her, yes, but hadn't entirely left her cold...

Stop it, she advised herself, then yawned with genuine weariness. It had been a big day, mentally and physically.

She'd had no intention of taking Slim's advice about delaying her unpacking and having a rest but the desire to lie down and close her eyes just for a few minutes was irresistible.

Two hours later she woke with a jerk. It was dark and for a moment she was completely disorientated, then she remembered and grimaced.

She groped for the bedside lamp and, by its soft glow, discovered it was six-thirty. She listened for a moment but heard no sounds.

'OK, boy, enough of this sloth,' she commanded as she got up.

Rich bounded up and together they descended to the lawn below the veranda. Slim had told Chattie that the station dogs were barred from the garden, but all the same, Chattie put a lead on the dog while they stretched their legs.

'Not much exercise but it will have to do,' Chattie murmured as they got back to the bedroom and went to take a shower.

She was just ready when someone knocked on her door. It was Slim.

'Dinner's nearly ready, miss, and Mr Kinane has asked you to join him for a drink.'

'Mark?'

Slim shook his head. 'By the way, I've made up a meal for your dog—think he'd come with me?'

Chattie thanked him warmly and was just about to hand over Rich when she was struck by a thought. 'How many Mr Kinanes are there? I mean, as far as I know, Mark has no father and only one brother.'

'That's him. I'll show you the way,' Slim offered.

Chattie swallowed, then tilted her chin. 'Thank you.'

Steve Kinane paused in the act of raising a glass of Scotch to his mouth as he heard Slim say, 'In here, miss.'

He turned to the lounge doorway—and encountered a pair of stunned grey eyes.

Charlotte Winslow had changed for dinner. So had he, for that matter, but only into clean jeans and a fresh, well-pressed khaki shirt, whereas she looked sensational.

Her hair was loose, in a curly bob to just above her shoulders, and very fair beneath the overhead light. Her outfit was simple yet elegant: cream trousers and a toffee-coloured silky blouse but, simple though it was, it showed off her lovely figure to perfection.

She was also, he realized, the only person he'd ever met who could look attractive with their mouth hanging open in disbelief.

He grimaced. 'Come in, Chattie. What would you like to drink?'

She shut her mouth then said through her teeth, 'Are you who I think you are?'

'I'm Steve Kinane, Mark's older brother—the dictator, no less.'

CHAPTER TWO

'WHY didn't you *tell* me?'

Steve shrugged. 'I wondered if there was something you weren't telling me, to be honest, Miss Winslow. *Would* you like a drink?'

Chattie considered him out of smouldering eyes. 'I could certainly do with one.'

He raised an eyebrow at her. 'Name your poison.'

'If you had anything resembling a glass of chilled white wine—'

'Done.' He put his glass down and opened a cabinet to reveal a bar fridge.

Chattie watched as he opened a bottle of wine.

Steve Kinane bore little resemblance to his brother Mark. He would be in his early thirties, but whereas Mark was fair and elegant with blue eyes, this man, with his dark hair and eyes, reminded her of a sturdy tree. He was as tall as Mark, over six feet, and, as she'd noted earlier, he was extremely fit-looking, but—how come she'd failed to pin down that elusive something about him as a definite air of command befitting the owner of Mount Helena?

None of it impressed her particularly at that moment, however, and her expression obviously gave this away as he handed her a glass of wine.

'Sit down and relax,' he invited with a dry little smile twisting his lips.

She glanced around and chose an armchair covered

20

in green velour. The lounge of Mount Helena homestead was furnished along the same grand lines as the guest bedroom—lots of mahogany and cedar but a rather attractive colour scheme of sage green and topaz.

He took his drink over to a matching armchair and sat down opposite. 'So?'

Chattie fortified herself with a sip of wine. 'I'm trying to guess what you imagine I'm *not* telling you,' she said coolly at last.

He observed that the finely sculptured chin he'd been admiring earlier was tilted to an ominous angle, and turned his glass in his hands. 'Why you're running after my brother—how about that for starters?' he suggested.

'What makes you think I'm running after him?'

'The manner of your—completely unexpected—arrival,' he answered thoughtfully. 'The fact that it *has* happened before and, I may as well tell you this right away, the fact that I plan to send you back where you came from just as soon as I can.'

She gasped. '*Why?*'

'Because Mark left Mount Helena two days ago.'

Chattie stared at him, and repeated herself. 'Why?'

Steve Kinane took a pull of his Scotch and watched her narrowly. 'When did you last hear from him?'

She blinked a couple of times. 'What does that have to do with it? Incidentally, what has any of this got to do with *you*? And if you knew Mark wasn't here why didn't you tell me immediately?'

He sat back. 'I didn't know. I've been out working on a bore for a couple of days. I only discovered his—er—defection this afternoon.'

Chattie licked her lips as she thought of Bridget sitting in Brisbane wringing her hands. 'Where has he gone?' she asked huskily. 'And why would he have gone so suddenly?'

'This is only an educated guess but his ex-fiancée—' he paused as he scanned Chattie thoroughly for any reaction but she only looked blank '—lives in Broome. He may be having second thoughts about her. As for why he went so suddenly, Mark and Mount Helena—' Steve Kinane looked satanically irritated '—only go together in small doses.'

Chattie couldn't restrain herself from making a strangled little sound of mixed emotions—frustration, confusion and a growing feeling of desperation.

'Did he neglect to tell you about her?' Steve enquired, his eyes dark and cool. 'I would imagine he broke off the engagement just before he met you.'

'I...that's...that is to say...' Chattie drained her wine and shuddered visibly.

'You would not be the only girl who thought herself madly in love with my brother only to find he had feet of clay,' Steve Kinane said dryly. 'Or the only girl to chase him round the countryside.'

'Dinner's ready,' Slim announced from the archway that led into the dining room.

'I don't feel hungry, thank you,' Chattie said automatically.

Slim came into the lounge with his hands on his hips. 'Not hungry? When I've spent all afternoon slaving over a hot stove to concoct a nice dinner?'

'Miss Winslow has had a bit of a shock,' Steve murmured.

'Lovie,' Slim addressed her, 'we all get those from

time to time and I have to tell you that's Mark all over again but life goes on! Come and have your dinner, there's a good girl—I won't take no for an answer!' He swung his pony-tail.

Chattie hesitated, feeling a bit like Alice about to sup at a Mad Hatter's dinner but also conscious that now was the time to clear up the confusion. She opened her mouth but Steve stood up and looked down at her with a glint of mockery.

'I'm not susceptible to girls going into a decline over my brother,' he said.

She got up and if looks could have killed Steve Kinane would have toppled to the floor. If anything, though, her flashing look seemed to amuse him and he said quite gently, 'After you.' He gestured. 'I'll bring the wine.'

She had no idea what prompted her to do it but she swished past him and walked into the dining room proudly. To show him she was not to be trifled with? she wondered. But at the same time she got the un-comfortable feeling she'd attracted his attention in a way she'd rather not—it was almost as if his dark eyes were boring into her back.

She swung round as she reached the table and their gazes clashed. To her mortification, she detected more amusement as well as appreciation in his—apprecia-tion of her figure. Then he looked away and picked up the wine.

She ground her teeth at the same time as a strange little sensation ran through her but she didn't have the time to identify it—Slim was holding a chair out for her.

In the event, she turned out to be hungrier than she'd thought. Either that or Slim's dinner was irresistible— Parma ham and melon followed by roast beef and Yorkshire pudding.

It was while she was tucking into the roast beef that Steve said, 'Tell me a bit more about yourself, Chattie. Were you born in Brisbane? Are your parents alive?'

She paused to take a sip of wine and told him the bare bones of her life story.

'That's rather unusual,' Steve commented.

Chattie neatly dissected a piece of beef and dabbed some mustard on it, but offered no further information.

'And you've lived in Brisbane all your life?'

The next bite she ate was a piece of Yorkshire pudding. 'Slim obviously knows his stuff; this is very good.'

'Slim does know his stuff. Why wouldn't you want me to know your background, Chattie?'

Grey eyes encountered dark brown ones.

'I can't see why my background is of any interest to you,' she said at last. 'I have no interest in yours.'

'I'm devastated.' Steve Kinane continued to eat his dinner without the least sign of devastation, however.

Chattie eyed a fine grandfather clock with a gold moon rising on its blue face, then finished her meal in silence.

Steve did the same and Slim appeared right on cue bearing a platter of cheese and fruit. 'Coffee's on its way,' he said.

Steve reached for a peach and started to peel it. His hands, she noticed again, despite her state of mind, were callused and strong but long, lean and scrubbed clean now. For some reason, it started her thinking along another tack…

She looked around. Some of it might be old-fashioned but there was an awful lot of substance to Mount Helena homestead. In fact, as her gaze travelled from painting to painting on the green-papered walls of the dining room and her eyes widened in recognition, some of that substance could be priceless. Then there was the china and crystal—she tapped a nail against her wineglass and the ping of crystal, Stuart, she guessed, resounded.

She resisted the temptation to turn over her side plate but thought the colourful, ornate, gilded and scrolled dinner service might be Rockingham or Coalport. The tablecloth was definitely fine white damask.

Her gaze returned to the grandfather clock but her mind's eye presented her with the vehicle Steve Kinane drove; dusty it might have been, but it was also a late model four-wheel drive with 'all the trimmings'.

She had not, she realized as all this impressed itself on her, given Mark Kinane's background a lot of thought. Now she was forced to wonder if it was very wealthy and that was why Steve Kinane was on his guard about girls running after his apparently profligate brother.

'So?'

She jumped and turned her head to Steve. 'So—what?'

'I gather you were making some assessments, checking the silver, testing the crystal and so on.'

She coloured faintly but answered evenly, '*I* gather your brother would be quite a catch?'

'He would. Have some grapes and cheese.'

Chattie took a bunch of grapes but studied the bloom on them instead of eating them. 'Is that why you feel entitled to police his love life?'

The air became literally electric between them. She saw the spark of anger in his eyes and the way his mouth hardened. In fact she quaked inwardly with fright but refused to allow herself to look away.

'You are a cool one, aren't you?' he drawled at last. 'No, I don't police his love life. What I do take exception to are girls "on the make", girls who succumb to unplanned pregnancies in the hope of trapping him into marriage—and the like. I do hope you're not about to tell me you're one of those, Miss Winslow?'

Chattie drew a deep breath as his eyes challenged her insolently, and all hope of explaining Bridget's predicament and getting a fair hearing flew out of the window.

So what to do now? she wondered. Go back home and tell her sister to forget about Mark Kinane because they'd never get past his definitely dictatorial if not to say dangerous brother Steve? Or hang in in whatever way she, Chattie, could until she found some way of getting in touch with Mark?

The thought resolved itself into speech almost simultaneously and was backed by a deep well of anger against this man.

'You need have no qualms on that score, Mr Kinane. I'm not pregnant. At the same time, whether you believe you're policing Mark's love life or not, there's no way you can police me, and I don't intend to leave here until I find out where Mark is.'

The silence reverberated with all the shivering strands of their mutual animosity. Heightened, Chattie found herself wondering suddenly, by their mutual curiosity about each other?

Then the sound of a motor intruded, and a squeal of tyres as a vehicle slammed to a stop outside. A little pulse of hope stirred within Chattie—that it was Mark Kinane.

But the person who pounded through the hall and into the lounge as Steve put his napkin down and rose was a girl, a girl in the grip of strong emotion, at that.

'Steve, you *won't* believe this,' she began as she saw him in the dining room, 'Jack's walked out on me! The two-timing bastard's done it again but if he thinks he's going to get away with it, he's mistaken.' She paused, panting, and her eyes fell on Chattie.

At the same time a boy of about six wandered into the lounge with his thumb in his mouth and a teddy bear tucked under his arm. He took no notice of anyone but climbed onto a settee and curled up as if sleeping wherever and whenever he could find a spot came quite naturally to him.

'For heaven's sake, Harriet,' Steve said in a grim undertone, 'couldn't you have rung rather than dragging Brett out at this time of night?'

Harriet opened her mouth, stopped, then, with an imperious jerk of her head, indicated Chattie. 'Who the hell is this?'

Chattie felt herself bridle instinctively. Whoever *she* was, this Harriet was a tall girl with an attitude. She had cropped chestnut hair, freckles, piercing blue eyes and her hands-on-hips stance indicated a belligerent nature, causing Chattie to feel some sympathy for the unknown Jack.

'This is Chattie Winslow,' Steve said. 'She's just passing through. Harriet—'

But Harriet burst into tears.

Steve Kinane raised his eyes to the ceiling and walked over to the liquor cabinet where he poured a tot of brandy.

'Here.' He led Harriet to a chair at the dining table. 'Drink this,' he said, not unkindly.

Harriet took a sip, then proceeded to pour out a disjointed tale of woe.

Chattie found herself rooted to the spot by the whole extraordinary rigmarole and the contradictions that emerged. For, at the same time as Harriet hated Jack Barlow passionately, she appeared to be devastated at the thought of losing him. At the same time as he could be the most frustrating husband and Harriet the most misunderstood wife in the world, there was no way any other woman was going to get her hooks into him...

Brett slept through it all but finally the flow was stemmed somewhat and Harriet raised drenched blue eyes to Steve. 'You do see that I have to go after him, don't you?' she said intensely.

He paused, and Chattie got the feeling Steve Kinane didn't see that at all but knew when he was fighting against thunder. 'Not right now, tomorrow morning will do,' he said finally.

'But—'

'No, Harriet,' he overrode her. 'If you want to leave Brett with me and Slim, that's the condition.'

Harriet hesitated, then got up and flung her arms around her him. 'You're a brick, Steve,' she told him. 'Mind if I sleep here tonight?'

He shook his head.

And, completely ignoring Chattie, Harriet scooped her offspring off the settee and waltzed out with him.

Chattie watched her go and blinked several times.

'I know, it's like being visited by a tornado.' Steve looked wry.

'I'm not sure if she loves him or hates him,' Chattie said involuntarily, then put her hand to her mouth as Slim came in with a tray of coffee. 'Pardon me, it has nothing to do with me.'

'She's besotted,' Slim said severely, 'but I've never known anyone with less tact or more capable of picking a fight than she is and the only way Jack can handle it at times is to run away. Excuse me, I'll go and make sure she has all she needs.'

Steve Kinane grimaced as his housekeeper departed, and Chattie had to chuckle at his expression.

'I would say Slim knows you all very well,' she said humorously.

For the life of him, Steve Kinane couldn't resist the glint of humour in those lovely grey eyes. 'He's the ultimate authority,' he replied ruefully, then shrugged. 'Harriet is a cousin but she lived with us after her parents separated so she's more like a sister. Jack is the station foreman and they have their own house on another part of the property.' His gaze narrowed on her then. 'Obviously Mark didn't tell you about her?'

Chattie shook her head as she got the feeling that the brief respite in their hostilities was over.

She was right. Steve Kinane joined his hands behind

his head and studied her expressionlessly but comprehensively.

To cover her nerves, she murmured, 'Why don't I be mother?' She picked up the silver coffee pot.

He let her pour the coffee, then added sugar but no milk to his.

Chattie did likewise and inhaled the fragrant aroma appreciatively.

'There's no way you can stay here against my wishes, Miss Winslow,' he said grimly.

'What about Mark's wishes?' she murmured. 'Do you ignore them entirely?'

'Since Mark neglected to advise me of any wishes at all in regard to you, I feel quite entitled to ignore them, whatever they are. I'm not even sure any exist,' he added.

'Look, I do know your brother and I'm perfectly entitled to...want to look him up,' she said evenly.

'How old are you?' he shot back.

She blinked. 'Twenty-two but why do you need to know?'

'I get the feeling you're too old for Mark,' he drawled.

'Well, as you now know, I'm not. We're the same age.'

He ignored that. 'How come you're sashaying around the countryside when you should be teaching little girls to cook and sew? Unless you're masquerading as a domestic science teacher?'

Chattie took a deep breath. 'I don't only teach girls, it's a TAFE college, adult education in other words, and we're on holiday at present.'

Steve Kinane formed one hand into a fist and laid

it on the table. 'That's the other thing—you just don't seem to be his type. Level-headed and domesticated are not what he usually goes for.'

'If that's a diplomatic way of saying I'm—' she paused and amended herself, Make that my sister! '—not *good* enough for your brother—'

'I didn't say that,' he broke in.

Chattie plaited her fingers and reproved herself for starting to lose her temper. She also found herself almost unbearably tempted to come clean with Mark's brother before this got any further out of hand.

However, he said then, musingly, 'No, if anything you're too good to be true. Because Mark, to date anyway, has always fallen for models, aspiring actresses or glamorous young things who would be totally at sea out here with no shops, no restaurants, no hairdressers and so on.'

Chattie bit her lip and felt her stomach sink. Despite the Rockingham, the Stuart crystal and the fortune on the walls, from what she'd seen of the countryside she couldn't doubt it would be an isolated lifestyle devoid of—as he'd just catalogued—just about everything that made up Bridget's life.

On the other hand, if Mark and Bridget decided they had a future together, would it have to be at Mount Helena? His own brother had, not that long ago, made mention of the fact that Mark and the station only went together in small doses.

'Got you there, Miss Winslow?'

Chattie came out of her reverie to find him smiling lethally at her.

'What you seem to misunderstand, persistently, is that Mark is a friend I'm trying to look up.'

'Bulldust,' he said softly. 'You're worried about something, Miss Winslow. You got much more of a shock than a mere acquaintance would have got to find he'd gone.'

Chattie cursed herself inwardly for being so transparent. At the same time, all desire to come clean with Steve Kinane left her as she made the decision that she would do anything she had to do to get her hands on his brother and not only for her sister's sake but just to annoy him...

'All right.' She shrugged. 'Let me put my cards on the table. Not quite in the backhanded way you've put it but, all the same, we seem to be in some agreement. I think I'd be good for Mark. And—' she looked around '—I prefer a challenging lifestyle over restaurants, hairdressers, shops and so on.'

For a moment his expression defied description.

'Got you there, Mr Kinane?'

What he would have said and done, she was never to know because Slim, with Rich pattering along behind, came into the room.

The dog grinned widely at Chattie, accorded Steve a brief glance and sat down at her feet to lay his nose adoringly on her knee.

'This is quite some dog, Miss Winslow,' Slim said. 'He's very well-mannered.'

'But just as capable of eating anyone alive,' Steve remarked acidly.

Slim laughed. 'You're not wrong. Had one myself years ago that nearly landed me in jail. Tore the pants off a policeman, he did! By the way, Mrs Barlow and young Master Barlow are asleep.'

'Thank you, Slim,' Steve said. 'I'm about to turn in

myself. Two nights at the bore camp, not to mention Miss Winslow's company, have quite worn me out.' He stood up. 'Please feel free to do whatever you would like to,' he said to Chattie, 'bar nicking any of the silver, and please be ready to depart straight after breakfast tomorrow. Goodnight.'

Slim watched him go with his hands on his hips, then began to clear the table. 'I wouldn't take that too much to heart,' he said to Chattie, still frozen to her chair. 'He has a lot of responsibilities.'

'I don't intend to,' she replied, 'but I've never met anyone as…' She paused, lost for words.

'Well, Mark flitting off into the wild blue yonder obviously hasn't improved his mood. There's a muster coming up, there's all sorts of things coming up, guests and what not, and not only has Mark done a bunk, so has Jack Barlow.' Slim shook his head. 'But Steve's OK, you know.'

Chattie rose. 'I'm not in the position to agree with you but I'd like to thank you for your hospitality, Slim. Can I give you hand?'

Although Slim looked gratified, and for a moment almost assessing, as if something had popped into his mind that had surprised him, he didn't reveal it and declined her offer.

'You pop off to bed,' he advised, 'but thanks all the same!'

CHAPTER THREE

AT TWO o'clock, the next morning, Chattie was wide awake beneath a sea of red silk quilt.

Rich was asleep on his favourite rug beside the bed and the house was quiet apart from the roof contracting in the cool night air with a series of creaks.

Not only was she wide awake but she was far from feeling serene as her mind's eye presented her with a recap of the previous day. In fact, her stomach was in knots as she contemplated all that had led up to her looking down the barrel of being booted off Mount Helena station.

Somehow or other, she had to discover Mark Kinane's whereabouts before that happened, but she had not the faintest idea how to go about it. If they didn't know where he was what hope did she have?

Also, it was all very well to, in the heat of the moment, take Steve Kinane head-on, but it was playing havoc with her nerves and her digestion. It had a distinctly 'playing with fire' feel to it, she acknowledged, and if it weren't for Bridget to fuel her defences and ingenuity, she would probably be only too grateful to be removed from his line of sight.

One thing she was sure of—that the curious frisson she'd experienced a couple of times beneath the onslaught of his looks and masculinity had been hammered to death by so many things he'd said or implied but the final blow had to be the 'nicking the silver' taunt.

She flinched as she recalled the mockery in his dark eyes as he'd said it, and anger started to seep through her veins again. Anger plus some of her famed—or would that be notorious? she wondered—level-headedness. Did they really not know Mark's where-abouts? Or was it a front?

Then it occurred to her that she had some sort of an ally in Slim. At least, she got the feeling that, for reasons best known to himself, Slim didn't share his boss's outright disapproval of her and, not that it came naturally to her to snoop, might she be able to get more information from the housekeeper?

After all, she told herself, she had been virtually pilloried as a girl on the make; a girl who'd deliber-ately got herself pregnant to trap Mark; a girl dubious enough to be warned against pinching the silver, so why should she bother about observing the niceties towards Steve Kinane?

It was also the only thing she could come up with, she thought forlornly.

By the time Chattie got up the next morning and pre-sented herself for breakfast, there was no sign of Harriet or Steve.

Breakfast, she discovered, was served in the vast kitchen. A bright, airy room, it overlooked the water tanks with their cloak of pink, purple and rusty bou-gainvillaea and yellow allamanda. It was also a cook's delight with cork-tiled floors, a wrought-iron pot-holder hanging from the ceiling and a butcher's chop-ping block on wheels.

There were herbs in pots on the window sill, a scullery that led off it and a big round table in an alcove set with chunky, colourful china.

Her companion at the table was Brett, stirring a bowl of oatmeal with little enthusiasm and swinging his legs at the same time.

Slim looked over his shoulder from the wood fire stove. 'Morning, miss. Sleep well?'

Chattie tipped a hand. 'On and off. Then I fell into this deep sleep and that's why I'm a bit later than normal.'

'Never mind! Sit down. What's your preference? Help yourself to juice, by the way.'

Seeing that he was tending bacon, sausages and eggs, she asked for one sausage and an egg, and poured herself some orange juice.

'Who are you?' Brett enquired. 'And why don't you have to have porridge?'

'Because I'm all grown up,' Chattie replied. 'When you're growing, porridge is an excellent body-builder.'

Brett rolled his eyes. 'That's what they say about nearly all the things I don't like. Are you Steve's girlfriend?'

'I am definitely *not* Steve's girlfriend,' Chattie said with emphasis at the same time as Steve Kinane appeared in the back doorway.

He pulled his boots off, tossed his broad-brimmed hat onto a hook on the wall and strolled over to the table in his socks. He looked big and there was something bracing about his presence. There was also something a little breathtaking about the width of his shoulders, his height and the way his dark hair flopped onto his forehead.

'That would be a fate worse than death,' he commented to Brett. 'Morning, Chattie.' Their gazes clashed and his was full of mockery but a different kind of mockery as once again he mentally stripped her.

'What does that mean?' Brett asked immediately.

Chattie had looked away in some confusion but she now turned back to Steve and surrendered the floor to him with a touch of malice in her eyes.

'It means...' Steve poured himself orange juice '...that—'

'It means,' Slim said severely as he placed a plate in front of Chattie, 'that these two don't quite see eye to eye, that's all. Brett, old son, if you don't finish that soon I will...' He paused, placed a hand over his heart, and keeled over onto the floor.

In their scramble to get to him, Steve knocked over his juice and Chattie's plate of sausage and egg went flying.

'What? What's wrong with him?' Chattie breathed, taking in the blue tinge to Slim's skin as she knelt beside him.

'He's got a dicky heart. Bring me the phone!' Steve commanded.

She glanced around wildly then spied what looked like a remote phone with an antenna on the kitchen counter. 'Here.' She pushed it into Steve's hand. 'Look, I know how to do CPR—'

'Good, you start it while I raise the flying doctor.'

An hour and a half later the three of them, Steve, Chattie and Brett, watched the flying doctor take off from the station's airstrip with Slim on board.

'Is he going to die?' Brett asked tearfully.

'Don't think so,' Steve said, 'but anyway he's in really good hands now.' He picked Brett up and put him on his shoulders for the short stroll back to the house.

'I don't like what happened, it made me really scared,' Brett said in his high, piping voice—and they stopped as an excited bark came from the direction of the house.

Chattie put a hand to her mouth. 'Rich! I forgot about him. Apart from a walk earlier he's been locked up on the veranda.'

'You've got a dog?' Brett queried alertly.

'Yes. Would you like to see him?'

Steve changed direction towards the guest bedroom veranda and put Brett down. He immediately raced towards the veranda.

'Rich adores kids,' Chattie said. 'And he might just distract Brett.'

Events proved exactly that. Rich streaked down the veranda steps as Brett opened the gate, flung himself up at Chattie briefly, ignored Steve totally, and then raced back to Brett with obvious delight.

'I see what you mean,' Steve commented.

'It makes my blood boil all over again, to think that anyone could have done that to a dog who gives so much pleasure,' she said.

He looked down at her with a faint frown, as if something was puzzling him about her, but in the end all he said was, 'It is hard to understand. Do you think we deserve a cup of coffee?'

She nodded after a moment.

'Stay here, I'll get it.'

Chattie stared after him, prey to some conflicting emotions. Thanks to his cool control and meticulous following of the flying doctor's instructions before the plane had arrived, Slim had had the best treatment he could have had in the circumstances and now had a good chance of recovery.

And it slid into her mind that Steve Kinane was a good man to have beside you in crisis—unless you happened to hate his guts.

He brought, not only coffee, but also buttered raisin toast to her veranda. Brett and Rich were now playing with a ball on the lawn.

It was a beautiful morning, clear and sunny, not a cloud in the sky and not too hot. She suspected that midsummer would be very hot at Mount Helena but at the moment, as April slid into May, autumn was a pleasure and the gold-cloaked hills behind the house stood out in such clarity, Chattie longed to have a paintbrush in her fingers.

'That's one problem in hand,' he said as he poured the coffee.

Chattie brought her mind back from the landscape. 'Brett?' she hazarded. 'I gather Harriet has already left?'

'At the crack of dawn.'

'What will you do?'

He studied her over the rim of his cup. She wore jeans and a blue blouse and her hair was plaited to one side. After her initial shock, she'd been both practical and very helpful with Slim and in dealing with Brett. Was that any reason to be contemplating what he was contemplating out of the blue, however? It just

didn't make sense to ask her to stay on for a while—
or, on one level, at least, did it? The level that this
mysterious girl intrigued him…

'My life,' he observed carefully after a long moment, 'has suddenly become extremely complicated. I
have no housekeeper, Brett has no parents, I'm minus
a station foreman as well as my brother and all in the
space of less than twenty-four hours.'

Chattie bit into a piece of toast and frowned but
said nothing.

'How much of your school holidays have you got
to go?' he asked then.

His intentions began to dawn on Chattie and she
took a sudden breath. 'Uh—just over three weeks.'

'You did tell me you were a girl of many domesticated talents. Not to put too fine a point on it, you
could help me out of a bit of a hole, Chattie Winslow,
but don't,' he said as she opened her mouth to speak,
'imagine it would be a one way street. I would be
more than happy to pay for your time.'

'Just what are you offering me?' she asked suspiciously.

'A temporary position as Slim's replacement.'

She chewed her lip.

'You did come up here to see a working cattle station, didn't you?'

'Yes. But…' She trailed off disjointedly for the
good reason that she was thinking furiously. Had the
opportunity to stay on until she discovered where
Mark was simply fallen into her lap?

'What's the difference?' He raised his eyebrows
ironically.

'Mark would have been here, should have been

here,' she said at last, then continued with more composure. 'It is completely different. I don't know *you* from a bar of soap—'

'Oh, come on, surely the old bar of soap doesn't wash,' he said with a tinge of impatience. 'You've had dinner with me, met my crazy cousin, you know my brother as you keep telling me—and you've just helped me to save someone's life.'

She hesitated as she wondered how to play it. Too much eagerness might arouse his already heightened suspicions of her... In the end she opted for, 'I don't like you. You don't like me.'

His lips twisted. 'It wouldn't be for long and I'm not suggesting we go to bed together, merely that you do a bit of housekeeping for me.'

Her eyes flashed, causing him to smile faintly.

She put down her plate and reached for her coffee. 'Aren't you worried about me pinching the silver?'

'No—'

'You were last night.'

'That was—' he looked amused '—a shot designed to annoy you more than the conviction you were a thief. And who knows?' he added idly. 'Mark might even turn up.'

The silence stretched as Chattie battled with her nervous tension at the thought of living with and working for this man, and weighed it against the possibility of securing her sister's future in some way.

'I pay well,' Steve Kinane added idly.

'What makes you think that's a consideration with me,' she asked with hauteur.

He shrugged. 'Just thought I'd mention it to reinforce the fact that we're talking about a business agreement.'

She eyed him. 'How much?'

He named a weekly figure, which, considering her food and board were all found, was astonishing.

'Is that how much you paid Slim?' she asked incredulously.

'No, I paid him more but he's been doing the job for the last five years since this heart condition has kept him out of the saddle so he's very experienced. Getting good staff out here is not that easy.'

She finished her coffee.

'Then again,' he drawled, 'I'd quite understand if you didn't feel up to the position. There is a bit more to it than appears on the surface.'

'Like what?'

'Let's see, I have a house party due to descend on Helena shortly, five people here for two nights, that's quite a bit of cooking and housework, and one meal is a formal dinner for ten. That kind of thing.'

'And you think I couldn't cope with that?' She raised her chin.

He shrugged. 'I'm asking you.'

'I could do it with my eyes shut,' she told him tartly, 'but on one condition.'

'Name it,' he murmured.

'If, at any time while I'm here, you find out where Mark is, I get to know too.'

Determined grey eyes engaged dark brown ones and the atmosphere between them couldn't have been more fraught if they'd been engaged in a duel.

Then Steve Kinane said flatly, 'Are you really madly in love with him?'

Chattie chose her words with care. 'That's none of your business. Do we have a deal?'

Something flickered in Steve's dark eyes. 'If he's driving to Broome—'

'He's driving? All the way to Broome?' Chattie interrupted. 'That's nearly right across the continent.'

'Yep.' He got up. 'But we country people are used to driving long distances. And I'm only assuming he's driving to Broome but, if he is, he'll be out of mobile range a lot of the time.'

'All the same, wouldn't he...' Chattie hesitated '...have more sophisticated equipment with him other than a mobile phone for such a long trip?'

'What did you have in mind?'

She gestured. 'A satellite phone?'

'Have you any idea how much satellite phones cost?'

'No, but you seem to have everything else that opens and shuts.'

He smiled satanically. 'How would you know?'

'Well, that phone you used to get in touch with the flying doctor—'

'Was a satellite phone,' he conceded, 'but it's kept for emergencies. Not...' he paused and continued with patent irony '...for Mark's personal use in sorting out his love life.'

Chattie came to her feet rather like a spring uncoiling as she was hit by Bridget's conviction that the root cause of all Mark's problems was this insufferable man. 'Has it ever occurred to you that Mark may have benefited from a less "superior" older brother, Mr Kinane?'

They eyed each other.

'He really did get you in, didn't he?' he said at last.

'He really did get me in, yes,' Chattie agreed, although she crossed her fingers behind her back and assured herself all was fair in this kind of war.

'So it's no good me telling you I've done my level best to steer Mark down the right road ever since he left school?'

'None at all,' she answered with dry economy.

He cocked his head to one side and frowned. 'Apart from the obvious—why is that?'

'What would the obvious be?' Chattie enquired.

'His skills in bed,' he drawled and ran his gaze up and down her body. 'Something, incidentally, I have no doubt he's very good at.'

Chattie went white. 'How dare you?'

He lifted an eyebrow. 'I can't imagine in the limited time you've known him that you've been able to assess his other qualities too accurately.'

For some insane reason, it occurred to Chattie to wonder how good Steve Kinane was in bed. She had no doubt he was a man's man, she had no doubt he was tough and strong, that he was also cool-headed under pressure and commanding at times, but was there another side to him?

From the way he was looking at her, she suddenly couldn't doubt that there was. His dark appraisal of her had all the hallmarks of a man who knew women well enough to be forming some opinions on how good *she* was in bed. The mere thought of it made her go hot and cold and feel quite panicky—why on earth was she thinking along these lines about a man she barely knew, even visualising his strong hands on her body with an inward little tremor?

'There is one quality I'm familiar with,' she said, wrenching her mind away from the unbelievable. 'He is not a dyed-in-the-wool grazier as you appear to be and forcing him to spend his life here when he hates it is diabolical.'

Steve Kinane folded his arms and, to Chattie's utter surprise, laughed softly. 'Is that what he told you?'

She gritted her teeth. 'Yes.'

'Then let me set the record straight, Miss Winslow. Mark is free to do what he likes. But if he expects Mount Helena to support him—and to date he's come up with no other visible means of support—then I expect *him* to put his shoulder to the wheel when he's needed. What's so unreasonable about that?'

Chattie gripped her hands together and took a deep breath. 'Families are still families even if they're going through trying times, even if they're much younger and seem to lack direction,' she said with quiet passion.

Surprise caused Steve's eyes to widen then narrow.

'The other thing is,' she went on, 'although I haven't experienced being old yet, I'm sure it's all too easy to forget what it's like to be young.'

He opened his mouth, closed it, then said incredulously, 'How bloody old do you think I am?'

'Thirty-two since Mark is twenty-two and you're about ten years older.'

'And you think that's *old*?'

She shook her head. 'Not so much in years but it can also be a state of mind.'

Fortunately, perhaps, Brett chose that moment to return to the veranda with Rich. 'We're hungry,' he announced.

'Just as well there's some raisin toast left,' Chattie said, and handed Brett a slice. 'I don't think Rich likes—oh, yes, he does!' she added with a gurgle of laughter as Rich pinched a piece of toast. 'Let's hope—' she raised her eyes to Steve '—this doesn't mean Brett will develop a liking for dog food!'

Steve Kinane had to smile but it was a perfunctory one as he grappled with the distinct feeling that Chattie Winslow had got the better of him. Not only that, as he watched her bend down to the dog and the boy, the more he got to know her, the more gorgeous she appeared to him. Dressed up or dressed down didn't seem to make much difference, her hips in blue denim were a delight...and therein could lie a problem for him.

A lovely body but the mind of an amateur philosopher, not to mention in love with his brother, he reminded himself ruefully—what could be more of a disaster for him?

Chattie straightened, and saw something in Steve Kinane's eyes as they rested on her again that was infinitely disturbing—why should the dark gaze of this man be so compelling? Wasn't she equally convinced that he was autocratic and insensitive even if he was—sexy?

Then he cut the eye contact. 'If you'd care to come with me,' he said as he turned away, 'we can try to raise Mark now.'

She hesitated but Brett and Rich appeared to be content so she followed him through her bedroom and across the other side of the house to the office.

It was a small, cluttered room with a map of the property on the wall and a battered old roll-top desk.

There was also a table with a computer, what looked to be a single side band radio and a phone.

He reached for a black covered phone book and leafed through it. 'I assume you would have tried his mobile?' he said then and Chattie held her breath because she had asked Bridget about a mobile number for Mark Kinane only to be told he kept losing them so didn't bother with one.

'He…appeared to have lost it,' she said.

Steve slammed the phone book down on the desk. 'Not again! Bloody hell! That must be the sixth one he's lost. I wonder if it's occurred to you that the man you're chasing across the country is almost criminally careless?'

Chattie failed to respond because Bridget was also careless with her keys, her purse—umbrellas were always disappearing, she'd even lost the car they shared in a multi-storey car park and it had taken her two hours to find it.

'What?' Steve Kinane asked.

My sister and your brother, if ever they do get together will either be wonderfully well suited or a disaster, it ran through her mind. 'Uh—nothing,' she said.

'No, it wasn't,' he contradicted irritably. 'Something struck you quite forcibly.'

Chattie lowered her eyes and castigated herself again for being transparent.

'Am I not allowed to be critical of Mark—is that it?' He looked at her incredulously.

She grasped the straw. 'I tried to make that point earlier.'

He said something unprintable, then took hold.

'Look, I have no idea how to get in touch with him, but you have my word, if he checks in I'll tell you. In the meantime, I have a muster to organize; I told you about the house party, I have a parentless kid on my hands—are you going to take the job or not?'

'Yes,' she said slowly, although she added the rider, 'but only for so long as I'm comfortable with it.'

He looked heavenwards but once again reined his feelings in. 'Thank you. By the way, I don't expect you to work yourself to death—if you keep us clean-clothed and fed to start with, I'd appreciate it. Slim did also have some help and...' he paused to listen '...from the sounds I hear in the kitchen, she has arrived. Come and meet Merlene.'

Merlene was in her thirties, well padded, at least six feet tall, she had a spiked haircut and if that didn't give her a belligerent look, her bikie attire and prominent chin did.

Steve passed on the information about Slim and introduced Chattie as his temporary replacement.

Merlene's eyebrows almost disappeared into her hair. 'That was fast work. So his old ticker is playing up again? Darn me.' She subjected Chattie to a thorough inspection and turned back to Steve. 'You serious?'

'Miss Winslow comes highly recommended,' he said gravely. 'All the same, I'd appreciate it if you could give her all the help you can, Merlene. And I'd appreciate it if you'd move into Slim's quarters in the annexe for the time being. In the meantime, I need to get back to work.'

*   *   *

'Here's the gist of it, Chattie,' Merlene said after Steve's departure. 'I do floors, windows, walls, the laundry and ironing and I chop the wood for the stove.'

'That must be an enormous help!'

'I do not,' Merlene continued, 'do bathrooms, I do not dust or polish furniture and knick-knacks, I do not cook or do dishes, and if that's Brett I hear, I do not run around after kids.'

'Naturally,' Chattie said a little faintly, beginning to wilt beneath the force of Merlene's strictures and intense blue gaze.

'Nor do I mend or sew, wait on tables or arrange flowers.'

'That's fine with me. Um—'

'And I do not take kindly to having my work picked over and criticized—which Slim had a nasty habit of doing!'

'I wouldn't dream of it,' Chattie said fervently, having gained the distinct impression that Merlene could pick her up with one hand. Her other thought was that Steve Kinane could have warned her before casting her upon the untender mercies of this woman.

'And—' Merlene pulled out a chair and sat down at the kitchen table '—I don't believe for one minute you're here as a replacement anything. Word has it one of Mark's fancy pieces followed him out to Helena only to find he'd done a bunk to Broome— least-wise that's what we're betting on.' She folded her arms.

Chattie digested this and decided she'd had enough. So she explained that she did know Mark but that was no one's business but her own and she didn't give a damn what anyone thought about her because she was quite secure in the knowledge that she was no one's *fancy* piece.

Merlene unfolded her arms. 'You and me could get along,' she said. 'How about a cuppa? I usually start my working day with one.'

Chattie breathed a little easier. 'Thank you.'

'Then I'll show you the ropes. By the way, I work three hours a day and you don't have to worry about feeding me while I'm sleeping in the annexe, I'll still take my meals down in the bunkhouse with the guys.'

Chattie looked bewildered. 'Why are you sleeping in the annexe, then?'

'Search me,' Merlene replied, then gave the matter some thought. 'I guess Steve likes to do things by the book and you two being alone here at nights mightn't look good.'

'Oh.'

'Although,' Merlene said, with her first flash of humour as she scanned Chattie from head to toe, 'whether it's your reputation he's worried about—or his—is a moot point. Now don't get your dander up! Only joking.'

By lunch time, Chattie had been instructed in all the core functionings of the Mount Helena homestead.

Along the way she'd also gathered snippets of information that fleshed out life on Mount Helena for her and gave her an insight into some of its inhabitants.

Slim and Merlene, for example, were sworn enemies but, she gathered, would probably be bereft without each other to fight.

Merlene herself had lived on Mount Helena all her life and had followed in her ringer father's footsteps until an accident had given her a reason to quit all the dust and toil of it. These days all she rode was her motor bike—much more predictable and better sprung than a horse. As well as her so clearly defined house duties, she operated a store for the workers, of which there were five permanent ones. She was the only woman on Mount Helena other than Harriet Barlow, of whom she had a low opinion.

She also imparted some knowledge to Chattie about the size of Mount Helena and how many head of cattle it ran, information that caused Chattie's eyes to widen.

And when Chattie commented on all the lovely things in the house, she told her that Steve and Mark's mother had been a great lady of great taste.

She didn't have anything to say on the subject of Mark Kinane—hard as it was to conceive, Chattie thought she was being tactful—but there was a definite flavour in her other observations that would have led Chattie to believe—had she not believed otherwise!—that the sun shone out of Steve Kinane.

Then it was one o'clock and Steve came home for lunch.

Mount Helena didn't have a fridge, it had a whole cold room, and out of it Chattie hastily assembled a simple meal of cold beef and salad.

'I'll be able to do better than this tomorrow,' she assured him, poured him a cup of tea and started to cut up Brett's beef for him. 'It's just that Merlene has been kind enough to—really show me the ropes.'

'This is fine,' he murmured. 'No calls?'

'No.'

'So you and Merlene hit it off?' he queried with his lips twisting.

'No thanks to you!'

'Nothing I could say would have made any difference.'

'I don't know about that.' Chattie sat down and smiled at him delightfully. 'I get the feeling you're the blue-eyed boy around here.'

'But you don't have to agree?' he hazarded.

'Bingo!'

'Chattie—' he laughed '—I am not an ogre.'

'What's that?' Brett asked.

'A scary person,' Chattie said.

'Mum says he can be,' Brett contributed. 'Mum says the only person she'd really rather not get on the wrong side of is Steve. Dad said he was amazed to hear it.'

Chattie shot Steve an I-told-you-so look.

But Brett continued, 'I can't see that he's worse than anyone else; actually I think he's a lot better.'

'Thank you, Brett. Do you think you could be parted from Rich long enough to come out into the paddocks with me this afternoon?' Steve asked.

Brett jumped up in his chair. 'Yes, sirree!'

'That way Chattie can have a bit of time to rest and recover her good humour.'

They gazed at each other until Chattie looked away and said stiffly, 'Thank you. I appreciate that. I haven't even unpacked yet,' she added with some amazement.

'By the way, please feel free to play the piano.'

Her eyes widened. 'Thank you again, but I haven't seen one.'

'The music room is off the dining room.' Steve finished his meal, drained his teacup and stood up. 'Let's go, young man.'

That was how, since Merlene had already left noisily on her bike, Chattie came to be alone in the homestead, apart from Rich, and able, for the first time, to think articulately about the surprising about-turn of events.

She poured herself another cup of tea and considered the fact that, whatever fix Steve Kinane found himself in, she would have thought one Chattie Winslow would be the last person he'd turn to for help.

Of course it was quite a fix but he could have contacted a pastoral employment agency, one would have thought, and have someone flown in. So, what did it have to do with her, personally?

She put her cup down and moved restlessly. Contrary to her 'certain sureness', a phrase she and Bridget had used as kids, that she could no longer feel one smidgeon of attraction towards Steve Kinane, there was still something there, to her amazement, something angry but electric at times.

Or was he, as his brother apparently was, a man who couldn't help sending out sensual vibes to any passable woman? Maybe it ran in the family, she mused. In which case, why was she responding? It didn't make sense. OK, he might be dynamic, but he could also be lethally insulting. He was also virtually hogging the high moral ground on the subject of his brother's love life, so...

She shook her head and got up to clear the lunch things and stack the dishwasher.

Then, in a bid to distract herself from all the things

she didn't understand, she went to find the piano. The door from the dining room to the music room was closed. She opened it gingerly—and gasped with delight.

The piano was a black baby grand in a perfect setting. It stood in the middle of the room. French windows with white curtains opened onto a side veranda and there was one divine armchair covered in navy velvet with a matching footstool. Like the dining room, the walls were covered with paintings but these were all vibrant, exotic ones of fruit and flowers, trees, gardens and birds.

A rosewood desk stood against one wall and another wall had built-in shelves laden with silver-framed photos interspersed between books and some lovely *objets d'art*.

It came to her from nowhere as she looked around that this had been the lady of the house's private retreat, and that lady had to have been Mark and Steve's mother, a lady she was starting to feel curious about.

She walked over to the instrument and lifted the lid. The keys were yellow and some of the ivories thin with much use but the tone, as she struck several, as clear as a bell.

She sat down on the stool, also upholstered in navy velvet, and played an air from Handel's 'Water Music', noting as her hands moved up and down that one B flat was a little stiff but otherwise it was the best piano she'd ever played.

She took her hands away from the keys and laid them in her lap as she looked around again, and came to a rather surprising decision. While she was in charge of the well-being of this house, she would take the opportunity to show Steve Kinane that she wasn't too good to be true.

Then she went to find her own mobile phone, and she spent the next ten minutes talking to Bridget and passing on a limited version of what had happened.

CHAPTER FOUR

STEVE dropped Brett off at five o'clock and told Chattie he had a few more things to do but would be back in time for dinner at seven.

Rich was ecstatic about being reunited with the boy, and Chattie let them play for a while. Then she insisted Brett had a bath and, perceiving signs of tiredness in Harriet Barlow's otherwise easygoing son, she gave him an early dinner, read him a story and put him to bed. He fell asleep immediately.

'Well, considering you don't really know me from a bar of soap—to use a well-worn phrase—and your parents have some strange ways,' she murmured with her finger on the light switch, 'you're an amazingly well-behaved child.'

'He is, isn't he?'

She turned to find Steve standing behind her. 'Oh! I didn't hear you come in.'

He studied her for a moment, then, 'Give me ten minutes and I'll be ready for dinner.' He turned away.

'Take as long as you like,' she recommended. 'It'll keep.'

But he was as good as his word.

'I hope this is all right,' she said as he came into the kitchen where she'd set the table for two. 'Merlene told me when it was only family that you eat in here.'

'It's fine. Care for a beer? Or a glass of wine?'

She looked surprised.

56

'Slim and I generally have a beer.'

'In that case, thank you, I'll have a glass of wine. Have you heard how he is?'

'Yes, I just rang the base hospital. He's resting comfortably but they've decided to fly him to Brisbane for a bypass operation.'

She digested this while she served up the soup and he got the drinks. She'd found some vegetable stock, added some cooked chicken she'd also found, some herbs and at the last minute swirled cream through it. And she placed a basket of crusty rolls she'd made in the bread machine on the table.

'Very good,' Steve Kinane said of the soup. 'That certainly didn't come out of a tin.'

'Is that what you were expecting?' she asked incredulously.

'My apologies to the cook,' he replied wryly. 'It is only your first day.'

'Well—' she got up to remove the soup bowls '—Slim has to take a lot of the credit. He has a very well-organized larder. I do hope you like curry?' She looked at him expectantly.

Steve took his time. She'd changed from her jeans into a three-quarter-length floral skirt and a white blouse. Her hair was tied back and she looked fresh and attractive. Also very slim about the waist, he noted, and wondered how he was going to broach the subject that still bothered him...

'Uh, yes, I do,' he said.

'Good,' she said briskly and moved away from the table. 'I make a mean curry. Not that I've made this one as hot as I can make them, just in case you're a mild curry person, but it should still be good.'

'You like a hot curry?' he queried.

She came back from the scullery and gestured with both hands outstretched. 'Love it.' Then she pirouetted towards the stove and began to dish up her curry.

Is it unconscious? Steve Kinane asked himself. Is she unaware that she has a lovely figure and does she swing her hips quite naturally because she's happy at the moment—or full of annoyed hauteur as she was last night—or is she perfectly aware of the effect she has on men?

Chattie turned from the stove with her eyebrows raised, to intercept his assessing gaze.

'You don't really like curry at all?' she asked with a suddenly and comically anxious expression.

He looked away. 'On the contrary, I also like it hot.'

He started to uncover the sambals already assembled on the table.

She paused, as if testing the air. As if she knew the atmosphere between them was about more than curry but she couldn't put her finger on it.

'My curry,' he murmured, but wondered at the same time what she would make of it if she could read his mind, which had flashed him a mental image of taking her to his bed and exploring every lovely inch of her in a way that would render things very hot between them.

She relaxed with a laugh. 'Wish I'd known!' She turned back to the stove.

His gaze narrowed on her back and he examined another question mark that had risen in his mind. This morning, he'd assured himself that to be attracted to a girl who was in love with his brother was the height of unwisdom. But was it happening whether he liked it or not, even when he wasn't sure he could trust her?

Would he be contemplating hot, steamy sex with her otherwise? he asked himself cynically. And was he imagining it or was she not entirely immune from his physical appreciation of her?

'You're right, it's very good,' he said some time later as he forked up some perfectly cooked, fluffy rice. 'You also seem to be in a very good mood, Chattie.'

Her eyes widened, then she looked wary as she remembered she should be posing as Mark's, possibly abandoned, girlfriend. 'I shouldn't be, I know. I guess I lost myself in my cooking.'

Steve Kinane went to broach one of the subjects he had on his mind but the phone rang, and Chattie sat up expectantly.

He took the call on the kitchen extension but it was Harriet.

'Are they—reconciled?' Chattie asked as he came back to the table.

He shrugged. 'They're talking, at least.'

'You didn't mention Slim,' she pointed out.

'Deliberately. In the event that Harriet felt she had to hare home before it's all resolved so we'd have to go through it all over again. Brett's no trouble, is he?'

'No. Not at all. Actually I like having kids around. He seems to be pretty keen on you.' She pushed her plate away and propped her chin on her hands. 'So I gather you like kids, too?'

'I like Brett, anyway.'

'Can I ask you something?'

He nodded.

She thought for a moment, unwilling to return to what was such a controversial issue between them, but it was concerning her. 'It seems an awful long way away for a fiancée to live, western Queensland to Broome, W.A.' She folded her napkin into a triangle.

'They met at university in Darwin. Mark got a place there he couldn't get in Queensland and, in Bryony's case, Darwin is closer than Perth.'

'Oh.'

'Chattie,' Steve said and paused for a moment to watch her carefully, 'is there something you haven't told me?'

Her lashes lifted. 'Like what?'

He finished his beer and twirled the glass in his fingers. 'You denied last night that you were pregnant, but is it true?' He raised his eyes to hers.

She swallowed as she wondered whether it was an opportunity to put Bridget's case and meet a rational response—but the events of the previous evening were too close to allow her to take the risk. 'No. I mean, no, I'm not pregnant.'

'Are you sure?'

'Of course I'm sure,' she said as colour rushed into her cheeks to think of him considering the state of her body in this light.

'Accidents do happen,' he said with irony.

'I'm sure they do.' She couldn't help herself from making the point with some emphasis and, on an impulse, added, 'If I were pregnant to Mark, what would you do?'

'Chattie—' his gaze was suddenly harsh '—it certainly won't help things if you've been lying to me.'

'I'm not,' she said quietly, but very conscious that

she was, in a way. Then she frowned. 'Why do you seem to be so concerned about it?'

'I couldn't help wondering if it was why you wanted to speak to Mark so desperately.'

She stared at him.

'Because,' he added, 'if I'd received the news you had, I don't think I'd have been that keen to speak to him at all. I mean, to all intents and purposes, he had a bit of a fling with you, invited you up here, then forgot all about it and took off.'

She folded her napkin into a smaller triangle. 'I see. Well, it's not that I'm pregnant but, speaking theoretically, how *would* you handle it if it—had happened?'

He smiled dryly. 'I'll cross that bridge when I come to it—if I ever come to it, and I just hope to hell I never do. May I ask you one more time—are you sure?'

More than ever sure I need to find Mark Kinane, she thought, but said, 'I am not pregnant.'

At that moment Merlene's motor bike made itself heard—her unlikely duenna had returned from the bunkhouse.

Chattie rose and added, 'I hope you like sticky date pudding?'

For a second Steve Kinane looked quite menacing, then he started to laugh.

He also said something that startled Chattie.

'I wonder if Mark knows what he's missing out on? Yes, I do like sticky date pudding, Miss Winslow.'

Two days later, Chattie had got quite settled into a routine at Mount Helena, and got to know a bit more about the station.

She was thinking of it as she, Brett and Rich were having a picnic lunch on the lawn under some shady gum-trees. Steve was away for the day, Rich and Brett were playing tirelessly with an old rubber tube and she gazed around, marvelling again at the colours of the landscape and thinking thoughts along the lines of how Mount Helena represented an empire of its own.

Yesterday, Steve had given her a short tour of the bunkhouse, the stables, the cattle yards and the mountain from which the station took its name. It was all impressive; you didn't have to have any experience of a cattle station to appreciate the solid fences, the well-maintained sheds and the expensive machinery they contained, including one helicopter.

Nor could you fail to see that, although Steve Kinane had an easy manner with his staff, he was still very much the boss. And it came to her again that she must have been mad ever to have mistaken him for one of his workers because there was—how to put it?—a touch of class about him?

She paused her thoughts in some surprise as this came to her. Considering the hostility she bore towards him, it was a surprising thought and she tried to gauge where it came from. Not solely to do with looks, she decided. So could it be because of a certain reserve about him that she sensed?

Now she knew him a bit better, he was obviously a more complex person than his brother. Not only that, she now saw that he did bear a lot of responsibility and did it well. He was also, so long as the thorny issue of Mark didn't rise between them, quite easy to get along with.

She plucked a blade of grass, chewed it, and wondered what she would have made of Steve Kinane in different circumstances…

'How was your day?'

'Fine, thanks,' Chattie said to Steve as she brought a chicken casserole to the table for dinner that evening. 'How was yours?'

'Complicated.' He lifted the lid on the casserole and sniffed appreciatively. 'I'm so under-staffed at the moment, I may have to postpone the muster. And it could rain tonight.'

'I noticed the clouds building up.' She glanced a little nervously out of the window. 'But rain has to be a good thing for the paddocks, surely?'

He shrugged. 'We've had a good season, now I need a bit of dry weather to get this mob in, but what will be will be. Looking forward to seeing your mum and dad, Brett?'

Brett was with them, having declared himself not tired at all—he was too excited because his mum and dad were reunited and would be returning shortly.

And as she busied herself serving the chicken, a potato pie and green beans she listened to Brett telling Steve there was only one cloud on his horizon—how was he going to bear being parted from Rich?

'Well,' Steve said, 'I would say you're old enough to have a dog of your own. Mind you, until that happens, you can always come over and play with Rich.'

'A dog of my own,' Brett mused. 'But how would I know he'd be as much fun as Rich?'

'Most dogs are pretty good if they're brought up properly. Isn't that so, Chattie?'

'Uh—yes,' she answered with a touch of caution. 'I did take Rich to training classes, though.'

Brett sat up excitedly. 'So you know how to do it? That means you could show me!'

'Well, I won't be here long enough for that,' she said, but added as the boy's face fell, 'I'm sure your dad or Steve could help. Does your mum—like dogs?'

'She doesn't like cleaning up after them,' Brett said. 'She reckons it always falls to the mum to have to do that kind of thing.'

'I see.' Steve thought for a bit. 'Well, maybe I could housetrain it first, then hand it over, but these things don't happen overnight, old son. First we have to find a suitable puppy.'

But Brett had stars in his eyes and after dinner the only way they could get him to bed was to play several games of dominoes with him.

'I just hope we haven't put ourselves beyond the pale with Harriet over a puppy,' Chattie said ruefully when she finally got him settled for the night.

Steve glanced at her humorously. 'So do I. We'll just have to present a united front.'

Chattie started to make some coffee at the same time as she examined the strange feeling of being united in humour and a co-conspirator with Steve Kinane. But before she could diagnose the feeling thoroughly, a clap of thunder tore the air, the lights went out and she dropped the coffee-pot.

Fortunately there was nothing in it but as a flash of brilliant lightning illuminated the kitchen briefly she clung to the kitchen counter.

'Chattie?' Steve stood up. 'Are you all right?'

Her voice wouldn't work at first, then it came out sounding strained and unnatural. 'Fine, thanks.'

'Like hell,' he said, and groped his way over to her. 'Are you scared of thunder and lightning?' he asked with a tinge of incredulity.

'That…' she swallowed '…was quite some thunder and lightning.' She flinched as another crack came.

'Well, well, I wouldn't have guessed it,' he said and put his arms around her waist.

She shivered against him as he pulled her closer. 'G-guessed what?'

'That the iron maiden had any cracks—this will pass over in about ten minutes and I doubt there'll be much rain,' he added before she could take issue with the 'iron maiden' crack. 'How long it will take for the electricity to come back on is anyone's guess. I'll get some hurricane lamps going.'

Chattie closed her eyes and felt a dew of sweat break out on her brow and down her spine as more lightning flashed. 'Would you mind,' she said with difficulty, 'not moving an inch just for the moment?'

And as a peal of thunder cracked right above them, she found herself clinging to Steve Kinane as if she'd never let him go.

'Chattie,' he said into her hair, 'I promise you you're quite safe. This old house has survived many a storm and we do have a lightning conductor.'

Chattie made a supreme effort but it wasn't enough, her knees felt like jelly and her heart was pounding. 'I'm sorry to be so stupid but my intellect and my…insides just won't co-ordinate over this.' She flinched as the storm continued to provide visual and audible pyrotechnics.

'OK.' He patted her back. 'Hang on, then, we'll ride it out together.'

'What about Brett?'

'He's not scared of storms even if it does wake him. What about Rich?'

'He's shut in my bedroom—he'll be under the bed by now. He's almost as much of a ninny as I am.'

Steve laughed. 'You make a good pair. Look, it's already starting to move away.'

Chattie listened and he was right. It had started to rain but the thunder and lightning were not as close. She sighed with relief, then tensed as another loud clap of thunder came.

'There could be a few last hurrahs before it goes away completely,' Steve said comfortably, 'but never mind, this is rather pleasant.'

She blinked up at him in the gloom. 'What?'

'An armful of Chattie Winslow,' he said gravely. 'Would you not agree?'

Her lips parted and her eyes widened. 'I... I...'

'Hadn't thought about it in that light?' He lifted a wry eyebrow at her.

'No! No, I hadn't,' she added, but less certainly because, now she did come to think of it, it was very pleasant. He felt like a strong, safe haven but it was more than that. Not only did she feel safe and secure, she felt her senses stirring as a delicious awareness of her contours against the strength of his tall body overcame her.

'Maybe you should?' he suggested. 'In general, I'm a much better bet than my brother. For one thing, I'm on the spot, so to speak.'

Chattie wrenched her mind from the sensations

starting to course through her—the sensitivity of her breasts, the tremor within that the feel of his hand on her hip created—and she tried to pull away, thunder or no thunder, but he wouldn't let her go.

'Not only do you feel very pleasant, but you're a good height for me,' he said musingly. 'Short girls can be tough on one's neck.'

Chattie gasped. 'How can you? I don't believe you're…saying these things!'

'Why not?' he asked lazily. 'We could hardly be closer.'

'If you think I was faking a fear of thunder and lightning,' she said through her teeth, 'if you think that wasn't just about the worst example of it I've ever experienced, you're mistaken. You…you have to be incredibly arrogant, not to mention even more of a typical man than I gave you credit for!'

He grinned. 'All charges accepted, ma'am. Well, one thing I do know, the very womanly way you feel in my arms at the moment has me feeling all man, arrogant or otherwise.'

Damn you, she thought, it's all too true. Her mind might take issue with it but her body was loving it, arrogant or whatever.

'You're taking advantage of me, Steve Kinane,' she accused.

'Mmm,' he agreed, but as the lights came on she could see that he looked entirely unrepentant.

'What happened to our purely business proposition?'

'Flew out the window. It's also occurred to me that since Rich is hiding under a bed I might as well make hay while the sun shines—terrible metaphor in the circumstances, but you know what I mean.'

'I know exactly what you mean but that makes it even worse!'

'Well, now,' he drawled, 'what makes it really *interesting* is that you should have felt so safe in my arms, Chattie. I doubt a man who was wholly repugnant to you would have had the same effect.'

She coloured delicately, she just couldn't help herself, but her eyes were defiant. 'I may have felt safe but I still haven't forgotten the quip about stealing the silver, however it was made.'

He looked down at her thoughtfully. 'And I'm still not sure what your intentions are, Miss Winslow, but it doesn't alter the fact that it's impossible for us to be like this and be physically unaffected.'

'If you would let me go—' she tried to keep her voice steady '—you would find that you're quite safe from…my intentions.'

He smiled fleetingly. 'Problem is, I don't want to be safe from you—not like this, anyway.'

They stared into each other's eyes. And Chattie discovered that, deep inside her, she didn't want to be safe from this man. There was something about him that attracted her, something elementary and strangely powerful, but it was accompanied by so much she couldn't rationalize, she'd be a fool to let herself be carried away…

'There's a little pulse at the base of your throat beating like a tom-tom,' he said softly, and put his fingertip lightly on it.

She bit her lip.

'And your mouth was made for kissing,' he added

barely audibly as that straying finger outlined her lips. 'Why don't we give it a test run?'

For the life of her, she couldn't control the quiver of her lips any more than she could block from her senses the sheer impact of Steve Kinane's body on hers. Hard and muscled, the impact was little short of electrifying.

'Let's not,' she said huskily as she tried desperately to gather her defences. 'This is ridiculous.'

'On the contrary, this is a force between a man and a woman who are attracted to each other—and it can happen with nothing so pale and wishy-washy as "liking" involved at all,' he said dryly.

'No,' she disagreed unevenly. 'This is your way of showing the contempt you really feel for me. For instance, I'd like to bet my bottom dollar that once you've kissed me you will make some cutting reference to me and your brother.'

Something glinted briefly in his eyes but she couldn't identify it. 'OK.' He shrugged. 'You be the judge—of whether you even remember my brother afterwards.'

'Steve,' she said urgently, 'no!'

'Chattie, yes. You can always lay the blame on the storm if you like, I probably will. Or—' his dark eyes glinted with something she could readily identify this time: wicked satire '—you could stick to the "typical man" bit but, whatever, I'm stuck on a course I can't get off.'

If you dare respond to this, Charlotte Winslow, I'll never speak to you again! she warned herself.

Only to have him read her mind—probably from the stubborn set of her lips. So he didn't bother with them. He cradled her hips to him. She had on the three-quarter-length skirt and white blouse she'd worn the night before, but the thin floral cotton and a pair of bikini briefs were little protection against the feel of his hands on her bottom and she started to breathe raggedly. He raised a wry eyebrow.

Then he slid his hands up to around her waist. 'I can nearly span this,' he said softly. 'Let me guess, twenty—twenty-one inches?'

'That's my business,' she said huskily.

'Well, I would…' those tantalizing hands moved upwards to her ribcage '…estimate thirty-two, twenty-one, thirty-two.'

'From your considerable experience of women, no doubt!' Her eyes flashed.

'Some,' he agreed.

'Then let me tell you, I despise men who go about mentally measuring busts, waists and hips!'

He smiled faintly. 'You're right, it's rather adolescent and not a common occupation of mine—must be something about the perfection of your figure that got to me.' He shrugged. 'Mind you, it doesn't help when you swing them.' His hands descended again to her hips.

'I don't, deliberately,' she denied. 'I just—walk.'

'Then it comes naturally? I'm glad,' he murmured. 'But it's still a bit of a trial. Then there's your skin. Another trial.' This time he slid his hands up her arms. 'Like silk,' he commented. He circled his arms around her again. 'And you're so fair, it comes as a bit of a shock to discover all this delicate beauty has a mind like a steel trap.'

'You better believe it,' she warned, but it was getting harder and harder to maintain her hostility for the fact of the matter was that she was in a trap, a silken trap, she thought bitterly, but one of her own making?

She had always been scared of thunder and lightning—it was the one area where Bridget was the stronger of the two of them. Bridget loved storms provided she was safe from the destructive effects of them. She even seemed to gather a kind of kinetic energy from them. But how foolish had she, Chattie, been to reveal this weakness of hers to this man in this way?

In other words, could she absolve him of some of the blame because she'd brought about the situation unthinkingly? And was as vulnerable to it as he was, if she was painfully honest?

'Miss Winslow?' he said very quietly.

She swallowed. Nestled in his arms like this she could breathe in the pure man aroma of him as well as the freshly laundered tang of the bush shirt and clean jeans he'd changed into. She could see the blue shadows on his jaw and the lines beside his mouth—and the question in his eyes.

A little sob of pure frustration escaped her and she raised her hands to cup his face, then stood on her toes and kissed him lightly on the mouth. And said against his lips, 'This may be my fault but it's still insanity and it changes nothing. Will you let me go now, please?'

'In a moment. I'm never one for leaving a task half finished.'

And he pulled her right into him, teased her lips apart and started to kiss her properly.

When he'd finished, she was quivering with desire,

surrounded sensually by his strength and masculinity and completely focused on Steve Kinane—her enemy.

'So,' he said to her dazed look as he let her go, 'what was so insane about that?'

She stared into his dark, saturnine eyes and did the only thing left for her to do—she swung on her heel and retreated to her bedroom.

Rich came out from under the bed to greet her eagerly and she patted him briefly, then leant back against the door to steady her breathing and take stock. But a more bizarre scenario she couldn't envisage.

To fall for a man who was going to hate her by association if nothing else once he learnt the truth was—asking for trouble, she thought shakily. And why wouldn't he put her in the same basket as Bridget? She was the one conniving to get Mark Kinane back to Bridget. Or, at least admit his responsibility towards her sister's unborn child.

Nor could Steve have made his sentiments clearer towards Mark being trapped into marriage.

She straightened and went to sit on the bed with a sigh.

'Tell him the truth now, Rich?' she said wearily. 'Before this gets totally out of hand? I think I'm going to have to. I don't know why I just didn't do it in the first place.'

She closed her eyes and mentally pictured Bridget at home and getting more and more disturbed as the days went by—and who knew how many more days would go by until Mark Kinane touched his home base?

Not only that but how many more days to endure in the company of a man who was diabolically attractive to you but didn't trust you and could only end up despising you?

'No, it's madness,' she said to Rich, and stood up. 'I'll tell him right now.'

She was halfway to the door when she heard a motor start up. Not Merlene's bike with its distinctive roar but the ute Steve drove around the property.

'Damn,' she muttered. 'Where's he going at this time of night?'

Wherever it was, two hours later he still hadn't returned and Chattie gave up and went to bed, but determined to have things out with Steve Kinane first thing in the morning.

Like many good intentions, it didn't happen that way.

CHAPTER FIVE

AT STEVE'S request, Merlene joined them at breakfast the next morning before Chattie got a chance to get him on his own. So that, when she did encounter him for the first time that morning, it was not only in Merlene's company, but Brett was labouring through his porridge as well.

Beyond exchanging cool glances, she and the boss of Mount Helena did not address each other but that cool, dark glance from Steve Kinane sent a shiver down her spine.

'Looks like a council of war,' Merlene commented as Chattie dished up steak and eggs.

'You could say so,' he said to Merlene. 'We've got a house party coming up in a few days. Five people, two couples—thank you—' Steve said to Chattie as she put his plate in front of him '—and a single. They'll be here for two nights, Tuesday and Wednesday, arriving late Tuesday afternoon and leaving on Thursday morning after breakfast. On Wednesday I'd like a formal dinner party for ten. The other four people will be Harriet and Jack and the shire chairman and his wife.'

'Uh-oh, it is a council of war!' Merlene buttered her toast. 'State of the roads, a drought relief fund for when the next one hits, noxious weed control?'

'Yes,' he agreed.

'And designed to bring home to the pompous old

git of a chairman the fact that he could get booted out at the next council election—good on yer!'

Steve grimaced. 'In a civilized manner but basically—yes.'

''Bout time you ran yourself,' Merlene commented. 'Your dad did an excellent job.'

'We'll see,' Steve said briefly. 'But Chattie is going to need some more of your time, Merlene,' he added.

Chattie opened her mouth to say that she wouldn't be available for the house party but Merlene spoke immediately.

'It's no good asking me to wait tables or cook. I'm all thumbs at that kind of thing. But I guess I could make an exception and do dishes and help with the cleaning and tidying up.'

'Thank you,' Steve said gravely. 'I'm sure Chattie would really appreciate it.'

'Uh—yes, but—'

Brett interrupted. 'Chattie, can I come and see Rich every day when Mum and Dad get home?'

'Uh—yes, but—'

It was Steve who interrupted this time. 'That's the second time you've sounded less than positive,' he said to her. 'Come into the office for a moment, please.' He got up.

Chattie took a very deep breath, and followed him.

He sat down at the desk but didn't invite her to sit in the only other chair. He swivelled his chair sideways so he could watch her and said coldly, 'You're about to do a bunk, aren't you?'

'It would hardly be a bunk, since I have no real reason to be here, as you've pointed out several times,' she commented.

'I would have thought you now had an excellent reason to stay on.' And he raked her from head to toe with a glance that was both insolent and contemptuous. 'Going to pretend it didn't happen, Chattie?'

She coloured but her eyes were steady. 'What happened was due to—an involuntary but all the same— thoughtlessness on my part and—'

'Like hell,' he shot back. 'Listen, if you feel you need some kind of a release from Mark to take up with his brother, you don't. He is obviously finished with you, Miss Winslow. Do you honestly think he'd be driving halfway round the country otherwise?'

'Look,' she began, 'things aren't quite what they seem—'

'Do you think I don't know that?' he broke in roughly. 'So tell me why you came and why you're about to scuttle away. Does Mark know something about you that mightn't appeal to me? Something that could be—awkward for you were it to be revealed later? I'm thinking along the lines of a history of promiscuity, perhaps?'

Chattie went white and immediately made a decision that was quite contrary to the decision she had made the night before. 'You misunderstand me, Mr Kinane,' she said icily. 'I was theorizing when I said that it would hardly be a bunk if I were to leave. In fact, I have no intention of leaving you in the lurch, not for the time being anyway, so you may relax.'

He sat up and frowned at her. 'What about the things that aren't quite what ''seem''?'

She shrugged. 'Another mistaken impression of yours. I was not asking to be kissed last night. I have no intention of allowing it to happen again and I wouldn't put it to the test if I were you otherwise you will find yourself even more short-staffed than you already are.'

His gaze narrowed and he rubbed his jaw. 'So why *were* you so bloody hesitant in the kitchen?'

Chattie thought swiftly. 'There are some things I need to know about this house party. It's all very well to dump numbers in my lap but I need more than that.'

'Like what?' He eyed her suspiciously.

Perhaps it helps to have a mind like a steel trap, she reflected as she pulled out a chair and sat down at the desk, assuming an earnest expression. 'Could you tell me a bit about these guests, please? It helps if you know who you're catering for.'

'On your present record, Chattie, which in my estimation is that you cook like an angel,' he said dryly, 'just keep on the way you've been going.'

She looked genuinely frustrated. 'But are they young, old, middle-aged or what?'

'What difference does it make?'

'In my experience, unless you're of Italian origin, for example, pasta and pizza are young to middle-aged dishes. The same goes for Thai, Chinese and Indian cuisine—it doesn't do much for older people who've been reared on roast beef unless they've done a stint in the Middle to Far East. Salads can be another touchy generational issue. A lot of older people would far rather have vegetables.'

'I see. You obviously take these things very seriously.' He looked amused for the first time.

'I do.' This was quite true too. 'So, although I can be a very traditional cook, it would be nice to know if I didn't have to stick to roast beef and three veg,' she said.

He grimaced. 'They're a mixed bag, I'm afraid. One couple—he's the local vet—are in their middle thirties. The second couple—they run the neighbouring property—are fiftyish but quite "with it". So are Harriet and Jack. The shire chairman and his lady, however—' he tilted his chair back and looked amused '—would definitely fit into the "roast beef, three veg" clan.'

Chattie wrinkled her brow. 'OK, so apart from the formal dinner, I can be a little adventurous, by the sound of it. What about the single? And you yourself?'

'I'm easy. The single? She's in her mid-twenties and very "with it". She's a journalist and she's doing a piece on the station.'

'Uh-huh!' She sat up, thoroughly on her mettle now. 'Would you like me to prepare a list of menus for your consideration?'

He laughed softly. 'No, thank you. Since there is no lady of the house, consider yourself the ultimate authority—just don't kill yourself in the process, Chattie,' he warned. 'We're not trying to be a five-star hotel.'

'All I'll be doing is making sure they're comfortable and well fed.' She got up. 'Oh, one other thing. I seem to be in the best guest bedroom—shall I move out?'

'No,' he said slowly. 'We've got plenty of bedrooms. Stay put.'

'Thank you. Well—' she got up '—back to the mill.'

They exchanged glances. Then she added softly but intently, 'I meant it.'

'Yes, miss,' he responded. 'Are you the terror teacher of your TAFE College?'

'No, but you'd be wise to take me seriously, Steve Kinane.'

'Oh, I do, Chattie. Well, until this blasted house party is over you've got me on a good behaviour bond so to speak.' He looked torn between supreme irritation and some wryly self-directed humour.

'Thank you,' she said gravely, and departed.

But Steve Kinane stared at the wall for some moments after she'd left and asked himself a few pointed questions. Why had he not sent this intriguing, mysterious, infuriating girl packing at the first opportunity despite being left in the lurch with Brett and no Slim? What was she hiding? How was he going to cope with living in the same house with her and not laying a finger on her?

'Bridget,' Chattie said into her phone, later in the day, 'as I explained, the problem is that no one knows where Mark is at the moment. He just took off apparently. But everyone seems to think that he will get in touch with the station so a few more days may be all I need. How are you?'

'Sick as a dog,' Bridget replied, then requested a reassurance from Chattie that she hadn't revealed the truth to Steve Kinane.

Chattie bit her lip. 'Bridge, no, I haven't, but if I can't find Mark I may have to. It—well, I won't do it without consulting you, so just hang in there. Listen, you're not going to believe this,' she said in a bid to cheer her sister up, 'but I've got a temporary job on the station. Which is just as well because I would have outworn my welcome well and truly by now otherwise!'

Several minutes later she ended the call feeling somewhat reassured that the rather comical account she'd given of being the temporary housekeeper at Mount Helena had cheered Bridget up.

The next couple of days were extraordinarily busy, but all the appearances of a truce between herself and Steve Kinane existed.

She wasn't sure how she did it—then it occurred to her he must have contributed—but she concentrated on being as natural as she could in his company. Deep thought had convinced her it was the only way to go, since she'd made the—insane? Angry certainly—decision to stay on. Being busy and doing the things she loved had to have helped, of course. And it was a particularly satisfying house to be in charge of.

Still, it was strange, she acknowledged, that they could be in such discord on one level yet, outwardly, almost 'matey' so that her natural liveliness, very much on the back burner until now, began to reappear. But he did provide her with one break that turned out to be a real treat, although it also provided a true test of their truce.

She and Brett got a tour of the property by helicopter and her enthusiasm for the flight, piloted by Steve, was almost as great as the little boy's—Brett's greatest ambition was to become a helicopter pilot.

It was a Sunday, the day before Jack and Harriet were due back, and Chattie had been asked to pack a picnic and bring along swimming costumes for herself and Brett.

'It's so big,' she said to Steve in wonderment as Mount Helena unfolded below her. They were wearing headphones and mikes so they could talk over the noise. 'Do you know every inch of it—is it possible?'

'Well, not every inch, but I've been flying over it since I was eighteen,' he replied.

'Do you muster by helicopter?' she asked as she spied a mob of cattle on the move towards a thread of green winding across the plain, indicating, she guessed, a water course.

'Sometimes. Over the really rough country it's easier but we also use motor bikes and ringers on horses or a combination of the three.'

'I would love to see a muster,' she said wistfully.

'If you're here long enough you will. OK—' he pointed through the wind screen '—see that big patch of green? It's a billabong and it has to be a pretty serious drought for it to dry up. We'll have lunch there.'

So they landed and spent a lovely couple of hours exploring the billabong, revelling in the shade of the gum-trees that lined it and splashing in the shallows.

'This is a very unique experience,' Chattie said as she set out her lunch on a rug. 'Let's see, egg and lettuce sandwiches, ham and tomato, Vegemite, which I happen to know goes down well with young Mr Barlow but you don't have to partake of them.' She glinted a dancing look at Steve. 'Uh—and some cold chicken. Do help yourselves. There are lamingtons and tea to follow.'

She'd slipped a white T-shirt over her swimming costume and she sat down cross-legged on the rug.

Steve and Brett wore only their swim wear, in

Steve's case dark green board shorts. He'd helped Brett construct an elementary raft with branches and some rope from the helicopter, and Brett was lying tummy down on it, scanning the depths of the billabong as he paddled it with his hands.

'Leave him,' Chattie said as Steve was about to call him to lunch. 'He'll come when he's hungry.'

'Tell me what's so unique about this?' he invited as he helped himself to a drumstick and several sandwiches.

'Well, I've got this picture in my mind of the map of Australia spread out all around us, and just the three of us on it.' She wrinkled her brow. 'Maybe some cattle as well, but that's all.'

'Funny you should say that,' he said slowly. 'I sometimes get the same feeling.'

'Do you enjoy the feeling?'

'I do enjoy the sensation of space, I sometimes revel in solitude, not that this is precisely solitude.'

She shaded her eyes with her hand and watched the way the sunlight filtered through the leaves above was dancing on the water. 'So do I.'

He glanced narrowly at her. 'Didn't you tell me you had a sister?'

Chattie tensed inwardly. 'Yes.'

'Do you live with her?'

'Yes. We're pretty close, actually, but this is different,' she said slowly.

He studied her thoughtfully, and suddenly realized he was on the receiving end of a similar, rather absorbed contemplation.

'What?' he queried, looking comically alarmed.

A faint blush stained her cheeks because she'd

found herself musing on the subject of just how much of a true loner he was; and how much the memory of the kiss they'd shared had occupied her mind ever since it had happened.

Of course, they had to be related topics, she realized. Nor was she in any way helped to forget that second topic as he lounged back in his board shorts on the rug.

If it weren't for Brett, I could happily do it again.

The thought raced through her mind and made her quite dizzy but a relaxed, slightly damp Steve Kinane, tanned, muscular and beautifully proportioned, was almost too much to bear. Then there was the desire she identified as a growing longing to get to know him better...

Be still, my crazy heart, she told herself, then leapt to her feet with a cry of pain as what felt like a very fine but red-hot skewer pierced the tender flesh under her arm. 'Ouch!' She swatted at the area frantically then felt another sting.

Steve was on his feet in a second and he picked her up with his hands about her waist and jumped into the billabong with her.

'What...why?' she gasped and swallowed some water.

'Green ants. They bite like the devil. Here. You can stand.'

She found her feet and he wrestled her T-shirt off, then unceremoniously pulled the straps of her swimming costume down, exposing her breasts.

'No...don't,' she spluttered. 'What are you doing?'

'No choice,' he said laconically and pushed her below the water to the level of her chin.

The relief was blessed. 'Holy smoke,' she said, forgetting her nakedness for the moment, 'that hurt!'

'They do,' he agreed. 'The longer you stay like that, the better.'

'He's right,' Brett called.

'That's all very well,' Chattie remarked, folding her arms over her chest, 'but they must be drowned by now and modesty prevents me from—'

'They would be drowned by now but the cold water will help soothe the sting and modesty is—well, you're quite safe from me if that's worrying you,' Steve said gravely.

She shot him a look. 'I should hope so.'

'Not,' he responded with an entirely wicked glint in his eyes, 'that it's easy to be unmoved by such sheer feminine perfection, but I am on a good-behaviour bond.'

Chattie's hair was dripping into her eyes and she raised her hands to smooth the water out of it.

'Even harder if you do that,' he added barely audibly.

She clamped her arms around herself speedily. 'Will you go away?' she requested *sotto voce*, but with her grey eyes growing stormy. 'You were the one who…got me like this.'

'Only in your best interests.' He looked quite serious but she knew he was laughing at her.

'Well, they've been well and truly served now!'

'Maybe.' He grimaced. 'Mine, however, are another matter. Still—' he shrugged '—I'm told cold water helps there too.'

Chattie took a breath as their gazes locked.

His dark hair was plastered to his head and his eyelashes clumped together—but he was breathtakingly attractive with his broad, wet shoulders and his white teeth. And for a moment it was impossible not to imagine them alone in the billabong. Alone, and matching her paler skin to his strong, tanned body, her curves to his lines and angles as the cool water swirled over and around them.

She closed her eyes for a long, sensuous moment and when she opened them it was to find that all humour, wicked or otherwise, had gone from his expression. She tensed. But he looked away first, then turned away and climbed out, calling to Brett at the same time, and things got back to normal.

Well, almost normal, she was to think later that evening. Nothing more had been said but there'd been one occasion when they'd been caught in a little world of their own again, she and Steve. When he'd helped her climb out of the helicopter his hand had lingered on her elbow.

It was the lightest pressure but she'd paused as her whole body had been invaded by an awareness of him and a strange but lovely sensation at the pit of her stomach had made her feel as if the world had tripped...

She'd stared into his eye with her heart starting to beat heavily but Brett had intervened, by jumping down beside her, and Steve had released her without a word—and the world had righted itself.

'You seem to know quite a few tricks of the trade,' Merlene said the next morning when they were dusting and polishing guest bedrooms and making up beds.

Chattie explained about her domestic-science training then straightened from the perfectly made bed with her hands on her hips. 'These guest bedrooms are kind of bare. No ornaments, no vases or that kind of thing.'

'Kid, when you got a house with six bedrooms excluding the annexe, and five bathrooms, it takes a powerful lot of work to keep it all dusted and clean. So Slim keeps one guest bedroom up to date, yours, and only breaks out the others when necessary, which ain't often.'

'Breaks out?' Chattie wrinkled her brow.

'There's a store room next to the linen press you may not have come across. It's full of knick-knacks and things.'

'Can I have a look?' Chattie asked with a tremor of excitement.

Merlene shrugged. 'Maybe Steve woulda mentioned it if he'd wanted—'

'He did say to consider myself the ultimate authority, well, below you, of course,' she hastened to assure Merlene quite untruthfully but most diplomatically.

'OK! I must say it all used to look lovely when his mum was alive and of course when—'

But she stopped as they heard a vehicle drive up to the garden gate. 'Who would that be?'

Brett solved the mystery by dashing past, yelling, 'Mum, Dad, guess what? You just have to buy me my very own dog or else I'll come and live with Steve and Chattie permam-m-m-ently!'

Merlene looked heavenwards. 'Her ladyship has returned. You watch yourself with her—she can be a right bitch.'

But Harriet Barlow had a glow about her of a woman deeply in love. She wafted into the house on the arm of a lean, freckled, fair-haired man and they shared an affectionate reunion with Brett, got introduced to Rich then became aware of Chattie—Merlene had retreated to the kitchen.

'You must be the godsend Steve mentioned—I'm Jack Barlow.' Brett's father extended his hand to Chattie. 'Thanks so much for looking after this young tyke!'

'It was my pleasure, but actually it was Rich who did most of it,' Chattie responded with a grin.

'Anyway, thanks,' Harriet remarked. 'I must say I got the impression the other night that you were just passing through but I may have been mistaken.'

'I was until Slim collapsed,' Chattie explained, then decided to get it over and done with. 'Actually I came up to see Mark but—we had a few crossed wires, I guess you could say.'

Harriet raised her eyebrows but that was all and they gathered Brett and his belongings and left.

'Tra-la, tra-la!' Merlene re-emerged. 'Until the next time.'

Chattie laughed. 'OK, lead me on to Aladdin's cave.'

The store room did turn out to be a bit like Aladdin's cave and Chattie had a marvellous time with all the neatly stored items she found: pretty scatter cushions for the armchairs, thick, thirsty monogrammed towels in jewel-bright colours, vases, ornaments and so on.

'That looks so much better,' she said to herself as she wandered through each bedroom on the afternoon the guests were due to arrive.

She'd consulted with the hand who looked after the

house garden and, although there weren't a lot of flowers to be had, there were some interesting shrubs with variegated or coloured leaves, tiny star-like blossoms and gum tips that filled the air with either a lemony or honey fragrance that she'd been allowed to plunder. She'd made up arrangements for each room and several for the lounge and dining room.

She was also confident she had everything else under control, and she'd taken an initiative. In a corner of the dining room she'd set up a trolley with a coffee machine she'd found, cups, milk, sugar, home-made biscuits in a barrel and a kettle for those who preferred tea.

She was studying it while trying to do up her fine gold chain necklace she always wore when Steve came up soundlessly behind her. 'Good thinking,' he pronounced. 'They can help themselves.'

She jumped.

'Sorry, didn't mean to startle you, Miss Winslow,' he said with a smile growing at the back of his eyes, 'but I must say you look the part. Can I help with that?'

Chattie looked down at herself, then at the necklace in her hand. She wore a chic slim corn-coloured three-quarter-length linen skirt and a sleeveless navy-blue top. Her hair was tied back with a colourful yellow and navy scarf and strappy low sandals completed her outfit.

'The part?'

'You look,' he paused, 'like the lady of the house.'

Colour rushed into her cheeks. 'I…only intend to be the housekeeper and to stay in the background as much as possible. Am I too—dressy?' she asked with concern.

He shook his head, took the chain from her and stepped round her to deal with the clasp. 'You're always dressy,' he said with his fingers lingering on the back of her neck, and causing the fine hairs to stand up all over her body. Then he went on his way—leaving Chattie electrified but frowning in confusion as she watched him go.

An hour later the first guests, from the neighbouring property, flew in followed closely by the vet and his wife, who brought the journalist with them.

'It's on for old and young,' Merlene said humorously. 'That woman, the journo, has been here before poking around and gathering info for some kind of book or article, but I wouldn't be surprised if she's got her eye on Steve and all the rest is humbug.'

Chattie looked up from the canapés she was preparing, to be served with sundowners on the veranda. 'Really?'

The 'journo' was a slim, elegant brunette with lavender-blue eyes and had been introduced to Chattie as Sasha Kelly. She'd contrived to be slim and elegant despite being all kitted out in khaki and wearing short boots, and, beyond the definite surprise in her lovely eyes on being presented to the housekeeper, she'd been rather nice.

They all had, Ray and Lucy Cook, the vet and his wife, and John and Joan Jackson, the triple Js as they called themselves, from the station next door—a hundred miles away.

Chattie had shown them all to their rooms, assured

them if they needed anything they only had to ask, and retired immediately to the kitchen.

She scooped some caviare onto the circle of hard-boiled egg atop a round biscuit, and paused for thought.

'It's a bit surprising he's not already married, isn't it?'

Merlene wiped her hands on her apron. 'Oh, he—'

She stopped as Steve came into the kitchen.

Chattie's eyes widened. He'd already surprised her twice today. Once, when he'd come upon her admiring the coffee trolley and again when, for the first time, she'd seen him out of jeans and a bush shirt and looking rather different but just as impressive, if not more so, in bone moleskins and a cream-and-red-checked shirt.

This time, though, it was his eyes that surprised her. They were hard and cool as he surveyed the scene in the kitchen and made her wonder nervously what she and Merlene had done wrong.

And a beat passed before he said with no particular inflection, also nerve-racking, 'I'm about to serve drinks and we should be ready for dinner in an hour.'

'Oh.' Chattie licked caviar from her fingertip and started to spoon it more rapidly. 'There, all done.' She indicated the two silver platters laden with artistic and delicious-looking bite-sized eats. 'Will I bring them through?'

'No, thanks.' He picked up the two platters and walked out.

Chattie turned to Merlene. 'What's gone wrong?'

Merlene merely shrugged, although Chattie did notice that she looked oddly embarrassed. But, from then on, Chattie was far too busy to give it further thought.

By ten-thirty the house was quiet, the last dish had been put away, the breakfast table laid and Chattie was able to retire to her bedroom with a cup of tea, which she took out to the veranda. Rich woke up and came to sit at her feet.

'Well,' she murmured to him, 'the entrée went down well. The main course of lamb and noodles with plum sauce and sesame seeds was much applauded and so was the apricot and sour cream slice.'

Rich yawned.

'Sorry—am I keeping you up? I was even,' Chattie continued, 'asked for my recipes, although I must confess Ms Sasha Kelly, who I first thought was quite nice, was the only one who did not appear to be impressed.'

She looked thoughtful for a moment, then shrugged. 'I think Merlene's right—Sasha may have her sights on Steve. The other thing is—the boss is not in a good mood. I can just *feel* it.'

This time Rich stiffened, growled, then leapt at the wire screen as a furry creature slipped down the outside of it from the veranda roof into the bushes. In the process Chattie upset her tea down her blouse and it was still hot enough to cause her to yelp in pain.

At the same time Steve Kinane loomed up out of the darkness.

'What are you doing here?' Chattie gasped, getting up and holding her top away from her skin. 'Sit, Rich,' she commanded.

'I usually take a stroll in the garden before I turn

in,' he replied, 'so I heard the kerfuffle—it was only a possum. No need to get your knickers in a twist.'

'I know it was only a possum! I'm not completely "citified",' she answered with some chagrin. 'Rich made me spill my tea, that's all.'

'Are you burnt? Let me see.' Without waiting for an answer, he pulled her top up and scanned her skin above the waistband of her skirt, and her breasts cupped in a navy bra trimmed with ivory and pink lace. His eyebrows rose but all he said was, 'Your skin's a bit pink. Go and splash yourself with cool water and I'll get us a drink.'

He let the top fall and walked away through her bedroom.

Chattie blinked several times, then shook her head bewilderedly and took herself to her bathroom.

When she reappeared on the veranda she had her pyjamas on beneath a yellow terry-towelling robe.

Steve was waiting for her with two glasses of brandy.

'Better?' he queried.

'Yes. I'll be fine.' She sat down. 'I don't even think I'm injured enough to deserve a brandy,' she added ruefully.

'Have it all the same,' he recommended. 'It's been quite a night for you, I would imagine.'

'I think it all went well, although at one stage Merlene got quite panic-stricken, which I didn't expect!' She laughed.

He grinned. 'It went exceptionally well. I'd like to pay my respects.'

Chattie's eyes widened. 'I thought you were upset with me.'

He lifted his dark eyes to her. 'No.'

'Well, about something, then.'

He paused. 'How could you tell?'

'I don't know, I just could,' she said slowly.

'Something came up, that's all. It's now—sorted.'

'Why do I get the feeling it isn't?' she said, barely audibly.

'Chattie, I know you have your finger on the pulse of this house as any good housekeeper would, but everything is OK. The guests are most impressed. So am I.'

Part of her harboured a little question mark still, but she had no choice but to allow it to rest.

'Thank you. So. You're all going out and about tomorrow?'

'Yes, we'll be out of your hair apart from breakfast, lunch and dinner.'

'What will you be doing?' she asked curiously.

'I've implemented a few changes recently, mainly to do with paddock and weed management. Often, when you do that, you hold an open day for the district, generally in conjunction with the manufacturers of a new piece of machinery, equipment or product of some kind. This is a test run for a proper open day.'

'Oh, that's interesting.' She looked into the dark night as if she was picturing Mount Helena in a new and rather fascinating way, then something struck her. 'Does it…' she hesitated '…also have to do with promoting oneself for election to the shire council?'

'No flies on you, Miss Winslow. Yes.'

She wrinkled her brow. 'May I make a comment?'

'Be my guest,' he said wryly.

'Only if you promise not to take offence.'

'I'll see.' He looked amused.

She took a breath. 'You seem to live and breathe Mount Helena and this "cattle" life.'

'You don't approve?'

She gestured. 'It's not that at all, I'm coming to think it's rather lovely, but...' she hesitated again '...I'm wondering how much of a loner you have to be to really stick to it.'

He grimaced. 'To do it properly does take a hell of a lot of time, but I'm not entirely uncultured, if that's what you're implying.'

'No, I wasn't!'

'Tell the truth, Chattie. Compared to such a multi-talented person as yourself, do you perceive me as a philistine?' He drained his brandy. 'Or perhaps you're comparing me to Mark?'

Her lips parted in surprise.

'Who is quite cultured but no good at running a cattle station.' He stood up.

She followed suit. 'I believe I've been misunder-stood. I—'

'No you haven't, Chattie. Goodnight,' he said abruptly and left via the garden.

She stared after him, then sat down again with a frown and the helpless feeling that she'd unwittingly brought back Steve Kinane's dark mood despite being no wiser as to its origin.

After the success of the evening it was a lowering and troubling thought.

CHAPTER SIX

THINGS began to go wrong almost from the start of the next day.

Chattie overslept and had an almighty rush to get breakfast on the table in time. And John Jackson sought her out to tell her that his wife, Joan, had a migraine and would be staying in bed.

'Oh, I'm sorry. I'll keep an eye on her, Mr Jackson,' she promised. 'Is there anything special you'd like me to do?'

'No, thanks, Miss Winslow. Dark, rest and quiet are what she needs, although, perhaps a small meal when it's over?'

'My pleasure,' Chattie murmured, suddenly conscious of Steve's dark gaze on her.

She had ignored him other than a formal greeting when she'd first encountered him at the breakfast table, not hard to do as she'd juggled a full breakfast for six people without giving off the vibes that she was in a rush.

But somehow she'd got through it all and the party was now leaving the table to get ready for their morning in the paddocks. As their gazes clashed, though, she got the feeling that Steve Kinane had divined her less-than-top-notch performance—or was she imagining the tinge of irony in his gaze?

Then Sasha Kelly, again kitted out in khaki, although the previous evening she'd looked stunning in midnight-blue, asked Chattie if she'd mind doing some washing and ironing for her.

'I've been on the hop for nearly a week now researching articles, and I just haven't had a chance to get to it,' she said airily. 'Besides which, I'm sure you're much better at laundry than I am.'

Whether intended as a sting in the tail or not, Chattie discovered herself in the mood to take it as such.

She flicked her hair back and put a hand on her hip. 'I'd be very happy to show you the washing machine and the ironing-board, Miss Kelly. Now—' she turned regally to the rest of the party '—just in case you get hungry during the morning, I've prepared an esky with some cool drinks and snacks—perhaps you'd like to be in charge of it, Steve?'

'Certainly, Miss Winslow,' he said with mock deference—it had to be mock, Chattie decided—although the rest of the party appeared to be electrified by her brush with Sasha Kelly.

'Fine. Well, off you go.' She waved a hand. 'Have a lovely morning!' And she strode purposefully towards the kitchen.

To find Merlene doubled up with laughter.

'You learn fast, kid!' she spluttered.

'You heard? Who does she think she is?' Chattie asked incredulously.

'I heard it all. Told you.'

'I am not in a good mood now, thanks to her.'

'Wouldn't be surprised if she isn't either,' Merlene commented.

'On the other hand,' Chattie said slowly, calming

down a little, 'am I supposed to do their washing and ironing?'

'Heaven's above, no!' Merlene looked horrified. 'None of the others would have dreamt of asking you.'

Chattie mulled this over. 'So she really meant to make me look like a domestic rather than an academic? Why?'

'Some women are just built that way. Can't tolerate "lookers" in any shape or form. And Steve is quite a catch.'

Before Chattie got a chance to respond to this, the phone rang. It was Harriet Barlow, distraught because Brett had disappeared and had they seen him?

'No,' Chattie said down the line. 'Why would we have?'

'He wanted to come and see your blasted dog, that's why. But I said I didn't have the time to drive him over this morning, and do you realize there are two dams between our house and yours and he is strictly forbidden to leave our garden on his own?'

'Then you should have kept an eye on him,' Chattie said crisply.

'Who the hell do you think you are? It's your stupid dog that's caused all the trouble!'

'Listen, lady, don't get sassy with me, I don't work for you. Get on your bicycle and start looking for him! We'll do the same from this end!' She put the phone down and explained things tersely to Merlene.

'The only thing is,' she finished up, 'what car are we going to use to look for him?'

'We'll use my bike—it's perfect and you can double up,' Merlene suggested. 'Poor little tyke,' she added.

So Chattie climbed up behind Merlene when they

should have been cleaning up after breakfast and starting to prepare lunch. And they roared around the property on the bike while picturing Brett drowned in a dam or lost in the wilderness, until they found him asleep under a tree about halfway between his house and the main homestead.

Harriet drove up not long afterwards and, to give her credit, she appeared to have been worried out of her mind, from the loving reunion she lavished on her son. Not that Brett seemed to understand what all the fuss was about.

'Look, he's welcome to come and spend a couple of hours with us,' Chattie offered. 'He and Rich just play for hours on end.'

'Thank you,' Harriet said stiffly. Then she sighed. 'I'm sorry. When I get worried I tend to let fly. You've been wonderful with Brett and I really appreciate it.'

Chattie blinked but Harriet was obviously genuine. 'Thanks. To be honest I don't usually let fly, but someone had already ruffled my feathers a bit. Oh, my stars!' She clapped a hand to her forehead. 'I forgot all about Mrs Jackson! If she's up and about she'll have no idea what's going on!'

But Joan Jackson, when Chattie cautiously peeped into her bedroom after they got back, was fast asleep.

'I'm beginning to feel as if I'm trying to run through heavy water,' she commented to Merlene as she got back to the kitchen and saw the time.

'Care for a bit of advice?'

'Only too happy to listen!'

'Stick the lunch out on the long table on the front veranda and let them fend for themselves. And you just concentrate on your cooking. I'll fix the rest, although I'll leave the dinner table to you.'

'Merlene, you're a doll!'

Lunch came and went without incident although Steve did enquire what Brett was doing amongst them.

Chattie explained briefly.

He raised his eyebrows. 'It never rains but pours.'

'Oh, he's no trouble, but it did wreak a bit of havoc with my timetable, that's all.'

'You look a little—frazzled.'

She subjected him to an annoyed glance and announced that she would be the essence of cool, calm collectedness for the evening.

His gaze lingered on her. 'That should be well worth seeing.'

'I don't know what you mean—I often find you hard to understand, in fact, but I'd appreciate it if you'd remove yourself and all these people as you promised you would!'

'Done,' he replied promptly, but added with a gleam of sheer satire in his eyes, 'Although I must tell you, you've taken the position of housekeeper to new—er—heights.'

He walked away without a backward glance.

Chattie bit her lip, and stayed where she was, lost in thought for a minute or two.

At four o'clock, she felt much more in control of things, having taken her advice to herself along the lines of being purely professional in this job.

She showered and changed—Brett had been retrieved by his mother—and, just to reaffirm her composure, she slipped into the music room for a couple of minutes. As her fingers slid across the ivories very softly a sense of peace came to her, as it always did. Then the door clicked open behind her and she turned to see Joan Jackson.

'Oh, Mrs Jackson! I hope I didn't wake you—how are you feeling?'

'No, you didn't wake me—may I call you Chattie? I've been coming out of it for about an hour now, but when I heard the piano I thought I must be dreaming. You play beautifully, my dear!'

'Thank you!' But Chattie looked perplexed. 'Dreaming?'

'Well, wafted back to the days when my good friend Christine—Steve's mother—used to play that piano. She was very musical too. Has he told you about her?'

'No,' Chattie said.

Joan looked around. 'I think there's a picture of her in here. Yes!' She walked over to the bookshelves. 'Here she is—so sad she's no longer with us; she was lovely in every way.' She lifted the silver-framed photo off the shelf and handed it to Chattie.

'Goodness me,' she went on as Chattie studied the fair woman in the photo who looked a lot like Mark, pictured with a tall man who reminded her of Steve, 'would you believe I was at Mark's christening?' she confided to Chattie with a twinkle.

Chattie smiled.

'And there used to be one of Steve's wedding,' Joan went on, 'but I'd be surprised if he allowed her to keep it—oh, yes!' She plucked a photo that Chattie hadn't previously noticed from behind an ornament.

Chattie's lips parted. 'Steve—has been married?'

'Yes, it didn't work out, though, and they're divorced. She was very beautiful but very much a city girl and she just didn't take to life out here. She often used to accuse him of having a one-track mind—cattle, cattle, cattle.'

It was as if a blinding light suddenly illuminated the dark corners of Chattie's mind—several blinding lights. Steve Kinane had thought she was accusing him of the same thing last night, and earlier he might have overheard her comment on the subject of his not being married—was that why Merlene had looked embarrassed? Just about to be caught discussing his private life by the boss might well do it.

She swallowed. 'I didn't know.'

'I'm sure it's all behind him now, although he hasn't taken the plunge again and it's been quite a while since they parted—years, actually—and there have been plenty who would have loved to attach themselves to him.'

Chattie studied the stunning girl on Steve's arm, the way he was looking down at her, then handed the picture back.

'Mrs Jackson, would you like a cup of tea? And perhaps a sandwich? I'd be happy to bring it to your room.'

Joan Jackson beamed at Chattie. 'That would be so kind, my dear! I don't get these wretched headaches often, but when I do…!'

But as she cut up the sandwiches and brewed some tea all Chattie could think of was Steve Kinane's failed marriage and the way he'd been looking down at his bride.

* * *

At six o'clock drinks were in progress in the lounge, the dining room was candlelit and resplendent, the kitchen was a model of good management—and the lights went off.

'Power failure,' Merlene said laconically. 'Happens all the time out here.'

'You're joking!' Chattie stared at her through the gloom. 'There are no storms in the offing, are there?' she asked nervously.

'No. It isn't only storms that do it, though.'

'What is wrong with this day? It seems determined to…flatten me!'

Steve came into the kitchen. 'We have a back-up generator, Chattie, don't panic.' He strode out of the back door.

Chattie took several deep breaths. 'I'm not panicking,' she assured Merlene. 'Well, only slightly.'

'We've still got the stove.' Merlene pointed to the wood-burning range. 'It's one reason why they kept it.'

Chattie nodded but thought of the use she'd planned to make of the microwave, the toaster, the electric coffee machine, the electric blender, and felt a little faint. 'How long does it take to get the generator going?'

'No time at all, usually.' Merlene shrugged. 'But I'll get some candles and paraffin lamps just to be on the safe side.'

The words struck a little chill in Chattie and, sure enough, fifteen minutes later Steve came back into the kitchen wiping his hands on a rag and looking grim.

'Don't tell me!' Chattie pleaded.

'Sorry, but the bloody thing has blown a fuse and it's short-circuited completely. It's a major repair job now that'll take hours. Look—' he looked around '—just size things down to what's ready, they'll understand, and I'll send Harriet in to give you a hand.'

Merlene snorted but Chattie had taken several deep breaths.

She said. 'If Harriet would help with the serving, we'd be most grateful, but I will not allow this day to defeat me even though it's been trying to *do* so all day!' She raised her chin. 'Please tell everyone dinner will be delayed by about half an hour but otherwise everything is fine.'

'Chattie—'

Steve Kinane paused and sighed as he observed his housekeeper. She'd chosen to wear slim floral trousers on a white background with an apple-green shirt. Over it, at the moment, she had a clear plastic apron, her hair was drawn back in a bunch and her feet were encased in green leather flat shoes. There could be no mistaking her determination from her expression, but she was so lovely at the same time, she reminded him of an avenging goddess of the very slim, very young variety.

'Hang on,' he said abruptly, and walked through to the dining room. He came back minutes later with two glasses of champagne, one of which he handed to her, the other to Merlene.

'There you go, troops,' he said with a wicked little smile. 'That should ease the pain a bit.'

'Why, thank you!' Chattie said in a genuine rush of good cheer. 'That's the best thing that's happened to me all day!' She raised her glass to toast him. 'Off you go, then; we'll be fine now!'

* * *

And, in due course, a delicate asparagus soup was served, followed by a magnificent beef Wellington and vegetables including cauliflower au gratin. And for dessert, a baked lemon cheesecake, topped with glacé lemon slices and a fruit salad, was served with hand-beaten cream.

By the time the dessert had gone into the dining room—Harriet had done all the ferrying in and out of food and dishes and tried to be as helpful as possible—the kitchen resembled a battlefield and Merlene was swearing audibly because she couldn't locate the manual coffee grinder.

'How are we going to grind these damn beans? I know there's one somewhere!'

'Merlene,' Chattie said, sinking into a chair, 'I'll let you into a little secret. A dash of something like Tia Maria gives a whole new meaning to instant coffee. Glory be—let there be light!' she added as the lights came on. Then she looked around and started to giggle. 'Let's go back to candles!'

Steve came in at that moment and looked around ruefully, and as the lights went out again said, 'That was a false alarm, thankfully, I agree with you. Uh—your presence is required in the dining room, Miss Winslow.'

Chattie put her hands to her cheeks, which were shiny with perspiration, touched her hair and knew it to be out of control, looked at her fingernails, and said decidedly, 'No way!'

'Then I'll bring them in here,' he murmured.

'Who?'

'The shire chairman and his lady—they're very desirous of making your acquaintance.'

'Don't you dare!' Chattie and Merlene chorused, with Merlene adding, 'Wash your hands, spit on your eyebrows, push your fingers through your hair, Chattie, but don't let 'em see this mess—I'll never live it down. And take your apron off,' she recommended.

Chattie did it all, even to licking a fingertip and smoothing her eyebrows, although she favoured Steve Kinane with a dark glance along the way. 'This is blackmail.'

'You'll probably change your mind when you hear what they have to say. One thing, don't accept any job offers—I wouldn't appreciate you leaving me in the lurch.'

'Well, ma'am,' the shire chairman, who was a large man with a large belly, said on Chattie's arrival in the dining room, and paused to do a double take, 'I have to tell you, you are going to make some lucky man a magnificent wife and I really would like to introduce you to my son!' He turned to his wife. 'Wouldn't you, Beryl?'

Beryl nodded enthusiastically. Ray Cook, Jack Barlow and John Jackson raised their glasses in heart-felt agreement, causing Harriet Barlow to look oddly thoughtful—and Sasha Kelly to look bored to tears. But the other women seconded this sentiment heartily and insisted Chattie sit down with them for a moment.

Two hours later when those driving had gone home and those staying had all gone to bed, Steve found his housekeeper asleep at the dining-room table.

She'd obviously been setting it for breakfast, but she

was now sitting at it with her head on her arms and dead to the world.

He surveyed her for a moment, and then said her name.

No response.

'Well, I can't leave you here all night,' he murmured wryly, and carefully manoeuvred her out of the chair and into his arms. She didn't wake as he carried her to her bedroom, and he quietly recommended to Rich to think twice about attacking him.

Then he went to put Chattie down on the bed, but she made a murmur of dissent and cuddled up against him with her arms around his neck, so he sat down on the bed with her in his lap instead. 'Chattie?'

'Mmm?' Her lashes fluttered but she was only half awake and she rubbed her cheek against his shoulder with a sigh of pleasure, and closed her eyes again.

A nerve flickered in his jaw as he looked down at the curvy, half-folded length of her. She was completely relaxed and felt soft and boneless against him. Her hair smelt of lemons, there was a streak of gravy down her blouse and a blob of blueberry on one knee of her trousers. She'd abandoned her shoes somewhere along the line.

But despite her exertions or even because of them—did it add a strength of character that made her irresistible?—she was quite lovely. Smooth-skinned, beautifully curved, delicately tinted—and from nowhere a vision came to Steve Kinane of the shire chairman's son, Ryan.

He grimaced at the thought. Ryan Winters was a brawny, good-looking young man of considerable ego. He was also considered the local stud, but had all the finesse of a front-row forward and it was simply unthinkable to imagine Charlotte Winslow in his arms.

Come to that, he thought grimly, he would have difficulty imagining her in anyone's arms but his own and therein lay a contretemps of the highest order for him.

Not only on account of her connection with his brother, he acknowledged, but because he'd considered himself immune from emotional entanglements now…

So how the hell, he asked himself, had he fallen for a girl who cherished the same negative sentiments about his state of mind as his ex-wife had?

Chattie moved in his arms, said drowsily, 'This is so nice after a hard day at the office!' And opened her eyes.

For a moment nothing registered in their grey depths, then comprehension dawned, consternation became shock and shock was coupled with deep embarrassment.

'Pardon me,' she whispered, going scarlet and scrambling to sit up. 'I…I don't know what you must think! I didn't realize it was you. I…' She got unsteadily to her feet at the same time as she anxiously patted her blouse into place, checked the buttons and smoothed her trousers. 'I am sorry but I guess I was overtired—'

'Or you thought I was Mark?' he suggested dryly.

'I'm not sure what I thought—' She stopped abruptly and her eyes widened.

'Unless you make a habit of it.'

'What?'

'Enjoying any man's arms around you,' he said flatly.

Indignation rushed to the surface. 'I do not!' she denied. 'How can you say that? You know, there are times when I quite like you, Steve Kinane, and times when you make it impossible!'

He shrugged. 'Then we'll have to go with the Mark scenario.'

It occurred to Chattie in a blinding instant that there was another scenario. Subconsciously she'd known all along it was Steve, and, again subconsciously, had felt safe with him yet again. Safe—*and as if she belonged in his arms...*

'I think,' she said, and patted her cheeks to hide her mortification, 'we should put it down to a long—extremely fraught, in fact—day. That's all.' She tilted her chin.

He smiled unexpectedly, and briefly. 'You'll be asking for danger money next.'

'I'm not saying it was above or beyond anything I expected to be called upon to do!' she countered with a flash of irritation. 'I'm using it to explain—oh, what's the use?' She turned away and sniffed. 'I think I better go to bed,' she said huskily, 'since we're destined to misunderstand each other completely, by the look of it.'

The moments ticked by as he said nothing and something compelled her to turn back. And she became conscious as they stared at each other of a rising tide between them of something elementary, something dangerous and disturbing but powerful at the same time. Like the peril of an emotional and physical storm about to break between them whether they liked it or not, whether they could rationalize it or not—and she certainly couldn't.

Because there was no way she felt safe with Steve Kinane at that moment. No way to guarantee that those dangerous, disturbing sensations racing through her at the way he was looking at her wouldn't push her into his arms unsure if she loved him or hated him but unable to resist him...

Her lips parted and her eyes widened in a stunned reaction. Never before in her life had a man stirred her like this for one thing, but to be unsure whether she hated him—or *loved* him, to have that spring into her mind was unbelievable.

He stood up and cut the eye contact. 'Might be a good idea for both of us to go to bed, but please don't think I haven't appreciated your efforts today. Even Slim would have been proud of you and he has very high standards. By the way, the bypass operation was successful and he's resting comfortably.'

It seemed to Chattie that her tongue was stuck to the roof of her mouth for some strange reason, so she swallowed visibly. 'That's good news.'

'Yes. Goodnight.'

She stared at the door after he'd closed it behind him, and wondered if she was going mad.

This roundabout of physical attraction, of liking, even respecting at times, and certainly feeling safe with Steve Kinane, then disliking him intensely, was impossible.

She shivered and got ready for bed distractedly. As she slid under the rose-red eiderdown it occurred to her that she might never get this man out of her system because, not only he, but also his damn cattle station was getting under her skin.

Face it, Chattie, she told herself, this would be a very fulfilling lifestyle for you, but how could it ever be?

Then another thought crept into her mind. She might not have had time to assess the impact it had had on her, but she couldn't get Steve Kinane's wedding photo out of her mind. Or the conviction that he'd been deeply in love with his bride.

CHAPTER SEVEN

CHATTIE was making an omelette for breakfast the next morning—full power had been restored—when someone came into the kitchen through the back door. Because it was very early, too early for Merlene normally and she was sure it had to be Steve, Chattie dropped the bowl and the egg, milk, mushrooms and finely diced onions spread in a wide, yellow-and-black-dotted stain across the floor.

It was Merlene, however, who stopped at the outer edge of the stain, looked down at it, then looked across at Chattie standing pale and transfixed. 'You OK, kid?'

'I'm jittery,' Chattie confessed ruefully. 'I don't know why but I feel as if something terrible is going to happen and it's all my fault.'

'Bloody hell,' Merlene replied.

Chattie grimaced. 'Don't take any notice of me, it will pass. Could you hand me a cloth?'

'What will pass?' It *was* Steve who came in this time, from the opposite direction. He also stopped at the outer edge of the stain, studied it, then studied Chattie and finally raised an eyebrow at Merlene.

'Chattie reckons the world's about to end and it's all her fault,' Merlene explained.

Sheer amusement lit his eyes but he said gravely to Merlene, 'Would you present my compliments to Miss Winslow? Would you also tell her that I had hoped to catch her before she started breakfast, to apprise her that she doesn't have to do a thing because I've organized a barbecue breakfast for the entire present population of Mount Helena down at the bunkhouse?'

'Good thinking, boss!' Merlene applauded. 'Seems to me our young godsend may have stretched herself a wee bit too far over the last couple of days.'

'I told her not to—' Steve started to say exasperatedly but concluded, 'Well, be that as it may, how does she respond?'

Chattie said it in her mind but the words echoed like a foghorn so it seemed impossible that the other two wouldn't hear—That has nothing to do with it! I'm bothered and bewildered because I don't know what's going on between, to be precise, Charlotte Winslow, spinster, and Steve Kinane, divorcee.

'She's really got the wobblies,' Merlene said for her after a moment, 'but I'll accept on her behalf. Why don't you take her out to…smell the flowers or something while I clean up the mess? Looks like she could do with it.'

Chattie came to life. 'Thanks, but that won't be necessary—I was only joking.'

Steve started to say something but the phone rang. Merlene picked it up, then handed it to him. 'Jack. He's got a bit of a problem.'

Steve listened for a couple of moments, then said down the line, 'I'll be there in five.' He handed the phone back to Merlene. 'You're in charge of getting this mob down to the bunkhouse, mate, and you—' he turned to Chattie '—can come with me.'

'Why? What's happened? Why do you need me?' Chattie asked dazedly.

'I do, that's all. Out you go.' He pushed her in the direction of the back door.

She was about to protest vigorously but she caught sight of Merlene out of the corner of her eye. And Merlene was clearly indicating by way of her thumb that Chattie should do as she was told.

'I still don't understand,' Chattie said breathlessly once she was in the Range Rover and Steve was climbing in beside her. Then her eyes grew suddenly fearful. 'It's not anything to do with Brett, is it?'

He switched the motor on and revved the engine. 'No, he's fine as far as I know. My favourite horse has got herself cast in her box.'

'Cast?' she repeated. 'What does that mean?'

'That she lay down or rolled over too close to the wall and now she's got no space to push off so she can't get up.'

'Why doesn't she just roll over again?'

'Sometimes that logic doesn't occur to a horse,' he said wryly. 'Sometimes they get so frightened they don't think straight. Sometimes, in their struggles, they really get themselves wedged in.'

Chattie's eyes all but stood out on stalks. 'You're not expecting me to help you, are you? I don't know a thing about horses!'

'No, I'm not expecting you to help,' he replied, ruefully this time. 'Just thought it would be good for you to get out and about a bit. Can't have my ace housekeeper worried about the end of the world.'

So that's the way it's going to be, Chattie thought as she stared down at her hands and the shiny red apple in them that she'd plucked from the fruit bowl while being propelled out of the kitchen. Swept under the carpet, unless I was imagining all sorts of weird things last night.

Then the supreme irony of that thought came to her. He was doing precisely what she'd tried to do after he'd kissed her on the night of the storm.

'You don't wish to comment?' he said.

She shook her head. 'But thanks for organizing me out of breakfast.'

'What else were we talking about?'

Chattie gazed at him coolly. 'I have no idea.'

'Uh-oh, one of those impasses.' His lips twisted

'Those?' she queried.

'Of the domestic dispute variety,' he quipped, and pulled to a stop in front of the stables. 'OK, let's see what we can do.'

Chattie stayed where she was with surprise and growing indignation colouring her expression.

'I get it,' he drawled. 'You're thinking MEN, in capital letters, but that's what I meant. I was thinking, WOMEN—along the same lines.'

'You know what I think? That you're one of those impossibly bright and bushy early morning people sent to torment the life out of the rest of the planet!' she retorted, and got out of the vehicle to close her door with a bang.

Steve Kinane flinched but a shrill whinny split the air and he turned away from the car immediately.

The scene inside the stables was horrifying—to Chattie at least.

Steve's favourite horse was a chestnut filly with one white sock and a white blaze. Sweat had darkened her coat and panic was sending tremors through her as she lay on her side wedged against the back wall of the stall.

'Every time we go near her,' Jack Barlow said, 'she tries to thrash about but she can't get over and I'm afraid she's going to injure herself. Like that,' he added as the filly strove mightily and convulsively to get to her feet to no avail.

'Get a couple of slings,' Steve ordered, then stepped into the stall and approached the horse's head. Chattie held her breath but immediately his tone changed as he knelt down beside the filly.

'Daisy, my darling,' he said soothingly, 'how did you get yourself into this mess?' He rubbed her neck and stroked her nose.

As Chattie watched in wonderment the horse relaxed, almost with a very human sigh of relief, and as Steve kept on talking to her and rubbing her he directed traffic with his other hand until Jack and one of the hands were in the positions he wanted them. Then, and Chattie wasn't quite sure how they did it, with one concerted movement they all heaved, Daisy flailed her legs and, scattering Jack and the hand, plunged to her feet.

She then, perhaps in an excess of exuberance at being freed, kicked out at the wall with both back legs.

Jack swore as he dodged just in time. At the same time Steve slipped a headstall onto her and admonished her with a grin. 'If you weren't such a darn good racehorse and hadn't just had a nasty experience, Miss Daisy, that kind of behaviour would not be overlooked.'

Daisy harrumphed and stuck her nose lovingly into his armpit. Steve submitted to this treatment for a couple of minutes, then he handed her over to Bill, the hand, and gave her a thorough running-over with his hands.

'Doesn't appear to be any damage but just trot her up and down a couple of times.'

Bill led the filly out into the central passageway and obliged while Jack and Steve studied her action.

'I reckon she's fine,' Jack said, and they all burst out laughing as Daisy turned her head as she passed Chattie and tried to pinch the apple out of her hand.

But instead of getting a fright Chattie was enchanted, and asked if she could feed it to the horse.

'Bite off bits and just lay them in your palm,' Steve said.

She did so and felt Daisy's velvety muzzle tickling her hand. Moreover, once the apple was consumed, she petted the horse before finally turning to Steve and saying, 'I don't know why I haven't had anything to do with horses! I'd love to learn to ride.'

'Yes, well, they are big and they do kick and bite sometimes,' Steve said and looked at her thoughtfully for a long moment. Then, 'OK, Bill, you can put her out in the paddock.' They strolled outside.

'Tell me a bit more about her,' Chattie invited as they leant against the Range Rover in the early morning sunlight.

'Her racing name is Miss Daisy. She's three years old and she's already won half a million dollars.'

'Wow! But do you...you don't train her yourself, do you?'

'No, but we own her dam, she was born and reared here, and she comes back here between preparations to spell.'

'So you've known her since the day she was born? That explains it,' Chattie murmured.

He cocked an eyebrow at her.

'Why she trusts you so much—is what I mean.'

He shrugged. 'Possibly. There's also a key to handling bright, spirited, flighty young things of the female persuasion. You need to kid to them a bit, you need to get them to trust you and you need them to know that when you put your foot down, that's it.'

'Only of the female persuasion?' Chattie asked gravely, then laughed with delight as Miss Daisy was released into the paddock where she put on a very spirited bucking exhibition before settling down and approaching the feed bin Bill had hooked over the fence rail.

'Colts,' Steve said, 'often need more authority, less kidding to.'

'I'm glad you qualified that very sexist statement, otherwise I could have got quite the wrong impression of you!' But her eyes were still dancing.

'In amongst all the other wrong impressions you have of me?' he queried.

'I was joking.' She sobered completely, and sighed.

He folded his arms and leant back against the Range Rover. Unlike her he wore no jumper against the chill of the air although they both wore jeans. And, unlike her earlier sentiments on the subject of men in general and Steve Kinane in particular, she was once again on the roundabout.

She'd started out the day feeling nervous and beleaguered because of him. Then she'd been most impressed by his physical and mental skills with Miss

Daisy, but in between she'd been thoroughly annoyed with him—even slamming his car door.

Now, though, she had no idea where she stood. Respect, admiration, and enjoyment of his company—all those things were there. There was also a whole lot about him she didn't know, not to mention that mixture of danger and delight he could arouse in her.

'Chattie—' she looked up to meet his dark gaze, and as it roamed briefly up and down her figure she literally experienced one of those dangerous moments '—tell me a couple of things. What will you do when you go back to Brisbane?'

Surprise caused her eyes to widen. 'Go back to my college, of course.'

'Will that be easy? And enjoyable?'

She looked around, shielding her eyes from the sun as she did so. And once again it swooped on her like a bird falling through the sky onto its prey—that Mount Helena was becoming more fascinating to her with every passing day.

She'd come to love the wide open spaces. She stood on her veranda every morning feeling liberated as she looked around. Feeling adventurous and with her painter's eye glorying in the colours and the width, depth and height of the canvas before her.

She also felt as if she'd grown, not physically but internally, with the job she was doing, the challenges she was meeting. And, not that she wanted to look forward to a career of housekeeping, but the life she was living was much more satisfying than her previous existence of teaching in a city, she realized.

Hang on right there, she cautioned herself, and the bird of her imagination soared back skywards out of reach... I can't stay on here after Bridget's news gets out so why am I even contemplating it?

'Chattie?'

She cleared her throat, then replied with a shrug, 'I'm a working girl.'

'Will you stay on here until the end of your holidays? That's about another two weeks, by my estimation.'

'I...' She paused and started to colour beneath his assessing gaze. 'No.'

'Why not?'

'Well—' she spread her hands and tried to think coherently '—you're not quite so much in the lurch now. Surely you could get a replacement for Slim from a pastoral agency? I don't know how long it will take him to recuperate, but if it's longer than two weeks you'll have to anyway.'

'What about Mark?'

'What about him?' she said absently, because her thoughts couldn't have been further from Mark Kinane or Bridget for that matter.

'Isn't he your *raison d'être* for being here in the first place?' he asked with palpable irony. 'Or are you starting to forget all about my brother, Chattie?'

She closed her eyes. 'No.'

'You don't lie very well.'

She bit her lip.

'Last night,' he said, 'you—'

'Please don't,' she whispered.

'Just another attack of involuntary thoughtlessness?' he suggested dryly.

Her lashes fluttered up to see he was focused on her intently.

'Which leads me to wonder if that's why you're going to go—because you can't help yourself with me. But the thing is, I have the same problem, so you would imagine it would make us—square.'

'Steve...' she took a shaken breath '...I—'

'No, Chattie, enough of this,' he said roughly, and took her in his arms. 'I don't know what game the hell you're playing but, the fact is, I don't care. Because sparks flew between us almost from the moment we met and I won't rest until you're honest about it.'

He lowered his mouth to hers.

'You promised you wouldn't do this,' she protested.

'To all intents and purposes the house party is over—and as you pointed out yourself I'm no longer completely in the lurch,' he growled against her lips.

'But anybody could see us!'

'Let 'em,' he said contemptuously. 'I've spent all bloody night wondering about you and how you like to be made love to. And you, my dear, were the one who fell asleep at the dining room table then didn't want me to let you go.'

Tears of confusion, of frustration, beaded her lashes but she blinked them away. 'I'm sorry,' she said huskily. 'I just...I just don't know what to say any more.'

'Good. Don't say a thing, then. Unless you'd like to tell me how you do like it.'

But he didn't give her a chance. He kissed the one tear that had escaped, then claimed her mouth possessively and hungrily.

When they finally drew apart, Chattie felt as if she'd come as close to being made love to as was possible without it actually happening. Her lips were bruised but her body was alive and singing with the desire that was coursing through her veins. She felt alive and intoxicated with the feel and the taste of him. She felt as if she was on a new threshold, but once again, as if she belonged in his arms,

'Anything thoughtless about that?' he queried.

'No. It's…lovely,' she admitted raggedly.

'Are you wearing a colourful bra?' he asked, with his hands beneath her jumper.

For a moment she couldn't remember what bra she was wearing. 'Why?'

'The one I saw a couple of nights ago was like no other I've seen.'

'I make my own bras,' she murmured and shivered as his fingers found her nipples.

'Is there anything you can't do?' he queried with a smile in his eyes.

'Cope with thunderstorms.'

'Will you stay on now? I'll see if I can organize a thunder-free period for the next two weeks.'

He was massaging her nipples with his thumbs and it was sending quivering tendrils of sheer delight to the pit of her stomach, and an intimation of further delight she could only marvel at with a breathless little gasp.

'Chattie?' he said softly but insistently.

That was when they heard hurried footsteps crunching along the gravel path from the stables.

She froze and Steve removed his hands from her breasts, pulled her jumper down decorously but kept her in his arms as he turned his head to look over the bonnet of the Range Rover to see who it was.

It was Jack Barlow, coming to a sudden stop. 'Pardon me,' he said in some confusion. 'I didn't realize—that is to say I...didn't realize—'

'That's OK,' Steve said abruptly. 'Got a problem?'

Jack scratched his head as if he was still getting to grips with the scene he was witnessing, then he looked urgent. 'You could say so. A chopper's come down on the property—not ours. Some guys surveying who strayed off course and then suffered a mechanical failure. The pilot's broken his leg—'

Steve swore and released Chattie. 'Badly?' he queried tersely.

Jack nodded. 'Compound fracture, by the sound of it. We're going to have to organize a search-and-rescue mission pronto.'

'One of those days,' Steve said dryly and turned back to Chattie. Could—' he paused '—could I ask you to handle the breakup of the house party?'

'Of course. Is there anything else I can do?' she asked anxiously.

'No, but thanks. Just—don't do anything I wouldn't,' he said and kissed her hair. 'Promise?'

She swallowed. 'I promise.'

'That's my girl.'

The news of the helicopter crash saw the house party break up rather quickly. All able-bodied men were seconded to the search, although John Jackson flew his wife home first.

Chattie received a warm hug from Joan Jackson and another from Lucy Cook. Sasha Kelly merely murmured goodbye in a languid manner. Harriet was on hand to farewell the guests, and, slightly to Chattie's surprise, suggested they have a cup of coffee once everyone had left.

Then again, she thought, Harriet had been really helpful as well as friendly the previous evening, so why not?

'I must say—' Harriet poured two steaming mugs '—you were inspired last night, Chattie.'

'Thanks. And thanks for your help.'

'Actually—' Harriet eyed Chattie over her mug '—you're exactly what Steve needs.'

Chattie went still. 'What do you mean?' Then enlightenment dawned. 'Jack didn't waste any time, did he?'

'No, he didn't.' But Harriet looked entirely unembarrassed. 'However, there is one thing you should know. Steve's been a different person since his wife, Nadine, left him. It hardened him and made him, well, pretty cynical about marriage.'

So that was her name: Nadine.

'Harriet,' Chattie said carefully, 'why are you telling me this?'

'Two reasons, I guess. It might help you to understand when you run into that wall of cynicism, as you're bound to. And he's done an awful lot for me so I wouldn't like to see him get hurt again.'

Chattie stared into Harriet's blue eyes and saw genuine concern. She looked away. 'Harriet, we've only known each other for such a short time it's impossible to say what will happen.'

'According to Jack all things looked possible this morning! And I get the feeling the mild interest Steve may have had in Sasha Kelly has—' Harriet theatrically thumped her palm on the table '—died.'

Chattie blinked.

'He was quite cool towards her when she tried to be—how can I say it?—possessive, last night,' Harriet added.

'Really? I—'

'And I believe you had a little run-in with her yourself?'

'Yes. Yes, I did.'

'Well, then.' Harriet looked complacent. 'Don't tell me you don't like it out here? You've fitted in so damn well, it's amazing. That is something Nadine did not do.'

Chattie simply couldn't help herself. 'Why did they marry, then?'

Harriet raised her eyebrows expressively. 'You should have seen her.' She shrugged. 'To all intents and purposes they made a fantastic couple but the isolation got to her. Actually, I think what really got to her was the fact that Steve could afford to have a full-time manager so they could have lived anywhere, but he wouldn't even contemplate it. He loves this place and this lifestyle.'

Chattie finished her coffee and rose, prey to a whole series of conflicting emotions. What would happen at the end of two weeks if she stayed? She had no doubt they would not be able to resist each other for much longer…

She stared out over the paddocks. Even without the complication of Bridget, would there be a future for her with Steve? Or, did he have in mind an affair for only as long as their passion lasted? Which led directly on to, she thought, was Harriet right about the cynicism he'd been left with towards marriage?

How *could* she leave Bridget out of the equation, though? She sighed inwardly and turned back to Harriet.

'Would you have any idea where Mark is?'

Harriet looked surprised. 'None. Why?'

'I—just wondered. Do you—obviously you know his ex-fiancée?'

Harriet shook her head. 'Never met her, none of us did, although I believe her name was Bryony. It was very much a uni kind of crush, from what I could gather.'

'So you don't think he's…gone back to her?'

Harriet waved a hand. 'Haven't a clue. Why?'

'Oh, nothing. Well…' Chattie shrugged '…that's how I came to be here in the first place—because I'd met Mark.'

The other girl wrinkled her nose. 'Forget about Mark. He's got a whole lot of growing up to do. I would have thought,' she added with a frown, 'Steve had quite wiped Mark from your mind.'

'You would be quite right,' Chattie replied with a burst of somewhat bitter honesty at the same time as Merlene came out onto the veranda.

They both turned to her. 'You got a sister called Bridget, Chattie?'

'Yes! Why?' Chattie sat up urgently.

'She's on the blower.'

'Oh, excuse me, Harriet—'

'Don't mind me, I'm about to go home anyway. Just remember what I said!'

'Bridget, it's me,' Chattie said into the kitchen connection. 'Are you all right?' She listened for about half a minute with her mouth falling open, then said, *'What?'*

Two minutes later she put the phone down and dropped her head into her hands in disbelief.

'Everything OK?' Merlene enquired.

'No. Well. My sister is on her way here. She's hitched a lift with a friend of a friend who is flying his light plane up to Longreach.'

'Is that such a disaster?' Merlene asked curiously.

'You have no idea,' Chattie said slowly. 'They expect to be here about mid-afternoon. Apparently this guy has flown into Helena before. He…' she paused *'he's* a friend of Mark's and he has a courier-run contract.'

'Oh, that'd be Andrew Watson,' Merlene said blithely. 'He often drops in with urgent packages. I still don't see what the problem is. The more the merrier!' she added jovially.

Chattie closed her eyes. 'I just hope he has plenty of airsick bags.'

CHAPTER EIGHT

OF COURSE it couldn't have happened any other way, Chattie marvelled bitterly.

Steve came back after the search-and-rescue operation had been successfully concluded and pulled the Range Rover up at the garden fence at the same time as Andrew Watson touched his smart little plane down on the airstrip.

Chattie had been alerted to its arrival when he'd buzzed the homestead and was waiting beside the strip.

Steve walked over to her with a frown as he observed the Watson Courier logo as the plane turned and taxied back.

'I'm not expecting anything,' he said. 'Something I don't know about?'

She took a deep breath. 'Yes. But I can explain.'

He looked down into her grey eyes and his frown grew. 'Like what?'

Chattie made a mental note to preserve how she and Steve Kinane had been in each other's arms that morning, to capture it and store it in her heart, because she was deadly afraid she might never be so close to him again.

'My sister,' she said.

'Your...' He paused as the plane stopped, the door opened, the steps lowered and Andrew Watson, who was a burly young man in his mid-twenties, got out.

Then he turned back to hand someone down and Bridget appeared, looking a wreck. She was pale, her dark hair was mussed and her clothes crumpled and entirely inappropriate—a filmy see-through skirt and a halter-neck top. She was also not too steady on her feet.

'That's your sister?' Steve said incredulously.

Chattie didn't answer. She went up to Bridget and put her arms around her. 'Bridge, you shouldn't have! Are you all right?'

'She's been a bit sick,' Andrew said. 'She's been very sick,' he amended with a rueful glance at Steve over his shoulder, 'but I guess that's normal. Took my wife the same way.'

Chattie blinked at him. 'You know?'

Bridget raised her head. 'I told him.' She cleared her throat. 'He needed to know why I have to find Mark. And,' she said, with tears falling down her cheeks, 'I don't care who knows now because I love Mark deeply, I'm having his baby and that's that.'

Steve Kinane froze.

'So all is explained,' he said.

Chattie swallowed nervously. It was an hour or so later. Bridget had been restored with a light snack and was fast asleep in Chattie's room. Seeing how exhausted she was, Chattie hadn't pressed for more of an explanation than the one Bridget had repeated several times—it had just come to her that she couldn't sit around twiddling her thumbs any longer, that she wasn't ashamed of being pregnant or of loving Mark Kinane.

Steve had been completely inscrutable on being introduced, but not unkind. He'd welcomed Bridget to Mount Helena and suggested that she have a rest before they discussed anything.

He'd then taken Andrew aside, leaving Chattie to shepherd her sister inside. A few minutes later, the plane had taken off and Chattie had heard Steve drive away.

Fortunately, Merlene had been down at the bunkhouse so no explanations for the state of her sister had had to be made immediately.

Then Steve had come home and Chattie had girded her loins, and gone to find him.

He'd been in the lounge, pouring a drink, and he'd accorded her another inscrutable glance but opened a bottle of wine.

It was as he'd handed her the glass that he'd made his comment about all being explained.

She took the glass he handed her and sat down because her legs felt like jelly.

'You don't know how many times I was on the verge of telling you,' she said, 'but you—' She gestured helplessly.

He sat down opposite, his eyes hard and cool. 'So it's my fault—is that what you're saying?'

She took a fortifying sip. 'No. Well, you made your sentiments so plain about your brother being trapped into marriage I—look, may I start at the beginning?'

'Be my guest,' he said dryly.

She put her glass down and twined her fingers. Ten minutes later she'd told him everything. How Bridget had depended on her since they'd been orphaned, how Bridget and Mark had met, the course of their affair and why, since Bridget was not only pregnant but the person she was anyway, she, Chattie, had decided to track Mark down for her.

'I see.' Steve swirled his drink. 'And what do you think Mark's reaction to this news will be?'

'I...I have no idea. But whatever happens for them, this baby deserves his support, and deserves, at least, to know who its father is.'

'Can we be quite sure Mark is the father?'

Chattie looked directly into his eyes with a fighting little glint in hers. 'I have no doubt whatsoever.'

'It's no good getting angry with me, Chattie,' he advised.

She stood up and paced across the room restlessly. 'Then don't say things like that.'

'I—or Mark, anyway—has every right to be sure this is his child. Incidentally, did you not try to talk any sense into your sister?' he queried.

'I tried my level best,' she replied grimly. Then she sighed. 'If you ever get to know Bridget any better you'll...well, she's not very wise at times. That doesn't mean to say she isn't warm, loyal and wonderful.'

'All of which Mark managed to walk away from with little difficulty, apparently,' he said with considerable irony.

'Bridget blames you for that.' Chattie bit her lip. 'Look, I don't know one way or the other—'

'You don't know?' he shot at her savagely.

Chattie gestured defensively. 'I have come to wonder about it,' she said, 'but the fact of the matter is, Bridget is convinced—from what Mark told her, obviously—that he has an inferiority complex, that he's all mixed-up and that he had to break up with her because you ordered him home.'

'How convenient,' he said scathingly.

'You mean for Mark?' she asked uncertainly.

'I mean for Mark,' he agreed. 'Sit down, Chattie,' he ordered. 'I'm getting a stiff neck watching you pace around.'

She took a breath and was on the verge of telling him to go to hell but changed her mind.

'All right.' He finished his drink. 'Since I'm the villain of the piece, let me tell you this. My mother tried for years to have another child after I was born. She didn't succeed until ten years later and after several miscarriages and two live births, but she lost both of them. I think she'd almost given up hope. Then Mark came along and she doted on him and was extremely protective. Not only that, she was very artistic and he seemed to inherit it.

'My father,' he said, 'resented the way she pampered him, which made for an uncomfortable upbringing for Mark and therein do lie the seeds of his restlessness. Nevertheless, I have never,' he said with emphasis, 'tried to make a cattleman out of Mark. Yes, when I need help, I have no conscience about roping him in and, to be honest, I don't think it does him any harm to be reminded where his bread comes from. But I will be only too happy for Mark to find his place in life, whatever it is.'

Chattie looked troubled.

'It could be we're in the same boat with our siblings,' Steve said after a moment.

She had to agree.

'And, contrary to what you may have decided,

Mark's happiness does matter to me.' He engaged her gaze deliberately and added, 'What I can't understand—OK, I may have contributed at the start—but how could you have deceived me for so long, Chattie?'

She stared into his dark eyes and shivered because she couldn't doubt he was deeply angry.

'My first concern had to be my sister,' she said quietly. 'I wasn't to know what kind of power you wielded over Mark or what lengths you'd go to protect him from this.'

'Do you think he's ready for marriage and children?' he fired at her.

Chattie looked helpless. 'I don't know. I mean, I liked him but, to be honest, I think they're two of a kind. Impetuous, immature—'

'Did you think he was as deeply in love with Bridget as she feels she is with him?'

'He certainly appeared to be, although...' She paused.

'Go on.'

'You haven't seen her at her best,' Chattie said. 'She is—gorgeous.'

Steve sat back. 'That goes without saying. What does she do? Anything?'

Chattie swallowed her ire. 'She's training to be a model.'

He lifted an eyebrow. 'I might have known. So the practical, down-to-earth genes bypassed her?'

'She is only nineteen,' Chattie said defensively. 'Look, this has happened. Aren't we better off working out what's best to be done rather than indulging in an orgy of recriminations? Believe me, it's no more my fault than it is yours!'

'So what are you expecting? That I drag Mark to the altar for you?'

'No,' Chattie cried exasperatedly, 'not if he has to be dragged! But some help, some support for Mark's child, some recognition.'

'In the form of dollars and cents?'

Chattie had picked up her glass but she put it down with a snap and went white. 'I can't believe you said that!'

'No? That's strange,' he drawled. 'You believe a lot of other things about me. You obviously cherish the suspicion that I'm some kind of monster, not to be trusted, not to be dealt with in honesty—no wonder you had such a battle with yourself when it came to being intimate with me.'

She went from white to pink beneath his intimately assessing gaze that stripped away her clothes and dwelt, reminiscently, on her breasts.

Nor was it a charge she could deny. 'Bridget is the only family I have,' she said wearily, then frowned. 'All right, I know this has come as a shock to you. When I found out I was—distraught. But if Mark and Bridget don't get together, by far the largest part of this burden will always be on her.'

'If they don't get together, the only real support we'll be able to give her is monetary,' he pointed out and stopped rather abruptly.

'What?' Chattie whispered, because of the way he was looking at her. As if he was honed in on her and her alone but in a curiously predatory manner.

'There is another way,' he said at last.

She blinked at him.

'You could marry me, Chattie Winslow.'

She gasped and for a moment the room spun round.

'What's so astonishing about that?' he asked with irony. 'We can barely keep our hands off each other.'

'You...I...'

'You've fitted in as if you were made for the place—in fact there've been times, Chattie, when I've seen you walk around this house as if you own it, as if you *are* the lady of the house.'

'I haven't,' she denied huskily and looked appalled.

He smiled twistedly. 'Believe me, you have. And it's not only the house—I get the feeling the whole of Helena appeals to you very much.'

She knitted her fingers, then unknitted them. 'I...I...it does, but that's no reason to...to marry you.'

'How about this, then?' he said sardonically. 'Since it weighs so heavily with you, it would secure your sister's future.'

She could only stare at him open-mouthed.

'Tell me this...' he paused and watched her narrowly '...are we in agreement that forcing them to marry, Bridget and Mark, unless it's what they *both* want, is not the solution?'

She cleared her throat. 'Yes, but—'

'If you married me, Chattie, Bridget and her child would always have a home at Mount Helena, the child would be recognized as Mark's and she would be treated as part of the family.'

'It should be recognized as Mark's anyway,' she protested.

He shrugged. 'Naturally. But if Mark doesn't come

to the party, it's not going to be of much benefit to Bridget unless you're here at Mount Helena.'

'But, say Mark doesn't come to the party, how awkward will it be to have Bridget and his child living here?'

'They'll have to handle it as best they can but in point of fact I don't see Mark ever settling down here. And contrary to your view of me...' he paused and eyed her insolently '...I would never have consented to a Kinane simply being abandoned.'

Chattie flinched. 'I...I still...would need to think about this.'

'What's to think about?' He searched her eyes. 'This morning—was quite a revelation I would have thought.'

'What do you mean?'

He looked mocking. 'You know what I mean, Chattie. You admitted you wanted me as much as I want you. Has that changed over the last few hours?'

'This morning,' she said with an effort, 'we were discussing the next two weeks.'

He shrugged. 'Your sister is the one who's pushed us up a few gears.'

'Steve,' she said, and shivered suddenly, 'how can you want to marry me when you're...angry with me at the same time?'

His gaze clashed with hers. 'I'm sure that will pass.' He smiled but not with his eyes. 'I could even tell you what would make it pass rather—delightfully. But as a business proposition it would be entirely beneficial for both of us as well as Bridget, don't you think?'

The look in her grey eyes said it all—disbelief and growing anger plus something he couldn't quite identify. Hurt, perhaps? he wondered, but even if it was it didn't appear to have the power to deflect him from the course he was on. A course apparently becoming more and more set in concrete in his mind since he'd discovered how he'd been duped.

'It's not often one gets the opportunity to mix business with pleasure the way we could, Chattie,' he added musingly.

That did it. The explosion he was waiting for—had even hoped to provoke?—came.

She sprang up with her fists clenched and opened her mouth.

'Let me guess,' he murmured and got up himself. 'I'd be the last man on the planet you'd marry? You'd rather consort with a snake?'

Chattie closed her mouth, almost biting her tongue as he took the words out of her mouth.

'Don't you think you're kidding yourself?' he added softly but lethally as he came to stand right in front of her.

She took a distraught breath. 'No.'

'Well, I do.' He reached for her. 'This morning you told me it was rather lovely, to be in my arms. What can have changed?'

'You've changed,' she said bitterly.

'In some essentials, not at all,' he assured her dryly. 'For instance—' he drew her closer '—all the while I was rescuing the guys who came down in their chopper, I was thinking of this.'

Chattie's eyes widened in disbelief.

'I know.' He looked momentarily wry. 'To have images of undressing you slowly and finding out what bra you're wearing today mixed in with the coordination of a search and rescue came as a bit of a surprise to me too. What have *you* been thinking about in the interim?'

Chattie closed her eyes. You, your wife, what you had in mind for us—until Bridget wiped it all out, she thought.

'Chattie?'

She couldn't speak as all the old magic began to course through her as his breath fanned her cheek and his hands moved slowly on her. She opened her eyes to see that he was looking down at her through half-closed lids in a way that left no doubt he desired her even, perhaps, in anger.

And she was mesmerized by that dark, intimate gaze to the extent of picturing him undressing her slowly—and the pleasure it would bring her. It was, in fact, almost as if it were happening so that her nipples peaked and she grew warm with her own desire. She dropped her face onto his shoulder with a husky little sound, a mixture of yearning and frustration.

How could it happen, though? How could this powerful physical force still exist between them when they were in more mental discord than they'd ever been?

Then his mouth met hers, and, if she knew anything, it was that 'how?' or 'why?' didn't come into it—it was simply happening.

What broke them apart was a strangled gasp coming from the doorway. And the voicer of that gasp was Bridget. Who then tottered into the room to sink into a chair saying, 'If this is what it looks to be, it's the best news I've had for weeks.'

Steve didn't release Chattie but he said to Bridget, 'So you don't mind me proposing to your sister?'

'Proposing!' Bridget's beautiful violet eyes rimmed by thick, dark, completely natural lashes almost fell out on stalks. 'Oh, my stars! No, of course I don't. I was beginning to think Chattie was so darn choosey she might never—' She broke off but began again immediately. 'And then there's the way she's always lectured me about rushing into things but—no! If it's what she wants, of course I don't!'

Steve looked down into Chattie's stunned eyes. 'How say you, Miss Winslow, the elder?'

If anyone had ever been saved by the bell, Chattie was to think later, she was at that critical moment, although the irony of it was that the outcome was to be the same…

At the time, however, her bell came in the form of a visitor who strode up the front steps, calling, 'Anyone home?'

This time Steve did let Chattie go. 'In the lounge, Ryan,' he called back with resignation.

The sound of boots being discarded came, then socked, though heavy footfalls padded down the hall and a large young man strolled into the lounge. 'Good day, mate! Come to meet the housekeeper from heaven,' he announced. 'Holy smoke! You sly dog, Steve, me boy,' he added as his eyes fell on Chattie and he came to a stop. 'Thought the old man was exaggerating but for once in his life he was spot on!'

Steve said irritably, 'This is Ryan Winters, Chattie. You met his mother and father last night.'

Ryan stuck his hand out to Chattie. 'It's a pleasure to meet you, ma'am, a real pleasure.' They shook hands, then Ryan noticed Bridget.

It was a different Bridget from the one who had

climbed off the plane. She'd changed into jeans, a figure-hugging cyclamen jumper, her hair was tidy, and
although she wore no make-up she looked exquisite.

So it came as no surprise to Chattie to see the shire
chairman's son do a double take rather as his father
had done.

He said, 'Bloody hell, Steve, no one told me you
had a harem of housekeepers from heaven!'

'I don't,' Steve replied abruptly. 'Bridget is
Chattie's sister. What can I do for you, Ryan? You
surely didn't drive all this way just to check out my
housekeeper?'

'It was an incentive, I cannot deny,' Ryan said ge-
nially, 'but the main thrust of my visit is that piece of
spraying equipment you promised to lend Dad last
night.'

Steve grimaced. 'Have you ever used one of them
before?'

'Nope. Thought that was the object of the exercise—if we find it practical and easy to use, we'll invest in one of our own. You got a minute to give me
a demo?'

'Yes, he has.' Chattie found her voice at last. 'Dinner won't be ready for an hour.' She glanced at her
watch and looked surprised. 'At least an hour,' she
added. 'So I'll have to get cracking. Bridget, you can
come and give me a hand. Nice to meet you, Ryan!'
And ignoring Steve's mockery-laden gaze, she
swished out of the room.

Bridget followed her into the kitchen looking confused.

'You don't really have to help,' Chattie said. 'I want to talk to you. Like a cuppa?'

'Thanks, yes, but I don't mind helping. Chattie, what is going on?'

Chattie boiled the kettle and, while she waited for it, got some peas for Bridget to shell. 'Sit down,' she advised. 'You can do them at the table. And just let me do this…' She put some wood into the stove, made the tea and took a cup to Bridget. 'And this…'

Several trips to the cold room and dry goods store yielded the ingredients for her dinner—a rack of lamb, a container of frozen soup, flour, sugar and butter to make an apple pie.

Bridget watched her narrowly as she sipped her tea, then she started to shell peas with a thoughtful frown, as if mentally viewing her sister through quite new eyes.

But Chattie, as she worked on the rack of lamb, inserting cloves of garlic and adding sprigs of rosemary, felt herself soothed and capable of starting to think straight for the first time for what seemed like hours. She put the lamb in the oven, the soup in a saucepan and got the rolling-pin and a pastry board.

'So he's not so bad, Mark's brother?' Bridget said tentatively.

'He—no.'

'Have you really fallen in love with him?'

Chattie measured flour and butter into a bowl and started to rub the butter into the flour. 'We—do seem to have clicked,' she said cautiously, 'but it's all so new and unexpected…' She gestured with floury fingers.

Bridget smiled faintly. 'You've been swept off your feet?' she suggested.

Chattie looked rueful. 'If you mean it's a reverse case of the pot calling the kettle black, perhaps. Bridge—' her busy fingers stilled and she looked across at her sister '—everyone here seems to think that Mark has gone back to his ex-fiancée, who lives in Broome of all places.'

'That's only because he doesn't know,' Bridget replied intensely.

'Honey,' Chattie sighed, 'I hate to be the one to say this, but I think we have to take into account the possibility that Mark won't be best pleased with your news. And we have to think of an alternative for you.'

'What do you mean?' Bridget asked, her eyes filling with tears.

'I mean we can't force Mark to marry you although Steve has indicated that they would provide some support and Mark would be recognized as the baby's father.'

A look of terror came to Bridget's eyes. 'But I don't want to do this on my own, Chattie!'

'You'll never have to do that. I'll always be there—'

'But I won't be able to work and you can't stop working—what kind of support?'

'Monetary,' Chattie said.

Bridget shivered. 'That sounds so cold and—'

'It's better than nothing,' Chattie pointed out.

Bridget laid her head on the table and started to weep.

Chattie went to the sink and washed her hands, then came back and put her arm around Bridget's shoulders. 'Please don't,' she said quietly and looked across the kitchen with unseeing eyes for a long moment. Then, much as Steve had said to her earlier, she said, 'There is another way.'

'What's that?' Bridget hiccupped.

Chattie drew out a chair and sat down. 'The one reason that would stop me from marrying Steve is you,' she said carefully.

Bridget sat up and licked some tears from her lip. *'Why?'*

'Well, it would be the perfect solution in most respects. Steve has said you and the baby could have a proper home here whatever happens with Mark. We'd be together, you and I. But, much as this place appeals to me—'

'I thought it must have,' Bridget broke in breathlessly. 'The last time you rang I got the feeling you were loving every minute of it. That's another reason I decided to come up.'

'Yes. Well. The downside, though, is how much it would appeal to *you*. It is isolated—'

'Chattie,' Bridget said tragically, 'ever since I found out I was pregnant I've felt as if I'm in…Siberia. Nothing could be as isolated as that feeling.'

Chattie's eyes filled with compassion but she knew she had to soldier on. 'The other thing is, if Mark doesn't want to marry you—' She held up a hand. 'I know, you don't even want to contemplate that, but we *have* to. If he doesn't—how hard will it be for you to live here?'

Bridget put her hands on her stomach and said nothing for almost a minute, but several expressions chased through her eyes. Then she drew a deep breath. 'Even if he doesn't want it, to know his baby has a home and at least some part of its heritage would be such a load off my mind. Oh, it would be hard, I guess, but I would do it for my baby.'

CHAPTER NINE

IN THE event, Chattie had to stretch her dinner because the Cooks popped in on their way past just as Steve came back from demonstrating the spray equipment.

She'd already experienced the hospitality the outback was famous for—although it obviously didn't extend to Ryan Winters and she wondered why—but it came as no surprise to hear Steve invite them to stay for dinner. No surprise, but quite some relief.

Mind you, she pointed out to herself, it's only delaying the evil moment.

But at least it provided some relief and normality from the tension, however temporary.

Bridget was introduced and Lucy Cook was delighted to meet Chattie's sister—it turned out that Lucy was an avid follower of fashion and dying to hear of all the latest trends.

It also, Chattie realised rather darkly, gave Bridget the opportunity to sum up Steve discreetly and be impressed as the meal progressed leisurely, companionably and with lots of laughter as Ray and Steve traded stories about the fixes cattle could get themselves into.

In fact she could see her sister relaxing visibly beneath the civilized aura of the evening—was she deciding that Mount Helena was not quite as isolated as she'd suspected and might even be a more enjoyable place to live than she'd thought? Chattie wondered.

But like all good things it came to an end. Bridget

helped her to clear up, then yawned hugely, so Chattie sent her to bed in the guest room next door to her own bedroom.

She was giving Rich a last walk in the garden when Steve found her. Rich had taken his time about bestowing his approval on Steve Kinane but he now walked up to him for a pat, wagging his tail, causing Chattie to wonder if it was some kind of an omen.

It was a crisp, clear night with a pale sliver of new moon, but the stars were huge and a lemon ironbark bush was scenting the dewy air.

'Quite a night,' he said.

'It's lovely,' Chattie replied, but pulled her jumper more closely around her.

'Quite a day, come to that. Do you often get these premonitions?'

She grimaced. 'No. Thank heavens.'

'Are we—talking to each other or not?'

She glanced at him. He'd leant his shoulders against the trunk of the ironbark, shoved his hands in his pockets and was regarding her thoughtfully. Throughout dinner he'd been perfectly normal towards her except for a couple of occasions when she'd discovered his dark eyes resting on her enigmatically.

'Steve…' she hesitated '…when did you plan to tell me about your ex-wife?'

'Right now, as a matter of fact—I had no doubt you'd already heard of her. I happened to overhear Merlene about to embark on that bit of gossip a couple of nights ago.'

Chattie frowned and remembered when she was making egg and caviare canapés. 'So that's why you were in a bad mood! I did wonder.'

'One of the reasons.'

'But—'

'Chattie, there is only one version of it you need to hear and that's mine,' he interrupted. 'As a matter of interest, who else has taken it upon themselves to enlighten you about Nadine?'

Chattie absolved Merlene, explained about Joan Jackson finding her in the music room and finding the wedding photo, but at the last moment decided to hold her peace about Harriet's two-bit worth. She finished by saying, 'I believe she was not suited to this kind of life.'

'No. She wasn't.'

'I can't help wondering if it's left you rather battle-scarred,' she said slowly.

'In what way?' He raised an eyebrow at her.

'Well, blackmailing me into a marriage of convenience could be a symptom of it, for example.'

'It wouldn't only be that, as you very well know.' She shivered.

'Nor am I still in love with Nadine, I got over it years ago and she's remarried but, yes,' he said, 'I did swear that if I ever married again, I'd be a whole lot more practical about it. I would have thought that might appeal to you because you're such a practical person yourself.' He raised an eyebrow at her.

How to tell a man you were harbouring a secret little hope that he would fall madly, passionately and quite impractically in love with you? Chattie wondered, but couldn't find the answer so she said nothing.

'Besides which,' he went on after a long moment, 'I'm tired of being a bachelor. I'd like to have my own kids rather than using Brett as a surrogate son.

I'd like to have someone to make plans with, someone whose company I enjoy and who enjoys this place, someone who'll keep me from becoming a dried-up, boring old cattle-man. You.'

Chattie felt her heart move in her breast because he'd spoken quietly but she got the feeling he meant every word and she couldn't help being curiously moved.

'And that's all without what we do to each other physically.' He straightened and she tensed but he made no move towards her. 'Would it be so inconceivable?' he asked.

Not at all, if I didn't suspect you're still angry with me, might never fully trust me or—could just say three little words—I love you, it ran through her mind.

Her next thought was that if it was so important for her to hear those three words, could she any longer doubt that she'd fallen in love with him?

'Steve—' She broke off.

He surprised her. 'Sleep on it,' he said, and this time he did move towards her, but only to take her face in his hands and add barely audibly, 'I think you'd make a wonderful wife, Chattie Winslow.'

He released her after a long, shared and searching glance, and walked away.

They were alone at breakfast the next morning.

'Morning—how is Bridget?' were his first words to her as he sat down to bacon and eggs.

'Dead to the world so I'll let her sleep in,' Chattie replied.

He studied her in a pair of caramel cord trousers and a pink crinkly cotton blouse with a drawstring neckline as she brought the toast. For some reason her hair was severely tamed into a tight-looking knot and there were faint blue shadows beneath her eyes as if she hadn't slept too well.

He waited for her to sit down before he said simply, 'So?'

Chattie reached for the butter. 'Thank you, the answer is yes.'

Their gazes clashed and for a moment Chattie was convinced she was right about something that had popped into her head during a long and difficult night. That this was some kind of a test, this proposal of marriage from Steve Kinane, a test she would fail if she agreed to marry him...

He went to say something but appeared to change his mind and said instead as he got up, 'Stay there.' And left the kitchen.

When he came back he had a small, old, leather-bound box in his hand. He flicked it open and put it beside her plate.

Chattie's eyes widened—it was an engagement ring. Obviously not new, it was nevertheless quite lovely, an oval ruby surrounded by tiny diamonds to make a flower shape and set on a gold band.

'But...whose...what...?' She looked up bewilderedly.

'It was my mother's.'

'Didn't...I mean your first wife, didn't she—?'

'No. My mother was still alive then,' he said, and, putting his hand over hers, drew her to her feet. 'This may not be the most romantic setting,' he added as he took the ring from the box and slid it on her finger, 'but my mother would have approved of you very much.'

It was all so unexpected, Chattie raised her grey eyes to his and they were deeply bewildered.

How had he managed to bridge the chasm that existed between them? A chasm caused by her deceiving him over Bridget and resulting in this proposal being made in the form of blackmail. Or rather, she thought, why was he doing it this way now? Had the cynicism he'd displayed yesterday dried up or was she being lured into a false sense of security?

'It's normal to kiss the bride-to-be in this situation,' he said softly and traced the outline of her mouth. 'Would it be permissible?'

She swallowed.

'Do you like the ring?'

'It's lovely.' She looked down at it on her finger. 'Uh—thank you.'

'My pleasure.' He enfolded the slim length of her against him. 'Mmm…you smell nice.'

She looked surprised. 'Must be my shampoo, I haven't used any perfume.'

'Might just be the essential you but, talking of shampoo, what have you done to your poor hair this morning?'

'I decided to look practical.'

Their gazes caught and his eyes told her he'd registered her attempt at a shot against him, but he was too clever for her. He countered it by fiddling with the bobbles restraining her hair until he got it free in all its fair, curly splendour.

'There, that's how I like it,' he murmured. 'Wayward and gorgeous, like the rest of you. In fact so much so I can no longer restrain myself from doing this.'

He put his arms around her again and lowered his mouth to hers.

Chattie thought of resisting but he foiled that too as his hands moved on her body to cup her breasts and trace the outline of her hips, then slide along the satiny skin of her upper arms—and she was lost.

Her nipples started to direct a stream of sensuous traffic throughout her slim figure, not only beneath the feel of his hands on her, but also the hard, warm feel of his body against hers. All sorts of secret areas of her body clamoured for his attentions and her breathing grew ragged as she felt herself budding and flowering like a thirsty garden crying out to be nurtured by Steve Kinane and Steve Kinane alone.

Then he untied the drawstring of her blouse and pulled it apart to reveal a hyacinth-blue bra trimmed with white and green flowers.

'It gets better and better,' he said against the corner of her mouth, and started to kiss the soft hollows at the base of her throat.

Chattie felt herself melting against him and she made a husky little sound of sheer need.

'Mmm, I'm rather a fan of it myself.' He pushed the shoulders of her blouse further down, then cupped her hips to him as he kissed, tasted and literally set her on fire as his mouth moved down towards her breasts.

From somewhere it came to Chattie that they were on a course they wouldn't be able to deflect themselves from very soon, unless she made a supreme effort.

'Maybe you shouldn't go there,' she whispered.

He raised his head and there was a wicked little glint in his eyes. 'No?'

'No. They seem to have a mind of their own as it is, but with your encouragement...' She trailed off.

'I like the sound of that.'

'All the same, perhaps this isn't the time or the place.'

'There are six bedrooms in this house,' he reminded her.

'I meant,' she said, barely audibly because it was difficult enough to talk, let alone going to be incredibly difficult to disengage from Steve Kinane now, 'I think we should wait until we're married.'

Surprise, or something, held him silent for a beat. Until he said. 'The sooner the better, then.'

And Merlene's motor bike made itself heard approaching.

He grimaced. 'Saved by the bell maybe. Because I get the feeling wherever we "go" in this manner could be problematic for us now.'

She licked her lips and tried to calm her breathing as well as all the lovely sensations running through her while he tied up her blouse. Then she realized he was watching her intently and expecting some kind of a response, some confirmation that they were in this together and there was no way—much as some instinct told her she might regret it—she could deny him that confirmation.

'Yes.'

Something flickered in his eyes and he took her hand and turned her towards the back door as Merlene strode in.

'Morning, boss! Morning, Chattie! Just went down to get the milk. Tell you what, it's a pleasure to have the place to ourselves, well, more...or...less,' Merlene wound down with a frown as she took in the picture Steve and Chattie made, only to demand then, 'Is this what I think it is?'

'Depends,' Steve replied. 'We're getting married.'

'I knew that!'

'How?' Chattie asked incredulously.

'What I mean to say is,' Merlene amended herself, 'I knew he'd do things by the book. Well, well, well! I don't think I could have done better for you if I'd chosen her myself.'

'Thank you,' Steve said gravely.

'OK! When? And where?'

'Here, of course—' He stopped. 'Actually, we haven't discussed that yet, Merlene.' He looked humorous.

'If the things I've been hearing are true,' Merlene said, 'the sooner you do, the better.'

Chattie blushed, Steve looked briefly irritated, then shrugged. 'The bush telegraph at its worst.'

'You shouldn't go around kissing her in public, then,' Merlene retorted, but came up to Chattie and shook her hand. 'You done good, kid. I have to tell you even Slim would approve and there's a hard man to please.'

Steve had to leave shortly after that but he promised he'd be back for lunch and had the afternoon free so they could make some plans.

'One thing,' he said just before he departed. 'What does Bridget know about all this?'

'She has no idea I'm—' She stopped abruptly as she wondered how to phrase it. Doing it all for her—was what she'd been about to say. But even if she was being pressured into marrying Steve, was that completely true?

'Chattie?'

She looked up at him at last. 'She doesn't know what precipitated it,' she said carefully.

'I see. Doesn't know that you're going to be a martyr on her behalf?' he suggested softly.

She stared into his dark eyes. 'I didn't say that.'

'No. But something's bothering you,' he countered. 'How many times do I have to kiss you and hold you to get you to believe—?'

'Don't say any more, Steve,' she advised. 'You've made that point and I accept it. I can't help feeling a little shell-shocked, though.' She gestured helplessly. 'We've only known each other for little more than a week.'

'Interesting you should make that point. Nadine and I knew each other for nine months before we got married.'

Chattie blinked. 'That long? So why…?'

'Why didn't it last?' he drawled. 'We didn't have enough in common. Why don't you reflect on that until I get back?' He turned to go but turned back. 'And this.' He pulled her into his arms and kissed her until she was breathless. Then he left without another word.

'So you're going to do it?'

Chattie had brought a breakfast tray for Bridget and her sister was sitting propped up in bed with the tray on her knees. She had immediately noticed the engagement ring on Chattie's left hand.

'Yes.' Chattie sat down in an armchair with the coffee she'd brought for herself, and added honestly, 'I don't know if I'm on my head or my heels.'

'That's just how I felt with Mark,' Bridget said reminiscently and began to look tearful, but she battled it resolutely and started to eat her boiled egg. 'Isn't it funny, though,' she said, 'that the two people I love most should have such differing views of Steve Kinane?'

Do we? Chattie wondered. I'm not so sure…

'Steve explained about the problems he and Mark have, Bridge,' she said, however. And she went on to tell Bridget what Steve had said.

'I guess that makes sense.' Bridget pushed her egg away and reached for her coffee. 'You know what he'd really like to do?'

'Mark? Something artistic?' Chattie hazarded.

Bridget shook her head. 'Apparently he's very good with horses.'

Chattie grimaced. 'Must run in the family, so is Steve. Go on.'

'Well, he'd love to be a racehorse trainer.'

'Why doesn't he?' Chattie asked slowly.

'I think it only came to him recently that the artistic side he inherited from his mother wasn't strong enough for any career in it. And, from what you've told me, I can't help wondering if he felt he would be letting his mother down somehow if he didn't go that way.'

'Perhaps,' Chattie conceded.

'It would be enough to make you a bit mixed-up, wouldn't it?' Bridget said.

'Yes.' Chattie drained her coffee.

'Still and all...' Bridget stretched '...that's enough of Mark. I've got to stop thinking about it, somehow. I will,' she assured Chattie.

Chattie got up. 'Have a shower and get dressed and I'll show you around a bit more.' But as she left the room she couldn't help wondering if Bridget might be growing up at last, and quite fast.

Steve didn't make it for lunch—Bill delivered the message to the homestead, adding that Chattie's presence was required at the bunkhouse at two o'clock.

'What for?' Chattie asked him.

He shrugged. 'Search me, I'm only the messenger. But the boss said wear jeans and boots if you've got any.'

Chattie frowned. 'A cross-country hike?'

'Dunno.'

At two o'clock Chattie and Bridget presented themselves at the bunkhouse, to find Harriet in attendance.

'You must be Chattie's sister,' Harriet said and shook Bridget's hand. 'I'm Mark and Steve's cousin—which will make me your baby's second cousin or something like that.'

Chattie took an unexpected breath, not sure whether to be angry or relieved that the news had been broken so summarily.

But Harriet turned to her with an engaging grin. 'And I guess we'll be cousins-in-law. Congratulations! Just don't forget what I told you,' she added in an undertone. 'OK, Steve's got plans for you and I've got plans for Bridget.'

Chattie opened her mouth but Steve came round the corner of the bunkhouse leading two saddled horses.

Half an hour later, Chattie was mounted on one of the horses, alongside Steve mounted on the other and connected by a leading rein. Bridget and Harriet had stayed to witness the initiation lesson Chattie had received—with some hilarity—then Harriet had shepherded Bridget towards her Range Rover.

'I don't know,' Chattie started to say anxiously.

'It'll be all right,' Steve assured her quietly. 'Harriet has pledged to be on her best behaviour. She's taking her home with her for coffee and a chat, that's all. Harriet's as bad as Lucy Cook when it comes to fashion and I thought the sooner we get all the awkwardness out of the way, the better it will be for Bridget.'

'Harriet can be staggeringly undiplomatic, though,' Chattie pointed out.

'Harriet will do exactly as I told her.' He folded his arms and regarded her gravely. 'Did you not once tell me, only yesterday as it happens, that you would love to ride a horse?'

'Well, yes, but—'

'Good. She's yours.' He indicated the chestnut one of the two horses.

Chattie's mouth fell open.

'She's a four-year-old mare, a stock horse with a lovely nature, and I'd already decided to turn her into a hack. Shall we give it a try?'

As a recipe for having the wind taken completely out of one's sails, being given your own horse and then to receive a riding lesson on it was unparalleled Chattie discovered.

Hard as she tried to bear in mind Steve's autocratic ways, she couldn't hold onto her resentment. Nor could she stifle the thought that he was right, the sooner the awkwardness of it all was banished, the better for, not only Bridget, but also all concerned. Finally, the pleasure in what she was doing took over completely.

'You could be a natural,' he told her as she gained the confidence to break into a slow canter. 'Don't forget the angle to have your feet in the stirrups—heels down, toes up.'

'Why is that?'

'Should you ever have to get off in hurry, you can just slip your feet out. Shall we have a bit of a break?' He indicated a patch of gum-trees beside a dam.

She nodded, and when they dismounted they gave the horses a drink and he showed her how to tie them to trees on a long rein so they could crop the grass.

'What's her name?' she asked as she stroked the mare's nose.

'Would you believe Cathy Freeman?'

Chattie looked amused. 'That's an odd name for a stock horse!'

'I know, but Bill names all the stock horse foals and he uses sportsmen and women. We have a Tiger Woods, a Pete Sampras and a Venus Williams.'

Chattie laughed delightedly, and when Steve sank down onto the grass she followed suit. 'Could we bring Rich along the next time we do this?'

'Sure. Rich is another one to take to this place almost as if he was born to it. Chattie, tell me about your parents?'

She pulled a stalk of grass, chewed it and looked at him questioningly.

'I just wondered what there might be in your background to account for...' he spread an arm '...the way you could almost have been born to this.'

A spark of interest lit her grey eyes. 'You could be right. My father was a stock and station agent. He said it was the next best thing to owning a station, which he couldn't afford. We lived in Toowoomba on what was really a hobby farm but, when they died, had to move to Brisbane to my mother's sister.'

'No other relations? Is she still alive?'

'No other relations and she passed away a year ago.'

'I see,' he said slowly. 'What about friends?'

'Oh, I've got plenty of those—is this conversation leading somewhere, Mr Kinane?' she asked with a glint of humour.

'Yep. Where to hold the wedding.'

Chattie sobered.

'Still shell-socked?' he queried.

She glanced across at him. He wore his usual jeans and bush shirt and as he lazily waved away some bush flies she was literally assaulted by everything that was fine, strong but also determined about him. A hard man to cross, it popped into her mind, a hard man to say no to...

She plucked another stalk of grass and was dismayed to find that her hand was trembling beneath all the things Steve Kinane did to her. I'll be a basket case shortly, it occurred to her, if I go on wanting him yet resenting him at times, like this.

'I have given it some thought,' she said cautiously. 'For Bridget's sake, something low key would be best.'

'Why?'

The way he said it told her she was in for a fight, and she took a deep breath. 'She's the one who was hoping to be married. A big wedding couldn't help but—well, make her think of what might have been for *her*.'

'Your devotion to your sister is commendable, Chattie, but there has to be a limit. No, listen to me,' he said quietly as she made a sudden move, and he put a hand over hers. 'There's going to be enormous curiosity in the district about this marriage as it is. For your sake, the best way to deal with it is not to be low-key or—hole-in-the-corner.'

'But—'

'I'm not,' he overrode her, 'suggesting anything flamboyant or over-the-top. But the ceremony and reception here at Helena should satisfy the district and, even more importantly—if we're going to do this, it would give me the reassurance that it's not all going to be hard labour for you.'

Their eyes met.

'We could fly in as many of your friends as you'd like,' he added. 'You could be the bride—of your choice.'

Chattie fixed her gaze on Cathy Freeman for a long moment, and commanded herself to think straight. What good would it do for any of them if she was giving off 'hard labour' vibes?

'OK,' she said. 'But I'll have to go back to Brisbane to wind up my—our lives there, first.'

'Your job?' he queried.

'I have two months' untaken leave up my sleeve,' she said slowly. 'I worked on preparation programs right through the last Christmas holidays, so I can use that as notice.' She gestured. 'Not how I would like to do it, but the best I can come up with.'

'Why don't we combine that trip to Brisbane with some shopping?' he suggested. 'We could fly down.'

'Bridget,' Chattie began.

'Bridget could come with us, if she's game to fly again.'

Chattie subsided. Then she asked, 'When—should we do it? Get married, I mean?'

'How about—three weeks from today?'

'Make it four and you've got a deal,' she said with another glint of humour.

He raised a wry eyebrow. 'Think we can last out that long?'

A tinge of pink entered her cheeks. 'We'll have to,' she said, however. 'I always wanted to design and make my own wedding dress, and, if we're going to satisfy the district and come up with a suitable wedding for them, and me, I'll need a month.' She got up and added gently, 'That's my last offer, incidentally, but you won't regret it.'

He rose to his feet. 'Talk about being caught by the short and curlies—my apologies—'

But Chattie started to laugh, she just couldn't help—as he looked extremely rueful.

He laughed with her. Then he helped her back on her horse, and they rode home with Chattie, mysteriously, feeling better than she had for a while.

CHAPTER TEN

MYSTERIOUSLY, also, Bridget had enjoyed her session with Harriet, Chattie discovered. Had Steve put the fear of God into his wayward cousin? Chattie wondered.

'She treated me as if I was one of the family,' Bridget said, wonderingly. 'I really thought they'd all hate me. And she gave me some tips about being pregnant, what to expect and so on. Apparently, the middle three months are best. Harriet got over all her morning sickness by then and she glowed!'

'That is good news!' Chattie responded wryly. 'Have you felt sick at all today?'

'Not really. Just a bit queasy after breakfast.'

'OK—I need to take a shower. Could you peel some potatoes for me?'

'Sure! What's for dinner?'

'Pork chops.'

'Would you like me to make that potato casserole with onions and tomatoes?'

'You're a honey, yes, please!' And Chattie closed herself into her bedroom to shower and change for dinner—and to think about the forthcoming expedition to Brisbane.

In the event, it wasn't Steve who took her to Brisbane, it was Joan Jackson.

While Chattie was showering she rang in to say that

John had insisted she visit a specialist about her migraines, and he was flying her down the next morning and leaving her there for a couple of days, so was there anything they needed from the Big Smoke?

Steve took the call, hesitated then asked her if he could call her back. And he went on to first find Bridget, then Chattie.

As he knocked then opened her bedroom door her head and arms emerged through the neckline and sleeves of a slate-blue dress that floated around her before subsiding against her figure.

'Sorry.' He leant back against the door.

'That's OK. I'm decent now,' she answered, although she looked faintly flustered. 'What can I do you for?'

He told her about Joan Jackson's call, and finished by saying, 'The thing is, I wondered if you'd like to go down with Joan rather than me.'

Chattie's lips parted. 'Why?'

'Because there's rain on the way, according to the weather forecast I've just heard, and there's a mob of cattle I'm particularly keen to muster before it gets here. The more hands I can muster, the better.'

Chattie smiled and was just about to comment on the joys of being a cattleman's wife, but something stopped her. 'Uh, well, but what about Bridget?'

'Nothing would induce Bridget to set foot on a light plane at the moment.'

'You've already checked with her?' Chattie looked surprised.

'Yep. I also rang Harriet and she'd be happy to have Bridget stay with her while you're away.'

'How on earth did you get Harriet to be

so…so…compliant and helpful?' she couldn't help asking.

His lips twisted. 'I told her what you told me—this has happened and we need to make the best of it rather than indulge in an orgy of recriminations. But, it so happens, Harriet is rather taken with your sister.'

'Most people are,' Chattie commented.

'Point taken.' Their gazes caught and held and he straightened and came towards her. 'Are you happy to go with Joan, then? She'd probably be a lot more helpful than I would be with the wedding preparations. She's married three daughters off.'

'All right,' Chattie said slowly.

'You don't sound convinced.'

'The speed with which you organize things takes my breath away at times, that's all.' She half smiled.

He hesitated, then, 'Sorry, but anyway, shouldn't most of the preparations be a surprise for the groom?'

'Traditionally, I guess so.'

'Why don't we opt for all tradition, then?' He suggested. 'After all, we're being very traditional in one area.'

She looked up at him with a question in her eyes, but comprehension came to them as his dark gaze slipped down her figure.

She stirred and drew an unsteady breath. Her dress was loose but its silky material clung to her breasts and she felt very much on display to Steve Kinane with all the attendant sensations that brought. And she was drawn, in her mind, to a vision of them preparing to make love. Of them kissing and discarding their clothes with sensual serenity as they gloried in each other's bodies.

It came to her that to be unclothed against the strong, hard planes of his body and to have his hands explore her nakedness might draw more from her than serenity—it might be a soul-liberating experience at the same time...

She swallowed and wiped the dew of sweat from her brow with the back of her hand as she wondered if he was as affected as she was.

Then, as he placed his hands on her shoulders and drew her into his arms, knew that he was. But he only kissed the top of her head—and released her.

'I think this might be a no-go zone—at this point in time, Chattie,' he said with a glint of humour in his eyes, but a tell-tale nerve beating in his jaw.

She smiled shakily. 'I think you could be right.'

'Should we—adjourn to dinner, then?'

'Definitely!'

Joan Jackson was almost as excited as if she were marrying a daughter off again.

By the time she and Chattie were ensconced in adjoining rooms at a luxury hotel the next day, she'd given Chattie and Steve her blessing. She'd told Chattie that at their first meeting she'd harboured the thought that Chattie was exactly what Steve needed. And, on Chattie venturing to say that some people might question the suddenness of it, she'd advised her that she and John Jackson had known within days of meeting that they were made for each other.

Then Chattie discovered that Joan was a mine of information on how to organize a wedding and she'd thought to bring along her diaries from the years of her daughter's weddings. Florists, bridal boutiques, printers, cake makers, caterers prepared to go up country and likewise hairdressers, plus a whole lot more came out of Joan's diaries.

Chattie attempted to stem the flow somewhat by telling Joan she meant to make her own dress and her own wedding cake, that she didn't need caterers or a hairdresser, and she wasn't planning on having bridesmaids.

Joan eventually backed down on the dress, the cake and the hairdresser, but stood quite firm on all the rest.

Until Chattie said with dawning suspicion in her eyes, 'Has Steve been laying down the law to you?'

Joan grimaced. 'In a way. He told me to make sure you didn't take too much upon yourself, and to spare no expense so that it will be a lovely, memorable occasion! Now, what more could you ask from a man?'

Chattie had to smile, although a shade ruefully. What indeed? Unless you resented being manipulated?

'And, of course, you must have your sister as a bridesmaid and I *know* Harriet would love to be the matron of honour.'

Three days later they flew back laden down with parcels.

Apart from her appointment with the specialist, Joan and Chattie had spent all their time together. As a shopper, Joan had proven to be intuitive with a keen eye for value and quality, and a terror when it came to laying down the law to caterers and florists, and deadlines to printers of wedding invitations.

She'd also been helpful with the winding up of Chattie's and Bridget's lives in Brisbane. All their belongings had been packed up to be trucked to Mount

Helena; the lease on their rented cottage renegotiated to a new tenant; their car placed with a car yard for sale. And Chattie had visited her TAFE college and broken the news of her marriage and defection.

The one thing she'd stopped short of doing was contacting any of her friends. She'd run out of time but, not only that, as she dismantled her previous life and prepared for an unexpected wedding she was often attacked by disbelief. Mostly she could stifle it, sometimes not and the thought of getting in touch with friends was one of those times.

It was late afternoon as Chattie disembarked at Mount Helena and Joan stayed aboard for the last leg of the flight. 'We done well!' she said to Chattie as she kissed her goodbye.

'Thanks to you!' Chattie responded warmly. 'I'll let you know when the dress is ready—perhaps John will fly you over for a sneak preview?'

It was John himself who answered, 'If I know a thing or two, Chattie, between now and the wedding, we'll be doing a lot of buzzing backwards and forwards. Bye now!'

Merlene came to meet the plane, not Steve and Bridget as Chattie had expected, and she brought the news that they'd had a bit of drama with the muster, one of the ringers had fallen off his horse and broken some ribs, and Steve was staying with him until they could helicopter him out.

'But he's OK himself?' Chattie asked.

'Yep. And your sister's fine, so is Rich. Glory be,' Merlene remarked as they loaded parcel after parcel into the back of the Range Rover. 'You leave anything back in the shops in Brissie, kid?'

Chattie laughed. 'I've just spent three days with the most determined shopper I've ever met in my life! She claims it comes from only being let loose twice a year—I wonder if I'll end up the same?'

'Could do! Can't say I go for it much myself,' Merlene opined, but she brought a pot of tea to Chattie's bedroom and sat down to go through all Chattie's purchases with keen interest.

'Where are they, by the way? Bridget and Rich?' Chattie asked.

'Still down at the Barlow abode—have those two ever clicked, which is a good thing for your sister in her condition! And of course you know what Brett thinks of Rich. How about we invite the Barlows up for dinner? You up to it?'

'Of course. But will Steve and Jack—?'

'Should be by then. I'll give Harriet a bell.'

Left on her own in the colourful chaos of her bedroom, Chattie sank down onto the bed and suddenly experienced one of those moments of disbelief, only it turned out to be much more than a niggle.

I can't believe this is happening to me, she thought, and suddenly felt as if she were suffocating. It's like being on a runaway train headed towards marriage to a man who wants me but hasn't fallen in love with me and I don't know if I can do it...

Do what? she asked herself.

'Stand the way I'm being railroaded into this,' she said aloud. 'Stand the thought of a marriage of convenience when I want to be loved. When I don't want the dark side of Steve Kinane to come between us but I know it's there.'

To her horror, she discovered tears rolling down her cheeks as she felt more shaky, emotional and scared than she'd ever felt in her life. And prey to a powerful instinct simply to run away.

Think of Bridget, she commanded herself. If nothing else, he has gone out of his way to make things as easy as possible for her. Hold onto that, Chattie, you must!

Steve came home just as Harriet, Bridget, Brett and Rich arrived at the homestead, and he had to wait his turn to greet her. Jack was on his way, having stopped to shower and change.

'Remember me?' he queried softly as he took her in his arms.

'The man who sent me to Brisbane?' she replied and attempted a teasing little smile. 'I think so.'

'What's wrong?' His gaze narrowed.

'Nothing! It's been a big three days, that's all.'

'Then why this bun fight?'

'It—was Merlene's idea. Plus—' she groped desperately for more humour '—you forgot to warn me about how stiff a novice horse rider would get.'

He looked wry. 'Bad?'

'My legs are killing me.'

'I know exactly how to help. A good massage works wonders.'

The thought of him massaging her thighs went straight to Chattie's head and she turned pink and trembled in his arms.

'That's better,' he murmured. 'I thought you'd gone away from me.'

'And if I had?' she asked barely audibly.

'I would not approve of that at all.' He stared down

into her eyes, and something incredibly determined glinted in his own.

But before Chattie could respond Harriet said teasingly, 'Now, enough of that, you two love birds, there are children present!'

They broke apart as everyone laughed.

It was a cheerful meal during which the wedding preparations were discussed. Cheerful, that was, apart from Bridget, who got quieter and quieter, causing Chattie to wonder helplessly how she was going to get her sister through it all.

But it broke up fairly early, the Barlows went home and she and Bridget were doing the dishes when another vehicle drove up to the garden gate.

'Who on earth could that be?' Chattie wondered aloud as she heard Steve walk out onto the veranda.

'I don't know about isolated, there seem to be an awful lot of comings and goings out here,' Bridget said ruefully and stiffened as a voice greeted Steve.

Chattie frowned and looked a question at her.

Mark! Bridget mouthed and moved convulsively.

But Chattie put a warning hand on her arm, then gestured to her sister to follow her into the passage where they could hear clearly.

'This is a surprise, Mark!' Steve said. 'Where the hell have you been?'

'Sorting out my life,' Mark Kinane replied, 'as you've so often recommended I do, big bro. Not that you're likely to approve of what I've done, but will you please just listen?'

There was a pause, then Steve said dryly, 'Go ahead.'

What came next was the sound of chairs being scraped back as the two men sat down.

Then Mark's voice came again. 'I've got a job. The one thing I really want to do is train racehorses so I applied to a Sydney trainer and he's taken me on for six months as his assistant. A house goes with the position. You know him, Brian Matthews, he's got a good record of training winners, and a lot that he could pass on. Then, in six months, I hope to be able to establish my own stables.'

'What could I object to about that?' Steve asked. 'I think you'd make a damn fine trainer and I'd be more than happy to give you some horses.'

'Thanks. It's not that, though, it's the reason behind it, the reason that made me see I had to stop drifting and do something with my life. The thing is, I'm getting married.'

Bridget froze.

'I know you'll say I'm too young,' Mark continued, 'we're too young and all that garbage, but I know she's the one for me and I won't be talked out of it. I just—can't live without her, I want a family with her and the hardest thing I've done lately is be away from her. But I thought I had to tell you this in person. I'm driving down to see her first thing tomorrow.'

'Who is she?'

'No one you know.'

'She has a name, I presume.'

'Bridget Winslow, and she's the loveliest girl in the world.'

Chattie took her hand off Bridget's arm and made a little shooing gesture. Her sister flew down the passage and out onto the veranda. Chattie followed, although more sedately, but in time to see Mark Kinane turn, look absolutely stunned, then rise in time to catch Bridget in his arms.

'Bridge, oh, Bridge, sweetheart! What are you doing here?'

'No one would believe me, but I knew you loved me as much as I love you, Mark, and I just knew you'd come back to me!'

'A double wedding?' Steve said.

Chattie was standing on the front veranda, staring out over the starlight silvered garden and paddocks. Both Mark and Bridget had just retired after a couple of hours of such joy, it had been hard not to be affected. And she had been affected, deeply affected for Bridget's sake. However immature and impetuous they might be, you couldn't doubt that Mark Kinane was deeply in love with her sister and she with him.

The discovery that Bridget was pregnant had drawn an awed response from Steve's brother, and together they'd barely been able to stop themselves speculating on which occasion they'd made love that it had happened.

But it was also outside Chattie's power to stop herself from being negatively affected, as she'd identified the difference between Bridget's situation and her own. The difference mutual love made as opposed to physical desire and a business arrangement, in other words.

She turned at last to find Steve standing right behind her. 'No, no double wedding. I can't do it, Steve.'

She thought his breath rasped in his throat and she tensed visibly.

'Why not?' he asked grimly.

'There is no reason for me to marry you now.'

'No *reason*?' he growled. 'It was never only Bridget and you damn well know it, Chattie.'

'It *was* Bridget—at least, she was the lever you used. Well,' she said bitterly, 'that lever has disappeared and what's left? A business arrangement, practicality, how well I'm suited to Mount Helena, how good I'd be for the place and you—but have you ever once stopped to wonder how well you and Mount Helena are suited to *me*?'

'If I had you in my arms,' he taunted, 'there would be no question of how well we suit each other.'

'Steve, I'm going on twenty-three and a virgin,' she said with tears slipping down her cheeks. 'That's fairly remarkable in this day and age, but I made a conscious decision that sex should be very special and reserved for a very special relationship: marriage. OK, I had to make some adjustments when I was desperate about Bridget, but now I don't because "practical" and "business arrangements" don't fall into that category.'

He was silent for an age. Silent, frowning and as watchful as a hawk. Until she took a hankie from her pocket to blow her nose, and went to turn away. Then he put a hand on her shoulder.

'So you really don't want to marry me, Chattie?'

'No, Steve, I don't. Not like this. I may have a down-to-earth side, but I'm not so firmly planted in the ground that I don't know the difference between real joy in a man and a woman—which is what I would need—and what you're offering me.'

'That's the best news I've heard for a while.'

Chattie's heart started to beat like a muffled drum as all hope slipped away. Then she swallowed. 'So, it's all sorted,' she said huskily. 'I may even get back to Brisbane in time to get my job back and stop them selling my car.'

'No, it's not all sorted,' he said and scanned her pale, strained face in the starlight. 'Because I've been trying to kid myself that I haven't fallen madly in love with you, Chattie, since the day we met.'

Her lips parted. 'You...have?'

'Yes.' He put his fingertips lightly on her cheek, then shoved his hands in his pocket as if he was afraid to touch her again. 'You see, I not only swore to be more practical about marriage if I did it again, but I swore never to fall in love again.'

'She hurt you that badly?' Chattie whispered.

'I thought so at the time. Now I know it was nothing compared to having to watch you walk away from me. My problem was, Nadine deceived me. She didn't want me, she wanted my money. She thought she could separate me from Helena and it drove her crazy when she couldn't. She had affairs to make me jealous, she...' He stopped and shrugged. 'I guess I thought I'd become an iron man emotionally.'

'And it didn't help when you discovered I'd deceived you too?' Chattie said on a breath.

'No, it didn't, although it probably couldn't have been in a better cause. If the way you take care of your sister is the way you would take care of anyone you love, Chattie, I couldn't admire you more. But, not thinking too rationally, I have to admit, it raised— I couldn't help thinking, Here I go again! In love with a woman who wants something from me, not just *me*.'

'Oh, Steve.' Her eyes were wet again. 'I couldn't help wondering if it was some kind of a test.'

'I know, crazy, wasn't it? Insane, even, because I would have married you come hell or high water, Chattie.' He closed his eyes briefly.

'And been suspicious and angry underneath at the same time,' she murmured. 'I knew that.' She paused and took a deep breath. 'May I ask you something?'

He nodded.

'Will you marry me, Steve?'

He moved abruptly. 'It's that—it is that special?' he queried unevenly.

'It's that special, now,' she agreed with no more tears slipping down her cheeks, with stars in her eyes instead. 'Because I too have been trying to pretend that I haven't fallen madly in love with you ever since we met.'

His taut, hawk-like stance relaxed at last. 'My darling Chattie,' he murmured and pulled her into his arms, 'if only you knew what a…damn roundabout I've been on since you walked into my life. How I've hated myself lately for even hoping I was hurting you because at least that would mean you felt the way I did or something of it.'

'I did, I do! And I've been on the same roundabout,' she confessed. 'Not that I wanted to hurt you, but sometimes I couldn't help hating you and—' She broke off and shivered.

'Never again.' He kissed her hair, then looked into her eyes with a little flame burning steadily in his eyes. 'Are you really sure you want to take me on, Chattie Winslow?'

'Certain sure,' she responded. 'Will you?'

'Marry you? Just let anyone try and stop me—I'll be honoured to.'

Three and a half weeks later, six light planes were parked on the Mount Helena airstrip, a variety of four-wheel drive vehicles stood outside the garden gate and a ceremony was about to take place on the front lawn.

Before a table clothed in white linen with a gossamer silver over-cloth, the crowd gathered were all in their Sunday best with many a colourful hat, and many a suit that had come out of mothballs.

Merlene was wearing a skirt rather than jeans for the first time for years. Brett was full of importance in a proper little suit and in charge of Rich, who had silver wedding bells on his collar.

Joan Jackson was there looking elegant but slightly harassed. Jack Barlow was alongside Bill and the other station workers.

Steve Kinane stood in front of the table in a dark suit with his brother Mark beside him, acting as his best man, and fiddling with the very new gold wedding band on his left hand. And the marriage celebrant glanced expectantly at the main steps to the homestead.

Just then a hum went through the crowd as Harriet and Bridget emerged through the front door as a recording of the 'Wedding March' rang out.

They both looked lovely in off-the-shoulder gowns, Harriet's in jacaranda-blue, Bridget's in hyacinth-pink, and they carried white bouquets. As they began to descend the steps, another, louder hum rose as Chattie appeared on Slim's arm.

Without his trademark pony-tail, few people would

have recognized Slim in a well-tailored grey suit, blue shirt and navy tie.

But it was Chattie towards whom all eyes were drawn as she paused at the top of the steps. Her dress was stunning. Pure white heavy satin, it was a strapless sheath with a small train. Over it she wore a bolero of delicately flower-patterned voile with puff sleeves and a stand-up collar encrusted with seed pearls.

A froth of veil beneath a pearl coronet covered her loose hair and face; she wore short white gloves and carried white roses starred with single blue agapanthus florets.

As she paused, she wasn't conscious of the crowd of guests, however, she was looking back over the last few weeks and some of the surprises they'd contained.

Bridget, for example, had refused even to consider a double wedding on the grounds that Chattie's special day should be hers alone.

'We'll do our wedding our way,' she'd said.

Accordingly, a week earlier, they'd all flown to the Gold Coast, the Barlows and the Jacksons as well, and Mark and Bridget had been married in the chapel of the private school both Mark and Steve had attended, then enjoyed a lively reception at a restaurant over-looking the beach.

But the biggest surprise, perhaps, had been Steve's insistence that they continue to be 'traditional' until their wedding day.

Nestled in his arms when he'd made the declaration, Chattie had thanked him gravely but expressed the doubt that they could handle the strain. He'd then embarked on a discourse on the efficacy of cold showers—until she'd been helpless with laughter.

'If you think it's funny—' He looked at her reproachfully.

'I do.'

'Well, I don't.' But he started to laugh too. Then he sobered. 'I suspect it will be good for my soul, a bit of discipline, but I also think, in your heart of hearts, you'd like to do it this way?' He searched her eyes.

'I must seem very old-fashioned but, yes, I would.'

'It's one of the things I love about you, Chattie. Your principles and your values.'

She came out of her reverie and walked down the steps on Slim's arm. There was, literally, not a cloud in the sky, and half an hour later as Steve raised her veil and kissed her the congregation cheered and Rich barked joyfully.

After the reception, Steve flew them to Brisbane where they picked up a commercial flight and winged their way to Cairns then drove north to Palm Cove.

They had the honeymoon suite in a marvellous hotel on the beach. Chattie looked round at the Javanese inspired décor of terracotta floor tiles, lovely fretted woodwork, bamboo and batik, the four poster-bed, and sighed with pleasure.

'There's more,' Steve said and took her hand to lead her out to their private courtyard with its own swimming pool and spa. He put his arms around her. 'Did I tell you what a stunning bride you made?'

She wrinkled her nose at him. 'Several times actually. Did I tell you that you took my breath away in a suit?'

'Several times, actually. Here's one thing I haven't

told you—I'm dying by degrees. Have been for over a month, come to think of it.'

'So have I. May I suggest a solution?'

'Be my guest.'

'A swim and a spa to freshen us up.' She paused as he looked alarmed, but continued resolutely, 'A leisurely consumption of those gorgeous pink cocktails they provided, to relax us, then—anything is possible.'

'I'm so glad you got to that bit. I had a horrible feeling you were going to recommend we went out for dinner as well!'

She looked into his dark eyes then stood on her toes to cup his face. 'As a matter of fact, I'm quite happy to reverse the—order of things.'

'Like this?' He started to kiss her.

Five minutes later Chattie was trembling against him with every nerve of her body pulsing, or so it felt.

'Steve,' she whispered raggedly.

'Come,' he answered, and picked her up to set her down on her feet again next to the bed. And he began to undress her item by item, stopping every so often to caress her.

Her going away outfit was a short-sleeved aquamarine linen suit. He took the jacket off and drew an unsteady breath because her bra was also aquamarine trimmed with white. He smiled into her eyes, and she smiled, wryly, back.

Then he reached for the zip of her skirt, and as it slipped down her legs matching briefs were revealed, plus a lacy garter belt holding up pale stockings.

She stepped out of the skirt and he put his hands on her waist and raised his eyebrows at her. 'Twenty-one?'

'Yes. You were right, thirty-two, twenty-one, thirty-two.'

'And all of it gorgeous. Especially these.' His hands moved to her hips. 'They have a way of swishing that is—was,' he amended, 'a sore trial to me.'

Chattie moved beneath his hands and slipped her arms around his waist. 'So you told me.'

'At least you're not cross about it this time.' His lips twisted.

'No. The opposite,' she said ruefully. 'May I?' And, without waiting for an answer, started to unbutton his shirt.

From then on things got quite hectic as they undressed each other and gloried in each other's bodies.

'I was wrong,' he said with an effort at one stage. 'Nearly everything about you drives me insane. Your lovely, satiny skin, your breasts, your perfume.' He stopped talking and buried his head beneath her breasts.

Then he picked her up again and laid her on the bed and lay down beside her. And what he did to her breasts and nipples with his hands and teeth brought her almost more delight than she could bear.

'Please,' she said on a sobbing little breath as she arched her body and tangled her fingers in his hair.

He raised his mouth and kissed her on the lips until she quietened. Then he slid his leg between hers and started to stroke her thighs with his fingers moving ever higher to that secret place that was at the core of her delight. And only when he felt her grow wet with desire did he ease his weight onto her and smile down into her eyes.

'How am I doing?' he asked her softly.

'Steve, I…got the feeling this would be a soul-liberating experience…between us,' she said disjointedly, 'I was right. You're *wonderful* and—'

But she couldn't go on because a shudder racked him and he said no more. But everything he did to her and the way he did it drew a rapturous response from her, until that moment when she was completely exposed to him and he claimed her for his own.

And, as they'd climbed the pinnacle of ecstasy together, so they came down in each other's arms, breathing heavily, dewed with sweat and immensely moved.

'That was…' Chattie paused '…like nothing else that's ever happened to me.'

He stroked her hair off her face. 'I didn't hurt you?'

'No,' she said wonderingly. 'There was so much pleasure I didn't even stop to think about it.'

He held her hard. 'So much pleasure,' he repeated. 'I can't even begin to tell you how much pleasure you bring me, soul and body.'

She breathed contentedly.

'Although,' he added, 'I have to tell you that discipline in these matters has become a thing of the past, Miss Winslow-that-was.'

She laughed softly and traced the line of his jaw. 'I have to tell you that, for a teacher, I've developed a strange aversion to discipline.'

He caught her wandering fingers and kissed them. 'I'm extremely glad we agreed to come away immediately after the reception.'

'Oh? So am I, but—why?'

'They'll party on for days.'

Chattie eased herself up on her elbow and as the

sheet slipped pulled it up to cover her breasts. 'Days!' she said incredulously. 'Without us?'

'Yep.' He pulled the sheet down.

'That's...unusual, isn't it?' She automatically reached for the sheet again but his fingers stopped hers.

'Why so modest?' His dark eyes glinted.

She coloured delicately. 'Habit, maybe?'

He pulled her into his arms. 'I was going to suggest a shower, a swim in the nude in our pool, then a spa, sipping those cocktails. Think you could cope?'

She opened her mouth, closed it, then said, 'Not until you tell me whether you're joking about them partying on for days without us.'

'I'm not joking,' he said solemnly. 'Old outback custom. Do you mind?'

'No. It's not my place to, anyway. I just—'

'Oh, but it is now you're Mrs Steve Kinane,' he interrupted.

Chattie lay back. 'I hadn't thought of it like that. But I certainly wouldn't interfere with any old outback customs.'

'What about customs affecting newly-weds?'

'Popping around in the nude and the like, do you mean?' she queried with the utmost gravity.

'Uh-huh.'

'I will...' her lips started to curve '...do my best!'

He hugged her until she could barely breathe, then looked into her eyes. 'You do know that I'd be lonely to the depths of my soul without you now. I *love* you.'

CHAPTER ELEVEN

TWELVE months later to the day, Patrick Charles Kinane was born to Charlotte and Steve Kinane, on their wedding anniversary. He was named after his grandfathers. Two and a half years later his sister, Francesca Christine Kinane, arrived.

By this time, Rich not only had Brett and Patrick to play with, but Brett's twin brothers, Luke and Jonathan, born nine months after Harriet had left the station the day after Chattie had first arrived at Mount Helena. And, on their frequent visits, Mark and Bridget's daughter, Louella, joined in. Mark and Bridget remained blissfully in love and his career as a racehorse trainer was going well.

Both Slim and Merlene still worked at the homestead in amicable disharmony and Miss Daisy, retired from racing, had produced a filly foal.

It was at Francesca's—universally known as Bubbles—christening that Steve Kinane looked around the garden at the festivities, and festivities they were. Once more there were planes on the airstrip and vehicles at the garden gate. Once again many of the district wore their Sunday best and a veritable feast had been produced. This time, though, there was a growing tribe of children underfoot.

But he couldn't see the person he sought so he went in search of his wife.

He found her in their bedroom. She'd just put the

baby down and was buttoning up her blouse. He closed the door and watched her, saying nothing. In nearly four years Chattie Winslow, as he still sometimes thought of her, had changed little.

Still the same fair curly hair, the musical laugh, the person you could depend on. Her figure was fuller but still enchanting and she had the lovely bloom and radiance of a contented mother and wife.

If it was possible, he reflected, he was more in love with her than ever—and more content himself than he would have believed possible.

'Why so serious?' she asked lightly as she came towards him. 'Don't tell me, Luke and Patrick are fighting? Merlene and Slim have fallen out? There's been a power failure or there's a storm lurking? Harriet is giving someone a piece of her mind or—'

He put a finger on her lips. 'None of those, although on past history they're all entirely possible. No. I just wanted to be alone with you.'

'Why?' she asked seriously, although her eyes were dancing.

'I have some matters on my mind, really weighty ones.'

'Oh, dear! That sounds ominous.'

'Mmm,' he agreed and looked her up and down from beneath half-closed lids. 'Much as I like this blouse—' he put his fingers on a couple of buttons '—and I think your skirt is very elegant—I would also like to rip them off and have my way with you here and now.'

She closed her fingers over his. 'Much as I *love* the sound of that, Steve, we are in the middle of a christening party.'

He took her in his arms. 'I have a solution. How about we muster this mob off to their prospective homes? They've been here all day anyway.'

Chattie slid her arms around his neck and looked thoughtful. 'Well, in about an hour Patrick will be ready for an early supper and bed. Bubbles has had such a big day, I confidently expect her to sleep for hours.'

'All of which means?' He stroked some of her curls behind her ear.

'The moon should be full tonight, so, when it rises, we could have a moonlit champagne supper ourselves—and an early night.'

'Done,' he replied and kissed her. 'I'll go and speed up the mustering process.'

'Just don't be too…obvious about it.' She looked comically alarmed.

'Obvious? Me? Whatever gave you that idea?'

'You did!'

'Listen, can we take a roll-call of our sentiments on the subject?' he asked rapidly and almost in military style.

Chattie removed her arms from his neck and he released her.

'Is it or is it not a known fact that, with very little prompting, our friends can sometimes take days to be gotten rid of?'

'Old outback custom—it has been known,' she answered precisely.

'Would it be fair to say—' his dark eyes roamed over her in a way she knew well and one that always thrilled her '—that, historically, when things get to this stage between us there is only one way to handle it?'

She moistened her lips but said crisply, 'That would be an accurate interpretation.'

His gaze rested on the hollows at the base of her throat where a little pulse was beating wildly.

'Then, having done our duty to our maximum ability, are we united in a desire to rid Mount Helena of all extraneous persons with courtesy, naturally, but also speed?'

'So long as you take responsibility for overturning old outback customs—' Chattie clicked her heels and saluted 'we are! I'll come and help you.'

But she collapsed against him, laughing, and he kissed her thoroughly before they left the room, hand in hand.

THE AUSTRALIAN'S MARRIAGE DEMAND

by

Melanie Milburne

Melanie Milburne is married to a surgeon, Steve, and has two gorgeous sons, Paul and Phil. She lives in Hobart, Tasmania, where she enjoys an active life as a long-distance runner and a nationally ranked swimmer. She also has a Master's Degree in Education, but her children totally turned her off the idea of teaching! When not running or swimming she writes, and when she's not doing all of the above she's reading. And if someone could invent a way for her to read during a four-kilometre swim she'd be even happier!

To Phil,
my second-born son, who constantly astounds me
with his intellect and wit and inbuilt talent for
cynicism. This one's for you, Phil!

CHAPTER ONE

IT WAS not quite light when Jasmine woke in the hotel bed.

She opened one sleepy eye and wondered what had wakened her. Perhaps it had been one of the wedding guests coming in late after a full night of partying, she thought, as she stretched out one cramped leg.

It had been a nice enough wedding as far as weddings went.

Her sister Sam had looked beautiful and happy, and Finn, Sam's new husband, had been glowing with pride, his handsome face wreathed in smiles all day and most of the night.

Her father had beamed down at everyone proudly from the pulpit of the Sydney suburban cathedral where he was the local bishop. He was pleased that he'd yet again been privileged with the honour of marrying another of his four daughters; her mother had dabbed at her eyes repeatedly and played the role of mother of the bride with thrice-practised aplomb.

It was a pity Finn's older stepbrother, Connor Harrowsmith, had to be the best man, but he'd more or less behaved himself, which was unusual, Jasmine reflected. He'd fulfilled his duties, producing the rings at the right moment, without mishap, even complimenting the three bridesmaids with no sign of his usual mocking humour until his dark brown gaze had singled her out. She'd smiled back sweetly, determined not to let anything or anyone spoil her sister's day, but inwardly she'd seethed.

She hated him and he knew it.

She could tell from the hard glitter that came into his eyes every time he looked at her, which was rather too often throughout the service and reception. It had been as if he were silently teasing her, the words filling the air between them even though he hadn't said a word: three times a bridesmaid

5

never a bride. She had heard it in her head each time his dark eyes had sought hers and she resented him for it.

Jasmine stretched her other leg and froze.

There was someone in the bed with her!

She held her breath, wondering if she should turn on the lamp but too frightened to do so in case it woke whoever was beside her. She edged herself away as carefully as she could, but even when she was practically hanging over the edge of the mattress she could still feel the warmth of the stranger's body as if it was reaching out to draw her back into the cocoon of the bed.

The room was cloaked in darkness, a darkness that was suddenly menacing.

She could hear the sound of rhythmic breathing, the slight rustle of the bedclothes as the stranger moved, stretching, reaching out hands to find her…

She leapt for the light switch and snapped it on, her eyes shrinking painfully as the bright glare filled the hotel room.

'Oh my God!' she gasped. *'You!'*

She stared in horror when she saw Connor Harrowsmith, his long, muscled body clearly outlined by the bedclothes straining against the hard male form lying beneath.

'Hello, Jasmine,' he drawled. 'Did you sleep well?'

She drew in a furious breath as she grabbed the hotel bathrobe to cover her near nakedness. Her matching bra and panties had cost a fortune but there was no way he was going to get a free peep show!

'Get out of my room!'

He arched one dark sardonic brow as he rolled on to his side to face her, the sheet falling away from his naked chest revealing a rock hard stomach, the ridges of muscle clearly visible.

'Your room?'

'Of course it's my room; now get out before I call Security.' Her eyes flew to where her suitcase should be but, to her shock, it wasn't there.

'Where are my things?' She glared at him.

'In your room.' He stretched again, which pulled the sheets even tighter across his pelvis.

Jasmine tore her eyes away and stormed towards the bathroom. She wrenched open the door but there was no sign of the neat little row of cosmetics she had left the afternoon before; instead there was an electric shaver, a bottle of expensive-looking aftershave, a male hairbrush and, to add insult to injury, a wet towel on the floor.

She stomped back out to the bedroom, her anger increasing at the sight of him propped up lazily against the pillows, his taunting gaze slowly moving over her.

'You've taken my things!' she accused, moving towards the bed to reach for the phone. 'I'm going to call Reception and have someone sent up to—'

A large male hand appeared over her wrist, the long fingers encircling the slender bones in a gentle but undeniably firm hold.

'I wouldn't if I were you,' he cautioned, his dark eyes meeting hers.

'Let me go.' She tested his hold but it remained firm.

'You'd look really silly complaining to management when actually it's you in the wrong room,' he said.

'I'm not in the wrong room,' she insisted. 'I used my key in the lock last night.'

'I didn't lock the door,' he said. 'I left the reception to dash up here to get something I'd promised Finn and forgot to lock it on the way out.'

'I don't believe you.'

He shrugged indifferently and let her hand drop. She rubbed at it furiously, not because he'd hurt her but more to take away the sensation of his warm fingers.

'Go and see for yourself,' he challenged her. 'Open the door and check the room number.'

Jasmine swung away and padded over to the door with a confidence that was visibly cracking. What if he was right?

What if she was in the wrong room? How would she live that down?

She opened the door and her heart sank when she saw the number. She was in the wrong room! And not just any wrong room—Connor Harrowsmith's room!

'All right.' She walked back in, her colour high. 'So I made a mistake, but that still doesn't explain why you got into this bed without telling me of my error.'

'I didn't want to wake you,' he said, his tone guileless.

'Oh, for God's sake!' she fumed. 'You had no right to take advantage of the situation!'

He propped his hands behind his head, his biceps bulging, as did Jasmine's eyes at the sheer size of their gym-toned strength.

'How do you know I took advantage of the situation?' he asked with a long leisurely slide of his dark eyes all over her outraged form.

She felt flustered and over-hot, as if he'd flicked a switch on her body while she'd slept, turning her usual cool control to a completely different setting.

She didn't know what to think.

How was she supposed to know what had happened during the night? He might have touched her for all she knew and she'd be none the wiser. Perhaps he'd even kissed her, stroked her breasts or…

'You snore, you know,' he said, interrupting her torturous thoughts.

'I do not!'

His eyes twinkled as he surveyed her outraged features. Her curly chestnut hair was looking very 'just out of bed' and her grey-blue eyes were flashing fire. Notwithstanding the delightfully clingy ice-blue bridesmaid's dress she'd worn the day before, he couldn't think of a time when she'd looked more beautiful.

'Come on, Jasmine,' he teased. 'Loosen up. You're safe with me.'

'No one with a pulse is safe with you,' she tossed back irritably.

He laughed and threw the bedcovers aside.

'What are you doing?' she shrieked.

'Getting out of bed.' He stood up.

She turned the other way so she didn't have to look at his naked maleness. Her breathing was hurried and shallow, her face aflame, her nerves stretching like tight wires underneath her pulsing flesh.

'For God's sake put something on!' she croaked.

'You're wearing my bathrobe,' he pointed out dryly.

She seriously considered giving it back to him. Anything was better than having to face such a blatant show of male flesh in its prime.

'I haven't anything to wear.' Her voice was hoarse.

She felt his smile as he drawled, 'The eternal female lament.'

She heard a rustle of fabric. Then, out of the corner of her eye, she saw her bridesmaid's dress sail through the air towards her.

'Here, put this back on,' he said. 'I'll turn my back.'

She knew he was still looking at her as she let the bathrobe slip. She didn't trust a word that came out of that sensual mouth but she wasn't brave enough to turn and check. She struggled into the blue dress and, once she was decently covered, tossed the bathrobe in his direction without turning around.

'You can turn around now,' he said.

She turned around cautiously and his eyes met hers. She was relieved to see the bathrobe covered him but it gave her a funny feeling to think that minutes before the soft white folds had been lying against her own skin and now they were lying intimately against his.

'I have to go.' She headed for the door, almost tripping over her own feet.

'Hey,' he called as she fumbled with the door knob. 'Aren't you forgetting something?'

'What?' She gave him a glance over her left shoulder.

He held up one long finger where her pair of strappy sandals dangled.

'Oh.' She let the door go and approached him. 'Thank you.' She went to snatch them out of his hold but his hand caught hers.

His dark eyes burned down into hers.

'I enjoyed sleeping with you.' His thumb began stroking along the underside of her wrist in slow, sensuous strokes that made her stomach give a sudden unexpected lurch.

She found it hard to hold his gaze.

'I hope I didn't disturb you too much,' she said, making an effort at lightness.

'Oh, you disturbed me a great deal,' he said, giving her wrist a little tug. 'A great deal indeed.'

She was up against him, her body pressed to his, her softness on his hardness. She felt the outline of his growing erection against her belly and her eyes widened in alarm.

'Please—' her plea was breathy and ragged '—let me go.'

'You didn't say that last night.'

Her eyes widened even further.

'What do you mean?'

His eyes gave nothing away.

'You were quite the little temptress.'

She felt sick with shame. Had she really? Had she? Oh, dear God, had she thrown herself at him? But, deep down, she was fairly sure she hadn't.

'I don't believe you.'

'Oh ye of little faith,' he goaded.

'You're making it up to poke fun at me,' she said.

'Now why would I do that?'

'Because you're an arrogant jerk who thinks every woman will automatically fall into your arms, that's why.'

'That's an interesting analysis of my character, but not exactly true.'

'Isn't it?' Her look was cynical.

'You've been reading too many gossipy magazines,' he said. 'Don't you know they make it up to fuel their readership?'

'Everything you do is news,' she pointed out. 'You deliberately court scandalous gossip just to annoy your stepfather.'

His eyes hardened and his hold on her arm tightened a fraction.

'Just because your sister managed to get her hooks into my stepbrother doesn't mean you get the right to comment on the affairs of my family.'

'I can say what I like,' she tossed back defiantly.

'Not without paying a price.'

'What price?' A tiny shiver of apprehension shimmied its way up her spine.

'This price,' he said and, bending his head, captured her mouth with his.

She should have fought him.

She knew she should, but her body wasn't listening to the frantic plea of her brain. It was as if her body was acting totally independently of all rational thought and reason, going on its own wilful way, relishing the feel of a very male mouth commandeering hers.

His tongue pushed her trembling lips apart and sank into her mouth, searching for her own tongue. He found it and played with it tantalisingly, drawing it into the heat of his own mouth. Jasmine could feel the liquefying impact on her legs and spine as she leant against him for support, certain that without it she'd slip to the floor in a pool at his feet. His arms were like bands of iron, drawing her even closer, making her irrevocably aware of his aroused body against the trembling weakness of hers.

The kiss went on and on. She was lost to the feel of his lips exploring the soft contours of hers, lost to the sensation of hot desire flooding her internally as if all her life she'd been waiting for this moment.

He lifted his head and she blinked open her eyes.

'You shouldn't have done that,' she said.

'Nor should you.' His eyes glinted with some indefinable emotion.

'I didn't do anything!'

'Yes, you did.' He grinned at her wolfishly. 'You kissed me back.'

'I…I…' There wasn't much she could say in her own defence. 'You caught me off guard. I was unprepared.'

'I'll have to remember that,' he said. 'It might be useful.'

She wrenched herself from his arms and flung herself towards the door, unconcerned that her shoes were still in his possession. She opened the door of his room and had only taken one step out into the corridor when a camera flash blinded her.

'What the—?' She held up her hands to her face but the camera flashed three more times.

She elbowed her way past the persistent photographer and quickly dashed to her room, opening it with trembling fingers and slamming the door behind her as if it were the devil himself she was trying to lock out.

She took several deep breaths as she leant her back against the door, trying to calm her over-stretched nerves.

Damn him! How dared he mock her? Connor had probably organised the press to be waiting outside the door to get the scoop of the week. She inwardly cringed when she thought about her father reading the news of his daughter's latest misdemeanour. Her mother would no doubt retreat to her room with a cold face-cloth over her face, mortified that yet again she'd have to face the other women at Tuesday morning's Bible group with her wayward daughter's exploits as the main focus of study.

Her three sisters would frown and shake their heads, each of them looking towards their successful husbands for emotional support as they faced yet another of their sister's scandals.

She pushed herself away from the door and began packing her things. She didn't bother to fold anything; she just shoved everything in viciously as if each and every item was a piece of Connor Harrowsmith's anatomy she wanted to injure.

She hated the way he mocked her. Every time she'd met him during the course of her sister's friendship and subsequent courtship with Finn she'd had to bear the brunt of his ridicule. She knew she was an easy target given her tarnished reputation but she resented him for latching on to it so assiduously. Her name had been dragged through the mud on more occasions than she cared to recall, each time damaging the high moral ground of her family's home.

She thrust her cosmetics haphazardly into a plastic bag.

OK, so she wasn't technically a virgin. So what? She bet her sisters hadn't exactly made it to the altar intact but she didn't hear anyone complaining, least of all her parents.

She'd never been able to please them.

No matter what she did, it upset their strict idea of what was good and proper. Of course her work at the drug centre in Sydney didn't help but she wasn't giving that up for anyone.

She slammed her suitcase shut and scowled at her reflection in the mirror above the dressing table.

No matter how hard she'd tried to fit in she'd never quite managed to cope with the stultifying existence of being the eldest of Bishop Byrne's daughters, all dressed up in their Sunday best, sitting in the church pew, their undivided attention on the erudite wisdom spouting forth from their father's mouth, droning on like a blowfly stuck in a milk bottle.

No, Jasmine had sat and squirmed in her seat for as long as she could remember. She'd hated the dour music and the way all of the women had tried to out-dress each other every week. She'd hated the way the Sunday School teachers frowned at her questions and talked behind their hands in reproving conspiracy at her wilful disobedience. She'd walked out of the gargoyle-appointed cathedral at the age of sixteen and had never looked back, except in anger. In anger at the way her choice of belief system had alienated her from her parents even as they preached tolerance and acceptance.

Jasmine hadn't even seen a copy of Monday morning's paper when her second youngest sister called her on the telephone.

'How could you do this?' Caitlin cried.

Jasmine stiffened in preparation for the damning tirade.

'After all you've put us through, you do this, as if that affair with Roy Holden wasn't enough!'

'I didn't have an affair with—'

'How could you sleep with Connor Harrowsmith? How could you? You know what he's like; Finn is always telling us about his playboy exploits.'

'I didn't exactly sleep with—'

'Of course Father is beside himself. The Archbishop has already called this morning and now Mother has a migraine and it's entirely your fault.'

Jasmine let her sister run herself out. There was no point in stating her case. No one would believe her if she tried, but her anger and resentment towards Connor increased by several notches.

'I just hope Samantha and Finn don't look at this morning's paper,' Caitlin continued. 'Otherwise their honeymoon is going to be completely spoilt by your foolish and reckless behaviour.'

Jasmine had heard enough.

'If Finn and Sam are reading the paper on the second day of their honeymoon then Finn isn't half the man he should be,' she said.

Caitlin's gasp was clearly audible.

'You're so shameless! How can you be so flippant? At least Finn has some sort of morals, unlike his wayward, philandering stepbrother.'

Strange though it seemed, Jasmine suddenly felt compelled to spring to Connor's defence.

'You hardly know the man,' she said. 'It's not fair to judge.'

'Not know him? Everyone knows him. Every movement he makes is splashed across the papers all the time. He's Sydney's biggest playboy and you were photographed half-dressed coming out of his room the morning after your sister's wedding.'

'I wasn't half-dressed,' Jasmine said more calmly than she felt. 'I just didn't have my shoes on.'

'And where were they?' Caitlin's tone was snide. 'Still underneath Connor Harrowsmith's bed?'

She didn't bother denying it.

'They were in his possession, yes.'

'I can't believe you can be so casual about this!'

'I'm not being casual.'

'Well, you won't be when you hear what Father has said.'

'What?'

'Father is outraged. He's threatening to prosecute Connor if he doesn't do something to immediately quell the scandal.'

'It's hardly a scandal—'

'You might like to remind yourself at this point that our father is a prominent member of the clergy. *This* is a scandal!'

'I think it's more of a scandal when people stick their noses into business that has absolutely nothing whatsoever to do with them,' Jasmine replied. 'I've got to go to work. Goodbye.'

She hung up the phone and fumed.

Damn him! This was entirely his fault!

The telephone rang again and she stared at it for a long moment before picking it up. The last thing she wanted was a tearful how-could-you-do-this-to-us-after-all-we've-done-for-you type of conversation from her distraught mother. Nor could she currently cope with a condescending, moralising lecture from her 'holier than thou' father.

'If you're ringing to criticise me then hang up right now,' she said into the receiver.

'I wasn't calling to criticise you.' Connor Harrowsmith's deep voice sounded in her ear.

Her hand tightened around the receiver.

'I take it you've seen the morning papers?' she asked.

'Have you?'

'Not as yet but I've been informed of their content.' Her tone was bitter. 'It seems I'm in the middle of yet another scandal, this time with you as my partner in crime.'

'Poor you.' He laughed. 'To have sunk so low.'

'This isn't funny!' she raged. 'This is all your doing.'

'I accept total responsibility.'

She frowned. 'What do you mean?'

'As you say, it's all my fault.'

Jasmine didn't think he sounded at all contrite; on the contrary, he sounded rather proud of the fact that he'd caused so much of a scandal.

'My father is furious,' she put in.

'So is my stepfather.'

'And my mother has a headache,' she added.

'I shouldn't wonder, having to listen to your father's sermons all the time.'

She opened her mouth to attack him but changed her mind.

'My sisters will probably never speak to me again,' she said instead.

'So?' She could almost sense his dismissive shrug. 'When was the last time they listened to what you had to say?'

She hated to allow him to be right but he was. Even as she privately marvelled at his insight into the dynamics of her family, another part of her still wanted to fight him.

'My family are very important to me,' she said.

'How admirable of you.'

'You're making fun of me.'

'No. I'm actually on your side in all this.'

'I don't believe you.'

'I can see why your father has such an issue with you,' he said wryly. 'Your lack of faith is lamentable.'

'You're making fun of me again.'

He laughed.

'Maybe I'm poking fun at life in general. Don't take it too personally.'

'Is your stepfather threatening to disinherit you too?' she asked.

'He shouldn't,' he said. 'I didn't do anything wrong.'

'You slept with me,' she said. 'Deflowering a bishop's daughter is pretty high up on the unforgivable sins chart.'

'But you're not the innocent virgin, are you?' he said.

Jasmine wasn't sure how to answer him. The papers had been full of her 'inappropriate relationship' with Roy Holden; Connor surely could not have been unaware of that. But while the press loved a scandal, they were less particular over the truth, and that lay within her, untouched.

'According to popular opinion I'm an "outright tart",' she quoted.

'I've never been one for popular opinion,' he said. 'I like to find out these sorts of things for myself.'

Jasmine felt a funny sensation rush through her at the thought of him examining her intimately. She dismissed the thought and schooled her voice into indifference.

'I need to get to work. Was there something you particularly wanted to discuss with me other than the contents of this morning's paper?'

'Actually there is something I wanted to discuss with you,' he said.

'Yes?' Her tone was abrupt.

He made her wait for his reply.

'I have a solution to our little problem.'

'What sort of solution?'

Again he let the silence continue unbearably.

'The sort of solution that will dispel all the rumours and restore family faith in the two miscreants.'

'A miracle?' she said with a rueful edge to her voice.

She heard him chuckle.

'Not quite a miracle but an amazing occurrence for all that.'

'What?'

'Marriage.'

'Marriage?' She almost choked on the word, 'Whose marriage?'

There was an infinitesimal pause.

'Our marriage.'

This time it was her who let the silence continue.

'I think we should get married as soon as possible,' he said evenly.

'I think you need to see a psychiatrist,' she shot back. 'I'm not marrying you!'

'Never say never, sweetheart.' He gave another little chuckle.

Jasmine felt as if someone had just walked over her grave. A cold shudder of fear ran through her and her fingers on the telephone grew white-knuckled in panic.

'My parents would never allow such a thing to happen,' she said with as much confidence as she could muster.

'Are you sure?'

'Of course I'm sure! My father would rather die than allow me to marry you.'

'You don't know your father very well then.'

'What do you mean by that?' A flicker of consternation settled in her chest, causing her breathing to trip and become erratic.

'I just spoke to him a few minutes ago.'

'And?'

'And he suggested we should get married as soon as possible.'

CHAPTER TWO

JASMINE felt as if she were going to faint.

The room tilted before her eyes and she had to grasp the edge of the telephone table to anchor her shaking body.

'You can't possibly mean to carry it out,' she managed to croak. 'I mean—it's unthinkable! We're strangers!'

'I don't know about that,' he countered. 'We're almost related now that your sister is married to my stepbrother. Besides, we've spent the night together; I'd say that covers a lot of ground.'

'Not the sort of ground I like to be on!' she shot back. 'I'm not marrying anyone and, even if I was, you'd be the very last person on my list.'

'Flattered, I'm sure,' he drawled insolently.

'I mean it, Connor,' she insisted. 'Marriage is an outdated institution constructed by men to gain control over women.'

'I'm sure your sisters would be very disappointed to hear your views considering that each of them have found and secured themselves a husband within the last year.'

'More fool them.'

He laughed. 'Come on, Jasmine. I promise to be a good husband.'

'You don't know the meaning of the word.'

'Which one? Good or husband?'

'Both.'

'It will have to be a quiet ceremony, of course,' he said.

'I'm not marrying you!'

'And I don't know if your parents will want you to wear white.'

'I'm not mar—'

'And I don't think we need bother with a long honeymoon.'

19

'I'm not going to—'

'But then again, it could be fun.'

She slammed the phone down in frustration. How dare he mock her?

The telephone pealed and she picked it up and thrust her finger on the answer button immediately.

'Go to hell, Connor Harrowsmith!'

She left the phone off the hook and wandered about her tiny apartment in agitation. She was already forty minutes late for the clinic. A few more wasn't going to make or break anything.

She had to sort out this misunderstanding, but how? Perhaps she could call her parents and explain.

She picked up the receiver and quickly dialled the number. Her father answered in his usual Eucharistic tones.

'Good morning. Bishop Byrne speaking.'

'Father, it's me.'

'Jasmine.' She heard him suck in a breath. 'I wondered when you'd get around to calling.'

'I wanted to explain—'

'Your mother is in a state,' he cut across her. 'I've had to call Dr Pullenby. It's been in every paper.'

'It's not my fault. You see it was—'

'Don't tell me the Devil made you do it.' His tone was impatient. 'Do you know how many times I hear that in a week? Do you?'

'Connor and I hardly know—'

'At least he's offered to do the decent thing.'

'Decent?' Jasmine was incredulous. Connor Harrowsmith didn't know the meaning of the word.

'But I'm not performing the ceremony,' he said. 'It would go against everything I believe in.'

'I'm not marrying him.'

'Yes you are,' her father said. 'Or you'll never see either your mother or me again.'

Jasmine couldn't believe her ears. Surely her parents' moral code wasn't more important than their own flesh and blood?

'I understand,' she answered in a detached tone.

'You'd better, young lady,' her father added. 'You've caused quite enough trouble as it is. I've had to negotiate my way through a conversation with the Archbishop this morning. I assured him that you and Finn's brother will be getting married within a month at the very latest.'

'A month!'

'I'd be happier if it were next week. For all we know you could already be carrying his child.'

Jasmine reared away from the telephone in shock.

'He's not the sort of husband I would've liked for you, of course, but then you've always been wilful and disobedient. Perhaps having a difficult husband will teach you the lessons you've always refused to learn.'

Jasmine was lost for words.

'I think it's best if you stay away from your mother for a few days at least,' he added. 'She's terribly upset.'

Jasmine knew enough about her parents to know both of them were upset and used each other's reactions as excuses not to see her. Her father's insistence over her mother's reluctance could be read as his own and, while it pained her, she knew from experience there was little she could do about it. Once their minds were made up they were set in stone; there was simply nothing she could say or do to change them.

She went to work with steps that dragged. Never had she felt less like facing the problems of others. Her own were banking up behind her, threatening to overwhelm her.

She sat listening with one ear to the lament of yet another recovering addict who had some sort of axe to grind over why he wasn't receiving the sort of support he wanted, all the time wondering to herself who was going to support her over this new obstacle.

Todd, the other counsellor, tossed the morning paper on the desk in front of her at lunch time.

'I didn't know we had someone famous working amongst us,' he said with a grin.

Jasmine gave him a twisted half-smile and opened the paper.

She was on page ten.

It wasn't a particularly flattering photo. One of the shoestring straps of her dress had slipped, revealing a little more of her upper cleavage than was commonly seen in the Montford parish.

She looked furtive and guilty.

She slammed the paper shut and scowled.

'I'll kill him.'

'Who?' Todd asked. 'The photographer?'

'No.' She spun herself out of the office chair. 'The man I slept with.'

Todd's eyebrows rose.

'It's not what you think.' She turned back to look at him.

'I'm not thinking anything.' Todd held up his hands in a gesture of innocence.

'I hate him to hell and back.'

'Strong words from a bishop's daughter.'

'I'm being disowned because of that jerk!'

'Maybe he's done you a favour.' Todd's expression was wry.

She turned away and shuffled the papers on her desk.

'I think I'll take some time off,' she said. 'I need to get away until the dust settles.'

'That's fine. I'll keep an eye on your clients for you.'

'Thanks, Todd.' She gave him a grateful half-smile. 'I really appreciate it.'

The New South Wales south coast had been a bolt-hole for Jasmine for as long as she could remember. For years she'd been driving out of the noise and activity of Sydney to the solitude of long, lonely beaches where her footprints in the sand were the only ones left there all day. She found the roar of the waves therapeutic, calming the inner tension she nearly always felt when surrounded by her family.

One of her mother's friends allowed her to use their little holiday house on their block, a short walk from Pelican Head. It wasn't flash, but it was safe and secure and without a telephone so no one could find her. Lately she'd found she needed more and more time alone; solitude was becoming as addictive as some of the substances her clients at the clinic were in the clutches of. It was only when she was alone she felt safe from her family's disapproval. She saw it in their eyes whenever they focused on her: Jezebel, temptress, sinner.

The trouble was, no one could understand.

No one could possibly understand.

She put her few things in the beach house and, hiding the key in its usual place under a log near the tallest of the three gum trees, made her way to the beach.

The autumn wind had picked up, stirring the waves into frenzy as they lashed at the shore. Jasmine tied her long hair back with a hair-tie and faced the wind full on, closing her eyes and breathing in the salt and spray like a restorative drug.

She sighed with pleasure and began walking, her feet sinking in the water-soaked sand. She trudged on, determined to walk off the image of Connor Harrowsmith's sardonic face.

She still couldn't believe she'd mistakenly gone into his room, especially as she hadn't really wanted to stay in the hotel in the first place. Sam had insisted, saying she didn't want her wedding day memories spoilt with the news of someone being killed on the way home through drink-driving. Well, her wedding memories were probably going to be spoilt anyway once she heard about the press release involving her sister and the best man.

The best man! Huh! He was the worst man. Just the sort of man she avoided at all costs—too handsome and too rich to be responsible for his reckless actions. He drove fast cars and gallivanted around the world's hot spots, all the time in search of the ultimate experience.

Finn had laughingly described some of his stepbrother's exploits—affairs with actresses, married women some of them, and of course his propensity to gamble. Her eyes had widened at the amount Finn had said Connor had won in Las Vegas. She hadn't thought people ever won that amount of money but it seemed Connor had and had used it to set himself up in some sort of computer business. From all accounts his business was expanding exponentially and he had branches in each Australian capital city and was now looking abroad.

Damn him! She skirted around a heap of twisted kelp and willed herself to stop thinking about him.

Marriage! Huh! As if he were any sort of husband a woman might want!

She kicked a piece of sponge with one foot and watched as the wind took over its journey, rolling it over and over until the raging water swallowed it whole.

She turned to go back the way she'd come and pulled up short when she noticed a tall figure coming in her direction.

She tensed; there was something very familiar about that long, easy gait. She blinked the grains of sand out of her eyes and peered a little harder. As he drew closer Jasmine knew there was only one man with that taunting smile.

She considered making a run for it but the sand beneath her feet was heavy with the wash from the high tide and she knew she'd stumble and twist an ankle before she covered any great distance. There was nothing else to do other than face him and ask him what the hell he thought he was doing here.

She waited until he was less than three strides away.

'What the hell do you think you're doing?' She had to almost shout the words over the roar of the surf.

'I'm beachcombing,' he said, holding up a rather nice shell for her inspection.

She slapped his hand away and stomped past him to head back.

'Go away! I don't want to see you.'

He fell into step beside her, his long legs making short work of the heavy sand.

'But I want to see you.'

'Why?' She spun to face him, her hair blowing into her mouth. She brushed it aside angrily and glared up at him. 'You're wasting your time. I have nothing to say to you other than get lost.'

'But I have something to say to you.'

'I don't want to hear it.'

'But it might be the most important news,' he pointed out. 'Something so significant that perhaps years later when you walk along this beach with your grandkids your mind will wander and you'll find yourself thinking, Now, what was it that nice young man had to say? You'll rebuke yourself for not having heard him out.'

'Don't be so ridiculous!' She began stomping through the sand once more. 'You're not a nice person and I don't care what you have to say. I've never cared and I never will!'

'I think you do care, Jasmine, but you choose to hide that from most people behind that gruff I-don't-give-a-damn façade you're always wearing.'

Jasmine didn't let him see how close to the mark his assessment came. She lifted her chin in the air and kept walking, determined to shake him off one way or the other.

'That's a nice place where you're staying,' he said after a stormy silence broken only by the sucking sound of the sand around their feet.

She stopped in her tracks and shot him an accusatory glance.

'How did you know where to find me?'

His dark eyes gleamed. 'Now wouldn't you like to know?'

'I would, actually.' Her tone was arctic. 'Did you have me followed?'

His expression gave nothing away and her frown deepened.

'Don't panic.' He smiled down at her. 'I won't tell anyone your little secret.'

She tore her eyes away from the glint of mockery shining in his. Fear churned in the cavity of her stomach at the thought of her haven being discovered by someone so invading as Connor Harrowsmith. She'd never be able to come here again without thinking about him; her private paradise was now occupied by the very Devil himself.

'You really shouldn't disappear without telling someone where you're going,' he said when still she didn't speak. 'It's not safe.'

'It was safe until five minutes ago,' she bit out.

'It's still safe.' His eyes had softened along with his voice. 'Now I'm here to protect you.'

'I don't need you to protect me.'

'I think you will be very glad of my protection when I tell you what's in the afternoon paper.'

She felt her breathing snag somewhere in the middle of her chest. Clenching her hands into fists she forced herself to meet his dark chocolate-brown gaze.

'What do you mean?'

The line of his mouth was grim. 'An interview with Roy Holden's wife.'

'Oh, my God!' She sucked in a shaky breath, her face blanching in shock.

'No doubt the lure of money for the interview put any of her previous scruples to rest.'

Jasmine's voice was hollow and emotionless when she finally found it. 'I can't see what this has to do with you.'

'It has everything to do with me,' he argued. 'You're now my fiancée.'

'I am nothing of the sort!'

His dark brows arched at the vehemence of her denial.

'Honey—' she felt herself shiver at his casually delivered endearment '—if you don't marry me within a month you'll find yourself without a family. Your father is serious; he's determined to denounce you. Harsh I know, but then he's on high moral ground.'

She stared at him. It was strange hearing him use the very words she'd used—was it only two days ago?—when thinking of her father's moral code?

'But you can't seriously want to marry me,' she said.

He gave a little shrug. 'I've got nothing else better to do.'

'Thanks.'

She spun back to face the climb up to the cliff path, her back stiff with pride. She felt him behind her with every clawing hold she took and wished she hadn't been so hasty. She could just imagine him tucked in behind her, grinning to himself at the uninterrupted view of her bottom as she scaled the track.

Damn him!

She lost her hold and slipped backwards, taking an uprooted plant with her.

'Hey.' He caught her between his legs, clamping his thighs to secure her. 'Watch your step. This path is lethal if you're not concentrating.'

She wasn't brave enough to look upwards. She'd already seen a glimpse of what was packaged between those strong thighs and she didn't want to remind herself of it.

She scrambled forward out of the vice of his legs and, with as much grace as she could gather, made her way to the top, her breathing hard and fast.

He joined her on the path, his own breathing steady and even.

'You need to get fit,' he said. 'Then you wouldn't be quite so puffed out.'

'I'm not puffed out!' she puffed. 'I'm angry.'

He grinned at her. 'I know of a very good exercise.'

'Shut up!' She clamped her hands over her ears. 'I don't want to hear about it.'

His hands covered hers and pulled them away from her

head. She wanted to tear them from his loose grasp but the drop behind her forestalled her.

'Jasmine, listen to me.'

She closed her eyes to shut him out.

'Go away. I don't even want to look at you.'

She heard him sigh but didn't open her eyes. Surely he'd just go away as long as she kept giving him the brush off. Most men would have left hours ago.

'You're a stubborn little thing, aren't you?' he observed.

'Say what you like,' she threw back at him. 'I'm not listening to you.'

'There's a whole lot I could say but now is perhaps not the right time. We seem to have company.'

Jasmine's eyes sprang open and she glanced past him to see who else was going to spoil her sanctuary.

'There's no one there.' She met his dark gaze once more.

'I beg to differ.' His hands tightened on hers a fraction as he inclined his head to the left of where she was standing.

She looked down and shrieked at the coiled brown snake no more than a metre and a half from her feet. She flung herself forward into Connor's arms, uncaring that he was the enemy and could probably do her more harm in the long run. She decided to take her chances; snakes were not her favourite creature.

Connor held her against him as he began backing slowly away from the snake's uncoiling form.

'It's OK.' His tone was enviably calm. 'He's not all that interested in us. I saw a couple of geckoes on my way down so that's probably why he's here.'

'I hate snakes.' She gave a little shudder.

She felt his laugh rumble against her cheek where she was pressed so tightly against his chest.

'I wouldn't have one as a pet either.'

He loosened his hold as they came to the end of the path well away from the snake.

'There, what did I tell you—safe and sound.'

She looked around, inspecting the rocky ground for snake trails, but it was all clear.

'Thank you.' It was the least she could say under the circumstances.

They both knew the drop behind her had been there and that one startled step backwards would have sent her over. She felt a funny sensation in the pit of her stomach that he of all people had come to her rescue.

'No problem,' he said, his tone light and unaffected by the recent presence of imminent danger. 'Snakes I can handle. Threatening fathers are another thing entirely.'

The wryness of his tone reminded her of his own family battles. She didn't really know all that much about the Harrowsmith family except what Sam had let slip once or twice. She knew Connor's mother had died not long after her marriage to Julian Harrowsmith, leaving Connor at the age of four under his guardianship. Connor's own father was unknown; apparently he was the consequence of a passionate affair his mother had while still in her teens. Finn, the child of Julian and his second wife Harriet, spoke of his stepbrother with affection, although she sensed they were not all that close.

'How has your family reacted to this latest scandal of yours?' she asked as they began to walk along the bush track to the road.

His expression was guarded. 'They've made the usual noises about disinheriting me and so on.'

'That's terrible! You should do something!'

'I don't have a lot of choice just now,' he answered. 'The sooner this thing settles down the better. I have some big financial commitments pending with my overseas interests and I don't want to let the money from my mother's estate be redirected.'

'Could your stepfather really do that?' She stopped to look up at him, her brow furrowed in concern.

'He's one of Sydney's leading lawyers.' His eyes hardened momentarily. 'He can do anything.'

She bit her lip and kept walking.

'But surely you have enough money of your own by now to call his bluff?'

Connor's hand on her arm stopped her. He turned her to face him, the silence of the bush enveloping them in a type of intimacy she'd never felt with anyone before. It unsettled her, making her feel as if he stepped past some sort of barrier she had carefully constructed around herself all her life.

'I have plenty of money, yes, but I can't access my mother's until I marry,' he answered.

'What?'

'It was the way the will was written. I suppose my mother didn't want some poor girl to go through what she had as a teenage single mother. She wasn't taking any chances, even if I were her son and only an infant at the time of writing her will.'

Jasmine gnawed at her lip once more.

'Marriage is such a big step.' She looked at the open neck of his shirt instead of into his dark eyes. 'I wish I could help you but...'

'What will you do about your family?' he asked.

'I can handle them.'

'And the Holden interview? Can you handle that?'

Her gaze was worried when it returned to his. 'I have been through all this before, you know.'

'Yes.' His half-smile was wry. 'You certainly know how to rock the religious boat, don't you?'

She found herself smiling reluctantly at his choice of words.

'It wasn't intentional, I assure you.'

'All the same, this recent calamity won't help your father's chances of promotion. Finn has indicated that Elias has set his sights on being the next Archbishop when the present one retires.'

Jasmine had heard it too and it only added to her worries.

She knew her father was grasping at Connor's marriage solution with thoughts of his own salvation in mind, not hers.

'Marriage has never been a particular goal of mine,' she said. 'I can't see myself chained to a kitchen sink for the next fifty years.'

'Not all marriages are like that.'

'Aren't they?'

His hand disturbed the thicket of his dark, windswept hair, giving him an even wilder out of control look. His jaw was heavily shadowed as if he hadn't shaved since the day of her sister's wedding. She wondered what it would feel like to have him kiss her now with his lean jaw all scratchy and intensely, disturbingly male.

She gave a little shiver and tore her eyes away from his face.

'Are you cold?' he asked.

'No.'

They walked on a bit further in silence.

Connor watched her covertly as she walked beside him, the sweet fragrance of her hair reaching his nostrils from time to time as the wind lifted the chestnut strands across her face.

He felt that familiar gut-tightening reaction he'd experienced the very first time he'd met her. She was so unlike all the women he'd known, and he was the first to admit he'd known rather too many of late. It was time to settle down after that last disastrous affair with the Texan heiress—he had to take stock and get his priorities sorted once and for all. He owed that to his mother's memory if nothing else.

He couldn't help thinking his mother would have approved of the defiant figure beside him. Jasmine was like a breath of fresh sea air with her spirited defiance and spitfire tongue, but he was almost certain that underneath that prickly exterior she was already starting to melt. He saw it in her grey-blue eyes when she thought he wasn't looking. There was a hunger there and he fully intended to satiate it…

Jasmine listened to the crunch of leaves and twigs under

their feet and the warble of the magpies in the gum trees overhead. The sound of cicadas filled the air; it was as if they knew the long, hot summer was over and the shortening days would silence their chorus soon.

'How long are you planning to stay here?' he asked after a few more minutes.

'A day or two,' she answered, not comfortable with revealing all her movements to him.

'I left my car up at the beach house,' he informed her.

'How did you find it?'

'I just drove up the driveway and there it was.'

She gave him a reproving look.

'I mean, how did you know I was here? It's not exactly on the beaten track.'

'Well, it's rather a long story but I was discussing real estate with someone and they mentioned a property down here they thought I might be interested in, and I bought it.'

Jasmine forced her feet to keep moving forward, hoping her voice sounded suitably uninterested. 'Oh, really?'

'You probably know it quite intimately,' he said. 'It's not all that far from you.'

She stopped so suddenly she almost stumbled over her own feet.

'Which place?'

His dark eyes glinted down at her.

'The old house down the road.'

She knew it well. She generally avoided it because it appeared deserted and dilapidated, sad almost, as if whoever had lived there had not been all that happy with life. The fact that Connor had bought it seemed to her to be a deliberate act on his part to force his presence on both her and the neglected property.

She wasn't sure which she was defending when she turned on him. 'You have no right to come here!'

'I beg to differ as I have every right in the world. The place is now mine, so I can come and go as I please.'

She gave him a venomous glare.

'You're doing this deliberately, aren't you? You're invading every area of my life to get your own way.'

'Don't be so prickly,' he chided. 'Nothing was further from my mind.'

'Don't lie to me!' She almost shouted the words. 'If you think this will make me marry you to get you out of trouble, forget it. There's nothing on this planet that would induce me to become your wife—nothing!'

He let her vent her spleen, standing quietly and calmly, which only served to infuriate her even more.

She turned abruptly and stomped away, her head down in case he caught a glimpse of her stinging tears of anger.

Somehow she lost him at the turn-off. She took the long way back to the house that few people knew and, when she was sure he wasn't following, sat by the creek bed and howled out her frustration, leaving it another hour before she finally returned to the little beach house.

When she got there Connor's car was gone. But when she looked down at the dusty gravel of the driveway she could see where his tyres had been and it made her feel uneasy.

He'd be back, she was sure; that much about him she did know.

He'd be back.

Jasmine decided after another hour of sickening dread, that Connor would reappear and find her still crying, that her best course of action would be to leave.

She packed with none of her usual attention to detail, thrusting things untidily into the back of her car as if the hounds of hell were on her tail.

She gave the beach house a cursory swipe with a dust cloth and mop and hightailed it out of the driveway before she changed her mind.

Thankfully there was hardly any traffic on the roads and

although she had to stop once for petrol the trip back to her inner city flat was uneventful.

Her flat seemed poky and stuffy after the fresh air of Pelican Head. She felt claustrophobic and cornered, as if her days were numbered like someone on death row.

Ever since Connor Harrowsmith had come into her life she'd felt unsafe. He made her feel things she didn't want to feel. He made her so angry she wanted to hit him. She wanted to tear at his mocking eyes and stop him laughing at her from behind those chocolate irises.

The telephone buzzed beside her as she sat on her bed.

She looked at it indecisively for five more rings before snatching up the receiver.

'Jasmine?' Her mother's voice was wobbly—probably from a recent bout of tears.

'Hello, Mum.'

'Jasmine, you have to marry him. Please, darling, if for no other reason, do it for me.'

Jasmine felt fresh tears at the back of her own eyes and she swallowed deeply.

'Mum, I—'

'The parish council has called a meeting. They're thinking of withdrawing their support for your father.' Her mother's voice cracked. 'And with the synod meeting in a matter of weeks, you know how this will impact on his plans for the position of Archbishop.'

'Mum—'

'Jasmine, I've done all I can but this is the last straw. I can't see your father ruined. The last time was bad enough and now we have to relive it all again, splashed all over the press.'

'That's not my fault.'

'It is all your fault!' her mother screeched.

Jasmine's hand around the telephone tightened as she fought to control her temper. It was so unfair! Was there no one on this earth who would suspend judgement long enough to find out all the details first?

'Your father has decided on an ultimatum,' her mother continued.

'Which is?'

'He doesn't wish to see you again unless you agree to marry Connor immediately.'

'What about you?' Jasmine asked pointedly. 'Will you see me again if I don't?'

There was a telling silence at the end of the line.

'Darling—' her mother paused for breath '—you know how difficult this is for me but your father and I agree—'

Jasmine had heard enough; she knew she was cornered and there was no point fighting any more. Whenever her mother used that tone of voice she felt guilty. It was like an intolerable load on her back to hear that defeated, long-suffering tone. She loved her mother and, deep down, knew she would do anything to relieve her suffering, even if it cost her dearly.

'All right,' she said after another tight silence. 'I'll do it.'

Her mother's gushing relief should have encouraged her but it didn't. Instead it made her realise she had just stepped into a noose that had been laid out especially for her.

And at the other end of the rope was Connor Harrowsmith, who would no doubt be smiling in victory at her final capitulation.

CHAPTER THREE

JASMINE had no way of contacting Connor but he must have known she'd changed her mind for when she got back home from the clinic the following day he was waiting for her outside her flat.

He was leaning up against his shiny black Maserati, this time dressed a little more formally in a business shirt, tie and black trousers which seemed to make his long legs look even longer.

His eyes meshed with hers as she came across the road from the bus stop.

'Hello.'

She found it hard to hold his look and inspected the cracked pavement at her feet.

'What brings you here?'

'What do you think?' he asked.

She gave a non-committal shrug before chancing a look at his handsome face.

'I don't suppose you've brought an engagement ring with you?' She hoped her tone sounded flippant enough to cover the trepidation she was currently feeling.

'I did, as a matter of fact,' he said, surprising her completely.

'Oh.' What else could she say?

'It was my grandmother's so I hope it fits. If it doesn't, we'll have it adjusted.' He slipped his hand into the top pocket of his shirt and handed her a little velvet box, the edges worn with age.

She took it from him, trying not to touch his fingers as she did so. She opened the box and for a long moment looked at the ruby surrounded by tiny diamonds.

'Go on, try it on.'

She took it out and slipped it on to her finger, somehow not at all surprised to find it was a perfect fit.

She lifted her troubled gaze to his. 'It's beautiful. It must be very valuable.'

'It is.'

She didn't know what to say. It seemed like sacrilege to be wearing such a ring for all the wrong reasons. It wasn't a proper engagement in any sense of the word, nor would it ever be a proper marriage.

'Would you like a drink or something?' She hunted for her keys in her bag, trying to cover her unease with forced politeness.

'Sure.'

He followed her up the pathway to the old terrace house where she occupied the top floor. She hoped he wasn't noticing the cracked and peeling paint on the stairwell as they went up. She imagined he lived in some sort of playboy mansion in an exclusive suburb and was probably turning his aristocratic nose up with distaste with each and every step he took behind her.

'This is cosy,' he said, surprising her again as he followed her into her tiny flat.

She tossed down her keys without answering.

'Have you lived here long?'

'A few months,' she answered. 'It's close to the clinic.'

'Ah, the clinic.' There was something in his tone that unsettled her. 'I've heard all about the clinic.'

'From whom?' Her words were sharpened by her anger at her parents' ultimatum. She could just imagine them describing the run-down building to him, lamenting the fact that their church school educated daughter had chosen such a career path, and an underpaid one at that.

'Not from anyone you'd know,' he said.

'My parents haven't talked to you about it?' She eyeballed him directly.

'I'm afraid my conversations with your parents so far have concentrated on other topics.'

She could just imagine!

'You weren't too put off by one of my father's interminable lectures about right and wrong?'

'Your father and I have come to an impasse. He thinks he's right and I think he's wrong.'

'About what?'

'About you.'

'Me?' She stared at him.

'Yes, you. He doesn't know you at all, does he?'

Jasmine couldn't help feeling a little bit overexposed. How had he come to that conclusion? He hardly knew her! Surely that one night in his bed, innocent as it was, couldn't have given him any sort of insight into her character?

'I'm not sure I know what you mean,' she hedged.

'Do you know, to an outsider you seem to be rather a misfit in your family,' he said, watching her intently.

She turned away from his all-seeing eyes to switch on a lamp. Her tiny flat didn't get much afternoon sun and the subdued lighting gave the room an intimate atmosphere she felt uncomfortable sharing with him.

'What makes you think that?' she asked off-handedly.

She watched him out of the corner of her eye as he sat down on her second-hand sofa chair, the one with the springs showing through the cushions, noticing he didn't even flinch as he sat on their protruding coils.

'Your hair for one thing.'

'My hair?' She touched the cascading strands around her face self-consciously; no matter what she did, her hair would just not stay up.

'Your sisters all have straight blonde hair; your hair is chestnut and curly.'

'So?'

'Your parents are both fair.'

'Perhaps I'm a throw-back.' She met his eyes across the room. 'It happens from time to time.'

His dark gaze held hers.

She felt increasingly uncomfortable under his scrutiny, frightened in case he would eventually see through the wall of indifference she'd erected around herself for protection.

'What would you like to drink?' she asked, desperate for a subject change even if it meant extending his visit, loath as she was to do it.

'What will you have?' he asked.

'I'm not a drinker,' she said without apology. 'So I've only juice, tea or coffee or water. The coffee's instant by the way.'

'Water's fine,' he said, surprising her yet again. 'It's been quite warm today, hasn't it?'

She wasn't so sure about the day but she was feeling increasingly warm with his dark eyes on her all the time!

'I didn't go outside much,' she answered. 'I was tied up with a workshop all day.' She went through to the kitchen and got two glasses out of the cupboard above the sink.

'What do you do at the clinic?' he asked from behind her.

She waited until she'd filled both glasses before turning to answer him. He took the glass she held out to him, his fingers brushing hers.

'I'm involved with the rehab team.' She cradled her own glass with both hands. 'We teach the patients life skills, help them find employment—that sort of thing.'

'Rewarding work.'

She gave him a rueful look.

'Sometimes.' She took a sip of water. 'But I'm afraid there aren't as many happy endings as I'd like.'

'People have free will. You can't always make them change unless they want it for themselves.'

'I know.' She put the glass down on the sink. 'But I have to try.'

'Because of your family background?' he asked.

She looked at him when he said that.

It amazed her later to think how close she had been to admitting to him how right he was, but something had stopped her. She didn't want him to have access to any part of her private life; it was less hurtful that way.

She pushed herself away from the sink and made to move past him.

'If you've finished your water I think you should be going. I have some calls to make.'

His hand came down on her arm and held her fast. She forced herself to meet his gaze but it took every ounce of her pride to hold it without blinking.

'I haven't finished talking to you,' he said. 'We have a wedding to plan.'

'Plan it without me.' Her tone was dismissive as if they were discussing a picnic she hadn't yet made her mind up to attend. 'I'm not fussy.'

'So it seems.' His tone was dry. 'But, all the same, I'd like your input.'

'I don't want a big wedding,' she insisted. 'A registry office will do and no guests.'

'What about photographs?'

'No photographs.'

'You might regret that one day when the kids ask to see them.'

She wrenched her arm out of his hold and glared up at him. 'What kids?'

She didn't care for the dark glitter that had suddenly come into his eyes. 'Ours, of course.'

She felt a flicker of heat pool traitorously in her belly at the thought of being swollen with his child but as quickly as she could she stamped it out.

'If you think this marriage will ever be consummated you're very much mistaken.'

He quirked one aristocratic brow.

'Never say never, sweetheart.' The corner of his mouth

twisted mockingly. 'Such emphatic statements have a nasty habit of coming back dressed up as humble pie.'

'I don't want to marry you in the first place!' she fumed. 'If I have to sleep with you it will make it a hundred times worse!'

'How so?'

'You know how so.' She clenched her fists in agitation.

'I'll be gentle—'

'Oh, for God's sake!' She wanted to stamp her foot over his toes in frustration. 'Stop making fun of me!'

'I'm not making fun of you; I'm simply informing you of my intentions.'

'Your intentions are to milk this situation for all it's worth. I know what you're up to. This is about getting back at your stepfather, isn't it?'

His eyes narrowed slightly and she continued heatedly. 'I'm known as a notorious tart; everyone knows it and, even if they'd forgotten, they were reminded of it in the papers two days in a row. What better way to rub your family's nose in it than to marry me to spite them?'

'If you'll remember, the notion of marrying you was your father's suggestion,' he pointed out in even tones.

She'd forgotten that little detail but it made no difference.

'Either way it's still his penance for you. It's all the same thing, isn't it? I've been cast as the devil's gateway in all this; it's irrelevant who's actually oiled the hinges.'

His chuckle of amusement broke the tension.

'What's so funny?' She frowned at him darkly, trying to suppress the twitch of her mouth that had been precipitated by his.

'You are.'

'I'm not trying to be funny.' She scowled.

'I know, and that's why you're so successful at making me laugh.' He touched her gently on the cheek. 'Not many people can make me laugh; not many people at all.'

Jasmine couldn't quite get rid of the feeling that something other than mutual amusement was being passed between them. It was more subtle than that; like a delicate, slender thread had passed across the room, linking them in an indefinable way.

Her cheek still tingled from his butterfly-like touch, her senses now on full alert at his nearness. He was half a step away from her. She could even feel the heat coming off his body as he stood looking down at her, his firm mouth relaxed in a small sexy smile that sent a silent message straight to her feminine core.

He closed the distance without appearing to have moved at all. For a fleeting moment she wondered if in fact it had been her who had shifted in response to a subconscious desire to feel his mouth on hers.

He bent his head as if in slow motion.

The anticipation was like torture to Jasmine's already throbbing lips, her snagging breath escaping in sharp, painful little intervals from between them. As his head came closer and closer her lips opened automatically as if commanded to do so by the flash of desire in his eyes.

His lips touched hers in a tentative 'hardly there' kiss that made her lips buzz with sensation even more. He did it again, and again, each time the pressure increasing a mere fraction as if he were tasting her for the very first time.

She'd had enough.

She wanted him to kiss her, really kiss her.

She grasped his dark head between her hands and took over the kiss with all the pent-up passion she'd been feeling from the first moment his eyes had met hers in the church at her sister's wedding. Her tongue found his and he tightened his hold around her waist, pulling her into his hard frame, leaving her in absolutely no doubt of his body's instant reaction.

He wanted her.

For whatever reason, he wanted her and knowing it made her own response to him fire out of control. Her mouth became frenzied on his, kissing him greedily as if he were the very air she needed to breathe to keep alive.

He returned the frantic pleas of her mouth with commandeering ones of his own, his tongue leaving no corner of her mouth unexplored, staked and claimed.

She felt as if she belonged to him now.

He'd branded her with an invisible brand that left her useless without his touch on her fevered skin.

She craved it.

She craved it like the thirsty crave water or the hungry hunger for food. Every cell in her body was rising up to greet him, every nerve leaping just under her skin to feel the pressure of his fingers running over her, caressing her. Her breasts felt heavy, their pointed buds tight against the cotton of her bra, straining, aching to get closer to him.

She felt the rasp of his evening shadow as he moved his mouth slightly, sending a sharp burst of sensation to the pit of her stomach. Never had she been more aware of his masculinity. Her heightened awareness fuelled the leaping flames of her desire into a conflagration; she was completely at his mercy, wanting him even more than her pride, which until now had been so important to her.

As if he sensed her surrender, his kiss changed to a seductive caress, his lips leaving hers to move down to the sensitive skin of her neck. She felt the warm brush of his fingers undoing the top three buttons of her simple white blouse, the fabric folding open to give him access to the creamy shadow of her breasts lying waiting, aching for his touch.

He gave her an opened mouth kiss on the upper side of her right breast; the heat of his mouth firing her senses to an intolerable level. He did the same to the other and she thought she would scream if he didn't finish the job properly by uncovering her breasts completely.

His hand came up to gently cup her cheek, lifting her face so she had no choice but to look up at him.

'You know I could do right now what most men would do

in this situation, yet something tells me it's not the right time.' His voice was deep and husky. 'But I promise you I will finish this. You have my word.'

Jasmine found the sparkle of unrelieved desire in his eyes compelling; she couldn't look away if she tried. She swallowed the restriction in her throat; her intake of breath catching in tiny little tugs all the way down into her lungs.

He released his hold and stepped away from her.

'I have to go now,' he said. 'Will you be all right?'

Pride came to her rescue. What did he think she was, some sort of sexual desperado?

'I think I'll just about manage,' she said tightly.

He smiled and touched her on the cheek once more.

'Till next time.'

She didn't answer him.

She didn't trust herself not to beg him to come back and finish what he'd started right here and now.

She watched as he walked from the room and then listened to his footsteps as he traversed the tiny hall, heard the door open and registered the click of the lock as it closed behind him, still without moving a millimetre from where he'd left her.

She was frozen to the spot by the sudden realisation that her hatred of him had vaporised, leaving in its place a much more destructive emotion. The sort of emotion she didn't want to feel for any man, the sort of emotion that would spell disaster for someone such as her.

She didn't want to love him.

Damn him!

She wasn't going to give in!

Jasmine did all she could to avoid Connor's calls.

She left the phone off the hook for hours and didn't answer the door if the doorbell rang. She worked the most unfriendly hours she could, repeatedly taking the graveyard shift to avoid facing him until she was ready.

She wasn't ready.

She wondered if she'd ever be ready.

She only had to think of him and her stomach would cave in, the sweet hollow feeling reminding her of an aching physical need of him.

As if summoned by her thoughts, he materialised just as she was leaving the clinic at midnight the following Friday. He was standing outside, leaning against his car, his dark, hooded gaze fixed on her.

He pushed himself away from the car and before she could say anything picked up her left hand and inspected it. He dropped it and asked, 'Where's your ring?'

She found the abruptness of his tone intensely irritating.

'I don't wear it in public.'

'Why not?' He almost barked the words at her.

Her eyebrows rose and she swung away from him to make her way to the bus stop. She hadn't taken three steps before he'd caught the tail of her untucked shirt and pulled her back.

'Hey!' She slapped at his hand. 'This is my best shirt!'

'It's too big for you and it's the wrong colour,' he said.

She felt herself bristle at his criticism.

'I like it.' She snatched the fabric out of his grasp and dusted herself off exaggeratedly.

'Why haven't you answered my calls?' he asked.

'I've been busy.'

'You've been avoiding me.'

'No I haven't,' she lied.

'Why don't you wear my ring?'

'I thought it was my ring?' she shot back.

'Don't split hairs.'

'It's too expensive.'

'Oh, for God's sweet sake, Jasmine, it's an engagement ring. It's supposed to be expensive.'

'I don't like wearing expensive jewellery.'

'Then I'll get you something cheaper.'

'I don't want something cheaper.'

'Then what the hell do you want?' His voice rang out over the deserted street.

'I...' She clamped her mouth shut. She was so close to shouting back that she wanted him—wanted him with every fibre of her being.

'I want to go home,' she said instead. 'It's been a long day.'

He sighed and, taking her arm, led her towards his car. 'It's been a long week,' he said, opening the door for her. 'And it's not over yet.'

She didn't respond. She slipped into the seat with uncharacteristic meekness and silently buckled her seatbelt. She watched as he came round to the driver's side and took his own seat, his glance wrathful as it came her way.

'Don't ever do that again, do you hear me?'

She gave him a frosty look. 'You don't own me.'

'Yet.' He started the car with a violent turn of the key.

She winced at the barely disguised anger simmering under the surface of his one hard-bitten word.

'Did you get out of the wrong side of the bed this morning?' She folded her arms across her chest huffily.

'You could say that.' He recalled the lonely emptiness of his bed that morning, adding with a rueful glance her way, 'It was certainly the wrong bed.'

Her heart sank. Surely he didn't have someone else? A sick feeling came into her stomach, a combination of fear and dashed hopes and mind-blowing jealousy.

'Perhaps you should be a little more careful in your choice of bed partner,' she tossed back.

'I intend to be very careful in future.'

She didn't know what to make of his statement so kept silent.

It was a while before he spoke.

'I suppose you saw the televised interview with Holden's wife on Channel One last night?'

She kept her eyes on her tightly crossed knees.

'No, I didn't.'

She felt his quick glance.

'Why not? Surely you'd want to know what's being said about you.'

She elevated one slim shoulder dismissively. 'What would be the point? It's not as if I can answer my critics.'

'You could give your own interview, tell them your side of the—'

'No!'

She felt his assessing glance once more.

'You sound very determined.'

'I am.'

'The money doesn't tempt you?'

She looked at him at that. 'No, the money doesn't tempt me.'

He turned back to the traffic, his brow creased in a heavy frown.

He knew she didn't know all the facts. How could she? The trouble was, he knew too much. The burden of his knowledge was like a thorn in his side. It niggled at him constantly, but he could hardly blurt out the truth. She would very likely be devastated to hear it so baldly. Better to let her begin to suspect something and then gradually help her to see it...

A wave of protectiveness washed over him, surprising him in its intensity. He wasn't usually the knight in shining armour type; God knew he'd exploited so many relationships in the past any decent white horse would have bucked him off years ago. But there was something about Jasmine that stirred him where no one had stirred him before. He wasn't all that sure he understood it but he knew he had to have her, and her parents' ultimatum was going to make it a whole lot easier than he'd expected.

'I had a call from your father today,' he said after a long pause.

She gave a cynical grunt as he pulled up alongside her terrace house.

'What did he want? A chance to inveigle himself into the registry office proceedings?'

'It seems he's having a rethink about us getting married.'

Jasmine tensed.

'Apparently he thinks you could do much better.'

'What did you say?' she asked, not brave enough to look his way.

He gave a deep chuckle that sent shivers up her spine.

'What I told him is not for a bishop's daughter's ears.' He gave her a wry glance. 'Unfortunately, it wasn't all that suitable for a bishop's ears either.'

A bubble of laughter came out of her mouth before she could stop it. She quickly covered it with a self-conscious cough but from the satisfied expression on his face when she looked at him she could tell he'd heard and noted it.

'So the wedding's off?' she asked.

'No, the wedding is not off.'

A funny sensation flickered between her thighs at his emphatic tone.

'Actually, he soon changed his mind again,' he added.

She looked at him warily, wondering what was going on behind that sexy half-smile playing at the corner of his mouth.

'Don't tell me you had to bribe him for my hand?'

He gave a deep rumble of laughter which sent another shiver of sensation right through her.

'Your father is very proud of his organ, isn't he?'

It took her a moment to grasp his meaning but by then it was already too late, her cheeks were fiery red.

'Yes, although it's in some need of repair,' she muttered, trying not to look his way.

'Not enough use?' He threw her a cheeky look.

She didn't answer, but the glance she sent his way spoke for her and he laughed again.

'Once your father cashes the cheque I just donated to the organ fund I don't think we'll hear another word about my unsuitability as a husband.'

'I thought you were short of money.' She frowned at him. 'Isn't that why you need to get married to access your mother's estate?'

His eyes were on the traffic ahead and he waited until someone turning right moved out of his way before he answered.

'I will never be short of money, but the money I want most in the world is what my mother left for me in her will. I guess compared to what I currently earn it may, to some people, seem rather a pittance, but she wanted me to have it and no one, and I mean no one, is going to stop me getting it.'

There was something in his tone that yet again alerted her to some undercurrent of ill-feeling towards his stepparents. She wished she knew more about his childhood, about the grief he must have felt on the death of his mother at such a young age, and his feeling of uncertainty for his future living in a household of people who bore no blood relationship to him. She didn't voice her thoughts, however; she didn't want him to think she had any feelings of any sort where he was concerned, and especially not feelings of empathy.

'You're making a big mistake tying yourself to me,' she warned as he turned the car into the kerb. 'Nothing good can come out of it.'

'Let's wait and see, shall we?' His eyes caught and held hers.

She had to look away; he had an uncanny knack of seeing things she didn't want him to see.

'Thanks for the lift home.' She reached for the door.

He reached across her to open it for her and she instantly shrank back as his muscled arm brushed against her breasts.

He heard her swift intake of breath and, leaning back, gave her a long, studied look.

'Jasmine, answer me one question.'

She turned back to face him. 'What is it?'

He waited a full thirty seconds before he spoke.

'Tell me something.' He paused. 'Are you agreeing to

marry me because of your parents' demands on you or because of my desire to claim my mother's estate?'

What could she say?

Neither?

That she was tempted to marry him just for herself? There was no way she was going to confess that to him! The truth was she did want to marry him. She wasn't entirely sure why. He annoyed her, agitated her, teased her and intrigued her as no one else had ever done but a secret part of her felt drawn to him, as if he alone held the key to her long search for happiness. His laughter stirred her, his touch inflamed her, and his eyes twinkled with passionate promise until she couldn't think straight. But she mustn't let him see the effect he had on her. That must be kept hidden at all costs.

'I've got nothing better to do.' She tossed his previous words back at him casually.

A small smile tugged at his mouth.

'Jasmine Byrne, what the hell am I going to do with you?'

'I don't know.' Her voice came out huskily.

'I know what I want to do.' He closed the distance between them, his arm coming around her shoulder and drawing her close.

She lifted her startled gaze to his descending mouth, her heart tripping in her chest as she felt his warm breath disturb the soft surface of her lips.

'W…what?' She barely breathed the word.

'You know what,' he said and covered her mouth with his.

She didn't want the kiss to end.

She was already mentally rehearsing her invitation for him to come upstairs when he broke the contact and looked down at her with a rueful half-smile.

'I'll call you tomorrow,' he said.

Her fingers reached and fumbled over the door handle and somehow she finally managed to get it open and drag herself from the car without caving in to the temptation to beg.

She stood awkwardly on the pavement, her hands twisted

in front of her just like a gauche schoolgirl coming back from her very first date.

'Go on in,' he said. 'I'll wait until you're safely indoors before I leave.'

She turned on her heels and walked the short distance to the front door, all the time resisting the urge to run back to the car and plead with him to...

'Jasmine?'

His voice stalled her.

She turned back around, faint hope flashing briefly on her features until she saw he was holding something out to her, suspended on the end of his long fingers.

'Your bag,' he said evenly, his expression unreadable.

She walked back to his car with as much dignity as she could and took her bag from him.

'Thank you,' she said stiffly.

He didn't say a word.

She walked back to the front door and after three attempts finally opened it and without a backward glance went inside and closed it behind her.

But even as she stood and listened as his powerful car drove off she was sure she could hear the sound of his mocking laughter filling the night air.

Damn him!

CHAPTER FOUR

THE date for the wedding had been set for the following Friday.

All the way to her parents' house Jasmine's anger had been steadily growing over her father's permission being granted for the mere price of a pipe organ overhaul. She wanted to be angry at Connor for suggesting it, but knew deep down it was her father she was most annoyed with for accepting it.

On her arrival, however, it seemed her mother still had some misgivings.

'Are you sure you know what you're doing?' Frances Byrne asked, her brow furrowed in a frown.

'Of course I know what I'm doing,' she answered, wondering if it were entirely true.

'But darling—' her mother's hands twisted together '—he's so…so…'

'Go on, say it, Frances,' her father cut in impatiently. 'He's a rake and he gambles.'

'And I'm an outrageous tart,' Jasmine shot back. 'A match made in heaven, if you ask me.'

Her father had always found it difficult to deal with her propensity for sarcasm and, as was his custom, shook his head and looked heavenward for guidance.

'Oh, for goodness sake, Elias,' her mother scolded.

'It's all right, Mum,' Jasmine said, sensing a showdown. 'I understand your concern, but this is now between Connor and me.'

Her mother's worried gaze flicked to her husband and back again.

'Jasmine…' She hesitated.

'No, Frances,' her father interrupted her. 'Leave it.'

'But Elias, she has to know some time—'

'If you mean about the organ fund, I already know about that.' She threw her father a caustic glance.

Her father shifted his gaze uncomfortably.

'Elias—' Her mother's voice sounded hollow and her features took on a sickening pallor.

Jasmine's eyes went back and forth between her parents, a sinking feeling coming into her stomach at the lines of tension she could see etched on their faces as they exchanged worried glances.

'What's going on?' she asked.

Her father's lips closed together like a purse being shut.

'Mum?' She turned back to her mother, her frown deepening.

'Nothing's going on,' her mother said, avoiding her eye. 'I'm just being silly, that's all. Too many weddings in one year, I suppose.' She dabbed at her eyes and once she was finished stuffed her handkerchief back up her sleeve, communicating that her brief lapse into sentimentality was now over.

'Jasmine, your mother and I want you to be happy,' her father said in the tone he used for a particularly serious sermon topic. 'But your tendency to rush headlong into things has always been of great concern to us.'

'I'm twenty-four years old,' she said with a touch of bitterness. 'Surely it's time I was left to deal with the consequences of my actions without your intervention.'

Her parents exchanged another nervous, agitated glance.

'What is it with you two?' Jasmine asked in frustration. 'You're acting unusually weird all of a sudden.'

'Darling—' her mother used the soothing tone she saved for emergencies '—of course we're not acting weird! We're both looking forward to seeing you happily married to Mr...I mean Connor, aren't we, Elias?'

Her father grunted and picked up the sermon notes he'd

been revising before his wife and daughter had interrupted him.

'I'll be in the breakfast room,' he said and closed the door behind him.

Jasmine looked at her mother.

'Mum?'

Frances Byrne gathered up the patchwork quilt she was making for the parish fair.

'Don't worry about your father,' she said, folding the quilt haphazardly. 'He's nervous about the synod, that's all.'

Jasmine sighed. 'I understand, Mum, I really do.'

'No, you don't,' her mother said, clutching her needlework to her chest like a shield. 'That's the whole trouble; you don't understand.'

Her mother left the room and Jasmine was left staring at the space she'd just vacated, her mind swirling with a kaleidoscope of doubt and fear.

Connor called on her the Monday before the wedding. She'd not long come home from the clinic after a particularly trying day when one of her 'hopefuls' had slipped through the hoop and gone back on the streets for 'a fix'.

She was in no mood to discuss weddings, parties or anything.

'What do you want?' she sniped as she thrust her key in the lock.

He followed her into the flat, deftly catching her bag as she flung it to one side carelessly.

'Hard day at the office?' he commented, hanging her bag over the back of the nearest chair.

She shot him a fiery look, frightened that if she relinquished her anger she'd howl like a baby instead. Ever since that strange exchange with her parents she'd felt on edge, as if she were on the cusp of some new change in her life, a change that would be both permanent and painful.

'Why are you here?'

'I've missed you.'

She gritted her teeth. 'I wish you wouldn't make fun of me all the time.'

'I'm not. I'm telling you the truth. I really missed you today.'

'You saw me three days ago.'

'I like seeing you every day.'

'Why?' She glared at him. 'So you can inspect the goods daily to make sure you aren't being short-changed?'

His dark eyes flashed a gentle but firm warning.

'Are you premenstrual?'

'*What?*' she gasped.

'Are you—'

'I heard you the first time!' She stomped to the other side of the tiny lounge and, crossing her arms over her chest, faced him. 'Why is it that women's anger is nearly always relegated as hormonal? Why can't women be allowed to be angry without a biological reason?'

'What are you angry about?'

'Everything.' She let out her breath in a rush.

'That's pretty broad.' He perched on the edge of her old sofa. 'Want to narrow it down a bit?'

She was close to tears and hated him for it. She turned her back and addressed the dismal brown curtains with the silver fish holes in them.

'One of my clients went back on the streets last night,' she said, her voice sounding hollow and defeated. 'No one can find him.'

'Then how do you know he's back on the streets?'

She turned to look at him. 'We have it on reasonably good authority he bought some drugs at about midnight. No one has seen him since.'

'Has someone checked where he lives?'

'He doesn't really live anywhere.' She sighed heavily. 'Occasionally he stays overnight at one of the homeless hostels, but…'

'It's hard to believe that in this western civilisation of ours, people still choose to live on the streets,' he commented.

'It's not a choice!' She rounded on him hotly. 'Oscar's family kicked him out when he was barely fourteen! His stepfather abused him repeatedly and his mother is an alcoholic. He'd been on the streets for three years before we came across him and began counselling him, to help him kick his heroin habit.'

'With any success?'

She sighed again. 'He'd agreed to go on a methadone programme but he's got a lot of anger stored up and whenever things get him down he has a relapse.'

'You really care about these people, don't you?' His question brought her head back up.

She met his eyes across the room and was surprised to find warmth in their depths.

'Yes, I do care.'

'So you work with them for next to nothing to do your bit to change the world?'

She hunted his face for signs of criticism but his expression remained largely impassive.

'I don't need a lot of money,' she answered.

'What about clothes?' His eyes ran over her worn jeans and faded pink T-shirt.

'I'm not a fashion follower.'

'Don't you ever wish you had what your sisters have?'

She found his question unsettling.

'My sisters finished their education. I didn't. Employment for me has been difficult.'

'Why didn't you finish your education?'

'Why all these questions?' she fired at him. 'You read the story in the press of how I nearly ruined Roy Holden's teaching career. You don't need to hear it all again from me.'

'On the contrary, I'd very much like to hear it from you.'

She was angrier than she'd ever been at being so cornered.

'It's an old story.' She gave him a blistering look. 'A

young, impressionable sixteen-year-old student spends too much time with one of her teachers. We were caught in what the witness claimed to be "a compromising situation". He was transferred to another school, his career prospects in shreds.'

'And you?'

She lowered her eyes. 'I left school the same day. I couldn't bear the furtive looks and whispered comments, so I quit.'

'Why are you still punishing yourself after all this time?'

Her eyes flew to his once more. 'I'm not punishing myself.'

'You were a child,' he said. 'You shouldn't have been cast as the wrongdoer if it was Roy Holden.'

'Roy Holden wasn't any such thing!' Her protestation was vehement. 'He did nothing wrong, nothing.'

Connor looked at her intently for a long moment.

'So you took the rap?'

She looked away. 'It was my fault.'

'Teenage girls are notorious for harmless flirting. It's natural.'

'I didn't flirt with him,' she said. 'I...I liked listening to him. He was knowledgeable and made the books we read come to life. I'd never had a teacher like him before. From the first moment he looked at me, I felt as if a part of me had come alive, and...' She suddenly realised how much she'd given away and clamped her mouth shut.

What was it about Connor Harrowsmith that made her speak so unguardedly?

'What was your parents' reaction when your relationship with Holden became public?' he asked after a stretching silence.

'They were devastated.' She sat down on the chair opposite. 'Especially my mother. She had a migraine for three days. My father simply brushed up on all his moralising lectures on why good Christian girls shouldn't give in to the temptation of fleshly desires and delivered them at every available opportunity.'

'But you hadn't, had you?' His dark eyes never left hers for an instant. 'Given in to fleshly desires,' he clarified when she remained silent.

She felt two flags of colour on her cheeks.

'Certainly not with Roy Holden,' she said. 'But after all the drama, as an act of rebellion, I had a one night stand with the captain of the football team.'

'And?'

She gave him a rueful look. 'It was dreadful.'

He smiled in empathy. 'My first time was a shocker too.'

She felt a smile tug at her mouth and quickly suppressed it. 'What did Mrs Holden say in the television interview?' she asked.

'Just that she supported her husband in his claim of innocence of any impropriety.'

''Did she say anything about me?'

'Not really.'

'Nothing at all?'

'Nothing too damning, if that's what's worrying you, but I think our marriage will definitely put out the remaining embers of gossip.'

Jasmine gnawed at her bottom lip. 'It was all so long ago. Eight years, in fact. I can't understand why anyone would be in the least bit interested after all this time.'

'Your father's a bishop,' he pointed out. 'Anything any member of his family does or has done is fuel for gossip. If he were a milkman no one would be interested.'

'I guess you're right.'

'Come on.' He got to his feet. 'Let's find somewhere to have a quick meal and then we can take a drive around the haunts you think your young absconder might be frequenting.'

Jasmine picked up her bag from where he'd placed it earlier and followed him to the door, all the time her feelings for him undergoing a rapid turnaround. Apart from her colleague, Todd, at the clinic she didn't know of a single man who'd willingly take out a weeknight of his time to trawl the down-trodden end of town to look for a person he didn't even know.

It made her see him in a totally different light.

It made her hatred retreat to a place where she could no longer access it.

It made her afraid.

After trawling the streets for an hour or so they stopped to share a Chinese meal in a small café in Chinatown. Jasmine picked at her food, her eyes avoiding Connor's across the small table.

'Are you nervous about Friday?' he asked after a few minutes of silence between them.

'Why should I be nervous?' She lifted her gaze to his, her chin slightly raised. 'It's not as if it's a real marriage, it's merely a formality so we both get what we want. I want to get my parents off my back and you want to secure your late mother's trust fund.'

He watched her face for endless seconds.

'I have every intention for this to be a proper marriage, Jasmine, and you know it.'

'You can hardly force me.' Her chin went a little higher.

A small smile lifted one corner of his mouth.

'No, but I have some persuasive tricks in my repertoire that should have the desired effect.' He picked up his wine. 'They haven't let me down in the past.'

She could feel the heat rise in her cheeks as she imagined him in the arms of God knew how many women, all of them gasping for the release only he could provide with his masterful mouth and intensely male body.

She covered her discomfiture with sarcasm.

'I suppose you're leaving a veritable legion of disappointed women behind you now that you're so intent on removing yourself from bachelordom?'

'Not as many as you probably think.' He smiled. 'But enough to make you jealous.'

'I'm not jealous!' Her insistence was perhaps a little too emphatic and she could tell from the glint in his eye he'd noted it.

'Of course you're not.' He leant back in his chair and surveyed her flushed features in a leisurely manner. 'You'd have to care about me to be jealous, wouldn't you?'

Without answering, she poked at a grain of rice with the end of her chopstick.

'How many lovers have you had?' he asked after a little pause.

She squashed the grain of rice before lifting her eyes to his.

'Not as many as you probably think but enough to make you jealous,' she threw his own answer back at him.

His dark eyes twinkled with amusement as he twirled his wine glass in his hand.

'Nice come-back. I'm impressed.'

She toyed with her own glass, her fingers restless and fumbling.

'It wasn't a come-back, it's the truth. No man wants to hear the intimate details of his future wife's past sexual exploits.'

'I don't know.' He put his glass down and leaned his elbows on the table to look at her closely. 'I think I'd be very interested to hear who's been in your bed.'

Hot colour suffused her face and she turned away to disguise it. He had seen too much as it was, and it wouldn't do to be too transparent; her pride would never survive it.

The waiter came to clear their plates and she was saved from having to respond. They declined dessert and, after the bill came and was settled, Connor got to his feet and, taking her arm, tucked it through his.

'Come on, where shall we look for Oscar now?'

Jasmine walked with him back along the streets of Darlinghurst and King's Cross, occasionally stopping to talk to someone she knew, but all the time she was conscious of Connor's arm linked through hers.

No one seemed to know where Oscar was, or if they did

they weren't saying. They'd walked back and forth along the main thoroughfares and into some of the less frequented ones. Even Connor began to balk as someone looking a little the worse for wear leered at Jasmine, making an obscene comment about her availability and price.

He quickly ushered her back into the brighter lights of the main street and, standing under the nearest street-light, frowned down at her.

'I want you to promise me you won't ever come here again by yourself. Do you promise?'

She met his determined gaze, her expression undaunted.

'Don't be silly, that was only Reggie. He's totally harmless, and besides—' she gave him a reassuring half-smile '—that was just the sweet sherry talking.'

'Sherry or not,' he growled as he led her back to his car, 'this place isn't even safe for the police, let alone civilians.'

'Are you frightened?' She gave him a teasing glance.

He glowered down at her, but she could see behind the frowning expression the glint of amusement in his eyes.

'Of course I'm not frightened, but I don't like the thought of you out here wandering amongst goodness knows what desperadoes.'

'They're people like you and me, Connor,' she said, her tone now serious. 'They've just made a couple of bad choices here and there. Any one of us could end up the same, given similar circumstances.'

He looked at her speculatively for a long moment before sighing. 'You're right, of course.' He took her arm again and continued walking the two blocks back towards his car.

Somehow she sensed a certain quality in his statement, as if he himself had at some point been in difficult circumstances but had managed to right himself. She realised with a prickle of conscience that she still hadn't asked him anything about his family. Most of the conversations they'd had about family members had concentrated on hers.

'What was your mother's name?' she asked, when they were back in his car.

He shot her a quick glance before turning back to start the engine.

'Ellen.'

'Do you remember her?'

'A bit.' His voice was gruff.

'What sorts of things do you remember?'

His car lurched forward with a jerk as if he'd let the clutch out too early.

'What is this?' His look towards her was frowning. 'Why the sudden interest in my background?'

'I was just making conversation.' She folded her arms defensively. 'You ask me intimate questions all the time so I don't see why I shouldn't do the same to you.'

'My mother has been dead for nearly thirty years,' he said after a tight little silence. 'I don't see any point in bringing it all up now.'

'I'm sorry.'

'Look.' He turned the car into the kerb and once it was stationary faced her. 'The script of my family doesn't exactly read like the happy families on TV.'

Even in the subdued lighting within the car she could see the normally handsome lines of his face grow harsh in remembrance.

'For most of my childhood it was a fight for survival,' he said. 'I couldn't wait to get away.'

'What about Finn?' she asked. 'Weren't you two ever close?'

His eyes hardened. 'Finn's my stepbrother, the child of Julian and Harriet. No blood relationship to me and I don't think a day went past without one or both of my step-parents reminding me of it.'

'It must have been so lonely for you.'

'Probably no lonelier than for you,' he said, his tone softening as he turned the car back into the traffic once more.

'What do you mean?' She gave him a narrow-eyed glance.

'It can't have been easy for you, surrounded by sisters who couldn't do a thing wrong.'

'I wasn't bad all the time.'

'You didn't need to be,' he said. 'Just being different was bad enough.'

Jasmine felt a trickle of alarm slide down her spine.

'W…what do you mean by that?'

He flicked another quick glance, taking in the tight clench of her hands in her lap, the worried look in her blue eyes and the anxious set of her slim body, sitting upright in the seat.

'I mentioned to you before that you don't seem to really belong in your family. Does that worry you?'

'I'm not a believer,' she answered quickly, 'in a church family. That is about as isolating as you can get.'

'The black sheep, eh?'

'You'd better believe it.' She tried to make her tone light to cover her unease at his probing questions.

'Good for you,' he said, surprising her yet again. 'Good for you.'

Jasmine opened her mouth to say something in return but just then she noticed a familiar figure out of the corner of her eye.

'Stop the car!' she cried.

'What?' Connor braked and she lurched forward. 'Here?'

She already had the door open and was half out before the car had completely stopped.

He watched as she disappeared down a dark alley off the main drag of The Rocks. He quickly parked in a loading zone, hoping his car wouldn't be towed away for contravening the parking restrictions, even though it was getting on for one a.m. in the morning.

He found her at the end of the alley with her arms around a scraggy-looking youth who smelt as if he'd recently been sick.

'Should we get an ambulance?' he asked.

She shook her head. 'He's fine, just a bit of a hangover.'

He helped her get the youth on his feet, carefully sidestepping what appeared to be the recently evacuated contents of his stomach on the cobblestones.

'Where to now?' he asked, looking at Jasmine.

'We'll have to take him to the hostel.'

'In my car?' He winced at the thought of whatever else was left in the lad's stomach waiting to make an untimely appearance on the leather interior.

'Of course in your car.' She hitched the boy's floppy arm across her shoulder and then eyeballed Connor with an accusing eye. 'Unless you'd rather not?'

Somehow he sensed it was some sort of test.

'My car it is.' He took the boy's other arm and half carried, half dragged the lad to his less than three months old, showroom perfect Maserati.

The hostel was a short drive away and as they hauled the lad inside a large man of Maori extraction greeted Jasmine warmly.

'Hey, girl. So you found him, eh?'

Jasmine handed over her young charge, who was mumbling something unintelligible as he flopped on the nearest chair and dropped his head between his knees. She absently stroked his straggly hair as she spoke to the hostel supervisor.

'I don't think he's had a fix, just a little too much to drink. He'll probably sleep it off.'

'I'll get the Doc to give him the once over. Just in case.'

'Thanks, Rangi.' She smiled up at him and then, turning to Connor, introduced them.

'Rangi, this is Connor Harrowsmith.'

The men shook hands and exchanged one or two comments about the All Blacks rugby team, which made them both laugh.

Jasmine watched the little exchange with interest. She hated to admit it but Connor wasn't exactly as she'd assumed he'd be. There was no sign of snobbery about him and he seemed at ease talking with anyone, from members of the clergy like her father to street kids, and those who looked after them, like Rangi. Just when she thought she'd got him all figured out he'd say or do something that would totally surprise her.

'You two want a coffee or something?' Rangi asked, glancing between them.

'Not this time.' Connor spoke for both of them. 'Jasmine's had a long day and I've got an early flight in the morning. Thanks, anyway.'

'No problem.' Rangi held out his hand once more. 'Come back some time and I'll show you round the place.'

'I'd like that.' Connor smiled and reached for Jasmine's hand. 'Come on, honey, let's get you home.'

She waited until they were outside before she spoke.

'Where are you flying to in the morning?'

He drew her closer to his side as a wobbling couple came towards them, the young woman tottering on impossibly high heels as her inebriated partner sang at the top of his voice.

He waited until they were well past before answering.

'I'm flying to Perth for two days, then to Adelaide, but don't worry, I'll be back in time for the wedding.'

Her heart sank at the thought of facing the rest of the week without him to banter with; she'd become so used to it she almost craved it now.

'Is there anyone you'd like to invite to the ceremony?' he asked as they came to his car.

She shook her head.

'I told you before: no guests, no photographs.'

He frowned as he deactivated the central locking.

'But what about friends, or a favourite relative, perhaps?'

She looked away. 'My mother's an only child and my father hasn't spoken to his younger sister in decades.'

He quirked one brow. 'Some sort of family feud?'

She gave a little shrug.

'I don't know. Ever since I can remember the topic of Aunt

Vanessa has been out of bounds. Apparently she did the unforgivable and brought shame on the Byrne name.'

'Like you?' His eyes held hers for a moment.

She returned his look without blinking.

'Yes,' she said. 'Just like me.'

He opened the door for her and she slipped under his arm to take her seat, her awareness of him intensifying a hundredfold as his hand lifted a lock of her trailing hair out of the way of the door just before he closed it.

She was silent on the journey back to her flat, Connor driving the short distance without even glancing once in her direction. She wondered if he was thinking about their wedding ceremony in four days' time and whether he had even half the misgivings she currently harboured about the union, or if he was secretly congratulating himself on finally bringing about a solution to his deceased mother's estate. His future would now be secure with a token wife in tow, while he carried on with his life just as he had before. It wasn't as if it were a love match; he'd made no promises to her and nor did she expect him to. When it came down to it, she hardly knew him, she realised with a little jolt when she sneaked a covert glance his way. What was going on inside that handsome, dark-haired head? What was he seeing from behind those dark brown eyes?

Her eyes lowered to his hands where they were resting on the steering wheel and she gave a tiny shiver. What were those hands planning to do once they had placed a wedding ring on her finger?

CHAPTER FIVE

IT ONLY took Jasmine half a day to pack her things ready to move into Connor's house. She sat back on her heels and sighed as she surveyed her five cardboard cartons on the floor in front of her. Her few meagre belongings wouldn't be taking up too much space in his Woollahra mansion but she refused to be ashamed. It had been her choice to live simply and just because she was marrying into the Harrowsmith family didn't mean she was going to rush out and buy a whole lot of designer wear.

Connor had organised a key for her and arranged for a removal firm to pick up her things while he was in Perth. Jasmine had just as quickly cancelled the removal van and caught a cab instead.

When she arrived with her things in the cab, it was the first time she'd seen his house. She was glad he was interstate so she could look around at her leisure, hoping she would learn something about the enigmatic man she was marrying in less than four days.

It was a big house but not really pretentious in either size or décor. The cab driver carried her things to the foyer for her and once he'd gone she closed the door and looked around.

The long, wide hallway had various doors leading off it and a Persian runner lined the floor over highly polished floorboards. A grandfather clock was ticking rhythmically in the background and a wide staircase wound itself in a half turn to the floor above.

Jasmine went to the first door and looked in. It was a large sitting room, tastefully appointed, comfortable sofas and stylish lighting with beautiful formal cream curtains at the bay windows. Again the polished floorboards were occasionally interrupted with Persian rugs, which looked as if they were velvet.

She went to the next room where she found a long cedar dining table with seating for at least twenty, the beautifully carved chairs each in themselves like works of art. The colour of the dining room walls was a dark forest green and the curtains at the windows a rust-coloured fabric with a gold edging.

The kitchen wasn't large but it was decorated all in white, giving it the appearance of space, and the high-tech appliances added to the overall affect of functionality.

She wandered through each of the remaining downstairs rooms, noting the tastefully decorated bathrooms, and the utility room near the back door which led out to a neatly landscaped garden, resplendent in the golds and reds of autumn from the various European trees situated there.

She left the upper floor till last. The closer she got to the main bedroom the more uncomfortable she became. She knew Connor was out of town and not likely to find her in his room but even as she cautiously opened the door she felt his dark eyes following her every movement even though he was at least a couple of thousand kilometres away.

His room was dominated by a huge bed, the linen of a caramel tone with white edging. There was one large rug which almost covered the entire floor except for a border of about a foot all round where the floorboards shone through.

A door to the right led to an *en suite* bathroom and, tempted as she was to check if there were any wet towels on the floor, she somehow resisted the urge to peek. Another door led to a walk-in wardrobe and, this time giving in to the temptation, she went in and looked at his clothes hanging in neat rows.

It was like being in the room with him.

She could even detect his distinctive male smell, a combination of a particular brand of aftershave and his own masculine scent. Almost of its own volition her hand went out and touched one of his shirts, holding the sleeve against her face, breathing in the fragrance, imagining his arms coming around her and...

'Looking for somewhere to hang your things?' His deep voice sounded behind her.

Jasmine swung around so quickly the shirt she'd been holding came off its hanger and landed in a heap at her feet.

'I...I thought you weren't coming back until tomorrow?' She knew her face was aflame for the walk-in wardrobe suddenly felt over-hot, as if someone had turned on a heater to full power.

'The Adelaide meeting was cancelled at the last minute.' His eyes flicked to his shirt on the floor.

She bent to pick it up, her fingers fumbling over the task of replacing it on the hanger. She hung it back with the rest of his shirts before facing him.

'My... My things are downstairs,' she stammered. 'I...I wasn't sure where you wanted me to put them.'

His expression was so hard to read in the soft light of the wardrobe. She felt increasingly uncomfortable in the small space, and her breathing instantly became shallow and hurried.

'There's plenty of room in here.' He reached past her and pushed the left row of his suits out of the way. 'Put what you can here and I'll have my housekeeper clear some space in the drawers later.'

While he was rearranging his clothes, Jasmine took the opportunity to back out of the wardrobe.

He followed her out and looked down at her standing before him with her bottom lip caught between her small white teeth.

'Will you have a problem sharing my wardrobe?' he asked.

'No.' She let her lip go. 'I have a problem sharing your bed.'

'But that's what married couples do,' he pointed out with a mocking twist to his mouth.

'But our…' she hesitated over the word '…marriage isn't going to be like an ordinary marriage.'

'How so?'

'I don't want to complicate things by sleeping with you.'

'Listen, honey.' His tone was dry. 'It will complicate things a whole lot more if you don't.'

'It seems so…so cold-blooded. We're practically strangers and we don't have any feelings for each other.'

'I don't know about that,' he drawled. 'I certainly feel something for you.'

She gave him a frosty look.

'Now you're making fun of me again. You can't possibly feel anything for me other than lust and I despise you for it.'

'Is that so?' His dark eyes glittered.

'Yes.' Her mouth was tight. 'I despise you for taking advantage of my…my little mistake and allowing it to go this far. One word from you and the baying hounds of the press would've gone elsewhere looking for blood, but no, you let them run me to the ground.'

'Perhaps I should point out that I have absolutely no control over what the press says or does. I was hounded myself as soon as I touched down in Perth and it was a hundred times worse at Mascot when I landed an hour ago.'

'Why?'

'It seems the marriage of a notorious playboy to a bishop's daughter sells papers. Everyone wants an exclusive. You only have to look outside if you don't believe me.'

Jasmine frowned and, hesitating for half a minute, moved across to the windows and looked down.

'Oh, my God!' She swung back around to face him. 'There must be twenty journalists out there!'

'I know.' His expression was rueful. 'And I've just told each and every one of them to go to hell.'

She sat on his bed and twisted her hands together in agitation. 'What can we do?'

He shrugged off his suit jacket and reached back inside the wardrobe for a hanger.

'Nothing until Friday. Once the marriage is finalised I think we'll be left alone.'

His eyes met hers across the room. 'Trust me, Jasmine. Our marriage will solve this little problem once and for all.'

Jasmine wondered if that were strictly true. Sure, it might resolve the public's interest in them and leave them to get on with their lives, but their marriage was going to produce some problems of its own, the first one being the increasing ambiguity of her feelings for him.

How was she supposed to keep them hidden? How was she supposed to walk away when she ceased to be useful to him, as was surely to happen at some time in the not too distant future?

How would she survive it?

She stayed where she was, perched on the edge of his bed, and watched as he unpacked his case, her eyes drinking in the sight of the muscles of his back as he bent to pick up something off the floor.

He turned suddenly and caught the tail end of her look and a teasing smile lit his eyes.

'Do your parents know we're going to be living in sin till Friday?'

She gave him an icy look and crossed her legs to stop the flow of heat from her lower body.

'We're not exactly living in sin,' she pointed out with as much primness as she could.

'No, more like living in lust,' he said, grinning.

'Don't be so ridiculous!' She crossed her arms as well.

He closed his suitcase and shoved it into the corner of the wardrobe before closing the door and leaning back against it with his customary indolence.

'Why does the thought of physical intimacy threaten you so much?'

She forced herself to meet his gaze.

'I'm not threatened; I just prefer to feel something other than hatred for my sexual partners.'

'If you truly hated me, Jasmine, you would've insisted on your father marrying us and preaching a forty minute sermon on the Seven Deadly Sins while he was at it.'

She felt a reluctant smile tug at her mouth and hastily looked away.

'What are the Seven Deadly Sins, by the way?' he asked.

She began rattling them off without thinking. 'Pride, wrath, envy, gluttony, avarice and...' She stopped and chanced a look at him.

'And?' he prompted with a glint in his dark eyes.

She sprang off the bed and stalked over to the window to see if the press had moved on, her back stiffly turned against his teasing smile.

'I can't stay locked up in here for the rest of the week,' she bit out. 'I just can't.'

She felt him move across the room to stand at her shoulder, with barely the width of a hair separating them.

She held her breath as his hand reached out to separate the curtains so he could inspect the scene below. The curtain fell back into place and he turned, his hands coming to rest on her shoulders as he looked down at her.

'The press gang has just about gone,' he reassured her. 'If we give it another half an hour it will be dark and we can go and have a meal somewhere in peace.'

She felt herself drowning in the chocolate pools of his eyes, the warmth of his hands penetrating the fabric of her top until she was sure his fingers would be permanently imprinted on her flesh.

She could feel the strength of his long thighs so close to hers, not quite touching, but her lower body already felt as if he was probing her intimately. She could feel the tug of her inner muscles preparing...anticipating...aching...

The sound of the telephone from the side of the bed broke

the moment. Jasmine wasn't sure whether to be relieved or annoyed at the intrusion.

'It's for you.' He handed her the extension and she took it from him with an unsteady hand.

'Hello?'

'Jasmine, it's Todd. Your mother told me I'd find you on this number. We need you at the clinic. Annie, that girl you've been working with, the one with the little kid, has been asking to see you for the past hour. I can't get rid of her and the kid is howling like a banshee. Casey called in sick and Rangi's got his hands full with two attempted suicides down at the hospital. Can you come?'

Her eyes met Connor's and she felt an unexpected sensation of warmth when she saw him reach for his car keys.

'I'll be there as soon as I can,' she promised and hung up the phone.

Connor pulled up outside the clinic and strode around to open her door.

'What time do you think you'll be finished?' he asked as she stepped out.

'I'm not sure.'

'Call me and I'll pick you up.'

'It might be very late.' She addressed the bottom of his chin, not wanting him to see the gratefulness in her eyes.

He tipped up her face with the end of one long, very male, finger.

'Call me, Jasmine. Promise.'

She felt her breath hitch in her chest as she held his unwavering gaze.

'I promise.'

He bent his head and sealed her mouth with his in a brief, hard kiss. Then, without another word, he stepped back from her to swing away to get back into his car.

She stood on the pavement as he deftly re-entered the traffic, listening to the roar of his powerful car as he skirted it around an off-loading cab, watching until his bright red tail-lights gradually disappeared into the distance.

One of her fingers went to her mouth and tentatively traced where his lips had been.

She dropped her hand and sighed as she turned to enter the clinic, but even hours later, whenever she sent her tongue out to moisten her lips, she was sure she could still taste him.

Annie Tulloch was clutching her young toddler to her chest when Jasmine entered her small office space. It was clear that, although the infant was now asleep, he hadn't been for all that long, judging from the tracks of tears down his grubby little face. It was also evident from the harried look on the young mother's face that this was not going to be a simple social call.

'I'm not using anything if that's what you're thinking,' she said even before Jasmine had shut the door.

Jasmine drew her chair close and sat down, touching the young woman on her thin arm encouragingly.

'I didn't think that at all. I know how determined you are now for Jake's sake. You've done so well, I'm very proud of you.'

Tears glittered in the young woman's eyes as she bent her head to her son's ruffled dark curls.

'Wade's coming out of jail,' she gulped. 'I know he'll come for us, I just know it.'

Jasmine drew in a painful breath. Wade Evert's criminal record already contained three accounts of domestic assault; she had no doubt he would have no hesitation in adding a fourth.

'What about the women's refuge?' she asked. 'You'd be safe there for a few days until the authorities inform you of his movements.'

'I came here from there,' Annie said. 'They're totally full. There wasn't even sleeping room on the floor.'

Jasmine chewed the end of her nail as she considered the possibilities.

'What about another suburb?' She reached for the telephone. 'I'll do a quick ring around to find a place for you and Jake.'

Even as she dialled the numbers she knew it was hopeless. Refuge places were few and far between. With the government dollar being squeezed so tightly, people like Annie and little Jake stood very little chance of being placed on priority. Annie's drug use history worked against her as surely as her dark colouring. It made Jasmine's blood boil at the injustice of it all.

After eight calls she put the telephone down in disgust. She drummed her fingers on the desk in front of her for a moment or two before snatching up the receiver again and quickly stabbing at the numbers.

The telephone seemed to ring for ages before it was picked up.

'Father?'

'Oh, Jasmine.' Her father's tone sounded somewhat distracted. 'Can I call you back? We're just in the middle of a prayer meeting. We should be through in about half an hour or so.'

She gritted her teeth. 'No, don't bother. It was nothing.'

She put the phone down and looked at the exhausted young mother in front of her.

'Will you excuse me for a minute?' she asked, pushing out her chair to get up. 'I need to make a private call. I won't be long.'

Annie nodded as she cuddled into her sleeping son's form, each and every sharp angle of her body defeated with tiredness.

Jasmine used the staff room extension and dialled Connor's number.

He answered on the second ring. 'Finished already?'

She couldn't help thinking his voice sounded disgustingly cheery considering the late hour. But then, she reminded herself, he'd probably been relaxing with his feet up on the plush leather sofa with a drink in one hand while she'd been fighting her way through a bureaucratic nightmare.

'No, I think this is going to be an all nighter.'

'Can I do anything to help?' he asked.

'Not unless you can find a safe house for a young mum and her toddler for a few days,' she said with a sigh.

'No room at the inn?' he quipped.

She was glad he couldn't see the way the corners of her mouth lifted in a reluctant smile.

'No room anywhere, I'm afraid.'

'What about a hotel?'

'My client hardly has enough money to feed her little boy let alone pay for a hotel.'

'What about a women's refuge centre?' he offered.

'I've rung all the ones in our area and they're all full.'

There was a small silence.

Jasmine suddenly felt embarrassed about calling him. She didn't really understand why she had, except somehow she'd felt as if she'd needed to hear the sound of his voice.

'Leave it with me.' His deep voice broke across her thoughts. 'I'll get back to you in half an hour or so, OK?'

'You don't have to get involved,' she said. 'This is my problem, not yours.'

'Then why did you ring me?'

'I…'

Her hesitation gave him all the answer he needed.

'Come on, admit it, Jasmine, you rang me because you need me.'

He was closer to the truth than he probably realised, she thought, even as she vehemently denied it.

'I don't need you. I can handle this on my own. I only rang to let you know I won't be home so you wouldn't wait up.'

She heard his soft chuckle of amusement and ground her teeth.

'I mean it, Connor.'

'Sure you do.'

'I'm hanging up.'

'Go right ahead.'

'And don't ring me back, I'm busy.'

'I won't.'

Her finger hesitated over the cut-off button. 'And I won't be back tonight.'

'That's fine.'

'You…you don't mind?' Uncertainty crept into her voice.

'Why should I mind?'

'But…but I thought you…'

'Listen, baby.' His sexy tone sent a shiver up her spine. 'In less than three days you'll be spending every night in my bed. I know it's hard, but if I can wait so can you.'

'I didn't mean that!'

He gave another deep laugh. 'Sure you didn't.'

'Go to hell!'

'I'm well on my way, or so your father told me not so long ago.'

'I don't think even hell is going to be hot enough for you,' she spat back.

'It certainly won't be if you're not there with me,' he teased.

She opened her mouth to throw back a stinging retort but he'd already hung up.

She glared at the telephone for half a minute, fighting the temptation to call him back just so she could have the last word, but a sound from the next room reminded her of her responsibilities to her client.

Annie turned in her chair when Jasmine came back in.

'Have you found somewhere for us to go?'

'Not as yet.' She held out her arms for the little boy who'd just woken. 'But I'm still working on it.'

The toddler stopped snivelling as soon as Jasmine cuddled him close to her chest. She stroked his little back as she sat on the edge of her desk, breathing in the soft baby smell of him as his tiny fingers curled around a strand of her hair.

'Annie, have you considered contacting your mother?'

Annie's expression closed over.

'Why should I? She gave me away when I was four years old. What sort of mother is that?'

'I understand how you feel, especially since you're now a mother yourself, but a few years ago things weren't all that easy for a single mother.'

'They're not easy now,' Annie put in dejectedly.

'I know, but your mother did what she thought was best at the time. You can't blame her for trying to give you the best chance.'

'I can manage on my own.' Annie's face was determined. 'I've had to ever since I was fourteen.'

Jasmine sighed. Annie was one of the saddest cases she'd ever had to deal with. Every time she took a couple of steps forward something would come along and send her three steps backwards.

Todd had warned her not to get so involved. Professional distance, he called it, but there was something about Annie Tulloch that had touched Jasmine from their first meeting. She wasn't exactly sure what it was about the fragile young woman that stirred her so much. Most of the street kids she worked with had similar tragic backgrounds and yet Annie had slipped under her professional guard right from the start.

Little Jake gave Jasmine's hair another tug and gurgled up at her.

'Hey, little guy,' she said, tickling him under the chin. 'Don't you know that's no way to treat a lady?'

'It certainly isn't,' said a very familiar male voice from the door.

Jasmine swung around to see Connor standing there with a take-away food bag in one hand and a hot drinks tray balanced in the other.

'Anyone for coffee?' he asked, stepping into the room.

It was clear from the look on Annie's face as she eyed the

paper bag he set before her that it had been quite some time since she'd eaten.

'I got chicken nuggets for the little one.' He took out the small container and handed it to Jasmine before turning back to Annie. 'I'm Connor, by the way. Jasmine's fiancé.'

Annie's eyes widened before turning to Jasmine.

'You're getting married?'

Jasmine gave a chicken nugget to Jake before answering. 'Yes…on Friday.'

'I thought you didn't believe in marriage?' Annie said, popping a French fry into her mouth.

'She's a very recent convert, aren't you, darling?' Connor smiled.

Jasmine sent him a quelling look before handing Jake another nugget.

'I've found accommodation for you, by the way,' Connor announced.

'You have?' Jasmine and Annie spoke in unison.

'As safe houses go this has got to be one of the safest. Beryl Hopper has spent the last twenty odd years looking after folk who need a break to get back on their feet. And don't be fooled by the blue rinse hair and the grandmotherly figure; she's got a black belt in just about every version of martial arts. No one but no one will get past her unless she says so.'

'I don't know what to say.' Annie smiled up at him shyly.

'Where does this Beryl woman live?' Jasmine asked.

'In the Blue Mountains.' He checked his wristwatch. 'She should be here shortly. She was visiting a friend in town but I managed to track her down before she left.'

'There are formalities to see to,' Jasmine said. 'I have to get police clearance and so on.'

Connor reached for the toddler who had held up his arms towards him.

'You do what you need to do while this little chap and I finish off these fries.'

Jasmine reached for the phone, trying not to notice how at ease he seemed to be with the little child.

A short while later Todd came to her office to announce the arrival of Beryl Hopper who within minutes had ushered Annie and Jake out to her car with the bustling efficiency of a mother hen.

Jasmine stood by Connor's side on the pavement and watched as the older woman's car drove off with an ignominious hiccough or two before merging into the late night traffic.

She felt his glance on her and faced him, meeting his eyes in the shadow cast by the streetlight.

'Thank you for what you did tonight.'

'It was nothing.'

She gave him a long, studied look.

'How did you meet Beryl Hopper?'

'She was a friend of my mother's,' he said with a fond smile. 'She's been there like a bull terrier in the backyard of my life making sure I don't go too far off the rails.'

'She's certainly had her work cut out for her then,' she said with an attempt at wry humour.

He looked down at her for a long moment without speaking, his dark gaze holding hers.

'You look exhausted.'

She gave a weary sigh as she lowered her eyes. 'I am.'

'Come on.' He put his arm around her shoulders and reached for his keys. 'Let's get you to bed where you belong.'

Jasmine didn't have the strength to argue with him about which bed she preferred to occupy.

Once in the car she closed her eyes and laid her head back against the soft leather upholstery, trying not to think about his hard-muscled thighs so close to hers, or about his strong, capable, long-fingered hands on the steering wheel.

Within a few minutes he pulled into his driveway and walked with her to the house, his arm still casually slung around her shoulders. She didn't move out of his hold, even though a part of her insisted she should.

He opened the door and let his arm drop as he tossed his keys on to the hall table.

'Do you want a drink or something?' he asked, shrugging his jacket off.

She hovered uncertainly, not sure what he was expecting of her.

'Hey.' He touched her cheek with one finger in a fleeting caress. 'Go to bed, sleepy eyes.'

'But—'

He pressed his finger to her lips. 'Goodnight, Jasmine.'

She turned and began treading the stairs, each and every step she took feeling like a marathon.

'I'll be in the spare room if you need me,' he said as she reached the upper landing.

She turned to look back down at him. She so wanted to say she didn't need him but it seemed like tempting fate to voice the very words that could in the end prove to be her downfall.

'Goodnight,' she said instead and took another step.

'Jasmine…'

Her hand stalled on the hand rail, her heart tripping over itself in her chest at the seductive sound of his voice.

'Yes?'

He seemed about to say something but then changed his mind.

'Nothing. It can wait. I'll see you in the morning.'

He turned and the study door closed behind him, the hall suddenly seeming empty without him.

Jasmine continued up the stairs and closed the bedroom door softly behind her, but even when she was curled up in the big bed a few minutes later she wondered what it would be like to sleep with his warm arms around her, their legs entwined, and his firm mouth on hers.

She pummelled the pillow and clamped her eyes shut but it was hours before she could relax enough to sleep.

When she woke the next morning there was a short note from Connor stating his absence due to a problem with one of his outlets in Brisbane. His hastily scrawled message informed her he would be back in time for the wedding.

She screwed up the note and threw it at the nearest wall. How like him to desert her just when she'd decided she needed him around!

Damn him!

CHAPTER SIX

IT SEEMED strange to Jasmine to be at a wedding where her father, in his whiter than white cassock, wasn't presiding over the proceedings, his booming voice echoing throughout the cathedral.

For one thing, the registry office wasn't big enough for a Bishop let alone an echo, and as she had insisted on no guests the ceremony was brief and impersonal.

She told herself she didn't mind. She wasn't the type to stand up in front of distant relatives, dressed like a meringue and feeling like every type of fraud for wearing a veil.

She was glad she'd worn a short bright red dress—very glad. She was the family tart, after all, so it seemed rather fitting.

However, when she first arrived, she caught Connor's eye and she felt a momentary flutter of unease at the glitter of anger in his eyes. She knew he was annoyed and his fury at her would be intensified by the fact that he couldn't speak to her about it until they were finally alone.

She hadn't been at his house the night before when he had returned from interstate. She'd left her own terse note informing him of her plans to spend the night with friends. She hadn't spent the night with anyone. She'd booked herself into a cheap hotel and spent the night eating her way through the mini bar chocolate supply, trying to convince herself she still had time to call it all off.

But she hadn't called it off.

She still wasn't sure why.

She wanted to put it down to her rebellious streak that insisted she do the exact opposite of what was expected of her, but deep down she knew it wasn't that at all.

When the celebrant gave permission to kiss the bride Jasmine was unprepared for the heat and fire of Connor's mouth on hers. It wasn't a kiss to seal a contract; it was a kiss to remind her she'd just tied herself to a man she barely knew, a man who held all the cards.

As soon as they left the registry office a huddle of photographers crowded around as they tried to get back to his car. Jasmine put her head down as he tugged her behind him, almost tripping over her own feet as she tried to negotiate the pavement in her high heels.

At last they were in the car, several camera lenses pressed right up against the windows even as Connor began to drive away.

There was a stiff silence until they'd made their way out of the main flow of traffic.

'I hope you've got a very good explanation,' he ground out as he deftly skirted around a driver trying to reverse park.

'I don't have to explain myself to you,' she bit back.

'Perhaps not, but have you thought of how your parents are going to feel when they see tomorrow's paper with you splashed all over the front of it dressed like a streetwalker?'

She hadn't given her family a thought and it made her resent him for pointing it out.

'I don't have an extensive wardrobe,' she said. 'I'll have you know this is my best dress.'

He gave her a look of frustration before turning back to the traffic slowing up ahead.

'Then why the hell didn't you tell me? I could've arranged for you to get some clothes. It's not as if I can't afford to dress you.'

'I thought your main intention was to get me out of my clothes.' She gave him a caustic glance.

'You know something?' He turned her way as the traffic came to a stop. 'You're one hell of a complicated young woman, do you know that?'

She folded her arms across her chest in a defensive pose.

'You surely didn't have to go to the length of marrying me to come to that conclusion, did you?'

His wry laugh broke the tension.

'No. I guess you're right; I didn't.'

'Then why did you?' She swivelled to look at him.

He gave her one of his long, studied looks before answering.

'It seemed like a good idea at the time.'

'And now?' She held his gaze without blinking.

'And now.' He put his foot back down on the accelerator as the traffic ahead began to move forwards. 'Now we've made our bed, so to speak, we're going home to lie on it.'

The car shot forward and she clutched at the armrest to steady herself. There was a promise in those dark eyes of his, and while she still didn't know him well, she did know that was one promise he was going to keep.

But he didn't take the turn-off to the eastern suburbs. Jasmine shot him a questioning glance as he headed for the freeway south.

'Where are we going?'

'I've got something to show you,' he answered. 'I got my housekeeper to pack a weekend bag for you.'

She wasn't sure what made her angrier—the fact that he'd instructed a housekeeper she'd somehow never met to go through her things or that he hadn't informed her of his plans for the weekend.

'Maria comes in a couple of times a week,' he said before she could fire up her stinging tirade. 'She doesn't speak much English but enough to tell me off for leaving my towels on the floor all the time.' He gave her a quick grin but she scowled back at him.

'I could've packed my own bag. I don't like other people going through my things.'

'You don't have all that much to go through,' he said dryly. 'But once we get back to town I'll make sure that's rectified.'

'If you think buying me a whole new wardrobe of clothes

is going to change anything, think again. If and when I want new clothes I'll get them myself.'

'With what?' He shot her a flinty glance.

She turned away from his probing eyes.

'I have some money, not the disgusting amount someone like you earns, but I manage.'

'You live like a bloody pauper!' he said. 'Why is that? Just so you can make the differences between you and your family even more marked?'

Jasmine tensed.

'I don't do anything of the sort. I just don't see the need for expensive clothes when there are kids on the streets without food and shelter.'

'Well, if those kids on the streets spent a little less on drugs and drink perhaps they would have somewhere to live and something to eat.'

She gave him a gelid glare.

'How typically middle class! You with your silver spoon still sticking out of the corner of your goddamned mouth!'

'Watch it,' he warned.

'You know people like you really make me sick,' she continued recklessly. 'You've never had to worry about where the next meal was coming from and yet you dare to criticise those who have nothing, not even a parent who loves them...' She stopped as she realised what she'd said. He'd grown up from the age of four without either of his parents and while he may never have had to worry about hunger she suspected love was something that had been in short supply.

'I'm sorry,' she mumbled. 'I shouldn't have said that. I wasn't thinking.'

'Forget it,' he said without glancing her way. 'I already have.'

He put his foot down and overtook four cars in one stretch. Jasmine stole a covert glance at him. His expression was inscrutable. However, she noticed his hands on the steering wheel were tense.

She felt terrible.

She sat in a miserable silence and wondered how she could apologise any further. She was used to his teasing, not his temper, and it made her realise how little she knew of him. She wished Sam had been back from her honeymoon so she could have asked her to fill her in. Surely being married to his stepbrother, Finn, would have given her some insight into his character?

After another silent half-an-hour Jasmine began to suspect where he was taking her—Pelican Head. He drove past her mother's friend's turnoff until he came to the end of the road to a large Victorian house. Jasmine had explored the grounds in the past, imagining it was haunted, with the shadowed windows of the old house looking like ghostly eyes as they surveyed whoever was game enough to trespass. Never in her wildest dreams had she ever expected to be driving up the pot-holed driveway with a new husband, bags packed to stay the weekend.

'I'll take our things inside,' Connor said. 'You want to have a look around by yourself for a while?'

How had he known she wanted to be alone just now?

'All right.' She avoided his eyes as she slipped off her high heels and pushed her feet into a pair of flat casuals.

He took their bags from the boot and made his way to the old house while she stood and breathed in the cooling evening air. The sun was sinking behind the screen of tall gum trees behind the house, casting rays of golden light across the iron-laced veranda.

She turned away from the house and walked towards the creek, where the soft sway of the she-oaks in the light breeze and the trickle of water over the river stones gradually began to calm her overstretched nerves.

She bent down to trail her fingers through the velvet softness of the maidenhair fern that was bowing towards the water and she breathed in the earthiness of moss and damp, a heady mix after the fumes of the bustling city.

So this was the first day of her married life.

She straightened and absently twirled the band on her finger, wondering if it would be there long enough to leave a mark.

It was certainly an unusual way to start a marriage. A rushed ceremony to satisfy her parents' need for propriety as well as to secure Connor's mother's estate, not to mention keeping the gossip-mongers at bay. It seemed a strange set of reasons for marriage, but then what else in her life wasn't strange? She was like a stranger in her own family. She looked different. She even felt different. All her life she'd felt as if some part of her was missing and, just like a small piece of a jigsaw, the picture wasn't complete.

It was nearly dark when she wound her way back through the bush to the old house.

Connor had turned on some lights, which took away from the haunted look she had been so used to seeing. In fact, the old house almost looked alive, as if it had been waiting all those years for someone to come along and switch on its lights so it could see through its dark windows again. Ever since she'd first skirted past the place on one of her walks she'd felt as if someone inside the house was watching her, but now it looked just as it was—a very old and rundown house in the middle of nowhere.

She shook her head at her musings and walked up the steps to the front door. When it opened in front of her she started and almost stumbled back down the steps.

'You look like you've just seen a ghost,' Connor said.

She covered her embarrassment with cynicism. 'I don't believe in the afterlife.' She made to brush past him but his arm came out to block her entry.

'Aren't I supposed to carry you over the threshold or something?' he said with a teasing light in his eyes.

She met his look with a hard light in her own.

'And aren't you supposed to love and cherish me till death us do part?'

His expression became unreadable as he dropped his arm.

'What I feel about you is irrelevant,' he said. 'What's more important is what you feel about yourself.'

She stared at him for a moment without speaking. Then, retreating into the protection of her usual sarcastic armour, she spat back at him, 'As much as we are both likely to regret it, you are my husband, not my psychoanalyst.'

'In that case I'd better carry you over the threshold.' Without any other warning, he scooped her up in his arms and carried her into the house.

'Put me down!' she shrieked, straining against him.

'When I'm ready.' He tightened his hold. 'Now stop struggling or I'll drop you.'

'I don't want you to—' Her words were suddenly cut off by his mouth coming over hers, stopping all sound.

She stopped fighting him and began fighting with herself— fighting to keep control of the yearning his kiss had ignited like a lighted taper to dry kindling. She was erupting into leaping flames of need; there wasn't a part of her untouched by the pressure of his mouth on hers. Her skin tingled all over, her heart leaping erratically when he deepened the kiss with a moist slide of his tongue through her parted lips.

The flames of need were now an inferno. She was aching for him inside and out, her arms tight about his neck, holding on as if he were the lifeline she needed to stay afloat in the sea of passion that was threatening to consume them both.

She felt him lower her feet to the floor, her body sliding down his erotically, snagging on the thrust of his aroused body, leaving her in no doubt of what he craved.

But then he lifted his mouth off hers and she opened her passion-glazed eyes to find him looking at her intently, a question lurking in the depths of his chocolate gaze.

She couldn't hold his gaze.

She pushed herself out of his hold, putting some much

needed distance between them. She couldn't think straight
when his hands were on her, her thoughts becoming as jum-
bled and erratic as her pulse. She had no idea how she was
going to get through the weekend without betraying herself;
her physical desire for him was already spiralling out of her
control just from one kiss!

She turned around and looked at the interior of the house
rather than face his sardonic half-smile.

'What plans do you have for this place?' she asked casually
as she picked at a flake of cracked paint on the nearest wall.

'I was hoping you'd help me with that.'

She glanced over her shoulder at him.

'I don't know anything about interior decorating.'

'But you're familiar with the house.'

She turned to face him.

'Before today I've never even stepped inside the place.'

He raised one brow. 'Not very neighbourly of you.'

'Look, I came to the shack down the road to escape, not
to socialise with whoever may have been living here.
Anyway, word has it the person who was last here was a
recluse.'

'Weren't you even a little bit tempted to come over and
look around?'

'No, why should I?' She gave him a reproachful glare. 'Unlike some, I do actually respect people's need for space.'

'But surely you must have wondered who was living here?
I thought all women were by nature curious.'

Jasmine found his question slightly disturbing. The truth
was she had been intensely curious about the occupant of the
old house but her own need for peace had prevented her from
investigating any further. She'd wandered through the
grounds once or twice, watching for any signs of movement
behind the half-drawn blinds before turning for the creek path
that ran through the property.

'All I know is whoever lived here wasn't keen on home

maintenance,' she said with a wry glance towards the peeling paint.

'Yes, it does look a little neglected but I like a challenge.'

He wandered over to the bookshelves where books were lying haphazardly amongst decades of dust. He picked up a copy of Thomas Hardy's *Tess of the D'Urbervilles* and blew off a cloud of dust. 'I thought the place needed some attention and, like you, I was drawn to the solitude.'

Her eyes connected with his across the room but she felt as if something more than the meeting of gazes had passed between them.

She realised then that she knew virtually nothing about his work, what sort of stresses he had to contend with. In fact, apart from what she'd occasionally read in the press and what she'd heard from Finn and Sam he was an unknown quantity. The fact that she was now married to him made her ignorance all the more intimidating.

'Do you enjoy your work?' She was pleased with her question; it demonstrated an interest without revealing her need to pry.

He put the old book down and dusted off his hands.

'It pays the bills and creates a few more,' he answered. 'Like most jobs.'

'Business is like that,' she said in response.

'What about you?' he asked. 'Do you have plans to move on from the clinic to a job with more sociable hours?'

'No.' Her reply was short and sharp.

He gave her a studied look.

'You have an insatiable desire to be needed, don't you?' he observed. 'That's why you work yourself into the ground on a wage that wouldn't feed a sparrow.'

'I don't see how it's any business of yours what I do or how much I earn doing it.'

She turned away from his penetrating look and inspected the bookshelves nearest her. She picked up a copy of Milton's poems and flicked idly through the yellowed pages.

'What made you buy this house?' she asked.

She sensed his casual shrug but didn't look up at him as she put the book carefully back amongst the others.

'I liked the mystery of the place,' he answered. 'Mystery intrigues me.'

Just then the lights flickered momentarily, went out completely, and then came back on all within the space of a few seconds.

Jasmine felt a tiny shiver run through her as she turned to look at him.

'Are you frightened?' he asked, a half-smile lurking at the corner of his mouth.

'Of course not!' She gave her head a toss.

A distant roll of thunder sounded and she visibly flinched. His smile widened.

'Sounds like we're in for a storm.' He watched the interplay of emotions on her expressive face. 'Don't worry, I'll protect you.'

She didn't need to tell him her biggest fear was him, not the approaching storm; she was sure he must see it for himself in the widening of her eyes as he stepped towards her.

She held her breath as he touched her gently on the cheek with the back of his hand.

'Don't be frightened, Jasmine.' His voice was like velvet running over her skin.

'I...I'm not frightened.' Her voice caught in her throat. 'I just don't like storms.'

'What is it you don't like, the thunder or the lightning?'

'I don't like the unpredictability of it.' She swallowed. 'You never know when the next strike is going to come; they seem to come from a long way off and then the next moment it's right on top of you, catching you off guard.'

'Like falling in love?' His eyes held hers for a moment.

'I'm not sure. Anyway, what would you know of love? I thought a playboy's credo was to keep things strictly on a physical plane?' She knew disapproval coloured her tone but couldn't check it in time.

His mouth lifted in one of his characteristic half-smiles.

'Even playboys can fall in love,' he answered smoothly. 'And just like thunder and lightning it can take them completely by surprise.'

She felt increasingly uncomfortable under his watchful gaze and lowered her own to inspect the floorboards at her feet.

'How often have you fallen in love?' She hoped her tone suggested indifference.

'Not often enough to be any expert on the subject,' he said.

She didn't understand why his answer had disappointed her.

'What about you?' he asked into the stretching silence.

She would have answered him with some carefully framed, suitably evasive reply but just then a bolt of savage lightning split the sky, turning the room a sickly shade of electric-green. She flinched as if someone had struck her from behind and flung herself forward into his arms. He held her against him as the thunder boomed like a cannon over their heads, his hard body like a fortress against the enemy at the gates. She heard a crackle and the light flickered and then finally snuffed out like a candle in a sudden breeze.

She squeezed her eyes shut as another bolt of lightning rent the sky, closely followed by the roar of angry thunder.

'It's all right.' His hand stroked the back of her head. 'It'll pass in a few minutes.'

'It's getting so dark,' she said into his chest.

She felt rather than heard his rumble of amusement.

'It is, now that the power's off.'

'Do you have a torch?' Her tone was hopeful as she looked up at him.

His eyes were like fathomless pools as he held her gaze. She was suddenly conscious of the hard length of him against her, its presence between them a reminder of the intimacy of both their circumstances and relationship. They were totally alone, without the distraction of either people or power; alone in a big old house still trembling with a host of memories seeping through every wind-borne crack in the windows.

'I don't have a torch,' he said.

'A candle?' She peered up at him in the ever increasing darkness.

He shook his head.

'But I have laid a fire in the fireplace and I have some matches.'

She didn't see any point in disguising her relief.

'Thank God.' She gave a tiny shudder against him. 'For a moment I thought we were in big trouble.'

There was a strange little silence.

'We are in big trouble,' he said.

'What sort of trouble?' She looked up at him again.

'This sort of trouble,' he answered and bent his head to hers.

CHAPTER SEVEN

ANOTHER shaft of lightning filled the room momentarily with green-tinged light but once it flashed Jasmine didn't even spare a thought for the thunder. When Connor's mouth covered hers she was lost to the violence of the storm outside, her only thought on the storm of need he'd awakened inside her with the first dart of his tongue into her warm mouth.

She was carried along by the maelstrom of desire pulsing between them, a desire she didn't want to feel but couldn't stop herself from feeling. It was as if the force of nature had taken over her body, making her act in ways totally unfamiliar to her. Her hands were already threading their way through his dark hair, her soft whimpering cries filling the silence of the room as he left her mouth to blaze a trail of kisses down her neck. She was on a wanton path to destruction but she didn't care any more. She heard the rasp of the zip at the back of her dress and stepped out of its silken folds, glad of the cloak of darkness as she stood before him in her underwear.

She felt the scorch of his eyes even through the darkness.

'I'll light the fire,' he said in a whispering tone.

She wanted to tell him he'd already lit a fire; her body felt as if it were going to burst into leaping flames right then and there. But she said nothing as he searched along the top of the mantelpiece for the box of matches.

The strike of one against the side of the box seemed loud now that the storm outside had faded to a distant rumble. She watched as the tiny glow of the match cast his features into relief, giving him a rakish look. He bent to the laid fire and it erupted into a warm glow, giving her a timely reminder that he must have done this a hundred times with a hundred different women in a hundred different locations.

He reached for her but she'd anticipated the move and put the old sofa between them. The fire lighting him from behind made him appear larger and more threatening as he loomed over her, his eyes scorching her from head to toe.

'Cold feet, Jasmine?' he asked in his customary mocking tone.

She set her chin at a defiant angle.

'I'm not on the Pill.'

'I have a condom.'

'Only one?' Her look was cynical.

'I came prepared.' There was an intent light in his eyes that frightened her.

'I bet you did,' she sniped back at him as he made a move towards her. 'In an array of colours and textures, no doubt.'

'I always aim to please.'

She tore her eyes away from his and did another round of the sofa.

'Will you stop following me like some nasty predator?' she railed at him crossly as he closed the distance with another stride. She didn't trust herself not to throw herself back in his arms and so retreated behind a wall of cold anger to disguise her need. 'Leave me alone, Connor, or I'll scream.'

His eyebrow lifted in amusement.

'Who do you think is going to hear you? God?'

'Believe me—' she gave him a fulminating look '—when I scream the whole universe will hear it.'

'A screamer, eh?' His eyes danced as he looked her over once more.

She felt herself blush from head to foot at his double meaning. Well, that was one thing on which he could reassure himself; her responses were hardly going to wake the neighbours if her track record was anything to go by, she thought bitterly.

She crossed her arms over her chest, wishing she could reach her dress on the other side of the sofa.

As if reading her mind, Connor bent down and, picking it up, dangled it from his fingers.

'You want this?'

She tightened her mouth. 'I'm cold.'

'There's a roaring fire over here,' he said, pointing back over his shoulder.

She ignored his comment and commanded, 'Hand me my dress.'

'Come and get it.'

She met the challenge in his eyes and, taking a swift intake of breath, strode across and snatched it out of his hand. She turned her back to him and stepped back into it with as much grace as her fumbling fingers would allow. Once she was decently covered she faced him once more, the light of rebellion still firing in her eyes.

'If you thought you could haul me down here for a weekend of seduction think again. I won't be any man's plaything.'

'The thought never crossed my mind.'

She glared at his guileless expression.

'You're making fun of me again and I won't stand for it.'

He laughed softly as he turned back to stoke the fire behind him.

'Don't worry, Jasmine—' he addressed the settling flames '—I won't suddenly leap on you and take you without your consent. That's not my style.'

'No.' She tightened her hands into fists. 'Your style is more the sneak up and take them when they're off guard, isn't it?'

'So you do confess to being a little tempted?' He looked over his shoulder at her standing stiffly on the other side of the sofa. 'That is, when your guard is down?'

'No!' Her protestation was far too vehement, sounding more defensive than convincing. 'I'm not tempted at all, guard down or not.'

She could see he didn't believe her, his dark eyes communicating as surely as if he'd spoken the words out loud.

'I'm not interested in casual relationships,' she added when he didn't speak.

'Our relationship is hardly what I'd call casual,' he pointed out wryly. 'After all, we've already shared the same bed and are now officially married.'

'You're really enjoying this, aren't you?' she said. 'It really suits your perverse sense of humour to have me in this unspeakable situation, doesn't it?'

'I can't deny the element of comedy in the situation.'

'*Comedy?*' She almost shrieked the word. 'You think this funny, me being imprisoned with you in this haunted mausoleum all weekend?'

'I thought you didn't believe in the after-life?'

She gave a shiver as the old house creaked, as if in protest.

'I don't, but this place still gives me the creeps.'

'It's just an old unloved house, Jasmine. By the time we've finished, all the ghosts will be well on their way.'

She didn't care for the glint of mischief in his dark gaze and hastily turned her back to inspect the nearest object of furniture, to cover her unease. It was a small escritoire, beautifully crafted and in good condition considering the state of the house.

'It's a nice piece.' He spoke from behind her left shoulder. 'I bought it at an auction a few days ago.'

She admired his taste but didn't say so.

'I bought a few other things, which will be delivered on Tuesday.'

She turned to look at him at that.

'You're planning to stay until Tuesday?'

'As honeymoons go it's still rather short but I thought we needed more than two nights to get to know one another.'

'We'd need a century.' She brushed past him agitatedly to go and warm herself by the fire. 'That is if I felt so inclined to get to know you at all.'

'I think by the time we leave here you'll know me very well.'

She knew he was using the biblical meaning of the word by the element of lazy humour in his teasing tone.

'I don't want to know you. I don't even like you.'

'The reason you don't like anyone, including me, is because you don't even like yourself.'

She rolled her eyes at him.

'You can quit the Freud impersonation right now,' she said tightly. 'Analyse your own behaviour before you start on mine. You're the one who got us into this unholy mess in the first place.'

'You were the one in the wrong room,' he pointed out neatly.

She was infuriated by his satirical tone.

'I made a simple mistake! Am I supposed to pay for it for the rest of my life?'

He gave an indifferent shrug of one shoulder.

'That's entirely up to you.'

'What do you mean by that?' She stared at him suspiciously.

'I mean this "unholy mess" we're in, as you so indelicately described it, could turn out to be a whole lot of fun.'

'I'd rather die than have fun with you.'

He raised his eyebrows at her.

'Careful, such careless untruths could call that old storm right on back.'

'Don't be ridiculous.' Her tone was scathing.

There was a very definite grumble of thunder in the distance. Connor winked at her and she turned back to the fire, her face glowing more than the flames still leaping there.

'Would you like something to eat?' he asked.

'How can we cook without power?'

Just then the lights gave a tentative flicker or two before coming on completely.

Connor lifted his head towards the ceiling with a grin.

She didn't know what to say. She even wondered if he'd

engineered the whole black out thing to suit his plan for seduction.

He could see her scepticism and he smiled.

'Come on. Let's see what's in the kitchen to eat.'

She frowned as she followed him from the room at a safe distance. When she saw how well-stocked the old refrigerator was as well as the walk-in pantry she had to concede that he had certainly gone to a lot of trouble; at the very least, there was enough food to keep them going for a month.

'Would you like some wine?' He took a bottle out of the door of the refrigerator and held it up for her inspection.

She didn't normally drink much alcohol but decided that she would this time. She needed something other than him to stimulate her senses!

'All right,' she said.

She watched as he uncorked the wine, poured some into the two glasses he'd taken from a cupboard. She took the glass he held out to her and took a tentative sip.

He raised his own in a salute.

'To a happy union.'

She refused to join him in the toast.

He took a generous mouthful and she watched the movement of his neck as he swallowed. She dragged her eyes away and stared into the contents of her own glass for a long moment.

'You have to drink it, not wait for it to evaporate,' he said.

His mockery made her reckless. She gritted her teeth and, with the barest hesitation, lifted the glass to her lips and downed the contents in one hit. She put the glass down on the counter and met his taunting gaze.

'Another?' he asked.

'Why not?' she said, and pushed it towards him.

After topping up his own he refilled it for her, leant back against the counter top and surveyed her defiant pose.

'Doesn't do to drink on an empty stomach,' he cautioned.

'I can handle it.' She drained the glass with three mouthfuls.

He pursed his lips as he watched her.

'I can see what you're up to.' He twirled the glass in his hand. 'But you'll regret it in the morning.'

'So?' She tossed her head at him. 'If I fell for your seductive plans I'd regret it in the morning too. The way I see it, this is the lesser of two evils.'

'I have no plans for seduction. When we make love it will be because we both want it so badly there's no other choice.'

'There's always a choice.'

He quirked an eyebrow at her.

'That high moral ground is unfamiliar territory for you. I thought you enjoyed playing devil's advocate?'

'I'm having a night off.' She suppressed a hiccough and steadied herself against the counter as the alcohol began to kick in. 'Anyway, my father's not here so I don't need to bother.'

'You enjoy needling him, don't you?'

She refused to acknowledge the question and reached to pour herself another glass of wine.

'I suppose you think it's your duty as the resident black sheep of the family,' he added.

She sipped at her wine before finally responding.

'I don't have a lot of time for people who are too heavenly good to be of any earthly use.'

'Strong words from the daughter of a man who wants to be the next archbishop,' he put in.

'Look, don't get me wrong. I care about both of my parents but their beliefs are not mine, and I won't be forced to do or say anything I don't want to.'

'I'll have to remember that.'

'Yes, you will.'

She was glad when he went to the refrigerator once more to organise some food for them. She was on shaky ground with so much alcohol in her system, and she didn't trust herself not to start saying things she had no right saying to him or anyone.

'How about some smoked salmon quiche and salad?'

'Fine by me,' she said as he brought over the food and set it out on the scrubbed pine table in the centre of the room.

'We could eat in the dining room but it's probably warmer in here,' he said, holding out her chair.

She sat down, conscious of his large frame leaning over her. She could smell his aftershave, a spicy, heady concoction that she knew she'd always associate with him. She held her breath until he moved to take the chair opposite, his eyes meeting and holding hers.

'More wine?'

'Why not?'

'Why not, indeed?' He reached behind himself for the bottle and topped up her glass, leaving his own as it was.

She bent her head to the food in front of her and, picking up her knife and fork, began applying herself to the task of eating to avoid having to make conversation rather than any particularly pressing need for food.

Her appetite had waned hours ago when she'd joined him in front of the marriage celebrant, her stomach hollowing as she'd taken her place by his tall side, his broad shoulder touching hers as they both turned to face the front. The enormity of what she'd been about to do had struck her then more than at any other moment. As they'd signed the marriage certificate a few minutes later she'd truly felt as if she'd signed her life away. The sinking feeling in her stomach hadn't gone away even now, all these hours later. A great yawning emptiness, reminding her of all she wanted but could never have…

'You don't seem all that hungry,' Connor observed after a few minutes watching her shred her salad into tiny pieces, none of them quite making the distance to her pensive mouth.

Jasmine blinked and looked down at her plate.

'Oh.' She gave a cherry tomato a little push with her fork

and it rolled like a beach ball to the side of her plate. She put her knife and fork down and met his compelling gaze.

'I'm sorry. I had a big breakfast.'

He studied her for a long moment, his handsome head on one side, his dark hair ruffled, making her fingers twitch with the desire to thread themselves through the silky curls. She thrust her hands in her lap and forced herself to hold his gaze.

'Is there a telephone?' she asked. 'I need to ring the clinic to tell them how long I'll be away.'

'I've already done that.'

She felt herself tense in growing annoyance at the way he kept stepping over her personal boundaries. First, having his housekeeper pack her things and then calling the clinic.

'You had no right to do that.' The air crackled with her anger.

He held her look, his eyes so intent she was sure he could see right through her to the back of the chair where her trembling shoulders were pressed.

'I had every right to ensure you have a decent honeymoon period.'

'Decent?' The word came out as a harsh grunt of cynicism. 'There is absolutely nothing about any of this that is decent!' She got to her feet in agitation, tossing the napkin on to the table with a slash of her hand.

'Jasmine…' His tone was cautionary, which made her all the angrier.

'Don't you "Jasmine" me,' she shot back with a passable imitation of his deep intonation. She caught the tail end of his little smile of amusement and stamped her foot at him. 'I told you to stop laughing at me.'

He got to his feet in a single movement, his sudden increase of height making her shiver in apprehension. She couldn't read his expression accurately but thought it was somewhere between anger and frustration as he laid his napkin down with exaggerated precision even though his eyes never once left hers.

'I think you should take yourself off to bed,' he said in a tone one might have expected to hear when speaking to a small, over-tired child. 'You're beginning to sound distinctly shrewish.'

She gasped at his effrontery.

'And why wouldn't I be shrewish? You've dragged me to this God-forsaken gothic gargoyle-adorned disintegrating dosshouse just so you can inveigle your way into my underwear.'

His brows rose in mocking admiration at her wordy diatribe.

'They say alcohol loosens the tongue. In your case it's just off-loaded half the dictionary.'

She was beyond containing her rage. She moved from her chair, uncaring that the action toppled over the glasses, spilling wine everywhere. His glass rolled off the table and shattered at his feet, the sound of it breaking filling the flinty silence with an ominous edge.

This time she was in no doubt of his expression. He was angry, possibly more so than she'd ever seen him. His jaw was tight, the evening shadow on his jaw not able to disguise the flicker of a pulse at the side of his firm mouth, the shadows cast by the single light bulb overhead unable to conceal the glitter of reproach in his darkly hooded gaze.

'That was not a very nice thing to do,' he said after an interminable pause.

'I don't care,' she tossed back recklessly. 'You deserved it. I wish it had been red wine and stained your trousers.'

'If that had been red wine you'd be flat on your back by now with me staking the claim that I should have staked the moment we walked into this house.'

Her head reared back at the crudity of his statement. A host of disturbing images flooded her mind—images of his large body pinning her to the floor of the sitting room, the flickering flames from the fire nothing compared to the heat and fire of his touch on her fevered skin. She felt her innermost intimate muscles clench involuntarily at the thought of his hard length filling her, his milky fluid bursting from him at the peak of his pleasure...

'I must remember to make sure you never consume red wine in my presence.' She made an attempt to lighten the atmosphere.

He wasn't letting her off that easily.

'After you've cleaned that up I'll show you where we'll both be sleeping.' He stepped over the broken glass and, before she could open her mouth to tell him what to do with his arrogant command, he'd gone from the room, clipping the door shut behind him.

Jasmine stared at the mess on the floor. She refused to feel ashamed about her loss of control. He'd asked for it, damn him! Teasing her all the time, laughing at her behind those chocolate eyes, biding his time until he made the final swoop and made her his in every sense of the word.

She'd show him! She snatched at a dustpan and brush and shoved the broken fragments into the bin. She gathered the dishes and, after giving them a cursory scrape, left them in the sink. She'd be damned if she'd turn into his galley slave as well as his sex slave.

She stomped from the kitchen, intent on tracking him down in the big old house to inform him that even if there was only one bed left on the planet she was *not* going to share it with *him*.

He was in the main bedroom, a lovely room with large bay windows which in daylight afforded a beautiful view over Pelican Head. The old bed seemed to dominate the room, even though by any standards the room was commodious.

He turned as she flung open the door with a theatrical shove of her hand.

'I'm not sleeping with you in that bed.'

'I see.'

She hunted his face for a clue to what was going on behind

that impenetrable mask but his cool indifference gave nothing away.

'It's unthinkable,' she added.

'Quite.'

She opened and closed her fists by her sides.

'It's not that you're not very attractive…' She gnawed her bottom lip as she tried to back out of that very obvious compliment. 'What I mean is…I can't do it. I just can't!'

'I understand.'

She pressed her lips together tightly, not trusting herself to continue confessing rather more than she wanted to confess.

'I'll sleep on the sofa downstairs,' he offered gallantly.

She ran her tongue across the parchment of her lips.

'That's very…kind of you.'

'No trouble.' He picked up his things off the bed, a small shaving bag and his bathrobe, and left her in the middle of the room—alone.

She stared at the now closed door and frowned. She knew she shouldn't be feeling this gnawing sense of disappointment but, damn it, she did!

She turned around and sat heavily on the big bed, instantly sinking into the depths of the old mattress. A cloud of dust rose in the air and she sneezed.

'Some honeymoon,' she said under her breath, giving the springy mattress a punch with her fist. She sneezed again and her eyes began to water.

Damn him! She sprang to her feet and, kicking off her shoes, padded back downstairs to have it out with him.

She opened the sitting room door and pulled up short when she encountered him standing totally naked in front of the sofa preparing to settle down for the night.

'Did you want something?' he asked with an air of nonchalance she assumed came from being viewed naked by legions of women.

'I…' She swallowed and forced her eyes north of the border with considerable difficulty. 'No, I was just going to say…'

'Is the bed not comfortable?' he asked.

'No, it's...' She clutched at the lifeline as a drowning person did a float. 'Yes! That's why I came down here. I'm allergic to that bed.'

'Allergic?' His dark brows rose in twin question marks on his forehead.

'I...I sneezed.'

'That hardly constitutes an allergy.'

'Twice,' she added hastily. 'And my eyes are watering.'

'They look fine to me.'

She stomped across the floor and stood right in front of him and pointed to her itching eyes.

'See?' She blinked a couple of times. 'That's what I'd call an allergic reaction.'

She opened her eyes to see him studying her features, as if seeing them for the very first time.

'Nope.' He shook his head. 'I think you're overreacting.'

'Overreacting?' she gasped. 'I won't sleep a wink tonight because of you!'

'Ditto, so we're square at least.'

It took her a moment to understand his meaning and when she did she blushed to the roots of her hair.

She swung away but in her haste her bare toes caught in the ragged edge of the worn carpet and she felt herself falling.

He caught her and pulled her upright against him, her back pressing into the wall of his chest and stomach, and what was just below...

'You need to take a little more care, Jasmine,' he said, his voice a soft rumble along her liquefying spine. 'With all that alcohol on board you might find yourself doing things you might not normally do.'

She turned without thinking, still pressed far too close to him but beyond caring.

'I'm not drunk if that's what you're implying.'

'I didn't say you were.'

'You hinted at it.'

His expression was all innocence. 'I did no such thing.'

'You're laughing at me again,' she tried to growl at him but somehow her voice came out husky instead. 'I told you not to laugh at me.'

'Believe me, Jasmine—' his tone was wry '—I'm not laughing.'

She felt the unmistakable heat against her stomach where her body was pressed up against his. Her legs went to jelly and her stomach clenched as she saw his physical reaction to her reflected in the dark, deep pools of his eyes.

It was hard to say who moved first. Jasmine assumed it had been him, but later, reflection caused her to wonder if it had been her mouth that had pressed itself against the firm line of his.

All she knew was his mouth was back on hers, his tongue seeking entry, and she gave it willingly, softening against his hardness, unfolding all her tight barriers in his commanding male presence.

She could feel the nectar of her need pooling between her thighs. Her body ached to be filled, its pulse of blood reminding her of a need she could no longer ignore—no matter the consequences. She couldn't resist him any longer. She didn't see the point. Surely it was inevitable that they would finally end up in each other's arms, however short the interval. Once he discovered how unresponsive she was she knew he'd be back off to bachelordom without a backward glance.

He pressed her to the floor with a gentleness that surprised her considering the highly aroused state of his body. He took his time, peeling away her dress, deftly removing her plain bra, her breasts spilling into his waiting warm hands.

She felt his mouth take each nipple in turn, subjecting them to an exploration of his teeth and tongue until she was writhing with the sensations gathering inside her.

He slid down her body and she sucked in her breath as his long fingers began sliding away her panties, the glide of fabric down her thigh a delicious torture in her state of heightened awareness. She felt his warm breath on her intimately, and instantly tensed.

He placed a palm on the flat plane of her belly and its heat seemed to seep through to the very core of her, melting her momentary resistance.

'Trust me, Jasmine.' He breathed the words against her tender flesh.

She shut her eyes and let herself feel as he explored her pulsing need, taking his time acquainting himself with her delicate detail.

She drew in a ragged breath as he found what he was looking for.

'Oh!' She couldn't stop the gasp in time. She clutched at his dark curls and held on as the spasm tightened her legs as it flew along her veins like a furious fire in search of fuel.

She clamped down on her lips to stop the cries coming out but it was no good. Her body was taking her on a journey she was unprepared for; there was nothing she could do to stop it.

He slid back up to anchor himself up on his elbows either side of her still gasping form. She felt his throbbing maleness so close she wanted to grasp at him but when she reached out a tentative hand his fingers closed over her arm, stalling her mission.

'I have to protect you,' he said and, rolling away, dug his fingers into his shaving bag by the sofa and retrieved a tiny foil packet. He took the edge of it in his straight white teeth and tore it, spitting the edge of it out of one side of his mouth in a bone-meltingly male fashion that made her almost mindless with lust.

She watched as he applied the protection with practised ease but this time she was beyond caring how many women had gone before. All she knew was that she was the one beneath his hard body now, and it was her desire he would be fulfilling.

He pressed her back down and gently slid into her warm

feminine cocoon with a deep groan that surprised her. Somehow she'd imagined someone with his depth of experience would find her body very humdrum but he appeared to be deeply moved by the feel of her muscles tightening around him.

'Am I hurting you?' His voice was just a whisper against her mouth.

'No,' she breathed back against his lips.

He increased his pace just a notch, gently at first; then as she welcomed him with increasing confidence he drove a fraction harder and deeper. She could hardly believe what she was feeling; it was so different from her first time. That time she had been embarrassed at her ineptness at insufficiently arousing a young man who on record had bedded most of her year as well as a considerable portion of the year above. This was nothing like it. Connor had drawn from her a response she hadn't known she'd been capable of. Great waves of feeling washed over her, rolling her over and over in their intensity. She heard her keening cries as he took her once more to the pinnacle with every deep surge of his body in hers. She went willingly, with abandon, with relish, with joy.

She was still coming back down to earth when his release sounded in her ear in a deep groan of expelled breath. She listened to the sounds of his pleasure—his faster than normal breathing, the tenseness of his muscles and then the swift descent into relaxation afterwards, his large body collapsing against her hers, spent in pleasure.

She wasn't game enough to move. She hardly breathed in case she disturbed the moment, frightened he would spoil it by mocking her inexperience, shaming her the way she'd been shamed before.

Sudden doubt assailed her.

Connor felt her tense beneath him. He rolled off and, leaning on one elbow, surveyed the complex emotions flickering over her features as he slowly trailed an idle finger down between her breasts.

He heard her swift intake of breath as his finger came up to circle one rosy nipple.

'You like that?' His eyes burned down into hers.

She didn't respond in words but his question had been answered all the same. He moved to the other breast and repeated the movement, watching as she struggled to disguise her reaction to him.

She intrigued him. The way she fought him at every turn, her defiance the biggest turn on he'd ever experienced. He'd wanted her from the first moment he'd seen her on the day of his stepbrother's engagement party. She'd glared at him from time to time, which had only served to inflame him even more. And now he had her in his arms where he wanted her to stay—permanently. He couldn't help smiling at how much he'd changed. Who would recognise the play hard playboy now?

'I need the bathroom.' The prosaic tone of Jasmine's voice was a little unnerving under the circumstances of their recent intimacy but he knew she was keen to put some distance between them.

'Be my guest.' He released her from his light hold, watching her as she fought with herself about whether to get up and reveal her nakedness to him as she left the room.

He heard her breath of resignation as she got to her feet and, snatching up her discarded dress, clutched it to her chest.

What did one say in this sort of situation, Jasmine wondered? Thank you for the lesson in sensuality. I'm sure it will come in very handy in the future?

She bit her lip.

Connor got to his feet and reached for his bathrobe, which was draped across the back of the sofa.

'Here.' He handed it to her. 'It's cold in the bathroom. You'd better wear this.'

She could smell his body's exclusive scent as she wrapped herself in his robe. The soft folds of fabric almost covered her, consuming her just as he had done a few minutes ago.

She felt a combination of gratitude at his sensitivity and shame at herself for needing it so badly. What was wrong with her? Why couldn't she just enjoy the moment for what it was—a pleasant interlude of passion and unrestrained lust? Why ask for anything else? What more could he give other than the heat of his body and the temporary comfort of his arms?

She stepped over his long, outstretched legs and left the room, but she felt his dark eyes on her all the way to the door and even when she closed it softly behind her.

CHAPTER EIGHT

JASMINE took her time in the bathroom. The ancient plumbing surprised her in allowing her to shower in relative comfort although, as Connor had warned, the old bathroom was a little cold.

She stared at her reflection in the speckled mirror, hardly recognising herself. Her eyes were different, pupils wide and extended as if she'd just woken up from a very long sleep. Her mouth was still slightly swollen from Connor's deep kisses, and when she pressed her thighs together she could feel the intimate place where he'd so recently been.

It felt strange to feel him on her skin. She could smell his presence even after her shower. It felt as if he'd indelibly marked her as his. She was sure no one else could ever make her feel the way he did. The only trouble was, she was just one of many to him. There was no future in a relationship that had come about the way theirs had.

She'd fought her feelings for him from the moment she'd met him; it was as if she'd innately sensed he was danger personified. But it hadn't done her any good because, in spite of her determination to keep him at arm's length, her heart had already capitulated to his disarming version of humour and charm. A deadly concoction that she was fiercely tempted to keep sipping for as long as she possibly could...

When she went back to the sitting room he had stoked the fire and was standing before its warm glow, the strong flanks of his muscled thighs cast in gold. He looked over his shoulder at her as she came in, a small smile lurking about the corners of his mouth.

He was still naked, she noted, with a sweep of her gaze

113

that this time lingered a little more than she'd allowed previously.

'Pleased to see me?' It was her first attempt at flirting with him and it gave her a heady feeling.

His eyes meshed with hers. 'What do you think?'

Her eyes lowered and she felt a trickle of excitement pool in her stomach at his extended arousal.

'On the evidence at hand I'd say that was a yes.'

He moved towards her. Her breath locked in her throat as he reached out a hand and captured a strand of long chestnut hair. He coiled it around his finger again and again until she could feel herself being pulled ever so gently and inexorably closer and closer into the waiting heat of his body.

'It's a very definite yes,' he said just above her mouth.

His mouth came down to hers and time ceased to exist once more. He sucked on her bottom lip, drawing it into the heat of his mouth. His slow-moving tongue unfolded and dipped into the recesses of her mouth, leaving her breathless with mindless need.

She pressed against him with female instinct, the softness of her body seeking the all conquering male strength of his. He lowered her to the floor and held her down with the weight of his frame, his arrant maleness slipping between her thighs like an arrow from a quiver. She gasped at his sudden entry, caught up in the wave of his urgent desire, wondering why it had taken until this very moment to realise she loved him. But then how could she not? His gentleness had been her undoing; he'd unravelled her just like a strand of yarn from a tightly wound ball. Even if she tried she knew she'd never be able to tighten her defences again. He'd slipped through and there was no going back.

She didn't want to remind herself of the temporary arrangement of their marriage, a marriage conducted solely to keep the baying hounds of the press and the more repressed members of both their families off their backs. It couldn't last, she knew that, but for the first time in her life she wanted to live in the moment only, take a risk, live out a dream, even though it would very likely end in a nightmare of hurt and rejection.

Connor felt the increasing urgency of her mouth and hands as she explored him, her small fingers running over the muscles of his back and shoulders, lingering in his hair, sending shivers of need up along his spine. He was losing control but it didn't matter as she was with him all the way, her body rising to greet his every deepening thrust.

There wasn't time for thinking; this was all about feeling and finding the fulfilment they both craved. He felt her slip over the edge, her slender body tightening around him, drawing him in and sucking on his heat as if within it was the breath which she needed to breathe.

It was an almost savage release for him, a violent burst of feeling that filled his head with a kaleidoscope of fragmenting colours cascading around his brain. Her ragged breathing filled his ears, her chest rising and falling in time with his, her breasts crushed between his pectoral muscles, their rounded mounds spilling upwards as if seeking his mouth.

Jasmine opened her eyes and found him looking at her, his body still encased in hers but relaxed now.

'You have such beautiful breasts,' he said.

She didn't know what to say. Thank you seemed so formal and polite, especially after the intimacy they'd just shared.

'Why the act?' he asked when she didn't speak.

'Act?' She looked at him blankly.

He coiled a strand of her hair around his finger once more, leaving her no choice but to hold his look.

'The look-at-me-I'm-an-outrageous-tart act.' A little smile accompanied his words.

She swallowed. 'You could tell?'

He nodded.

'Was I...so bad?' Doubt seeped into her tone, her cheeks already growing hot at the thought of her failure to please him.

His mouth lifted in a sexy smile.

'You ask *that* after what we just shared?'

She pressed her lips together and tasted him.

'I...I'm not an expert on these situations,' she said. 'As you no doubt can tell.'

'You're a very sexy young woman, Jasmine.' His pupils widened as his gaze swept over her full breasts again. 'You make me lose control. No one has done that in years.'

'I'm sorry.'

He threw back his head and laughed and she felt it in her stomach as his abdomen rippled along hers.

'You're also one of the most amusing women I've ever met,' he added, still smiling down at her. 'And that's the biggest turn-on in the world.'

'It is?' She sneaked her tongue out to moisten the dryness of her lips. He followed the movement with his eyes, his own mouth coming closer and closer until it was barely a millimetre away.

'You bet it is,' he said and covered her mouth with his.

It was a long and languorous coupling, slow and sensuous, bringing Jasmine bit by bit towards a higher level of physical consciousness. Her body seemed to be melting in the heat and passion of his, her softness swallowed by his hardness. She felt a sort of completeness in his arms that went further than simply the appeasement of fleshly desires.

When the storm of passion had receded, Connor kissed the tip of her nose before getting to his feet with the sort of agility she privately envied. Her body felt as if someone had loosened all its joints, leaving her boneless, too relaxed to move.

She watched him as he scooped up the cushions off the sofa and laid them on the floor next to her in front of the glowing fire. He picked up the throw rug and, once she was settled on the cushions, gathered it around them both. She felt cocooned in sensual warmth, the scent of their spent desire filling the air around them.

They lay in a silence broken only by the occasional spitting of a log as it released some sap into the fire. Jasmine had never realised before how deeply erotic a fire could be—the heat of glowing embers, the leap of flames as more fuel was laid down, the hiss and spit of released juices as the wood was consumed.

She felt Connor shift his arm from under her neck, turning slightly so he could look at her in the incandescent glow of the fire.

'Where are you in your cycle?'

The question seemed to come from nowhere and it took her a while to grasp the context.

'I'm due any time,' she found herself saying.

His relief was almost palpable.

'I didn't wear a condom after the first time, sorry.' A brief frown of contrition flicked across his forehead. 'I got carried away and put you at risk.'

'I'll be fine,' she said, hoping it was true.

'I don't have any nasty diseases, if that's what's bothering you,' he added when he saw her frown forming.

'The thought never crossed my mind.'

He traced the line of her mouth with one lazy finger.

'You should mind,' he said. 'Encounters like this could change your life in a second.'

She wanted to tell him it had changed her life permanently, but bit back the words.

'I'm sure I'll live to tell the tale.'

He hunted her face for a few moments, as if he could see behind her miserable attempt at humour and was going to call her to account. But after a while he simply dropped another swift kiss on to the tip of her nose and slid back down beside her, gathering her back into his warm embrace.

'Let's get some sleep.' His voice was a soft burr in her ear.

She shut her eyes and concentrated on listening to the sound of the fire. After a few minutes Connor's even breathing informed her he had drifted off to sleep. She laid her head on his chest and breathed in the scent of his skin and wondered if he'd still be there in her arms in the morning.

* * *

Jasmine woke up alone but she could hear the sounds of Connor moving about the house. She rolled on to her other side and listened to the chorus of birds outside the bay windows, their cheery song failing to lift her spirits at all.

She dragged herself from the warmth of the makeshift bed, her body protesting inside and out at the movement. She hunted for some clothes but only found Connor's bathrobe. She slipped her arms through the sleeves and, stepping over the disarray of the sofa cushions, made her way to the bathroom.

Her mood hadn't lifted even after her shower. With the morning had come the recriminations from her behaviour the night before. She scowled at herself in the steamed up mirror, hating herself for having capitulated so readily. A couple of glasses of wine and she was anybody's—and not just anybody's, but Connor Harrowsmith's, one of the biggest playboys of all time. It didn't salve her conscience one iota to remind herself she was in love with him and had every right to express that physically. Somehow it made it so much worse. It wasn't as if she could come right out and say, 'By the way, I really love you in spite of the bizarre circumstances surrounding our marriage'. She'd look a fool and no doubt his response would be to laugh or, even worse, smile one of those mocking smiles.

She tossed her towel to the floor on top of Connor's with a spurt of defiance. Let him pick them up, she wasn't going to be running around after him like some downtrodden housewife while he went off and charmed the birds from the trees, the office, nightclub or wherever he found his latest conquests.

She found him in the back garden, hanging out the bed linen from the master bedroom she'd refused to sleep in. He turned to look her way, even though she was absolutely sure she'd made no sound. She wondered if he had a sixth sense where she was concerned, or whether he could read her mind.

'How are you feeling?' he asked, ducking under the clothes line.

'I'm sore,' she said bluntly, forcing herself to look him in the eyes.

His small smile had a trace of apology about it.

'If you had been straight with me about your level of experience perhaps I would've compensated a little more.'

'I wasn't exactly a virgin.'

'No, perhaps not technically, but you're hardly a seasoned tart though, are you?'

'I am now.'

He frowned heavily. 'What's that supposed to mean?'

She scowled at him darkly. 'What number am I on your bedpost, Connor? Do you keep a running record?'

He stood looking at her assessingly, his continued silence intimidating her into further reckless speech.

'Or maybe you have a little black book in which you write all the details, such as how enjoyable it was for you, whether you'd like to continue the relationship or not, or whether she was fat or thin or had big boobs or—'

'If this attack is expressly aimed at alleviating some of your own guilt over your responses to me, then stop right now.'

His terse words brought her head up straight.

'My guilt?' she threw at him incredulously. 'What about yours?'

'I did nothing you didn't want me to do.'

'Yes, you did. I told you I didn't want to sleep with you and you took advantage of my...of the fact that I'd had a couple of drinks and wasn't thinking clearly.'

His jaw tightened, which should have warned her to drop it right there, but her fighting spirit and her pride had already combined forces.

'I despise men like you; your selfishness knows no bounds. It's all about getting laid at whatever cost, even marriage in your case.'

'I think you've said quite enough, Jasmine.' His tone was steely. 'I can see you're having second thoughts about last night but don't make me your scapegoat. You came to me quite willingly and I did what any normal man would do under the circumstances.'

'I want to go home right now!' she said. 'I don't want to stay another minute here with you.'

'Don't be so melodramatic.' His tone was impatient. 'If we go back to the city after less than twenty-four hours it will cause the sort of speculation neither of us need right now.'

'I'd rather face the press than spend another night in your arms.'

'We both know that isn't true.' His dark eyes held hers challengingly, daring her to contradict him.

She glared back at him rebelliously.

'Why did you bring me here? Why not a decent hotel instead of this rat-infested place?'

'I got rid of the rats last week and, as for the cobwebs, I was going to do that this afternoon.'

Jasmine gaped at him speechlessly.

'I know it's not exactly The Ritz, but with a little attention it could be made very comfortable. Anyway, no one but us knows about this place so, for a few days at least, we're safe,' he continued calmly.

She found her tongue at last. 'There were *rats* here last week?' She couldn't help a tiny shudder and a furtive glance around her feet.

'Not many.'

'H…how many?' her eyes were wide with fear.

'You don't like rats?'

'Give me a snake any day.' She gave another shudder.

Connor smiled and picked up the clothes basket.

'Come on, let's have some breakfast before we go down to the beach.'

Jasmine found herself following him into the house despite her earlier determination to avoid him at all costs. Her eyes darted about the kitchen as he filled the kettle with water, fully expecting tiny black eyes to be staring from between the gaps in the skirting boards, waiting for their chance to flash past under her feet.

Connor handed her a cup but it slipped from her grasp and landed at his feet in a myriad of pieces.

He gave her a wry look.

'You're really on edge, aren't you?'

'I'm fine.' She paid no attention to his comment as she went to get the dustpan and broom she'd used the night before.

It was unfortunate she hadn't put it away properly for when she opened the broom cupboard door the small brush with its grey-black bristles dropped near her foot.

Her scream filled every corner of the room. Connor swung around to find her on the table, her face a ghostly white, her limbs trembling like the autumn leaves outside.

'Hey there, sweetheart.' His tone was instantly placating as he reached up a hand to her. 'Did the big bad old brush give you a terrible fright?'

She glowered down at him, ignoring his hand.

'Don't you dare laugh at me, just don't you dare.'

He held up his hands in a gesture of complete innocence.

'Now would I do that?'

'Yes, you would.'

He gave a mock pout.

'I'm hurt, crushed in fact, that you think so poorly of me.'

She clambered down from the table and stood fuming in front of him.

'You are one of the most annoying men I've ever had the misfortune to meet, do you know that?'

He gave her a sweeping bow.

'At your service, ma'am.'

She flung herself away and stomped out of the kitchen without a backward glance, all her appetite for breakfast completely gone.

She found her clothes in the upstairs bedroom, where she saw Connor had stripped the bed and opened all the windows to air the room. She dressed in track pants and top, relieved that she didn't sneeze once. Making her way back downstairs, she left the house through a side door so she didn't run into him.

Only when she was finally on the beach did she start to relax enough to gather her thoughts. She walked along the water's edge, the swell hissing and retreating at her feet, the crunch of shells like percussion in her ears. Two gulls soared above her head and then, catching an up-draught of air, flew off to the cliff face once more.

The slight breeze was chilly but refreshing as she walked towards the first group of rock pools about two kilometres away in the distance. When she got there she bent down to inspect the contents of the biggest pools, dangling her fingers in the slightly warmer water where the morning sun had lingered. Two purple anemones, their white spines close to their round bodies, lay undisturbed amongst the bright green seaweed.

She sat on the bump of a rock and stared out to sea. The rolling waves were soothing as they crashed against the shore, every fifth or sixth one spilling over the rock pools before draining away once more.

It was a noisy peace. The harsh cries of gulls and the roar of the sea, combined with the deepening breathing of the wind, made her sigh with tentative pleasure. Her paradise was not the same with Connor there to invade her sense of peace. He made her feel edgy and on guard, especially now as he'd broken down another barrier to brand her as his.

She knew she was being unreasonable towards him, blaming him for what after all was her own fault. She'd practically thrown herself at him, subconsciously at least, when she'd gone to have it out with him over the sleeping arrangements. A tiny part of her mind had to admit the risks she'd been taking in going back to confront him, but she'd ignored those warnings to rush headlong into a situation that would in the end only hurt her.

He was invincible. His heart was whole and untouched while hers was now his and very likely to be destroyed.

She took shelter from the wind in a sea cave she'd found on one of her walks previously. It was tucked into the cliff face, its steep access making it almost invisible from the beach.

She sat on the rocky ledge and listened to the roar of the sea below, lifting her face every now and again to catch the fine mist of sea spray in the air. She brushed at her eyes once or twice, refusing to give in to the desire to cry. She hadn't cried in years and had no intention of resurrecting the habit, no matter how vulnerable Connor made her feel.

The wind had died down when she left the cave a long time later. She retraced her steps along the sand, her head down, concentrating on placing one foot in front of the other in the steps she'd trod earlier, not wanting to disturb the long stretch of sand any more than she had. She managed to get to the first rock pool without a step out of place but when she came off the rocks to retrace her earlier footsteps she saw that her small ones had been crushed by a much larger foot.

She spun around and saw the culprit bending down over one of the rock pools to her right. She hadn't seen him before as her head had been down, retracing her steps, but she knew before he stood up to his full height it was Connor.

She considered pretending she hadn't seen him but before she could escape he turned and faced her. She waited until he skirted around the rock pools to get to her, his steps unhurried, but she could tell from the tight look about his mouth he was annoyed with her.

She straightened her spine as he closed the distance.

'You've been gone over three hours.' His tone was curt.

'So?'

'So you should tell me where you're going.'

'Why should I?'

He clenched his teeth. 'Because it's polite to tell people where you're going, that's why.'

'It's no one's business where I go.'

'As much as it pains me to disagree with you, I'm afraid it is very much my business.'

'You take your responsibilities as a husband a little too far, as I told you earlier.' Sarcasm laced her tone.

His eyes ran over her, taking in her wind-blown hair and reddened eyes.

'Have you been crying?' he asked, his tone gentled.

'Of course not.' She spun away to walk back to the cliff path. 'I got sand in my eyes. It was windy earlier.'

He seemed satisfied with her answer and adjusted his stride to hers as they traversed the rest of the beach to the path.

'You must be starving,' he said after a few minutes. 'You didn't have breakfast and its way past lunch.'

'It won't hurt me; I need to lose some weight anyway.'

'As it is, you look as if a gust of wind would blow you over,' he observed.

'I'm sure you're used to the very best in female figures,' she said with a trace of bitterness. 'Sorry to disappoint you.'

'You'd be surprised.'

'I'm sure.'

He gave her a sideways smile.

'If I didn't know you better I'd say you were just a tiny bit jealous.'

She stopped at the base of the cliff path and faced him.

'Sorry to disappoint you, but I don't feel anything towards you except dislike.'

'That's not the message I was getting last night.'

'I was not myself last night.'

'Ah yes, last night was an aberration never to be repeated, is that right?'

'Yes, that's exactly right.'

He gestured for her to precede him on the cliff path. 'You go first; I'll be here in case you fall.'

'You go first,' she insisted. 'I'm not going to fall.'

He shrugged his shoulders and leapt up the path like a

mountain goat, leaving her to clamber up by herself a little more circumspectly. He was waiting for her at the top, his expression showing signs of amusement as she joined him.

'What's so funny?' she asked irritably.

'You are.'

'Why?'

'Because you hide behind anger to cover other more dangerous emotions.'

She made to brush past him. 'I don't know what you're talking about.'

His arm caught hers on the way past and he turned her to face him. She schooled her features into resentful defiance but she knew the sheen of fresh tears was in her eyes.

'Yes, you do,' he said. 'Whenever anyone gets within touching distance you put up a great wall of anger to warn them off. That's why you're so cross with me about last night because you let your guard slip, but it's not really me you're angry with, is it, Jasmine?'

She averted her gaze and aimed it at a point to the left of his broad shoulder.

'Strange as it may seem, I am actually angry with you. I suppose it's a kind of novelty for you to have a woman tell you that but it's true.'

'Look me in the eyes and say that,' he challenged her.

She locked eyes with his. 'I'm angry with you, Connor.'

Somehow the way she said his name took away from the conviction of her other words; it came out huskily, like a caress, instead of sharply and implacably as she'd intended.

His wry smile was back in place.

'I like you being angry with me,' he said.

She blinked up at him in confusion. 'Why?'

'Because it shows you feel something towards me.'

'I don't feel—'

His fingers gently pinched her two lips together, halting her speech.

'Don't,' he said as softly as the breeze moving through her

hair. 'You keep on being angry with me. In fact, you should be furious with me, speechless with rage.'

He let go of her lips in time for her to ask somewhat ironically, 'Why?'

He bent his mouth to hers and kissed her deeply before responding.

'Is that a good enough reason?'

She opened and closed her throbbing mouth, uncertain of how to respond.

'I'll take that as a yes, then,' he said and, before she could reply, he disappeared along the path, leaving her to stand staring at the space he'd vacated.

CHAPTER NINE

JASMINE took the long way back to the old house.

She knew it was being cowardly but she couldn't help thinking that Connor had manipulated her into confessing something she hadn't wanted to confess. She replayed the conversation in her head and had to concede that he was a master at playing conversational games, cutting her off at every pass, anticipating her every move as if he were able to see through the tangle of her thoughts.

She entered the house the same way she'd exited it and, listening out for sounds of his presence, made her way cautiously to the kitchen for something to ease the gnaw of hunger in her stomach.

She'd not long finished a tomato sandwich when he came in, brandishing a long-handled broom.

'I've finished the cobwebs but I was wondering if you'd give me a hand in the study.'

She looked at him warily.

'Doing what?'

'I promise you—no rats, spiders or snakes, just a whole heap of books.'

'Books?'

He nodded.

'I'm not a classics fan but even I can see value in some of those titles. Some of them look like they might be first editions.'

He'd won her without a fight. Books were her passion and old ones in particular.

'All right.' She got to her feet, noting the tiny gleam of victory in his dark eyes. She felt as if she'd been cleverly manipulated again but for the life of her couldn't imagine what he'd be up to this time.

She followed him down the dark hall and tried not to let her eyes wander to the cracks in the skirting boards nor flinch at the creak of old floorboards.

The study smelt musty but she managed to suppress her reactive sneeze long enough to look around.

The shelves along three walls were floor to ceiling and each of them was lined with books. A leather-top desk was in front of the window and the maroon velvet curtains were heavily faded with tiny holes in the aged fabric letting pinholes of sunlight through. Dust motes rose in the air each time either of them moved but Jasmine hardly noticed. Her attention was on the gold-embossed spines of the books on the shelves before her at eye level, some of the higher ones looking even more impressive.

She sucked in a breath of excitement.

'This is amazing.' Her eyes shone as she reached out and touched a first edition of a children's book from the turn of the last century.

She turned to face him.

'Some of these books are priceless, do you realise that?'

He studied the excitement on her face for a long moment as if committing it to memory.

'I'm sure one or two will prove to be so.'

She would have frowned at his strange reply but the books were all she could think about at present. She turned back and, with fingers almost reverent, reached out and touched the spines at her level.

'I wish I'd known these books were here all this time.'

'Why?' Connor's voice sounded from somewhere behind her.

She didn't turn around but kept looking at the titles in front of her.

'I love old books. I love the smell of the pages and the thought of generations of people reading the same words time and time again.' She turned to frown at him. 'But why didn't the previous owner take them when they left?'

'I'm not sure,' he answered as he made his way to the door. 'I'll leave you to have a play while I make some inroads on dinner.'

She turned back to look at him.

'You don't mind if I stay here a while?'

He shook his head. 'Go right ahead. The closest I get to reading is the sports page in *The Herald*,' he confessed with a wry grin.

Of course she didn't believe him. How else would he have known the value of the books he'd led her to? But he closed the door before she could respond and she was left alone with a crowd of aged titles and a host of memories as she reached for the book nearest her.

He found her curled up on the cracked chesterfield an hour and a half later, her chestnut head buried in an early edition of Constance Mackness's *Di-Double-Di*.

'Good book?'

She looked up and smiled; the first genuine smile he'd seen on her beautiful face.

'Yes, I love this old book.'

He sat on the sofa beside her and peered over her shoulder at the book she had in her lap.

'What's it about?'

She closed the book, suddenly feeling embarrassed.

'Go on,' he urged. 'Tell me.'

'It's about two girls at boarding school who find a gap in the fence through to an adjoining property.'

'A girls' own adventure?' he guessed.

'Yes, you could call it that.'

'Happy ending?'

She nodded. 'Very happy.'

His eyes held hers for a fraction longer than necessary.

'Dinner is just about ready, if you're hungry.'

She gave him a guilty glance. 'I should be helping you with the cooking.'

'No problem. I enjoy it really; my housekeeper, Maria, has taught me a thing or two over the years.' He got to his feet and stretched.

Jasmine's eyes were instantly drawn to the ridged muscles of his abdomen that his close-fitting T-shirt revealed. His body was magnificent in every way possible—toned, tanned, taut, tall and devastatingly handsome, his firm mouth with its fuller bottom lip promising mind-blowing passion...

She tore her eyes away and got to her feet, barely registering the soft thud of the book as it slid to the floor at her feet.

'Connor, I...'

'Yes?' His tall body stood motionless, his eyes dark mysterious pools of some indefinable emotion as he looked down at her.

The intensity of his gaze made her hesitate. She caught her bottom lip between her teeth momentarily.

'What did you want to tell me, Jasmine?' he probed gently.

At the last minute she decided she couldn't do it. She'd wanted to tell him of her shifting feelings about him but when push came to shove the words just wouldn't come. She just couldn't allow herself to beg for a few crumbs of affection when what she really wanted was the whole package. She wanted him to love her. She wanted him to feel the same stomach-jerking pangs she felt every time she looked at him.

She stared at him blankly for a long minute before bending to pick up the book from the floor.

'Nothing.' She dusted off its fragile cover with a gentle brush of her hand. 'It was nothing important.'

Connor didn't press her, which made her feel grateful at a time when she wanted to distance herself in every way possible. He made her feel vulnerable and exposed as she wasn't used to someone being close enough to see through the mask she wore to cover her inner loneliness.

He held the door for her and she slipped past him with her

head down, not stopping until she came to the kitchen, conscious of his heavy tread behind her every step of the way.

Connor suggested they eat in the dining room, where he'd laid two places on one end of the long table. Jasmine took her seat as he dished up the veal and tomato casserole he'd prepared earlier, the deft movements of his hands reminding her all over again of what it felt like to have those hands on her, exploring her intimate contours, drawing from her a response she could still feel in her innermost body…

'Would you like some wine?' He poised the bottle near her glass.

Her eyes connected with his, her face instantly heating when she recalled how the wine had made her act so out of character the evening before.

'I think I'll give it a miss, if you don't mind,' she answered after the tiniest pause.

'Shame.' He filled his own glass and she was left to speculate on what exactly he meant by that one word delivered so dryly.

'This is very good,' she said after tasting the meal.

'Thank you.' He picked up his glass and took a sip.

Jasmine ate the meal in front of her more for something to do other than feast her eyes on his features all the time like some sort of lovesick schoolgirl. She took her time over every mouthful, stringing out the process so as to avoid making conversation.

Connor had finished his meal and, sipping his wine, watched her as she cut the last few morsels into the tiniest pieces, chewing them slowly, almost exaggeratedly.

He put his glass down and, leaning his elbows on the table in front of him, gave her a knowing smile.

'You find my company disturbing, don't you?'

She hoped her expression was suitably guileless as she looked across at him.

'Not at all.'

He raised a brow as he reached for his wine once more.

'What is it that threatens you the most?' he asked after a little pause.

She put her knife and fork down and dabbed at the corners of her mouth with her napkin to stall her reply.

'I don't find you threatening. I find you annoying.'

'Why?'

'Because you push me too far.'

'In what way?'

'In every way.'

'Be more specific.' He leant back in his chair, one arm slung casually over the back.

Jasmine pursed her lips before responding.

'You don't respect my personal space, for one thing.'

'You mean I come too close?'

'Far too close.'

'What else?'

'You don't take no for an answer.'

'I take it if I see it,' he said.

'What do you mean by that?' she asked.

He ran a finger around the lip of his glass, his eyes never once leaving hers.

'You might say no with your mouth but your body says yes every time.'

'That's not true.'

'What about last night?'

'What about it?'

'You wanted me as much as I wanted you. You spent most of the day saying no but when it came down to the crunch your body decided for you.'

'Last night was a mistake,' she said quickly, her colour high.

'It probably appeases your sense of propriety to see it that way, but I prefer to see it as two people who have a chemistry thing happening which they responded to instinctively.'

'You make it sound as if we had no choice in the matter.'

'We didn't,' he said. 'What happened was meant to happen.'

'Only because you were determined to make it happen.'

'Not at all,' he protested. 'I wasn't going to push you into something you weren't ready to do. I waited until you made the first move.'

'Define the first move.' Her tone was cynical. 'What did I do? Look at you for more than fifteen seconds or something?'

He smiled. 'You really won't admit it, will you?'

'Admit what?' She scowled at him.

'That you wanted me.'

'I did not want you. You took advantage of the situation.' He picked up his glass and took a contemplative sip.

'You're not being honest with me or yourself. Why is it so hard for you to admit what you actually feel?'

'Damn it, Connor!' she almost shouted at him. 'You make me feel things I don't want to feel!'

'Like what?'

'Nothing.' She bit her lip. 'I feel nothing.'

'Tell me what you feel, Jasmine.'

Her fingers around her glass tightened agitatedly.

'I...I feel like...like someone else.'

'When you're with me?'

She nodded. 'I'm usually so in control, so neat, so tidy, everything in its place, you know?'

He nodded.

'But when I'm with you I feel...I feel...' She paused, searching for the right words.

'What do you feel, Jasmine?'

'I feel...out of control,' she confessed at last, lifting her eyes to his.

'Control is important to you, isn't it?' he asked.

She toyed with her glass distractedly.

'I don't like unpredictability. I like to know what's going on so I can be prepared. I don't feel like that around you. I don't know what's going on and I don't know how to prepare myself.'

'You don't need to prepare yourself at all,' he said gently. 'Just be yourself.'

'I don't know how to be myself any more.'

'Because of what happened with Roy Holden?'

She lifted her eyes to his briefly.

'That… And other things.'

'What other things?'

She lowered her gaze. 'Things I don't want to talk about.'

She bit her lip, trying not to give in to the threatening tears. She felt his hand reach out to touch her on her arm, the warmth of his palm seeping through her cold, stiff flesh, making it suddenly come alive with the pulse of blood. She lifted her gaze to find him looking at her, his expression serious but encouraging.

'Why don't you go and relax in the sitting room while I clear up here? I'll bring in some coffee shortly.'

She gave him a grateful half-smile and left the table, glad of an opportunity to gather her crumbling demeanour away from his all-seeing eyes.

Connor had laid a fire earlier and it was crackling merrily as she went into the room, its golden glow welcoming in spite of the aged furnishings and décor.

She deliberately avoided thinking about what the room had witnessed the night before and sat on the sofa and leafed through an old *National Geographic* magazine while she waited for him to join her.

He came in a few minutes later with freshly brewed coffee and two mugs on a tray, setting them down in front of her on the old coffee table.

'How do you have it?' he asked.

'Straight black,' she answered and took the mug from him, cradling her cold fingers around its warmth.

She sipped the hot liquid and watched as he stirred two

teaspoons of sugar in his own along with a generous splash of milk. He caught her eyes on him and gave a rueful smile. 'I know it's bad for the teeth, but so far so good.'

She couldn't argue with him over that; his straight, even teeth were the whitest she'd ever seen.

Connor allowed a little silence to settle between them. He sat back and drank his coffee, his eyes on the fire in the fireplace, his long legs stretched out before him, his feet crossed at the ankles.

Jasmine was sitting within touching distance and just knowing she could reach out with her fingers and stroke her hand along his firm thigh suddenly made it all the more tempting to do so.

She didn't know what was wrong with her. She'd been determined that the physical intimacy they'd shared was not to be repeated, for several reasons. Firstly she didn't want to complicate things between them, and secondly she wanted to be able to walk away with her pride intact when the time came. She couldn't imagine him staying married to anyone very long, least of all to her.

She sat on her hands to stop them from betraying her, but her movement caused him to look at her which somehow made things a whole lot worse. His dark eyes bored into her grey-blue ones, pinning her to the spot.

She ran her tongue over her dry lips in a nervous action that shifted his gaze to the fullness of her mouth. His face was shadowed with a day's growth of beard and she wanted to rasp her fingertips across the lean jaw, linger beside his mouth where his skin creased slightly whenever he smiled his bone-melting smile. She wanted to trace the fullness of his lower lip, run her fingertip down the length of his patrician nose and back up to his dark eyes, those eyes that sent shivers of anticipation down her spine each and every time they rested on her.

Her eyelids fluttered closed as his head came towards her,

her shoulders relaxing as his mouth pressed hers once in a kiss as soft as the brush of a feather.

He leant back and she opened her eyes, giving his features a searching look.

He tucked a wayward strand of her hair behind one of her ears, the tiny movement sending an arc of feeling straight to the hollowness of her belly.

She wanted him to kiss her again, properly. She wondered he didn't see it in her eyes and the slight lean of her body towards him.

'Connor…' She breathed his name.

His hand cupped the side of her face, holding her gaze to his.

'Jasmine, I want you right now.'

'I know.' The thought thrilled her even as it terrified her.

He got to his feet and, taking her hand, pulled her up to stand before him. She could feel the warmth of his body emanating towards her, drawing her to him like a moth to a flame. She knew ultimately she was going to get hurt but she couldn't seem to help herself. She needed him, wanted him and to hell with the consequences—she was going to have him.

He led her upstairs, neither of them speaking. It was as if a silent agreement had passed between them, neither of them wanting to speak in case it changed the atmosphere of heightened physical awareness.

He laid her on the old bed and she sank into the soft mattress, her bones melting as his dark eyes ran over her, lingering over her breasts, dipping to where her womanhood was secretly pulsing in anticipation of his invasion.

He pulled his T-shirt over his head and tossed it to the floor. Her stomach gave a funny little flip-flop when his hands went to his belt, the unclipping of the buckle the only sound in the room apart from her racing pulse which she was sure must be audible to him.

He stepped out of his trousers and his shoes thudded to the

floor as he came towards her, his eyes pinning her to the bed as surely as any bondage.

His fingers were gentle in their task to remove her clothes, so gentle she grew impatient and, brushing away his hand, she tore at them, wriggling out of them unashamedly.

He came down beside her on one knee, his hand stroking along her thigh, gradually going higher until his palm cupped her face once more. He lowered his mouth to hers in a lingering kiss, so leisurely she grew impatient. She nipped at his bottom lip and he suddenly stilled, his eyes growing darker as he looked down at her.

'I detect a tinge of impatience here.' His voice was a soft rumble against her breasts.

'I want you, Connor.' Her eyes held his without shame. 'Not tomorrow, not next week, but now.'

'Now it is.'

He reached for a condom and deftly positioned it before coming back over her, his thighs nudging hers apart.

'Are you sure about this?' he asked, searching her face for a sign of a change of mind. 'I don't want you to beat me over the head with this tomorrow when rationality returns.'

'I promise I won't.'

'I'm tempted—' he gave her body an intimate nudge '— but then, as I think about it—'

She grasped at him with clawing fingers.

'Connor, if you don't make love to me right this instant I'll call the press and tell them you're a lousy husband.'

He grinned down at her wickedly.

'I just love it when you beg.'

She would have said something but his body surged forward into her waiting warmth and all thoughts were immediately driven from her head. His groan of pleasure as her muscles enclosed him was like music to her ears, the weight of his body over hers a delight, the heat of his mouth a salve to her pride, knowing he wanted her just as much as she wanted him.

When his kiss deepened so too did his body in hers, driving her to a new level of feeling. Gone was the delicate brush of yesterday's tentative fingers. In their place were the ravenous hands of heightened desire, grabbing at their prize with greedy, insatiable fingers.

Jasmine almost screamed with the pleasure his lips and tongue called out of her. She was on fire, great leaping flames of desire licking at her flesh like a whip, scalding her until she could bear it no more. She wanted release but it was just out of reach. She had to climb and climb, but he kept her dangling until she was almost sobbing with her need.

'Please…' She nipped at his mouth and then his shoulder. 'Please, I want to…'

He slipped a hand down between their writhing bodies and found the swollen nub of her frantic desire, his touch gentle but determined. Jasmine sunk her teeth into his shoulder as the spasms hit her in great rolling waves that threatened to toss her to the floor of the ocean when they were over. She felt him tense as he prepared to let himself go, his body tight with sexual energy ready to burst forward.

He groaned his release beside her ear, sending delicious shudders of vicarious feeling through her. It made her feel so vital, so alive, so energised to think she had brought him to that.

He rolled to one side, his breathing still out of control.

'God.' He flung a hand over his eyes, his chest rising and falling as she watched him with hungry eyes. 'You're unbelievable.'

He rolled to his side in one fluid movement, propping himself up on one elbow to look at her.

'So are you.' She lowered her eyes, her shyness returning.

He hitched up her chin with one long finger.

'Hey, don't look away. I want to see that satisfied look in your eyes.'

She had no choice but to look at him.

'I'm sure you're very used to seeing very many satisfied women in your bed.'

'I prefer to concentrate on one at a time,' he said. 'And for now you're it.'

'For how long?' she couldn't stop herself from asking.

There was a funny little silence.

'For as long as it takes.'

She didn't know what to make of his answer. She supposed he was referring to the press interest. Perhaps he was planning to terminate their marriage once the hue and cry had died down.

She shut her eyes in case he could see her distress, her fingers plucking at the edge of the quilt in an absent manner.

'Don't worry, Jasmine.' His tone was teasing. 'I won't make you stay with me for ever if you don't want to.'

'I'm not the least bit worried,' she said tersely. 'I know this is a temporary arrangement.'

'It doesn't have to be temporary.'

Her eyes flew to his but his closed expression gave nothing away.

'What do you mean?' Her frown deepened.

'I mean we don't have to end our marriage unless we both want to.'

'But—' she bit her lip '—surely you won't want to tie yourself to me indefinitely?'

He shrugged noncommittally. 'It might be fun, you know, having kids and all.'

'You can't be serious!' She got off the bed in her agitation and snatched at the nearest article of clothing to cover herself.

'Why not?' His eyes sought hers. 'You think I won't be a good father?'

She opened and closed her mouth, uncertain how to respond.

'Well?'

A vision of him cradling a tiny dark-haired infant flitted

unbidden to her mind, his large hands gentle around the precious bundle.

'No.'

'No?'

'I mean yes, you'd make a wonderful father.'

'So what's the problem?'

'We don't love each other,' she said.

Another casual shrug. 'Most couples don't after a few years of marriage, so I can't see the problem.'

'Your cynicism is not reassuring.' She frowned at him.

He grinned. 'I know, but neither is the truth. More than two-thirds of all marriages end in divorce, most of them because one or the other has fallen out of love.'

'So where does that leave us?'

'It leaves us with a good chance of making a success of it because we haven't got the issue of blind love to cloud the issue.'

She bit her lip once more as she thought about his words. It was obvious he didn't love her, otherwise he'd have said so, surely?

'I don't think it's a good idea to bring a child into a relationship where hate is the dominant emotion,' she said, avoiding his eyes.

'You don't hate me, Jasmine.'

She lifted her chin, pride coming to her rescue. 'You seem very sure about that.'

'Sure enough.'

'Well, sorry to disappoint you but I'm very likely going to go to hell for the way I feel about you.'

He laughed. 'So am I.'

She couldn't stop her own smile at his wry tone.

'You find most things in life amusing, don't you?' she said.

'I find it pointless to torture myself with useless guilt and regret. We have one shot at life; my credo is to make it a good one.'

'So you flit from woman to woman in search of the ultimate physical experience?'

'You have a woeful view of my morality,' he quipped. 'I'm not a serial dater—I'm selective, that's all.'

'Am I supposed to be flattered?'

His mouth stretched into another quick, sexy grin. 'Of course.'

She looked away, not trusting herself not to give in to the temptation of returning to his bed and his arms for the pleasure promised in that smile.

'I think I'll have a bath,' she said.

'Want some company?'

She shook her head. 'The tub isn't big enough.'

'We can economise on space.' The wicked grin was back as was the twinkle in his dark eyes.

'Don't you ever think about anything else?' She scowled at him as she snatched at a bathrobe.

'Not much else when you're around,' he confessed unashamedly.

She felt a warm pool of pleasure fill her at his words but hastily reminded herself it was all about male physicality, nothing whatsoever to do with love.

The bathroom was cold but once she turned the hot tap on full it soon filled with steam and with a sigh she sank into the warmth of the water. As she soaped her body she couldn't stop herself from recalling how Connor's hands had explored every inch of her flesh in glorious mind-blowing detail. She lifted her leg free of the suds and immediately felt the pull of inner muscles and a quick spurt of remembered delight arrowed through her belly. She slid down beneath the water level.

She had to stop thinking about him all the time!

Was she so desperate for his attention that she'd put up with years of his womanising just so she could call herself his wife? That was surely the path to personal destruction.

How could she ignore his track record where women were concerned? If she did it would only come back to haunt her some time in the future, no doubt when he grew tired of her and went looking elsewhere. The thought of bringing a child into such a tenuous arrangement was beyond all rational thought. It was asking for trouble. The sort of trouble she had to deal with daily at the clinic. Broken people who turned to substance abuse to mask the pain of fractured relationships, bowed by bitterness and regret until they no longer functioned as normal people.

No. She was not going down that path.

She came up for air to find Connor looking down at her.

'You could have knocked!' She clutched at a face cloth to cover herself.

'I did but you were under the water.'

'You should have waited until I responded.'

'I thought I'd come in and wait for you to come up for air. The view is much nicer this side of the door.' His eyes ran over her thoroughly.

'You're being disgusting.'

'You're being unnecessarily coy.'

'I'm not being coy; I'm just not used to people waltzing into the bathroom when I'm having a bath.'

'I'm sure you'll get used to it in time.'

She gave him a black look. 'You have no respect for personal boundaries.'

'I have the greatest respect for your boundaries.' He trailed a long finger in the water right next to her thigh. The movement of the water where his finger disturbed the surface caressed her thigh in gentle laps, reminding her of the feel of his tongue…

'In fact,' he continued in a smoky tone, 'I was thinking about revisiting those boundaries.'

'Don't…' Her breath caught at the look in his dark eyes.

His finger moved up and traced the surface of the water in front of her breasts. He hadn't touched her once and yet she could feel herself melting, her intimate moisture gathering in anticipation.

It was a battle she could never win; she knew that and so did he, if the smouldering look he gave her was any judge.

She made room for him in the bath without a word. His eyes communicated his pleasure at her capitulation, lingering on her curves possessively until the blood ran thick and fast through her veins. He reached for her, sending a huge slosh of water over the sides, but she was beyond caring. His mouth was on hers, his hands were on her body, his thighs were between hers—this was heaven.

Her head thumped on the back of the bath as he sent her backwards with his first forceful thrust but she made no demur. She welcomed him with abandon, her limbs stretching apart to give him more room. He took her with him on a tidal wave of passion, his hands and mouth joining in the task of delivering her at ecstasy's door with harsh cries of release echoing his own.

The bathroom floor looked as if someone had left a tap on. Connor lay back in the almost empty tub and eyed it ruefully.

'You're one messy woman. Look at that.'

She gave him a playful poke in the ribs with her big toe.

'How like a man to blame someone else for the mess they made themselves.'

He caught her foot and gave her toe a quick hard suck, sending shudders of sensation along her spine.

'Hey!' She wriggled ineffectually. 'Let me go. That tickles!'

He sucked harder.

'Connor, I'm warning you,' she gasped. 'I can't think straight when you do that.'

'I don't want you to think straight,' he growled, dropping her foot to reach for her arms to haul her upwards towards him. 'I want you to think crookedly, sinfully, shamelessly—like me.'

She felt the unmistakable pulse of his growing erection between her legs as she slid on to his chest, but it was the only thought she had for quite some time…

Jasmine woke in the early hours of the morning. It was still dark but the moon made several brief appearances before the curtains of cloud created another interval for its performance.

She lay and watched Connor relaxed in sleep. His breathing was deep and even, his long frame taking up far too much room in the bed, but she wasn't going to wake him by pointing out that fact. Without his penetrating gaze to disturb her she could drink her fill of his features.

She sighed and allowed herself the luxury of reaching out a hand to his chest where his heart lay beating, her fingers nestling against the light sprinkle of masculine hair.

He muttered something in his sleep and turned over, taking her hand with him. She was right up against his back, her legs fitting in the crook of his, her cold body soaking up his tempting warmth…

Connor woke to the soft murmur of her voice near his ear. At first it was just a few indistinguishable sounds, nothing he could make any sense of. But then it changed. Her body tightened, her limbs rigid with fear as the nightmare took hold, her desperate cries filling all four corners of the room.

'Jasmine.' He shook her gently. 'Honey, wake up.'

'No!' She tossed her head as she thrust against his restraining hands. 'No!'

'Baby,' he soothed. 'Hey, it's just a dream; you're having a bad dream.'

She opened her eyes and stared at him blankly for a few seconds.

'Hey, sweetheart, you were having a nightmare.'

She pushed against his hands and got out of the bed, her body stiff as she faced him.

'You should have woken me.'

He gave her a bewildered look. 'I was doing my best.'

She turned away, her arms tight across her chest at the chill of the room.

'What did I say?' she asked, still with her back to him.

'Nothing I could make any sense of,' he answered.

She turned around to glare at him through the pallid light of the reappearing moon.

'Are you telling me the truth?'

'Of course I'm telling the truth. Why would I lie?'

'Because lying is second nature to you, that's why.'

He frowned. 'Jasmine, I know sharing a bed with someone is new to you but people say and do things in their sleep all the time. It's no great drama, believe me.'

'It is to me.'

'What are you trying to hide?'

'Nothing.'

'Then you've got nothing to worry about. Now come back to bed before you turn to ice out there.'

'I don't want to come back to bed.'

'I promise I won't touch you.' His tone was growing impatient as he switched on the lamp. 'Just get back in the damn bed before I lose my temper.'

'Lose your temper, I don't care.'

He thrust the quilt aside with an angry scowl.

'All right then.' His feet hit the floor with an ominous thud. 'You've asked for it.'

Jasmine stood her ground, determined not to be intimidated by him. He came to stand in front of her, glaring down at her in the soft lighting of the bedside lamp.

'I'm in no mood for this push and pull game you're so intent on playing,' he growled.

'I'm in no mood for your games either,' she shot back.

'Fine.' He held his hands up in the air in a gesture of surrender. 'I promise not to touch you, OK? I just want you to get back in the bed and go back to sleep. That's it, all right?'

She felt a bubble of emotion spring in her chest and, before

she could stop them, two tears squeezed past the tight clamp
of her eyes.

'Oh, for God's sweet sake.' He reached for her and hauled
her into the shelter of his warm chest.

She sobbed against his thudding heart, all her normal control disappearing as if he'd turned a switch.

'Hey, this is new,' he mused as he stroked the silk of her
hair. 'I've never seen you cry before.'

'It's not a show!' she howled.

'I know that,' he soothed, his palm gentle against the back
of her head. 'I'm just surprised you trust me enough to let
your guard down.'

'I don't trust you,' she sobbed.

'I know you don't think you do but you do underneath
where it counts.'

'I don't! I don't trust anyone!'

'Yes, you do.' His voice was like a caress as he held her
against him. 'You just don't like admitting it.'

'I want to be alone.'

'No, you don't.'

'You don't know what I want.'

'Yes, I do.'

'I hate you.'

'No, you don't.'

'I do so.'

'You don't.'

'I don't want to talk to you.'

'Then don't talk.'

She looked up at him through tear-washed eyes.

'Why are you so annoying?'

He smiled. 'Because it's my job.'

'You're fired.'

He laughed and gathered her back into his chest.

'Jasmine, I'm sure I'm getting laughter lines just because
of you.'

She didn't know what to say in response. He had the most

disarming manner at times, dissolving anger in a matter of seconds with a phrase that sent a smile to her lips and another arrow of love to her heart.

'I wish I'd never met you,' she said, not meaning it at all.

'I know.' He laced his fingers through the silk of her hair. 'I know exactly what you mean.' He tilted her chin and planted a soft kiss on the bow of her mouth.

She sighed into his mouth, her limbs already loosening at the probe of his determined tongue. What was the point in fighting it? She was his for as long as he wanted her and surely that was all that mattered?

CHAPTER TEN

WHEN she woke the next time she was alone in the bed. The birds outside the window were chirping with the vigour of early morning energy, a type of energy she couldn't help envying.

Her body felt languorous, sleepy and contented from the early morning activity Connor had insisted would be a sure cure for her insomnia. It had certainly worked for him for within minutes of their passionate exchange he'd been asleep, his arms still around her, his legs still entwined with hers.

Her own sleep had been slightly less forthcoming. She'd lain looking at the shadows of dawn dancing across the ceiling until they were shadows no more but streaks of golden light.

Connor had sighed and turned her over with him in a single movement. She'd closed her eyes and breathed in the scent of him, wondering how many mornings she had allotted to her before he would be on to new, more exciting, pastures.

They spent the next few days in much the same way. Jasmine went for long walks along the seashore while he worked on the house. Occasionally he'd join her at the tail end of her walk, his arm slung casually around her shoulders, his smile frequent as he recounted some anecdote that brought a reluctant smile to her own mouth.

She liked watching him work. Having grown up with father who thought handyman tasks beneath his theological intellect, it was quite a novelty for Jasmine to see Connor up and down a ladder while he repaired a crack in the plaster of a high wall or ceiling. Sometimes she handed him a tool from the toolbox at the foot of the ladder, her fingers touching his as she held it up to him. His dark eyes would send her a sil message as he took the instrument and she would look away, frightened he'd be able to see the desperate longing reflected in her gaze.

The nights they shared with a passion she hadn't known she'd been capable of. Time and time again he delivered her to the threshold of fulfilment with him in hot pursuit, their groans of delight a single sound. It made her shiver every time she recalled the way he collapsed against her, his great body wrecked by passion spent.

Tuesday came before she wanted it to. With it came the realisation that their privacy would end abruptly as they each took up their responsibilities once more.

The drive back to town was silent by tacit agreement. Jasmine sat and thought about her work at the clinic and wondered how she'd juggle her new role as Connor's wife while supporting the needy the way she'd done previously. The hours she worked were unforgiving at times, leaving her worn out both physically and emotionally, and within the context of their sudden marriage she knew she might have to make some adjustments.

She sneaked a glance his way once or twice but if he was worried about his own adjustments he showed no sign of it. He drove with quiet competence all the way up the freeway and then on to the highway interchange.

Finally they arrived at his house in Woollahra and once the car had stopped she got out and stretched her legs before he could get to her door.

He took their bags from the rear of the car as she went to open the front door with the key he'd given her previously.

Before she could use the key the housekeeper, Maria, opened the door and greeted her in rapid fire broken English. Jasmine caught one or two words that sounded a little like Italian but she wasn't sure.

Connor came up behind her and smiled at the older woman.

He proceeded to speak in the other woman's language, which made Jasmine turn her head to stare at him.

He caught her surprised expression and flashed a quick grin.

'I learnt to speak it when I lived in Sicily for six months.'

He turned back to the housekeeper and made brief introductions. Jasmine held out her hand and it was taken humbly by the older woman, who said something in her strange, unintelligible dialect.

Jasmine turned to Connor for an interpretation, her brow clouded with uncertainty.

'Maria speaks a little English but it's slow and it embarrasses her. I'll teach you a few phrases to get you through but for the time being just smile and nod your head as if you understand.'

She turned back to the housekeeper and smiled shyly. Connor said something in Italian and Maria's face lit up as she scuttled away to do whatever it was he suggested.

'What did you say to her?' Jasmine looked up at him.

'I told her to have the rest of the day off.'

'Why?'

His eyes twinkled with mischief.

'Because I want you to myself, that's why.'

Her stomach somersaulted as he reached for her, his mouth coming down on hers before she could say a word. He pressed her back against the nearest wall, his hands feeling her breasts through her thin sweater where her heart was leaping towards the warmth of his spread palm.

He was like a drug in her system. She could never have enough of him and with every kiss her need increased until she was breathless with wanting. She tore at his shirt with needy fingers, wanting the silk of his flesh beneath her fingertips, wanting to shape him intimately from head to foot as he had to her.

He tore his mouth off hers and, scooping her effortlessly into his arms, carried her up the stairs, shouldering open his bedroom door. Jasmine's breath was caught somewhere in the back of her throat at the look of masculine intent in his dark eyes.

He laid her on the bed and finished the task she'd begun of removing his shirt. His trousers were next and then his under shorts. He came towards her, his eyes dark with desire while hers widened in anticipation. His hands went to the waistband of her jeans and she lay back, stretching her arms above her head as he bent his head to her belly button, his tongue dipping into its tiny cave. A whirlpool of shivery sensations spiralled through her as his warm mouth moved lower to seek her feminine folds, separating them delicately, intruding into the dark secrecy of her core with bold strokes, leaving her writhing in exultant ecstasy.

He moved over her once more, lifting her sweater out of the path of his mouth and hands. She arched her back as his tongue circled her tight nipples in turn, the knife-hot feel of him against her a torture in itself.

She touched him, shaping him with fingers that trembled in their task. He sucked in his breath as she intensified the movement, lingering over his most sensitive spot until he grabbed at her hand and, holding it above her head, entered her with a harsh grunt of pleasure as her tender form caught and held him tight.

She was on another journey to paradise as his body stroked hers with deep, pulsing strokes, drawing from her a response she could never withhold even if she'd wanted to for pride's sake. Her cries of release were beyond suppressing as they leapt from her throat in high, gasping sounds that, when over, left her breathless and spent in his embrace.

Connor timed his own release, leaving it until she was supine in his arms before letting himself fall towards oblivion in deep throbbing waves that shook him to the core of his being.

He lay listening to the soft sound of Jasmine's breathing and wondered why it had taken him till now to finally realise he loved her. He'd kidded himself he desired her just as he'd desired many women in the past, but who was he fooling now? Her heart was beating against his, her body was curled into him and her feminine scent was like a drug he had to breathe in just to survive.

She shifted in his arms, her chin burrowing into his chest as she searched for warmth.

He trickled his fingers through the silky curtain of hair and speculated on what she'd say if he woke her to tell her. But then he remembered there were other things she needed to know and, besides, he didn't want to be the one to burst her bubble. But he was going to make damn sure he was there to help her pick up the pieces.

When Jasmine arrived at the clinic the next morning she was a little unprepared for the intrusive interest her sudden marriage had stirred amongst the other staff and even some of the clients. She spent most of the morning fielding questions with as much tact as she could manage but towards the end of the afternoon she was getting to the point of screaming. It wasn't hard to pretend she was in love, for she was; it was more because every time she thought about Connor she was assailed by a sinking feeling of hopelessness as she recalled his motivations for marrying her. He'd married her to secure his late mother's estate—nothing more, nothing less. It was about money, not his feelings.

She had only been home a few minutes when the telephone rang.

'Jasmine! You sly old thing!' her sister Sam exclaimed. 'I couldn't believe it when Mum told me you and Connor were married!'

'Yes, well, it's been rather a shock to most people.'

'I thought you didn't like him?' Sam said.

'I don't—didn't,' she said. 'But things are different now.'

'Love is like that,' Sam rattled on happily. 'I didn't like

Finn the first time I saw him either but one kiss and that was it—whammo! Love, lust and—'

'How was the honeymoon?' Jasmine cut across her sister's intimate revelation.

'Great.' Sam's tone was instantly dreamy. 'Everything I could have wished for, in fact.'

'Lucky you.'

'I guess Connor didn't have much time to organise a honeymoon?'

'No.'

'He's a great guy, Jasmine. I'm sure you'll be very happy.'

'Yes.'

'You're not still upset with Mum and Dad, are you?'

'Why should I be upset?'

'I heard they were pretty strong on the idea of marriage, given you'd been found in his bed.'

'There was a certain amount of pressure, yes.'

Sam giggled.

'I think it's terribly romantic, don't you? The outraged parents insisting on the poor man making an honest woman out of you, just like in one of those Victorian dramas.'

'Yes, it was very romantic.'

'You shouldn't take too much notice of what Mum and Dad think about him,' Sam advised. 'He's not the man he's been made out to be, if you know what I mean.'

'I know exactly what you mean.'

'I thought you would. I mean, he hasn't had it all that easy with his mother dying so young and no father and so on. He was left with nothing, not a penny. He had to depend on the charity of Julian and Harriet until he could make his own fortune, which he did rather spectacularly. He's incredibly wealthy now.'

Jasmine frowned as she took in her sister's words.

'But I thought his mother left an estate?'

'No, Finn told me about it just recently. He'd overheard his parents discussing it. Anyway, even if there was money,

Harriet would've spent it by now. Did you see the outfit she wore to the wedding? Finn told me how much it cost. Phew! I couldn't believe it when I heard.'

Jasmine needed time to think.

'Sam, I have to go. I've left something on the stove.'

'Call me soon,' Sam said cheerily. 'I want to show you the wedding photographs. There's a great one of you looking daggers at Connor at the reception. It will be great to show your children one day.'

Jasmine replaced the receiver once Sam had trilled her last goodbye and sat heavily on the nearest sofa, her hands shaking as she clasped them in her lap.

He'd lied to her. He'd expressly told her he needed to be married to access his mother's money. He'd tricked her into a loveless, pointless marriage. How had she fallen so neatly in with his plans? She felt like kicking herself for her own blind stupidity. He'd seized the opportunity when her parents had applied a bit of pressure, concocting his own tale of woe to draw her in. She'd fallen for it so gullibly. It made her sick to think of how easy it had been for him to get her to do what he had wanted. How he must be laughing at her behind her back. He couldn't have chosen a better victim. Who better than a high profile young woman such as herself, with a tainted reputation to match—a Bishop's wayward daughter, who had already caused one man's career to tumble. She'd been an easy target for his ruthless machinations, and to add to his victory she'd foolishly fallen in love with him. She'd even allowed him to make love to her, filling her head with stupid, empty dreams of happy-ever-afters that could never be.

Connor turned his key in the lock whilst balancing his briefcase under his other arm. His temples were tight with a tension headache which had grown steadily worse as the day had progressed.

He'd met his stepfather that morning to discuss accessing

his mother's estate, handing Julian his marriage certificate with an element of pride. His stepfather, however, had dismissed him with a wave of one hand.

'You surely don't think there's any of your mother's money left after all this time, do you?' Julian looked at him from beneath his grey bushy brows.

Connor felt himself stiffen.

'She left it to me,' he said. 'I'm here to collect it.'

Julian shuffled some papers on his desk, something in his manner suggesting he wasn't entirely comfortable with the discussion.

'I'm sure I don't need to remind you of the costs in raising a child,' he said. 'And since you were expelled from several schools the fees we had to pay for the Academy had to be met somehow.'

Connor's frown deepened.

'You mean there's nothing left?'

'Your mother wanted you to have a good education,' Julian said. 'I felt I owed it to her to ensure you got one even though you were hell-bent on sabotaging it at every opportunity.'

Connor had left his stepfather's rooms in an anger induced daze. He didn't trust Julian's explanation but knew that unless he was prepared to take him on in a court case he had no guarantee of winning he had no choice but to accept it as a lesson well learnt.

The only trouble was that his primary reason for marrying Jasmine no longer existed. And if she were to ever find out…

He closed the door behind him and, tossing his keys to the hall table, ran a hand through his hair, squinting against the pain across his forehead.

'Good day at the office?' Jasmine's tone was cool as she stepped out from the shadow of the sitting room doorway.

'Oh, hello, Jasmine.' He winced as his head gave another sickening pound. 'You would not believe the day I've had.' He shrugged himself out of his coat and flung it towards the hall stand with another flinch of pain.

'I'm sure I wouldn't.'

His eyes went to hers. 'Is everything all right?'

'What could possibly be wrong?' She held his narrowed-eyed look.

He ran a hand across his eyes and sighed.

'I have the most appalling headache.'

'Poor you.'

He hunted her face for the sincerity he'd sensed had been lacking in her tone.

'Has someone upset you?' he asked after a tiny pause.

'Who would do such a thing?' she asked.

'I don't know; your parents, perhaps?'

'I haven't spoken to my parents since the wedding.'

'Who have you been talking to?'

'No one you'd be interested in.'

'I don't know about that.' He loosened his tie. 'Why don't you tell me and I'll be the judge?'

'I was talking to my sister.'

'Sam?'

She gave a single nod.

'Finn called me too. Seems they had a great time,' he said, leading the way into the kitchen.

She stood silently watching him as he took a glass from the cupboard and filled it with water. He pressed two pain-killers from a foil strip and tossed back his head to swallow them.

'God, I feel like a construction team has started up inside my head,' he said, rubbing a hand across his forehead.

'My heart bleeds.'

He frowned, then leant his hips back against the bench and looked at her closely.

'At the risk of repeating myself, are you all right?'

She lifted her chin a fraction. 'You seem very determined that something must be wrong. Why, Connor? Is your conscience pricking you?'

His eyes fell away from hers as he put the glass down.

'I'm not sure what you're talking about but no doubt you're going to enlighten me.'

She drew in an angry breath. 'Why did you lie to me?'

'About what?' His eyes came back to hers, but this time she noted they were clouded with wariness.

'Lots of things, but the one that immediately springs to mind is the true nature of your financial affairs.'

There was a pulsing silence.

'You lied to me about your mother's estate, didn't you?' She glared at him furiously.

He didn't answer but she could see the flare of guilt in his dark eyes.

'You told me you needed to get married to access your late mother's estate.'

'I know what I said.'

'There is no estate, is there, Connor?'

He drew in a breath. 'Not any more.'

'There never was!' She threw the words at him. 'You lied to me to make me do what you wanted. I should have seen it from the start but I was fool enough to fall…to fall for it,' she tacked on quickly.

'Jasmine, you're jumping to the sort of conclusions you're very likely to regret when I explain—'

'I don't want your explanations or your bare-faced lies! I don't want anything from you but the truth, but you can't do that, can you? You wouldn't know how to tell the truth if it were tattooed on your tongue!'

'Oh, for God's sake!' Connor slammed his fist against the bench in frustration. 'Will you let me tell you my side of this?'

'Do you think I even care what story you're busily rehearsing in your head?'

'I'm not rehearsing anything.' He raked a hand through his hair. 'I intended telling you eventually, but I only found out about it—'

'*Eventually?*' She threw him a fulminating look. 'You

should have told me before I was stupid enough to sign my name on that marriage certificate!'

He needed time to think.

Her anger was justified, he knew, but he wanted to be in a better frame of mind than he currently was before he explained.

He garnered his pride with an effort and glared back at her. 'What is this? I come home with a fierce headache to this!'

'You shouldn't have come home at all,' she said bitterly. 'You should have gone to your latest lover's waiting arms instead.'

His eyes flashed with some indefinable emotion.

'Well, then.' His voice was a harsh scratch of sound in his throat. 'Maybe that's exactly what I will do.'

CHAPTER ELEVEN

JASMINE stared after his stiff back when Connor strode from the room, flinching as the woodwork protested as he slammed the door behind him. If a confession was what she was after she was sure she'd just received it; she'd never seen someone so guilty in all her life.

He didn't come home that night or the night after. Jasmine carried on as if nothing was the matter, mostly for appearance's sake, under the watchful, silent gaze of Maria the housekeeper.

She filled her days at the clinic, working a double shift to keep from facing the aching emptiness of Connor's house. She tortured herself with images of him with someone else—a tall, leggy blonde with a figure to die for, or a raven-haired temptress with smouldering eyes.

On the evening of the third day she'd had enough. She called the clinic and told them she needed some time off and, quickly packing a bag, made her way to the garage where the second of Connor's cars was parked.

The drive to the south coast was lengthened by the snarl of traffic at the start of the freeway due to an accident. She drummed her fingers on the steering wheel impatiently as she waited for the tow truck to clear the debris.

The old house was cold and dark, its shadowy verandas like heavy brows over sightless eyes.

She unlocked the door and after carrying her few things in shut it behind her, breathing in the empty silence.

She turned on one small light, somehow content with the creeping darkness. She struck a match to the fire Connor had left laid ready in the fireplace and waited for its warmth to seep into the stiff coldness of her bones.

It was hard to sit in front of the flames without thinking of him. She could almost feel his touch, the slide of his warm fingers down her arm, the rasp of his unshaven jaw on her breasts as she lay in his embrace.

She sighed as she poked at the fire once or twice. She'd have to learn to live without him, that was all.

She woke to the dawn chorus and her own low spirits. The sun was a pale imitation of its usual self, which did nothing to lift her low mood. The old house seemed to creak around her with every step she took within it, as if it were asking her, Where is he? Where is he?

In the end, she gave up and went for a long walk along the beach, striding with a vigour she couldn't feel through the heavy sand. The thunderous waves pounded at the shore in great lashing strokes, trying to soak her feet as she went past. The air was fresh with sea spray and the hoarse cries of the gulls echoed the silent cries of her heart as she faced the prospect of a future alone.

When she got back to the house she picked at some scraps of food she'd brought with her with little enthusiasm. Everything she touched reminded her of Connor. She saw his smile reflected in the glass of the windows, tasted his kiss on the afternoon breeze against her lips, felt his presence in the big bed when she lay down and tried to force herself to sleep. He was everywhere; she couldn't escape, for she'd brought him with her in her heart.

Some time during the night something woke her. At first she thought it must have been a possum on the roof but when she sat up to listen there was no sound except the soft brush of the branches of the old elm tree outside the bedroom window.

She watched the play of moonlit shadows on the ceiling for a while before finally giving up on the whole notion of further sleep. She threw back the bedcovers and, wrapping herself in the bathrobe Connor had left behind, made her way in moonlit darkness to the library to find something to read to take her mind off her worries.

The library floor creaked in protest as she stepped into the room. The rows of books seemed to have developed accusing eyes as they looked down at who had disturbed their solitude.

Jasmine gave herself a mental shake and switched on the desk lamp, but the sensation of being watched remained.

She reached for the book nearest her, which happened to be a family Bible, its spine encrusted with gold. Pulling out a chair and tucking her feet underneath her, she sat with the Bible in her lap and began turning the yellowed pages with careful fingers.

A single photograph fluttered to the floor as she turned from Genesis to Exodus. She reached down and, picking it up, turned it over and froze.

It was a photograph of her.

The heavy Bible slipped from her knees as she unfolded her legs, her startled eyes still on the photograph in her shaking hands.

She knew the photograph well. It was exactly the same as the one in the photograph album her mother had made her for her tenth birthday. She was a few months old, lying on a rug in a garden she didn't recognise, rosy cheeks and her wide, mostly toothless, smile.

How had it come to be between the leaves of this particular Bible? A host of questions flew around her brain, but none of the answers she needed.

She picked up the Bible and began leafing through the rest of the fragile pages, past Leviticus, Numbers, Deuteronomy and then on to Joshua and Judges. Another photograph was pressed between the pages of Ruth. This time she was a little older, a year or so, and the garden she did recognise as that of her childhood home.

There was another photograph of her in 1 and 2 Chronicles, one in Proverbs, a school photograph in Hosea and her confirmation photograph in the New Testament section between Acts and Romans.

She put the Bible back down and leafed through the collection of photographs in her trembling hands, her mind whirling with a magnitude of unanswerable questions.

After what seemed hours, she suddenly sprang to her feet, tossing the photographs to one side. She stared at the rows of books in front of her for a moment, before she began pulling them at random from the shelves, her fingers searching through the pages of every single volume.

She found a lock of curly chestnut hair in Charles Dickens' *Great Expectations*. She stared at it for endless minutes, her brain darting off in all directions but unable to make sense of it.

She put the lock of hair to one side and ran her eyes along the top shelves where the last books remained.

Only one book along the row had no gold-embossed title on its spine.

She reached for it with nerveless fingers, somehow not all that surprised to find it was a diary.

She sat on the dusty sofa and, taking a painful breath, turned the first page.

It was addressed to God.

> *I saw her today.*
> *She came to the house on her way to the beach. I wanted to call out to her but, as you know, I gave up that right a long time ago.*
> *At least I have the photos. She looks so like me, which I suppose is a rough sort of justice. How that must annoy your avid disciple!*
> *You'd better look after her while I'm gone. She's the only thing I'm proud of in my life. The one thing I did properly. I would have loved to have kept her but I was told you wouldn't approve.*
> *As for me, I'm not so sure…*

Jasmine sat in the quiet stillness of the old house, cradling the diary in her hands, her eyes moving over the various entries to find out the identity of the owner but to no avail—the diary was as anonymous as the 'disciple' referred to within it.

She knew she could put it off no longer; the creeping shadows of doubt could not be contained any more. She had to know the truth, even though she knew it was going to be painful.

She knew she had to visit her parents and ask them who would be watching her from afar, entering details about her in a nameless diary, for who but they was likely to know?

With that resolution in mind she tucked the photographs and diary beneath her pillow and shut her eyes, willing herself to sleep.

Her mother answered the door first thing the next morning with her hair still in the soft rollers she customarily wore to bed.

'Jasmine!' She put her hand to the plastic assortment on her head in what Jasmine knew to be a nervous gesture.

'Hello, Mum.'

'Darling, you don't have to knock,' her mother chided as she ushered her inside. 'Just because you're married now doesn't mean you're not our daughter any more.'

Jasmine couldn't have asked for a better opening.

'But I'm not your daughter, am I?'

Frances Byrne visibly blanched.

'I...I don't know what you mean, darling.' She recovered quickly. 'Is...is everything all right between you and Connor?'

'I'm not here to discuss my...Connor,' Jasmine said firmly. 'I've come to discuss these.' She handed her mother the small clutch of photographs but kept the leather-bound diary in her bag.

Frances took the photographs with an unsteady hand.

Jasmine watched as she turned each one over, her expression clouding as each image was revealed.

There was a hollow silence.

After a few moments her mother handed her back the photographs, carefully avoiding her eyes.

'I can't imagine where you found those,' she said, dusting off her hands.

'Can't you?'

Frances disturbed the neat perfection of her coral lipstick with her teeth.

'Darling, your father will be very sorry he missed you and as you see, I'm getting ready to go to church and—'

'I want to know the truth,' Jasmine said. 'The gospel truth.'

'Darling—' her mother's hands fluttered near her throat '— I'm not sure I can handle you in this mood.'

'I'm not leaving here until I have the truth,' Jasmine said implacably. 'And if you won't speak to me here then I'll have to go to the synod gathering and have it out with Father there.'

'Oh, dear Lord, don't do that!' Desperation crept into her mother's voice.

'Why ever not?' Jasmine asked. 'He's my father, isn't he? Surely I should be able to call him out of a meeting to speak with me?'

The silence this time was agonising.

'Darling—' her mother's face was pale with anguish as she wrung her hands '—your father and I—'

'Leave this to me, Frances.' Elias Byrne's voice sounded from behind Jasmine.

She spun around to find her father standing in the open doorway.

'I hope you've got a very good explanation for coming here and upsetting your mother like this.' He closed the door behind him with an ominous click.

Jasmine refused to be intimidated.

'I want to know the truth. Surely you owe me that?'

'We've taught you the truth since you were an infant but ou've wilfully and rebelliously refused to acknowledge it.'

'Not that sort of truth!' Tears smarted in her eyes. 'Why ust you always preach at me?'

'You've got a defiant streak, Jasmine. We've done all we an to school you out of it but it seems you're determined to gnore our admonitions.'

'I didn't come here for a sermon.' Jasmine's tone was cold. want you to tell me why those photographs of me were in family Bible in the old house next to the shack at Pelican lead.'

Her parents exchanged glances.

Elias's face drained of colour and her mother's hand flut-red back to her string of pearls.

'I'm not leaving until I know the truth,' Jasmine added eterminedly.

After a stretching silence her father appeared to come to me sort of decision. He straightened his spine and met her efiant grey-blue gaze with the cool ice blue of his own.

'All right, then.' He ignored the choked sound from Frances eside him. 'I'll tell you the truth but you must promise me is to go no further than the four walls of this room.'

She hated having to make such a promise but she needed know so desperately. She nodded her head, her stomach urning as she waited for him to continue.

Elias disturbed the neat comb-over he'd perfected that orning with a nervous flick of his hand.

'It's true that you're not our biological daughter,' he said. Your mother and I adopted you when you were six weeks d.'

Jasmine stared at them both.

'We would have told you but when Samantha came along few months later you both looked so alike and we thought best for all concerned to retain the secrecy. Of course, now ou and the girls are all grown up the differences between ou are more marked than we would have liked, but—'

'So sorry not to have fitted in as you wanted,' Jasmine put in bitterly.

Her father's brows drew together in a frown.

'Your propensity to speak before you think is one of those differences. It got your mother into trouble too, which is why we offered to take you in.'

'Who is my mother?'

'Your mother is dead.'

Jasmine's stomach hollowed.

'I still want to know who she was.'

Elias and Frances exchanged glances once more.

'Your mother was a rebellious drug addict who found herself pregnant. She gave you up and soon after disappeared. We've since heard that she had passed away some time ago.'

Jasmine felt as if the world was spinning out of control within the confines of her head.

'What about my father?' she managed to ask through the cold stiffness of her lips. 'Who was he?'

'We were never told his name. Your mother wouldn't say.'

She absorbed this information for a moment or two in silence.

'As for the photographs, I have no idea how they came to be where you said they were. Perhaps it's one of those coincidences that just happens from time to time,' Elias offered.

'A coincidence?' Jasmine frowned heavily.

'Of course—' he was obviously pleased with his explanation '—perhaps someone bought the Bible at a second-hand store or church fair and didn't check inside.'

'You surely can't expect me to believe in that sort of coincidence?'

'You have always shown a deplorable lack of faith in the miraculous,' Elias pointed out. 'But I have no idea how the photographs were obtained, do you, Frances?'

Frances shook her head, her eyes bright with tears.

Jasmine took out the diary and handed it to them both.

'What's this?' Elias frowned.

'It's a diary,' she said.

'Whose diary?' He turned a few pages with fumbling fingers.

'I was hoping you could tell me,' she said.

She watched as his throat moved up and down in an agitated swallow and assumed he'd come to the 'avid disciple' entry.

Elias handed the diary back, meticulously avoiding her eye as he did so.

'I realise this has come as somewhat of a shock to you but you must believe us when we tell you we kept the details of your birth quiet with the very best of intentions. You had no future with your mother; she was beyond redemption. We took you in as our own. Your mother—Frances, I mean—' he gave his wife a brief glance '—had not long had a miscarriage and was feeling low. You were a wonderful solution to her unhappiness and brought us much joy in those early years.'

But not in latter years. Jasmine filled in the rest in her head.

'Darling, no one else needs to know about this.' Frances was struggling to hold back her emotion. 'It would upset your sisters terribly if they were to find out at this late stage.'

'What about me?' Jasmine's own tears sprang to her eyes. 'Am I not allowed to be upset?'

'It's understandable under the circumstances, but—' Elias began.

'You don't mind upsetting me because I'm not really your daughter, but we mustn't upset the girls because they are? How unfair is that? Don't you understand how this is for me?'

'Of course we do but surely you must understand how difficult this is,' Frances said. 'Your father and I—'

'Don't call yourselves that!' Jasmine almost screamed the words at them. 'You're not my parents.'

'Darling, please—'

'Jasmine, control yourself. You're a married woman now, not a teenage girl. Go home to your husband and be grateful for the life you've had; it was a whole lot more promising than your birth mother had to offer.'

Jasmine wrenched the front door open and slammed it behind her, almost stumbling down the front steps with blinding bitter tears. She drove away with a squeal of tyres she knew would annoy her father—no Elias Byrne, her adopted father she corrected herself with another choking sob.

She drove around in circles, not sure whether she should go back to the old house or drive straight to Connor's place. So many questions were leaping in her head, each one vying for her attention, but she could barely think straight let alone attempt to frame any answers.

As she did another round of the block she recalled the cryptic comment Connor had made when he'd shown her the library at the old house for the first time. She'd told him the old books were very likely priceless and he'd said, *'I'm sure one or two will prove to be so.'*

She gnawed at her lip, trying to decipher the meaning of his words. Had he known something? Had he stumbled across the photographs and diary himself or had he known the previous occupant of the house? She had to know, even if it meant facing him again, which she wasn't sure she wanted to do right now.

Her curiosity got the better of her. She turned the car at the next roundabout and tracked back across the flow of traffic to make her way to Woollahra, determined to have it out with him.

When she arrived, she was relieved to find Connor's car in the garage and made her way to the front door, mentally rehearsing what she wanted to say. She went to unlock the door but before she could put the key in the lock it opened and he stood before her.

'Jasmine, I need to talk to you.'

She brushed past him to enter the house, not sure she wanted to pick up the threads of their last conversation just yet; she had more pressing things on her mind.

'I want to apologise.'

Her head came around at that. He sounded genuine but she wasn't quite sure what he was apologising for. Was it for not telling her the truth about his mother's estate or for his abrupt manner when he'd stormed from the house the other evening?

'I see.'

'No, you don't see.'

She followed him into the sitting room, where he proceeded to pour two generous shots of brandy. She took hers but didn't lift it to her mouth, simply cradling it in her hands as she faced him.

He ran a hand through his already disordered hair.

'I was out of line the other night,' he began. 'I had the mother of all headaches and when you threwe the issue of my mother's estate in my face, I lost it.'

'You lied to me.'

'I didn't lie to you.'

'You expect me to believe you?'

'Yes.' He thrust his own glass aside untouched. 'I'd like to explain about my mother's estate.'

'Please don't put yourself to any bother.' Her tone was laced with scorn.

'Jasmine, I know you think the worst of me right now but I can explain.'

'Go right ahead.' She gave him the floor with a theatrical sweep of her hand. 'God knows I could do with another good story after what I've already heard today.'

'What have you heard?'

She turned away. 'Nothing that's relevant to this conversation.'

'Jasmine, there's something you should know—'

'Why did you lie to me about your mother's estate?'

'Until a few days ago I didn't even know my mother's estate no longer existed.'

She wasn't sure she wanted to believe him but something

in his tone suggested he found the task of speaking about it difficult, so she stayed silent.

'But I want you to know that even if I had found out in time I would still have wanted to marry you.'

'Why?' she asked. 'Why did you want to marry me?'

His eyes shifted away from hers. 'I wanted to settle down.'

'With me?'

'Why not you?'

'I'm hardly perfect wife material.'

'I don't know about that and, besides, I'm not the perfect catch either, so what's the problem?'

'The problem is I'm not who you think I am.'

'I know you're not the wayward rebel people have made you out to be.'

'I don't mean that.' She chanced a quick glance at his face. 'I mean I'm not really a bishop's daughter.'

His dark eyes meshed with hers.

'Whose daughter are you?'

She lowered her gaze. 'I don't know.'

'I see.'

'No, you don't see,' she said, not caring that they'd each recycled each other's words several times in the space of a few minutes. 'I'm not my parents' daughter.'

'Do you have any idea whose daughter you might be?'

She couldn't meet his eyes.

'I don't know,' she answered raggedly. 'I don't know.'

She heard him move across the room and the chink of a bottle against a glass as he topped up his brandy.

'I take it Elias and Frances didn't enlighten you?'

She felt almost grateful he hadn't referred to them as her parents.

'No,' she said hollowly. 'They didn't enlighten me.'

'And Sam, Caitlin, Bianca—do they know about this?'

She shook her head, not trusting herself to speak.

'I see,' he said again.

She seriously questioned that; how could he possibly know what she was going through?

'I don't know what to do,' she found herself confessing. 'I've always suspected something wasn't quite right in my family but I could never put my finger on exactly what.'

'They should've told you.'

She bit her lip as she thought about her parents' dilemma. 'They did what they thought was best, I see that now.'

'You're very gracious.'

'You wouldn't say that if you heard what I said to them a few hours ago.'

'It's been such a shock,' he said. 'It's understandable.'

She sat down on the nearest sofa with a heavy sigh. 'I feel like an alien.'

'You don't have green skin, if that's any consolation.'

She couldn't stop her smile in time.

'Trust you to find something to laugh about in all of this,' she said.

He took a sip of his brandy. 'It's not really a laughing matter, though, is it?'

'No.' She met his dark eyes. 'It's not.'

'What will you do?'

'Do?' She frowned at him. 'What can I do?'

He put his glass down and folded his arms across his chest as he leant back against the drinks cabinet.

'For a start you could go and speak to Roy Holden.'

'Roy Holden?' Jasmine gaped at him. 'Why? What has he got to do with any of this?'

Connor met and held her startled gaze across the room.

'Because Roy Holden is your father.'

CHAPTER TWELVE

JASMINE genuinely thought she was going to faint. The room spun around her, the sofa opposite intermingling with the tall figure of Connor as he stood watching her reaction to his bombshell.

'My father?' she gasped. *'He's my father?'*

Connor nodded.

'How do you know?' She grasped the nearest surface to anchor herself. 'How can you possibly know that?'

'I found out some time ago.'

She sucked in a painful breath and sat down heavily on the sofa behind her.

'I can't believe it,' she said, almost to herself. 'I can't believe it.'

She felt Connor move across the room to join her on the sofa.

'Does he know?' she asked, turning to look at him.

He nodded. 'Yes. He's known from the start.'

Jasmine buried her head in her lap. She felt the gentle stroke of his hand on her hair and had to fight even harder against the sobs that threatened to consume her.

'I felt a connection with him when I had him as my teacher.' She lifted her tear-stained face towards him. 'I must have known subconsciously at least.'

'Yes.' He threaded his fingers through her hair. 'You must have sensed something.'

'Do you know who my mother was?'

He didn't see any point in denying it now. 'Yes, I do.'

She swallowed deeply, her hands like two tight knots in her lap.

'Who?'

His eyes held hers.

'Your mother was Vanessa Byrne—your aunt.'

Jasmine's jaw dropped.

'My aunt?'

He nodded. 'It seems she had a bit of a rebellious streak and went somewhat off the rails. She was disowned by the family. Her brother, your adopted father Elias, insisted she never darken the doorstep again. When she fell pregnant she was under a lot of family pressure; she finally decided, once you were born, to give you up.'

Jasmine's brow was deeply furrowed as she took it all in. After a long silence she lifted her pained expression to his.

'I found some photographs.' She rummaged in her bag and handed them to him. 'They were in the old Bible at the house.'

He gave the photographs a cursory glance and put them aside. Something in his manner alerted her to the possibility that it wasn't the first time he'd seen them.

'You don't seem very surprised,' she said.

He turned back to face her.

'I'm not.'

'You knew my aunt lived in that house, didn't you?' She stared at him.

He gave a single nod without speaking.

'I...I found a diary as well.' She handed it to him, her voice cracking slightly.

He flipped through the pages, smiling wryly when he came to the lock of hair she'd tucked inside.

'Do you know who gave the photographs and my hair to my aunt?' she asked after a pause.

'I have a fair idea.'

'But you're not going to tell me?'

His eyes came back to hers, his expression regretful.

'It's not my place to tell you.'

'My mother was watching me,' she said after a long silence. 'All those years she was so close and I didn't know.'

'Yes, your intuition was right after all. She was watching you whenever you came past, desperate for a glance at the daughter she'd been forced to give up.'

'I can't believe it.' She sank to the sofa once more. 'It's all so bizarre.'

'Yes, it is certainly that,' he agreed.

'It's so weird.' She lifted her gaze to his. 'Do you know I never realised it till this minute that I've never seen a photograph of my mother?'

'That doesn't surprise me,' he said. 'You were the spitting image of her when she was young. Your parents wouldn't have been able to explain away the likeness, especially as your three sisters are all so alike. From the first, Roy Holden saw it, but assumed it was one of those coincidences. You know, someone having a double somewhere in the world. After a while he stumbled across the truth, but he could do nothing about it. He was married with a child. How could he tell them of a child he hadn't known he'd had? After the scandal he couldn't even clear his own name, let alone yours, without inadvertently revealing the truth.'

Jasmine stared at her hands as she recalled the way it had all blown up in her face. Her favourite teacher blighted by scandal when all the time he was actually her father! He'd done nothing wrong other than listen to a lonely, confused girl who'd felt drawn to his quiet empathetic nature.

When a staff member had interrupted them one afternoon it had all been blown out of proportion. The teacher's aide had scurried off to inform the principal that Jasmine had been in Roy Holden's arms but it hadn't been like that at all. She'd stayed back after class to discuss her English paper with him, only to find herself confessing how unhappy she was over an argument she'd had with her parents that morning. He'd listened as she had off-loaded her frustration, reaching out when the first tears fell to take her hand in his.

The door had opened and they'd sprung apart with unnecessary guilt but it had been too late. It was all over the staff-room by lunchtime and all over the school by the time the home bell sounded. The heightened awareness of inappropriate student-teacher relationships at the time had made it very difficult to stop the hint of a scandal spreading. The climate of suspicion had been too intense to circumvent. Jasmine had watched in mute desperation as exaggerated lie after lie hit the headlines, her total bewilderment leaving deep emotional scars with each fire and brimstone lecture her father had delivered, her devastated mother's distress almost matching her own.

She'd left the school in disgrace and had blamed herself ever since for the damage she'd inadvertently done to Roy Holden's career.

'Does his wife know?' she asked.

'No, he couldn't tell her either without compromising you or your adoptive parents.'

'Secrets everywhere.' Jasmine sighed. 'So many secrets.'

'What will you do?'

'Do?' She looked at him blankly.

'Now that you know the truth, you do have some options.'

'Such as?'

'Such as seeing Roy Holden. You could also insist on finding out more about Vanessa from Elias and Frances.'

'But what about my sisters?'

'What about them?' he asked. 'They need to know the truth as well. I don't think it will harm them all that much. Maybe it will knock a bit of sense into them. Besides, the only one who makes any effort to be worthy of the title sister is Sam.'

'Yes, I know what you mean.' Her tone was wry.

Connor stood up and, draining his brandy, put the empty glass aside.

'You look tired; you should go up to bed. It's been a heck of a day.'

'Yes.' She lowered her gaze from the all-seeing intensity of his. There was still so much she wanted to ask him, like how he knew so much about her family, and things she wanted to tell him but she didn't know where to start.

'I'll sleep in the guest room for the time being,' he said into the telling silence.

'I understand.' She turned away.

'Jasmine?'

She stopped in her tracks and turned back to face him uncertainly.

'I realise this is difficult for you but there are still things we need to discuss,' he said.

'Such as?'

'The future of our marriage.'

'Where were you the last few nights?' she asked, giving him a pointed look.

'I was staying with a friend.'

'Was the friend a woman?'

'Yes, but it was—'

She gave him a chilling glance.

'Our marriage doesn't have a future, Connor.'

His eyes darkened with some indefinable emotion as he took in her simple statement.

'I see.'

'I'm going to bed.' She swung away, frightened he'd see the betraying moisture in her eyes. 'Goodnight.'

He didn't answer but she felt his dark, brooding gaze on her back as she left the room.

The next week passed in a blur of high emotion and recriminations, finally coming to a head when Jasmine confronted Elias and Frances once more. She demanded to see a photograph of her mother and, when they refused, she threatened to go to the press and tell them the whole story.

Elias was under no illusion as to whether or not she meant it.

'I should have known you'd be trouble from the first day

we took you in,' he said through clenched teeth, beads of perspiration sprouting on his receding brow.

'Elias!' Frances gasped.

He gave his wife a dismissive glance before turning back to Jasmine.

'You're on the same path to destruction your poor deluded mother took. I did everything in my power to make her see reason, but she refused to listen.'

'At least she wasn't a hypocrite!' Jasmine threw at him.

'You know nothing of what she put my family through. My parents, your grandparents were never the same again; she destroyed them with her scandalous behaviour.'

'Elias, please.' Frances's voice cracked with a growing anger. 'Vanessa wasn't all that bad.'

He gave her a quelling look but she stood her ground with uncharacteristic defiance.

'You were too hard on her, you know you were,' she continued. 'She wasn't an angel but neither was she the demon you made her out to be.'

'You sent her the photographs, didn't you?' Elias's frown was suddenly accusing.

'Yes,' Frances said with an element of pride in her tone. 'She had the right to see her child, a right you should never have denied her. I also organised for her to stay at the old house so she could at least be close whenever Jasmine went to stay next door.'

'You went behind my back,' Elias said as if he still couldn't quite believe it. 'You deliberately disobeyed my instructions and broke your vow of wifely obedience.'

'Oh, for God's sake, Elias!' Frances got to her feet in agitation. 'I had to do something to heal the hurt before she died.' She turned to Jasmine, her expression softening. 'Darling, your…mother loved you very dearly. I know she did.'

Jasmine could barely make out Frances's features from behind the blur of tears.

'She had an addiction problem she never quite got over.

She tried so hard but her kidneys were permanently damaged. She thought you'd be happier in the long run with us, but maybe...' Her words trailed off as she choked on a sob.

'It's all right.' Jasmine touched her on the arm. 'I understand.'

'It was God's will,' Elias put in gravely. 'All things work together for good.'

'Oh, for Christ's sake, Elias, shut up!' Frances said.

Jasmine couldn't help smiling at the shocked bewilderment on her adoptive father's face. It was certainly a novelty to hear her mother blaspheme but she didn't want to hang around to hear any more. She had more important things to do.

'I have to go,' she said. 'I need to speak to Connor.'

She left after giving them both an awkward hug, knowing it would take much more than a brief show of affection to heal the hurt and misunderstandings that had grown between them. But somehow in that quick embrace she felt something had shifted and settled inside her.

When she returned to Connor's house there was no sign of him having been there recently. She even pushed open the bathroom door to check the floor for towels but the floor was clear. She felt like crying and, just for the heck of it, tore one neatly folded towel from the rail and dropped it to the floor.

She considered asking the housekeeper where he was but changed her mind when she thought about what sort of conclusions Maria would draw, notwithstanding her limited understanding of English.

She wandered aimlessly around the house for a couple of hours when all of a sudden it came to her. She snatched up the keys to the second car and, without even stopping to throw a few things in a bag, rushed out to the garage.

The Friday evening traffic had begun to thin out by the time she hit the freeway and it wasn't all that much after nine p.m. when she pulled up in front of the old house and parked behind Connor's black Maserati.

There were a couple of lights on downstairs and she made

her way to the front door with trepidation in her breast, suddenly uncertain now that she was actually here.

The door was unlocked. She closed it softly behind her and made her way to the nearest door, where a thin beam of light was shining beneath.

The door opened and Connor stood looking down at her, his brows drawn together in a frown.

'What brings you here at this late hour, Jasmine?'

She stepped past him to enter the room, trying not to be too intimidated by his less than enthusiastic greeting.

'I wanted to talk to you about something.' She turned to face him. 'I think you owe me that.'

'Oh, really?' He moved across to the brandy bottle and poured himself a generous measure.

'Yes.'

He took a sip of brandy, holding it in his mouth for a short while before swallowing.

She wasn't sure what to make of his mood.

'I want to know how you came to know Roy Holden was my father.'

He took another sip of brandy before responding.

'Your real mother, Vanessa, told me.'

She stared at him. 'You met my...mother?'

'I met her about three years ago.'

'Where?'

'She was staying at Beryl Hopper's house in the Blue Mountains.'

Jasmine felt her legs weaken and reached for the sofa.

'I was going through a rough time of my own,' he continued. 'I'd just come out of a relationship which had cut me deeply. I landed on Beryl's doorstep as I had done on various occasions in the past. Vanessa was there and we got talking. I can't remember the details exactly but I think I might have mentioned Finn and Sam's relationship. Once she heard the Byrne name she told me of her past, how she had given up her daughter. It didn't take me too long to figure out just which of the Byrne girls she was referring to.'

'You should have told me.'

'How could I?'

'How did you know my mother, I mean Frances, sent the photographs?' she asked.

'Vanessa told me. She also told me Frances had organised for you to have access to the shack at Pelican Head whenever you wanted it.'

Jasmine's mind ran back to all the occasions she'd called her mother's friend to ask if she could use the property. She couldn't recall a single time when it hadn't been immediately available to her.

'I still don't understand.' She lifted her troubled gaze to his. 'Where do you fit in with all this?'

He gave her an unreadable look.

'When I met you first at Finn and Sam's engagement party I couldn't stop myself staring at you. I felt drawn to you even though you kept glaring at me. Vanessa had died a few months earlier, and I guess I wanted to get to know you for her sake, if not for my own. But within a very short time I realised I had rather a task on my hands to win you over. Then we woke up together.'

'So you decided to force me into marrying you?'

He met her scathing gaze.

'Neither knowing Vanessa nor the matter of my mother's estate were the only reasons for marrying you.'

'Oh, really?' Her look was cynical. 'I can just imagine what the other reason might have been! I must have been quite a novelty to you in that I spent a whole night in your bed without throwing myself into your arms.'

'You were certainly a novelty,' he admitted wryly.

'How could you do it, Connor?' Tears sprang to her eyes. 'How could you string me along with such a lie?'

'How could I tell you what I knew?' he asked. 'It wasn't my truth to tell.'

She fought against the tears with difficulty.

'You kept asking me about my family, pointing out the differences all the time. Why did you do that if you were never going to enlighten me?'

He ran a hand through his dark hair.

'I was so close to telling you so many times. It didn't seem fair that you were torturing yourself all the time, hating yourself for being something you could never be. I guess I was hoping you'd come to it yourself. I'm surprised you didn't actually.'

'I think I always knew deep down,' she found herself confessing. 'I just didn't want to come right out and say it.'

'Vanessa was so thrilled that you wanted to work at a drug clinic. It meant the world to her to know you were helping others triumph over the obstacles she never quite managed to overcome. She had no money to speak of, having been cast off by the family, but it pleased her to think you'd developed a social conscience all by yourself.'

'What about the old house?' She frowned at him. 'Didn't she own that?'

He shook his head.

'I bought it a couple of years ago from the person who rented it to her.'

'So then you rented it back to her?'

'No.'

'You let her stay there for nothing?'

Connor shifted his gaze from the tight scrutiny of hers.

'She needed a break. I gave it to her. She found happiness at Pelican Head and a sort of peace.'

She didn't know what to make of this latest development. It was hard to think of Connor being so intimately involved in her life for years without her knowing it.

'Jasmine—' he made a move towards her '—there's something else you need to know.'

Her eyes went to his, her breath suddenly tight in her throat.

'The woman I spent those few nights with was old Beryl

Hopper,' he said. 'I always go there when things get a bit sticky. I was trying to tell you that but I'd only just found out about the unscrupulous dealings of my stepfather over my mother's estate. I guess I wasn't thinking straight so I let you think the worst. I'm sorry.'

Jasmine didn't trust herself to respond without crying.

'I'm not proud of my past,' he continued when she didn't speak. 'I've left a string of broken relationships behind me, flitting from person to person looking for something that up until recently has proved to be elusive.'

She frowned, wondering if she'd missed something.

'When I saw you again at Sam and Finn's wedding I was taken aback. I couldn't stop myself from looking at you all the time; it was as if my whole life I'd been waiting for that moment. It completely rocked me and, I'm ashamed to admit, I hid my reaction behind a cloak of what could only be described as cowardly mockery, when all the time all I felt was the most amazing sense of rightness.'

She blinked up at him in confusion.

'You see, I fell for you the moment you first looked across the church and glared at me.'

'I...I really glared at you?'

He smiled. 'You sure did. I decided then and there I was going to marry you, no matter what. When you turned up in my bed that night I wasn't sure what to do. I know I probably should've woken you and told you of your mistake, but when I saw you curled up in my bed with your beautiful hair spread out over my pillow... Well, it was just too tempting.'

Jasmine couldn't believe her ears.

'I didn't, however, organise the photographer,' he added. 'I had no idea the press would make such a fuss, or indeed your father, or even my stepfather, but when they did it seemed a perfect opportunity to take you out of the firing line by marrying you. I thought that in time you'd get to know me and, hopefully, fall in love with me. I know it was a long shot, but I was desperate.'

'Are you saying what I think you're saying?' she asked.

'What do you think I'm saying?'

'I think you're trying to say what I've wanted to say for ages.'

'Oh?' His chocolate-brown eyes were twinkling and her heart gave a sudden lurch. 'What would that be?'

'I love you.'

He reached for her and enfolded her in his arms, burying his face in her hair.

'I can't believe you just said that.'

Jasmine smiled into the warmth of his chest.

'I can't believe I said it either.'

He put her from him and looked down at her, his eyes dark with desire.

'Do you mean it?'

She crossed her heart with one finger.

'Swear to God and hope to die.'

'I thought you didn't believe in God?' He gave her a mock frown.

She smiled back, her eyes alight with happiness.

'I think I'll give it some further thought,' she said, lifting her mouth for him to kiss.

He grinned as he planted a firm kiss on her up-tilted mouth.

'Thanks be to God,' he said, as once more he gathered her into his arms. 'I love you, Jasmine.'

EPILOGUE

CONNOR put down his paintbrush for the last time and turned to watch Jasmine come up the front steps of the old house.

'Finished?' she asked with a smile.

'Yes, and just in time for me to carry you over the threshold.' He dusted off his hands and reached for her.

'I'm too heavy!' she squealed as he scooped her up.

'And whose fault it that?' He grinned down at her wolfishly.

'Yours,' she said, laying a protective hand over the swell of her belly. 'All yours.'

He kissed her lingeringly before carefully setting her down. 'How are you feeling?'

'I'm fine.' She rested her hands against his chest and smiled up at him. 'I'm just nervous about tomorrow evening.'

'Don't worry, honey,' he reassured her. 'Roy assured me his wife took it all very well. She's just having a little trouble seeing him as a grandfather, that's all.'

Connor had arranged a quiet Christmas celebration at Pelican Head with Elias, Frances, Roy Holden and his wife, Leanne. Jasmine felt touched that he'd gone to so much trouble on her behalf to restore peace and goodwill after months of strained relationships.

'I just hope this baby doesn't make an untimely entrance.' She winced as her belly tightened as it had been doing for the last half hour or so.

'It's not due until New Year,' he reminded her.

'I know but babies often have a mind of their own.'

'Just like their mothers.'

'And their fathers.' She poked at him playfully.

'Yes, but you love me for it, don't you?' he asked with a sexy grin.

'I adore you for it,' she said, pressing a kiss to his neck. 'Even if you still leave your wet towels on the floor all the time.'

'I wouldn't do that if you didn't saunter into the bathroom with absolutely nothing on. I find it distracting, to say the least.'

'But you love me for it, don't you?'

'I adore you for it.' He gathered her closer. 'And you know it.'

Jasmine pressed herself against him for a long moment, breathing in the scent of him, marvelling at how he had turned her life around, filling it with unbelievable love and contentment.

An unmistakable contraction hit her with a sharp jolt.

'Connor?'

'Mmm?' He breathed in the fragrance of her hair.

'Do you think everyone will be upset if they arrive and we're not here?'

Connor lifted her off his chest to look down at her.

'What do you mean we won't be here?' he asked. 'Where else will we be?'

She took his hand and let him feel the contortion of her belly and his eyes widened.

'You mean this is it?'

'I think so.'

'Right now?'

She nodded.

'But what about Christmas? I've bought a turkey!' he exclaimed in panic.

Jasmine laughed.

'I think your baby has decided it wants to celebrate Christmas with us in person.'

'Well, then,' he said, picking up his car keys and taking her arm. 'Let's go see if there's room at the Inn.'

'The Inn?'

'Or, failing that, a stable.' He smiled and gently tapped the end of her nose with one finger. 'And we need to find three wise men and a very bright star.'

She couldn't help giggling at him.

'Connor, you're so irreverent at times.'

'I know.' He winked at her devilishly. 'But I love to see you smile.'

'Why?'

'Because it's heaven on earth, that's why,' he said and kissed her smiling mouth.

Elias and Frances arrived at the old house just as Roy Holden and his wife pulled up. They all went to the front door and peered at the note hastily scrawled there.

Jennifer Vanessa Harrowsmith was born on Christmas Day at five-thirty p.m., six pounds four ounces. Mother and baby doing well, father beside himself. Please help yourself to champagne and nibbles, Oh, and apologise to the turkey—I forgot to tell him he won't be needed this year!